Books and Reading

Noah Porter

Contents

BOOKS AND READING

BY

Noah Porter

BOOKS AND READING: OR,

WHAT BOOKS SHALL I READ, AND HOW SHALL I READ THEM?

CHAPTER I.

INTRODUCTORY.

WERE a South-sea Islander to be suddenly taken up from his savage home and set down in one of the great cities of Europe,—among the many strange objects which he would see, one of the most incomprehensible would be a *public library.*

A cathedral he would at once understand. Its vast area would suggest a counterpart in the inclosure which from his childhood onward he had known and feared as a place of worship. Its clustered pillars and lofty arches would bring to mind a well-remembered grove of old and stately trees, "with sounding walks between;" the dreaded dwelling of some cruel deity, or the fit arena for some "abhorred rite." The altar, the priests, the reverent worshipers, would speak to his mind their own meaning.

A military parade he might comprehend without an in-terpreter's aid. The measured tread of gathered legions, would, indeed, differ not a little from the wild rush of his own barbarous clan; the inspiring call of trumpet and horn, of fife and drum, blending with all those nameless instruments which make the music of war so splendid and so spirit-stirring, would be unlike the horrid, dissonant noises, with which the savage sounds out his bloody errand; but the object and purpose of the show would be seen at a glance, and would wake up all the warrior in his bosom.

A festive gathering of lords and ladies gay would be quite an intelligible affair, and the more closely he should look into the particulars of the transaction, the more numerous, it is possible, might be the points of resemblance between the barbaric and the fashionable assembly.

A gallery of paintings, adorned with the proudest tro-phies of genius, might not be altogether without meaning; for though the savage would look upon the creations of Raphael or Titian with somewhat such an eye as that with which Caliban looked upon Miranda, yet the uses of such a collection, which the price of his own kingdom could not buy, would not be entirely beyond his comprehension.

But a *public library* would be too much for him. It would prove a mystery quite beyond his reach. Its design and its utility would be alike incomprehensible. The front of the edifice within which the library was placed, might indeed command his admiration: and within, the lofty arches, the lengthened aisles and the labyrinthine succession of apartments, might attract and bewilder him. The books even, rising one above another in splendid lines, and dressed in gilt and purple and green, might seem to his savage eye a very pretty sight; though they would please that eye just as well if carved and colored upon the solid wall, or if, as has been the fancy of certain owners of libraries, the volumes had been wrought from solid wood—fit books for the wooden heads that owned them.

The mystery of the library to the savage, would be *the boohs in it,*—what they were, what they were for, and why they were thought worthy to be lodged in a building so imposing, and watched with such jealous care. If he should linger among the apartments for reading, and watch the movements of the inmates, his wonder would be likely to increase. His eye might rest upon Dr. Dryasdust, the antiquarian, as with anxious look and bustling air he rushes into one closet after another, takes volume after volume from its dusty retreat, looks into each as the conjuring priest at home looks into a tree or a stone to see the spirit within, and after copying from each in strange characters, stuffs the manuscript into his pocket, and walks off as proudly as though, like the self-same priest, he had caught and bagged the spirit in some fetish, amulet, or medicine-bag. The man of science sits for hours unconscious of the presence of the wondering savage, and grows more and more bewildered as he gazes upon a single page. The savage watches the poet reading a favorite author, and marvels at the mysterious influence that dilates his eye and kindles his cheek, and sends madness through his frame. He is astonished at the reader of fiction, look-ing upon what seems to him a vacant page, and yet seeming to see in its enchanted lines a world of spirits,—living, moving, talking, walking, loving, hating, fighting, dying. Should he seek an explanation of the mystery, the expla-nation would rather deepen than solve the enigma. Here is a volume, his interpreter might say, by the aid of whose characters the shipmaster can guide his vessel to your island-home as easily as you can follow a forest path. From this volume you can learn the story of that famous white captain who first landed upon your shores, in the days of your great-grandfather, and was there killed and buried; and—mystery above mystery—in this little book which gives an account of the discovery of your country by the white man, will be found the sufficient reason why his majesty, our king, has a right to burn your towns, to shoot down your people, to take possession of your land and bring you hither as a captive; all by the right of discovery, and of a title-deed from some king or' other potentate who never saw the country which he gave away.

This lesson concerning the nature and value of books would probably be quite enough for once, and would send the poor barbarian away, well satisfied that a book was indeed a very wonderful thing, and that a collection of books well deserved to be deposited in a dwelling so adorned and so secure.

Were our savage to remain longer among his civilized brethren, and gradu-ally to master the mysteries of their social state, his estimate of the influence of books would be likely to gather strength. To say nothing of their past influence in bringing a nation up to a point at .which he could only wonder and be silent, their present power to determine the character and destiny of single individuals might startle and surprise him. A few pages in a single volume fall as it were by chance under the eye of a boy in his leisure hours. They fascinate and fix his attention; they charm and hold his mind; and the result is, that the boy becomes a sailor and is wedded to the sea for his life. No force nor influence can undo the work "begun by those few pages; no love of father or mother, no temptation of money or honor, no fear of suffering or disgrace, is an overmatch for the enchantment conjured up and sustained by that exciting volume. A single book has made the boy a seaman for life; perhaps a pirate, wretched in his life and death. Another book meets the eye of another youth, and wakes in his bosom holy aspirations, which, all his life after, burn on in the useless flames of a painful asceticism, or in a kindly love to God and man. Another youth in an unhappy hour meets still another volume, and it makes him a hater of his fellow-man and a blasphemer of his God. One book makes one man a believer in goodness and love and truth; another book makes another man a denier or doubter of these sacred verities.

These thoughts may serve to introduce our subject and to suggest its importance. BOOKS AND READING are the theme—or rather the themes—on which it is proposed to offer a series of free and familiar thoughts, principally of a practical nature. The importance of the subject is not only great, but it is constantly increasing. Books, as an element of influence, are becoming more and more important, and reading is the employment of a widening circle. Books of all sorts are now brought within the reach of most persons who desire to read them. The time has gone by when the mass of the community were restricted to a score or two of volumes: the Bible, one or two works of devotion, two or three standard histories, and a half-dozen novels. Many intelligent men can recollect the time when all the books on which they could lay their hands were few, and were read and re-read till they were dry as a remainder biscuit, or as empty as a thrice-threshed sheaf.

There are ladies now living, who were well educated for their time, to whom the loan or the gift of a new book was an important event in their history, making a winter memorable, and now their daughters or grand-daughters dispatch a novel or a poem before dinner. All the known books for children, two generations ago, were some half a score; whereas, at present, new "juveniles" are prepared by the hundred a year, and the library of a child ten years old is very often more numerous and costly than was that of many a substantial and intelligent household. The minds of tens of thousands are stimulated and occupied with **books, boohs, boohs,** from three years old onward through youth and manhood. We read when we sit, when we lie down, and when we ride; sometimes when we eat and when we walk. When we travel we encounter a moving library on every railway car, and a fixed library at every railway station. Books are prepared for railway reading, and **Railway Library** is the title of more than one series of books in America, England, France, and Germany. We read when we are well and when we are ill, when we are busy and when we are idle, and some even die with a book in hand. There is little use for the caution now-a-days, " Beware of the man of one book." If it be true, as it may be, that single books make an impression less marked and decisive than formerly, so that a bad or inferior book may do less harm than it once did, it is also true that bad books and inferior books are far more common than they once were. Their poison is also more subtle and less easily detected, for as the taste of readers becomes omnivorous, it becomes less discriminating. Besides, the readiness with which good men, and men sturdy in their principles too, read books which they despise and abhor, has introduced a freedom of practice on this subject, at which other generations would have stood aghast. In many cases too, if the principles are not corrupted by reading, the taste is vitiated. Or if nothing worse happens, delicacy of appreciation suffers from the amount of intellectual food which is forced upon us, and the satisfaction is far less keen and exquisite than was enjoyed by readers of a few books of superior merit.

The number of persons who ask the questions: WHAT BOOKS SHALL I READ? AND HOW SHALL I READ THEM? is very great. Those who are beginning to feel an interest in books and reading, and who long for friendly direction, ask these questions more frequently than they receive wise and satisfactory answers. Intelligent young men, who have finished their education at school—clerks, apprentices, farmers, teachers who are moved by a wise and sincere desire for self-culture and self-improvement—ask the same questions of thems2lves and others. If they go into a bookstore, they are bewildered by the number and variety of the books from which they are to select, and their chance selection is as likely, to say the least, to be bad as good. It will rarely happen that it is the best which could be made. "The bookseller can tell them what books are popular and have a run, but this recommendation is of a doubtful character. They may have access to a well-selected library, but still they are at fault, not knowing how or what to choose for their immediate and individual wants. Students also, who are in a course of education at school or college, or who, having finished their course, would mark out for themselves a generous plan of private reading, are often greatly at a loss for the best answers to the questions which they would ask. Their time is limited, and they pertinaciously inquire:— What books ought I to read first of all, and what next in order ? In what way can a student form and direct a taste for the highest kind of literature ? How far can he trust, and ought he to follow his fancy; how far should he thwart and oppose his taste, and seek to form it anew ? Are there any fixed principles of criticism, by which the best books may be known, and a taste for them formed and fixed ? Young ladies, too, who are earlier released from the confinement of school-life and the drudgery of imposed studies—who often set the taste and prescribe the fashion for the reading of the village or the circle in which they move—often sadly suffer for the want of a little direction. Their sensibility is fresh, their fancy is wakeful, their taste is easily moulded. If guided aright, they might attain to a cultivated acquaintance with those ima-ginative writers who would inspire the purest and tenderest emotions and enrich the fancy with the noblest images; who would elevate their tastes and confirm good and noble principles. For the want of such direction, it often happens that ***such young ladies*** read themselves down into an utter waste and frivolity of thought, feeling, and purpose. The trashy literature in which they delight, becomes the cheap and vapid representative of their empty minds, their heartless affections, and their frivolous characters. Besides the classes already, named, there are heads of families who wish to form libraries, smaller or greater, which may instruct and amuse both themselves and their households, but who often choose books that defeat the very aims which they propose to accomplish, and react with more or less evil upon their children. What books shall they buy and how shall they judge of books ? Above all, how shall they train themselves and others to the best use of the books which they possess and read ?

We would in these papers meet this variety of wants; not completely—to attempt which would be idle—but in part, so far as our limits will allow. To give a complete catalogue of the best books, even in a few departments of literature, would be quite impossible. Such a catalogue would be dry reading at best—as dry as a volume of statistics, or a report of the census, and of far less interest and authority; for no man, on such a subject, would blindly yield himself to the direction of any single mind. A partial catalogue with a critique upon each author, would be little better. All that can be accomplished is to furnish thoughts and principles which may awaken the mind to wise activity, and illustrate them by examples from books and authors. We would show that the books which we read even carelessly, exert an influence upon us which is far more potent than we are apt to think, and that we ought to select our books—above all our favorite books—with, a more jealous care than we choose our friends and intimates. We would also show that reading is more than the amusement of an hour and the gratification of a capricious fancy: that it is an employment which may leave behind the most powerful impress for good, or which may reduce the soul to utter barrenness and waste, and even scathe it as with devouring fire. We would treat .also of the different kinds of books and the methods of reading appropriate to each. We hope also to give some direction to the taste, and this without the dry and formal precepts of the schools, or the captious and positive dogmatism of the professed critic. The taste, as applied to books and reading, like the eye for color and form, may be-educated, or rather it may be taught how to educate itself. We would aid in this effort at self-culture; especially would we indicate what are the methods and ways of reading imaginative literature, which may cause it to yield pure and exquisite delight, to add power to the intellect, and to impart a grace and finish to the character and life.

We are not insensible to the perils which are incident to our attempt. Not a few have undertaken to answer the questions which we have proposed, and have succeeded very indifferently. Many a young man has asked his respected teacher or trusted adviser " What and how shall I read?" and been put off with tiresome platitudes and solemn commonplaces for an answer, coupled with the titles of half a score of works, which every person is supposed to be acquainted with, and which are deemed eminently judicious and safe reading. The manuals usually known as " Courses of Reading," though useful to a certain extent, usually lack the germinant force of fundamental principles in respect to the object of reading and the estimate of authors. The list of books which Dr. Johnson recommended to a clerical friend, is a good example of most of the catalogues which are hastily prepared even by eminent critics. " *Universal History* (ancient)—*Rollin's Ancient History — Puffendorf's Introduction to History — Vertot's History of the Knights of Malta — Vertot's Revolutions of Portugai — Vertot's Revolutions of Sweden — Carte's History of England — Present State of England — Geographical Grammar — Prideaux's Connection — Nelson's Feasts and Fasts — Duty of Man — Gentleman's Religion — Clarendon's History — Watts' Improvement of the Mind — Watts' Logic —Nature Displayed — Lowth's English Grammar — Blaclcwall on the Classics — Sherlock's Sermons — Burnet's Life of Hale — Dupuis' History of the Church — Shuck-ford's Connections — Law's Serious Call — Walton's Complete Angler* — Sandys' Travels—Sprat's History of the Royal Society — *England's Gazetteer Goldsmith's Roman History — some Commentaries on the Bible"* This list seems to include works of three different classes. Books of standard authority and permanent value; books which had happened to please Dr. Johnson's permanent or temporary humor; books which had happened to occur to his mind when he was writing out the catalogue for his young friend. The most exciting and satisfactory comments on books and reading are not usually found in formal treatises, but in such incidental remarks as those which are recorded by Boswell of Dr. Johnson, or are met with in Montaigne's rambling and free-spoken essay *" Of Books,"* or in the pithy and pregnant essay of Bacon on *"Studies"* with *What eley's Commentary,* or in Charles Lamb's *"Detached Thoughts on Books and Reading,"* or in Hazlitt's many incisive essays and Coleridge's wonderfully stimulating criticisms, or in two or three good thoughts from Carlyle's address at Edinburgh mis-named *" On the Choice of Books,"* or the essay of B. W. Emerson on "Books" in the volume entitled *"Society and Solitude, "* which is characteristic of the author, even to his remarks about "Jesus " and "the Bibles of the world." All manuals entitled " Courses of Reading" must be exposed to the objection noticed by the elder D'Israeli, that they necessarily fall behind the times the moment they come up to them. A course of reading that should be complete in one month must begin to be defective the next.

Courses of reading from an elder adviser or friend to a pupil or ***protege,*** even if they are hastily prepared, serve a good purpose as pictures of the times. They cast more or less light upon the culture and knowledge which prevailed when they were written. A very distinguished clergyman of New England, furnishes the following list of books for a young pastor in 1792. " In Divinity, you will not wonder if I recommend President Edwards' writings in general; Br. Bellamy's and Dr. Hopkins'; ***President Davies' Sermons; Robert Walker's Sermons; Howe's do; Addison's Evidences ; Seattle's Evidences of Christianity; Leland's View of Deistical Writers; Berry Street Sermons;*** — in History ***Prideaux's Connection; Rollin's Ancient History ; Goldsmith's Roman History; do. History of England, or Rider's History of England*** which is more prolix and particular; ***Robertson's History of South America ; do. History of Charles V; Hutchinson's History of Massachusetts ; Ramsay's History of the War ; Guthrie's and Morse's Geography ; Josephus' History of the Jews ;— Watts on the Mind; Locke on the Human Understanding; — Specta-tor; Guardian; Tattler; Rambler; Pamela; Clarissa; Grandison; Telemachus; Don Quixote; Anderson's Voyage ; Cook's Voyages ; Milton ; Young's Night Thoughts; Vicesimus Knox's Essays ; Do. On Education ;— Buchan's Family Physician; Tissot on Health.-These*** may be sufficient—but additions may be easily made. The great danger will be of getting useless and hurtful books, especially Novels and Romances which generally corrupt, especially young minds; beside the loss of the purchase money and the time spent in the reading of them."

Another paper of a later date was prepared by a clergy-man, of some reputation for literature, for a young lady, whose mind the writer sought to direct, and, as is very likely, whose heart and hand he sought to win. It is as follows: "List of Books for a young lady's Library." *" Cann's small Bible* (with marginal references); *Home's Paraphrase on the Psalms ; Mrs. Hannah More's Strictures on Female Education; Mrs. Chapone's Letters to her Niece; Grove on the Sacrament; Mason on Self-Knowledge; Doddridge's Pise and Progress, etc. ; Newton on the Prophecies*

; Guide to Domestic Happiness and the refuge ; Cowper's Works, 2 vols.: *Young's Night Thoughts ; Elegant Extracts in Poetry; Rasselas, Prince of Abyssinia; The Rambler; Thomson's Seasons ; Dwight's Conquest of Canaan ; Washington's Life ; Trumbull's History of Connecticut.* This list of books might be enlarged, and perhaps upon recollection some alteration might be made, but these are well calculated to mend the heart, to direct the imagination and thoughts to proper objects, and to give command over them upon good principles. To read profitably we should always then have some object in view more than merely to pass away time, by letting words run off our tongue or through our minds. * * * Order and system in any business, and certainly in cultivating the mind, is really necessary, if we would be benefited by study. It is by having a few books well chosen and attentively and perseveringly read, that we fix in our mind useful principles. Books are multiplied without number, and it becomes perplexing to run from one to another, and none are well understood when we read in this manner. The Bible should always stand first in our esteem and be read first daily. It affords every species of reading,—history, biography, poetry, etc.,—and shows the heart in its true character."

If anything would discourage us from prosecuting the plan of writing upon Books and Reading, it would be the perusal of this paper of well-meant truisms and well-worn commonplaces. It does not follow, however, because advice upon any subject is especially liable to degenerate into meaningless generalities, that advice should never be given ; nor, because it is comparatively easy to discourse safely with uplifted eye-brows about the books we read and the companions we choose, that such counsel should never be given at all. The much-needed pilot-boat must run the risk of being itself stranded upon dangerous *flats* and beguiling *shallows,* if it would preserve the vessel from being ingulfed in the deeper seas, and the more terrible breakers.

There are not a few readers who reject all guidance and restraint—some from inclination, and some from a theory that counsel and selection interfere with the freedom of individual taste and the spontaneity of individual genius. Their motto in general is: "of all the sorts of VICE that prevail ADVICE is the most vexatious." So far as reading is concerned, it is, " In brief, sir, study what you most affect." One person, they insist, cannot advise for another, because one cannot put himself in the place of another. "Read what speaks to your heart and mind; let your own feelings be your guide, and leave critics and advisers to their stupid analyses and narrow or prejudiced judgments. Read that you may enjoy, not that you may judge; that you may gather impulse and inspiration, not that you may understand the reasons or explore the sources of the instruction and enjoyment which you unconsciously derive from the books in which you most delight." There is truth and force in this position, we grant. No man can read with profit that which he cannot learn to read with pleasure. If I do not myself find in a book something which I myself am looking for, or am ready to receive, then the book is no book for me whatever, however much it may be for another man. But to assert that one cannot help another to select and to judge of books is, in principle, to renounce all instruction and dependence on those who are older and wiser than we. To be consistent, it would turn every man into a hermit or a savage. Such a position is sometimes silly self-conceit; sometimes simple pride; sometimes it is a voluptuous animalism that would find in literature both stimulus and excuse for sensual indulgence. The wise adviser would respect the tastes of each reader, and would even bid him both gratify and follow them, but he. can do something to aid him in discerning what they are, and why, and how far they are to be allowed, or, if need be, restrained. Inspiration, genius, individual tastes, elective affinities, do not necessarily exclude self-knowledge, self-criticism, or self-control. If the genius of a man lies in the development of the individual person that he is, his manhood lies in finding out by self-study what he is and what he may become, and in wisely using the means that are fitted to form and perfect his individuality.

Others are especially jealous of the use of any *moral standard* in the critical judgments of books, or in the advice which is furnished concerning methods of reading. Such persons would be instinctively repelled from the papers which we propose to write, as they may have already inferred that we intend to use ethical considerations very freely, and perhaps severely. Against this they will inwardly protest in thoughts like these:—What has literature to do with morality? Poetry and fiction, essays and the drama, history and biography—everything in short which we usually call literature—aim to present man and his experiences as they are, and not as they ought to be. It is the aim and end of all these to describe, and not to judge, to paint to the life, and not to praise or condemn. The reader, not the writer, may judge if he will and as he will. But, in order to be able to judge, one must see all sides of human nature and human life, and these must be portrayed with energy and truth as they are; he must survey every manifestation of the human soul, the evil as well as the good, the passionate as truly as the self-controlled. The censor who brings the laws of duty to measure and regulate our reading, who judges of books as he judges of men, interferes with the freedom that gives all its life to literature and most of the zest and value to reading.

There is some truth in all this; or rather, there is a truth which is perverted into this caricature and error. What the truth is, and how far it may be carried without perversion and danger, we will show as we proceed. For the present, we observe that no mistake can be more serious than to suppose that the law of conscience and the rules of duty have nothing to do with the production and enjoyment of literature, as many modern libertines in the field of imaginative writing would have us believe. Ethical ideals are produced by the same creative imagination which furnishes the poet and the novelist their materials and their power. Ethical truth is but another name for imagination holding "the mirror up to nature," i. e., to nature in man, or human nature. Nature in man invariably prescribes ethical standards, and to these the imagination responds when she sets forth fiction as fact, poetry as truth, and history as reality in its highest import and loftiest significance. Not only is this true, but much more than this can be shown most satisfactorily.

If the lessons of these facts teach anything, they teach that literature must respect ethical truth if it is to reach its highest achievements, or attain that place in the admiration and love of the human race which we call fame. The literature which does not respect ethical truth, ordinarily survives as literature but a single generation. The writer who gives himself to any of the untruths which are known as superficial, sensual, Satanic, godless, or unchristian, ordinarily gains for himself either a brief notoriety or an unenviable immortality. He is either lost, or damned to fame. Of all the shams that pass current, with those who write or with those who .read, that is the flimsiest which hopes to outrage or cheat the human conscience.

While, then, on the one hand we contend for a somewhat liberal construction of the ethical and religious code as applied to the production and use of literary works, we insist that certain rules on this subject can be easily ascertained, and should be uncompromisingly enforced. But we as earnestly affirm that neither ethical truth, nor even religious earnestness, does of itself qualify a writer to produce, or require the reader to read a work which has no other ground on which to enforce its claims to attention and respect. It is not enough to say of a book, that it is good or good-ish, that it is Christian or safe, in order to justify its having been written or printed. There prevails not a little cant and hollowness, if not gross imposition and down-right dishonesty, in the use of the phrases *" Christian literature"* and *"safe or wholesome reading"* as we may have occasion to illustrate at some length.

We Wish it to be understood that we do not write for scholars or *litterateurs*, but for readers of English; not for bibliographers or bibliomaniacs, to whom literature and reading are a profession, a trade, or a passion; but for those earnest readers to whom books and reading are instruction and amusement, rest and refreshment, inspiration and re-laxation. Our papers will be familiar and free, not affected or constrained. Usefulness is their aim and object, and this aim will control the selection and illustration of the topics which may suggest themselves as we proceed.

But enough of this premising. We promise nothing, and yet we would attempt something. What we propose, if accomplished, will make these papers useful rather than exciting. They will be the minister of pleasure in their remote results, rather than by immediate excitement. "While then, as all well-mannered writers do, we ask the attention of the reader, we trust it will be given with a clear understanding of the character of what we propose to offer him, and with no extravagant expectations concerning its interest or its worth.

CHAPTER II

WHAT IS A BOOK? AND WHAT IS IT TO BEAD?

IT may appear very' much like trifling to ask these questions. Nothing is more familiar and nothing seems better understood. We may, however, find it useful to define, somewhat formally, what a book is, and what it is to read a book. Children, as we know, are very generally taught that whatever is printed is to be regarded with deference. The fiction is useful if not necessary, first, to prevent them from tearing books, and next, to train them to listen to the wisdom of books with a teachable spirit. In consequence, they learn very easily to esteem all books as alike oracles of wisdom and truth.

Mr. H. Crabb Robinson tells us that when a child he was corrected for mis-spelling a word on the authority of his spelling-book. On being told that the word was wrongly printed he says "I was quite confounded. I believed as firmly in the in-fallibility of print as any good Catholic can in the infallibility of his Church. I knew that naughty boys would tell stories, but how a book could contain a falsehood was quite incomprehensible." —

Diary, Chap. ii.

Not a few men live and die with a similar impression, and never cease to esteem a book as in some way endowed with a mysterious authority by the very fact that it is a book. This opinion is well expressed in the lines

" 'Tis pleasant, sure, to see one's name in print ;
A book's a book, although there's nothing in't

Following this tradition there are very intelligent men who. would never think of spending fifteen minutes in listening to stupidity or commonplace from a man's lips, who make it their duty and imagine it useful, solemnly to read, to weigh, and consider, any amount of dullness which an accredited author chooses to print, especially if it is done on expensive white paper and with a fair and wide margin. Men who will detect and spurn a lie, if it is spoken, will **read** lies by the hundred, if they are only printed; and when they read two books which contradict each other flatly in respect to statements of fact, will wonder how it can be possible that both should be worthy of credit, and yet as they are **books** they must of course **be true,** though they cannot see **how.** Very grave and Christian citizens —the stiff asserters of law and order—will read arguments that tend to the destruction of the family, with its sacred confidence and endearments—which would overturn every tribunal, unlock every prison, and make murder and arson as common as a change of the wind, and admire the profoundness of their wisdom. Nay—let it not be spoken above a whisper—modest and virtuous ladies, who would blush at an innocent remark, if it happens to be unfortunate or equivocal in its language, will read sentences, nay, pages, that are equivocal neither in language nor in sentiment, and pronounce them enchanting and delightful.

Let it be observed and remembered, that a book is always written by a man, and that it is never by any magic or mystery any better than its author makes it to be. This author may be a wise man or a fool. He may be an honest man or a knave. He may be a man of the best intentions, but slightly, or more than slightly, elevated with a little " too gude a conceit o' himsel" he may have something to say which it is worth the while should be said, and yet not know how to say it. But whatever he is, or knows, and has the power to communicate, that will he write down in his book, whether he thereby writes himself down a sage, or writes himself down after the earnest desire of Justice Dogberry.

"When we set ourselves to read a book, what do we do ? we place ourselves in communication with a living man. We go back with him to the time when he penned the volume. We think over the thoughts which he then thought, we sympathize with the feelings which he experienced, we behold the wondrous creations which his eye, " in fine frenzy rolling," saw enter his door and live and move about him—the men and women, or the spirits of heaven and hell, to which he gave being in his mind then, and which he re-creates in our minds now.

The theme may be God and man's concerns with God: and we sympathize, it may be, with the inspired Psalmist, as he utters the language of bitter repentance, of exulting hope, of unshaken fortitude, or earnest supplication; we follow the thoughts of the eloquent apostle, who discourses so sublimely of the loftiest themes; or we listen, in the attitude of love or of worship, to the words of Him who spake as never man spake. Or perhaps Barrow pours out before us a redundantly flowing stream of thoughts, weighty for sense and copious in diction; or Baxter speaks to our hearts in fiery directness; or Taylor amazes us by his mellifluent speech and his never-ending imagery; or South astonishes us by his wit, while he instructs us with his wisdom. Or, we confer with Bacon, who drops like pearls those pregnant observations that come home to " men's business and bosoms," or, after taking us by a rapid survey over what had already been accomplished in the field of science, leads us to a, height from which his prophetic eye can discern fields yet undiscovered. Spenser conducts us by devious but beguiling wanderings through the long pilgrimage of " Una and the milk-white lamb," till the Fairy Queen and fairy land become real to our thoughts and familiar to our memory. Shakspeare lets loose upon us a host of beings, the most wonderful that were ever created by a human fancy, or that can be gazed upon by the " mind's eye " of the re-creating reader. Mil-ton opens before us the gates of heaven, and we are dazzled at the magnificence of the scene, overwhelmed by the splendid array of the angelic host, or confounded by the glimpses which we catch of the infinite glories of the Un-created and Eternal. Or

> " On a sudden open fly
> With impetuous recoil and jarring sound,
> Th' infernal doors,"

and the archangel ruined stands before us, with his com-peers—sublime in intellect, degraded by sin, scarred and seared by suffering, yet proud and unsubdued in their relentless wills. Scott, "the magician of the North," marshals before us, with breathless haste, those marvellous creations of his genius, which are as familiar as household words. Dickens and Thackeray, " George Eliot" and Mrs. Oliphant, with many others, send us almost weekly, regular installments from their brain and bid us review with them the creations which they produce for our pleasure. The journalist or reviewer takes us into his closet, and discourses to us with wisdom or wildness, in soberness or extravagance, of the interests that concern the common weal, or the themes which are uppermost for the hour or the week.

To read an author is, however, more than to hold com-munion with a mind in its ordinary state, or by the usual method of hearing the conversation of a person, even in his happiest mood. For by the act of writing the mind is ordinarily raised to its highest energy both of thought and feeling. It condenses as it were and intensifies itself: whatever is good into what is doubly good—whatever is bad into what is doubly bad. It is deliberate. It does not proceed in haste. If a fact is to be stated, it may be examined with care and its truth established. If an opinion is to be expressed, it may be looked at from every side and in all its relations. What is spoken cannot be recalled, but what is ***written*** can be revised. The mind in its calmer mood can qualify and withdraw what it penned in fervid haste. New thoughts may modify its first conclusions, new energy may be concentered into some sinewy epithet, and new fervor may be expressed in a " winged word."

It follows from this, that a book does not merely represent its author, but it represents the best part of him, —or it may be the worst. It gives the picture of his inner self in forms enlarged and ideally improved. The colors are more intense and more finely contrasted than in the reality of his ordinary experience. Hence, reading a man's book is often worth far more than listening to his conversation. Hence, too, a good book is of more value to the world than a good man—for it is the best part of a good man— the good without the evil. Thus when a wise man dies, while his spirit is living on in one immortal life, he may be also living another immortality on earth—occupying perhaps a wider sphere than when he was in the body— his thoughts quickening the thoughts of others, as if he were present to speak them, his feelings inspiring the noblest feelings of others, and his principles prompting to worthy deeds after his own last action is done. It was by more than a figure that Milton wrote, in his ***Areopagitica:*** " for books are not absolutely dead things, but do contain a progeny of life in them as active as that soul whose progeny they are; nay, they do preserve as in a vial, the purest efficacy and extraction of that living intellect that bred them." " As good almost kill a man as kill a good book ; who kills a man kills a reasonable creature, God's image, but he who destroys a good book, kills reason itself, kills the image of God as it were in the eye."

The thought will doubtless occur, that this suggestion towards answering the questions, " what is a book, and what is it to read ?" applies to certain classes of books, but not to all. There are many books, it may be said, which might as well have been written by an automaton as a man, —books from which we can by no means gather what kind of a man produced them—books which have little or no flavor of the personality of their author. "We grant this of a few books, but the number is smaller than we should at first suspect, and it is literally true of no book whatever, that its character and value are not greatly determined by the intellect and culture, the honor and honesty, of the man who made it. The traces of personality are also oftener to be discerned than we imagine. Not only does the man make the book in more respects than we are wont to believe, but he can be known and detected in his book and through his book, more frequently than many readers notice.

A dictionary seems to be removed the farthest from any savor or aspect of human personality; and yet in any copious dictionary it is not difficult to discover the feelings and even the prejudices of its author. Those of Dr. Johnson are sufficiently manifest in respect to Excisemen, Pensioners, and his neighbors beyond the Tweed, by his definitions of *Excise, Pension, and Oats. Excise* he defines as " A hateful tax, levied on commodities, and adjudged not by the common judges of property, but wretches hired by those to whom excise is paid." *Pension,* he says, is "An allowance made to any one without an equivalent. In England it is generally understood to mean pay given to a state hireling for treason to his country." *Pensioner* is defined to be "A slave of state hired by stipend to obey his master." *Oats* he describes as "A grain which in England is generally given to horses, but in Scotland supports the people." The private opinions of Noah Webster look out very plainly through the judicial gravity with which he lays down the law concerning scores of words; as for example, when he defines *Dandy* thus : " In *modern* usage, a male of the human species who dresses himself like a doll and who carries his character on his back."

Every history purports to be an impartial record of facts, and a faithful transcript of the great truths which may be inferred from them. The historian, at the first thought, might be " set down " as nothing more nor less than an impersonal chronicler of actual events and facts. And yet who reads a history, even the most concise or rigidly impartial, who may not also read in the record of his facts the record of the author's partialities, and in his philosophy a transcript of individual prejudices as well as of universal principles ? The pithy Tacitus, by a pungent epithet and antithetic phrase, does not more effectually damn some hero in crime to everlasting fame, than he impresses you with a distinct and abiding image of his own strong and fervid character. Gibbon and Hume, Lingard and Macaulay, Bancroft and hildreth arnold and Froude, have not simply written out the story of the countries which have been their themes, but have also more or less distinctly recorded an abiding memorial of their own characters and principles, if indeed they have not now and then given to the world a distinct expression of their own prejudices and passions.

The poet, the dramatist, and the novelist may personate as many characters as they will, and put into the mouths of their fictitious personages the words most appropriate to the character of each—words seemingly very far removed from their own sentiments and feelings; but yet, when it chances that their own private opinions have to be spoken or their individual feelings expressed, it will be done with an energy of words, an intensity of expression, which betrays them as the author's own. Dante and Milton, Goethe and Schiller, Byron and Bulwer, introduce upon their shifting stage an immense variety of characters, and speak or sing through each of them the thoughts and emotions that belong to each. Their own genius lies in the power to forget themselves completely in their characters, or rather to transform themselves into the heroes whom they personate. But now and then occurs a sentence which is weighty with a double meaning, because the author speaks his own cherished opinions through his hero, or a strain will recur so often and in a character so peculiar, that we recognize it as the sad refrain of the poet's own sorrow. Herein is seen the man, and hereby does the individual man assert his right over the impersonal genius. Scott and Shakspeare are the least personal and subjective, the most completely objective and dramatic of all modern writers. Scott was large-hearted and many-sided enough ordinarily to lose himself in his characters. But now and then the reader can detect the humane Scotch sheriff, as well as the romantic and prejudiced tory, in characters and sayings in which neither would confess himself to be present. Shakspeare is rightly called the " myriad-minded:" and it may be hard to discern the man Shakspeare through the countless and strange variety of personages into which he so successfully transforms himself. But the man will speak out in the sonnets, which have been thought by many to have been written in order to satisfy even Shakspeare's longing at times to write in his own character and to give utterance to his own individuality. There are serious and solemn passages in his dramas in which no imitated voice is uttered: in which it is no masked histrionist who speaks, but Shakspeare's self utters sentiments and emotions that he could not repress. It is almost idle to observe that neither Dickens nor Thackeray, Trollope nor George Eliot, can always hide themselves in the motley of men whom their fancy has created. Coleridge and Southey, Wordsworth and Tennyson, usually sing their own songs, and from a loving, or, it may be, a saddened heart. We may truly utter the seeming paradox, that while it is the proof and triumph of genius to be able to overcome and overrule the individual man, yet where the genius is not rooted in, and does not grow out of the intense affections and the earnest character of the writer's own individuality, he shows the art of a dexterous histrionist rather than the earnestness of a great nature.

As for those authors who write to amuse the public, the perpetrators of humor of all sorts, and the producers of every variety of bagatelle to suit the reading-market, it is not easy for the man to hide his individuality behind the mask which he assumes, however grotesque and comical that mask may be. The features of the man will always shine through the mask—if indeed there be *a man* beneath it. For very great is the difference whether it be a *clown* or a *man* which is behind—whether we see, through the disguise, the look half-vacant and half-villainous of which the venal and frivolous Bohemian can never rid himself, with all his tact and art, or the broad swimming eyes of love, with which Hood always looked out through his fun, or the sad earnestness into which Lamb relaxed so soon as he had stammered out his joke or his pun.

It is scarcely needful to add that essayists and critics, the authors of moral, political and religious tracts and books, are supposed of course to write their own opinions, which, though they be also the opinions of large masses of men, will be shaded by the color and hue of the minds from which they come, and be warmed with the feelings which glow in the hearts of all thoughtful and eloquent souls.

Let it not be thought for a moment, that the assertions—that a book is written by a man, and is just what its author makes it to be, and that to read a book is to converse with a living man—are barren truisms. We believe them to be fertile in important suggestions, and that if held fast in the mind they will serve as a clue to guide us safely and wisely through the labyrinth of books —which may mislead and bewilder as well as amuse and ennoble. We invite the reader's attention to the suggestions which may be derived from them.

These thoughts may suggest the principles which we need to guide us as we judge of books and read them— and may help us distinguish the books which are books, from those which are only " things in books' clothing," as well as teach us how to make the best use of those which are books indeed.

CHAPTER III.

HOW TO READ-ATTENTION IN READING

LET US then take our clue in hand and follow it out, feeling our way along, in the suggestions and applications to which it will naturally conduct us.

It is thought a great feat for a child to learn to read. The process is not a trivial one which is accomplished every day, and is going on in our nurseries and schoolhouses, by which the infant learns to distinguish letters, to spell them into words, to look through written characters, to interpret words into thoughts and feelings, and do ail these so readily that the skill seems literally to have "come by nature." It is indeed a great feat, as we see plainly when a full-grown man or woman attempts it for the first time, and as we mark the slow and painful steps by which such persons must halt and stumble for years, in order to master the mechanical part of the process. It is very rightly thought to be a most important step that is gained when either the child or the man has finished this apprenticeship, and to make a great difference with him to have overcome these obstacles. But why is it so important? "What makes the difference so great? Who asks: what is all this for, and how may a man best use the power which is thus gained? It is not enough to say that it enables a person to transact business, to read his own accounts and letters from other people, to know what is going on at New York or "Washington, to pore over newspapers, to gape over a few tales of blood and murder, or now and then to extract a thought from a good book on Sunday. If this were all, it were indeed worth all the cost, as the experience and the common sense of the world shows. The transactions and intercourse of civilized life depend on this acquisition; and the unconscious discipline of civilized man that comes from the process, even in the limited and careless uses to which it is applied, reward the pains-taking a thousand-fold.

But suppose the question were asked more distinctly and more frequently: How may the power thus attained be used to the best advantage, and what are the uses to which it may be applied ? Shall we say or think that the instrument is too common to admit of improvement? Then would one method of plowing be as good as another, and one plow would be as good as another; when all the world knows that from good plows and good plowing—to say nothing of the best looms and best weaving—come the wealth and luxury and civilization of millions of men. If the applications to which a common instrument may be turned are of no consequence whatever, then are potatoes as good as wheat because both are products of the plow, and the coarsest serge is as desirable as broadcloth from Leeds or silk from Lyons.

But all this is too obvious to need an argument or illus-tration ; yet it is well to bestow a thought on truths so simple, for sometimes we are surprised by their extensive reach and even their tremendous import. Surely if a man should form and use principles in regard to any subject, he should form and use them in respect to what and how he reads, and for what ends. If life is not all a holiday or a day dream, then reading should be pursued in an earnest and reflecting spirit. For he that opens a book does by this very act begin to converse with a man—good, bad or indifferent as the case may be—with a man perhaps in his very best or worst phase or condition. If then you would scorn to take lessons or receive influences from an ignoramus, a knave, or a known deceiver and seducer of the good; why not scorn to come nearer to any such man by reading what is the image, the expression, nay perhaps the essence or embodiment of himself? If, when you are admitted to the society of a wise or amusing man who gives instruction or entertainment in a winning and graceful manner, you think it important to be wakeful in his society and to catch and weigh every word; why should you not feel the same necessity when he speaks to you through the written page ? And yet how many neglect the whole matter of what books they or their children read, or suffer it to take its chance, for evil or for good! Very good persons who would be slow to provide unwholesome or poisonous food, or to associate with mean or dangerous men, do both these things by the books with which they and their families come into close and frequent contact. They and their children read such books as come in their way, or are talked about, or are cheap, or attractive. Or, if they are careful in choosing books, they have little care as to the way in which they read them. This is not as it should be. It may involve a fearful and lasting wrong. If a man has but little time to read, he has no right to allow these golden hours of his life to be wasted and worse than wasted. If he reads a great deal, he has no right to allow influences which are silently but most powerfully affecting his whole character, to be what the chance or the mood of the hour decides them—to bring disease or health, life or death, to that which makes him a man. These influences might be most healthful and exhilarating; they might do much to make him a better, a more cheerful and self-relying man: and yet his time, it may be, is dawdled away in reading he knows not what, or in reading a good book in such a way that he knows not what he has read, any more than one can tell what he has said after being jaded by an evening party or wasted by a round of morning-calls.

Reading ought not to be aimless, even though its aim be to while away an hour. And reading when allowed for the merest relaxation is not exempt from the guid-

ance of principles and, if need be, the restraints of conscience. As to habits of reading, and the attitude with which we are accustomed to present ourselves before our
book and its .author, these are of so great importance that our success or failure in
the use of books is determined by them. We are not so stupid or pedantic as to desire to form the reading of two persons after the same model, or to Jay down formal
rules, for the mechanical adjustment and direction of the mental processes. But we
earnestly desire to awaken each person to the dignity of forming his own rules for
reading; and of making his converse with books to contribute to and to grow from
a character that is individual because it is formed by reflection.

The first rule which we prescribe is: read with attention. This is the rule that
takes precedence of all others. It stands instead of a score of minor directions. Indeed it comprehends them all, and is the golden rule. To gain the power and habit
of attention, is the great difficulty to be overcome by young readers when they
begin. The one reason why reading is so dull to multitudes of active and eager
minds is that they have not acquired the habit of attending to books. The eye may
be fastened upon the page, and the mind may follow the lines, and yet the mind
not be half awake to the thoughts of the author, or the best half of its energies may
be abroad on some wandering errand. The one evil that comes from omnivorous
and indiscriminate reading is that the attention is wearied and overborne by the
multitude of the objects that pass before it; that the miserable habit is formed and
strengthened of seeming to follow the author when he is half comprehended, of va-
cantly gazing upon the page that serves just to occupy and excite the fancy without
leaving distinct and lasting impressions.

It was said of Edmund Burke, who was a great reader and a great thinker also,
that he read every book as if he were never to see it a second time, and thus made
it his own, a possession for life. Were his example imitated, much time would be
saved that is spent in recalling things half remembered, and in taking up the stitches
of lost thoughts. A greater loss than that of time would be avoided: the loss of the
dignity and power which are possessed by him who keeps his mind tense, active
and wake-ful. It is very common to give the rule thus, " Whatever is worth reading at all, is worth reading well." If by " well" is intended with the utmost stretch

of attention, it is not literally true, for there are books which serve for pastime and amusement, books which can be run through when we are more or less fagged or ill,and cannot and ought not to put forth our utmost energies of body and mind. Then there are books which we may look through, as a merchant runs over the advertisements in a newspaper —-taking up the thoughts that interest and concern us especially, as the magnet takes and holds the iron filings that are scattered through a handful of sand. But if every part of a book be equally worthy our regard, as the writings of Arnold, Grote, Merivale, Gibbon, Burke, Webster, Milton, Shakspeare, or Scott, then should the entire energy of attention be aroused during the time of reading. The page should be read as if it were never to be seen a second time; the mental eye should be fixed as if there were no other object to think of; the memory should grasp the facts, (i. e.) the dates, incidents, etc., like a vise; the impressions should be distinctly and sharply received; the feelings should glow intensely at all that is worthy and burn with indignation at everything which is bad. For the want of this habit, thoroughly matured and made permanent, time is wasted, negligent habits are formed, the powers of the mind are systematically weakened by the very exercise which should give them strength, and reading, which ought to arouse and strengthen the intellect, produces, with many, no deeper and more abiding impression than the shifting pictures of a magic lantern, or the fantastic groupings of the kaleidoscope—first a bewildering show, then confusion and vacancy.

There is now-a-days a special danger from this inattention. So many books are written, which are good enough in their way, .and yet are the food for easy, *4. e.* lazy, reading, and they are so cheap withal; so much excitement prevails in respect to them, that an active mind is in danger of knowing many things superficially and nothing well, of being driven through one volume after another with such breathless haste as to receive few clear impressions and no lasting influences.

Passive reading is the evil habit against which most readers need to be guarded, and to overcome which, when formed, requires the most manful and persevering efforts. The habit is the natural result of a profusion of books and the indolence of our natures and our times, which desires to receive thoughts,—or more exactly pictures, many of which are thin, hazy, and evanescent—rather than vigorously to react against them by an effort that thinks them over and makes them one's own. It is the intellectual dyspepsia which is induced by a plethora of intellectual diet, if that may be called intellectual which is the weak dilution of thought. Almost better not read at all, than to read in such a way. Certainly it is better to be forced to steal a half-hour from sleep, after a day of bodily toil, or to depend for your reading on an hour at a midday nooning when your fellow-laborers are asleep, if you but fix your whole mind on what you read, than to dawdle away weeks and months in turning over the leaves of hundreds of volumes in search for something new, which is feebly conceived, as lazily dismissed, and as stupidly forgotten. Better read one history, one poem, or one novel, well, if it takes a year to despatch it at stolen intervals of time, than lazily to consume twelve hours of the day in a process which wastes the time, and, what is worse, wastes the intellect, the fancy, and the living soul.

But how is the attention to be controlled? How can this miserable passiveness be prevented or overcome? Rules in great number have been prescribed. All sorts of directions have been devised. An ingenious author has advised that each sentence should be read through at a single breath; the breath being retained until the sentence is finished. Some advise to read with the pen in hand; others to make a formal analysis of every volume ; others to repeat to ourselves, or to recite to others, the substance of each page and chapter. These, and other devices, are all of service in their way, and some of them we will consider in their appropriate place. But their chief value turns upon this, that they induce an interest or require an interest, either direct or indirect, in the subject-matter which is read. Whatever awakens the interest will be certain to fix and hold the attention. The hired lad in the country who steals an hour from sleep or rest, that he may get on.a few pages in the odd volume of Plutarch or Rollin, which, having fallen in his way, has begun to unfold before his astonished gaze the till then unknown history of the ancient world; the errand-boy of the city, who stands trembling at the book-stall, lest the surly proprietor should out short his borrowed pleasure from the page which he devours; these need no artificial devices to teach them to hold the mind to the book, or to retain its contents. The great secret of their attention is to be found in the fresh interest with which they lay hold of the thoughts of the pictured page, and this remains ever the great secret of the habit of successful reading even to the mind that has been disciplined to the most amazing feats of application. There are no arts of attention, no arts of memory, which can be compared with this natural and certain condition of success.

Daniel Webster was one of the most earnest and intelligent* of readers all his life long. His favorite authors were read and re-read with a passionate fondness. His critical conversations upon the standard poets and essayists and orators of the English tongue are still remembered and quoted by those who were present to hear when the mood and opportunity of discourse were upon him. In one of the last evenings of his life he beguiled the weariness of his attendants by reciting a poem from Cowper. How he came to be so successful and so intelligent a reader is explained in his autobiography. Whatever he read he read so often and so earnestly that he learned to repeat it.

" We had so few books," he says, " that to read them once or twice was nothing ; we thought they were all to be got by heart." A. small circulating library had been established in the neighborhood by his father and other persons, and among the books which he obtained from it was the Spectator. " I could not understand why it Was necessary that the author of the Spectator should take such great pains to prove that Chevy Chase was a good story ; that was the last thing I doubted." He tells us, " In those boyish days there were two things which I did dearly love, viz: reading and playing—passions which did not cease to struggle when boyhood was over."

The man or boy who reads with attention thus quickened cannot read amiss if what he reads is worth perusing. Of his habits when a student he says : "Many other students read more than I did and knew more than I did. But so much as I read I made my own. When a half hour or an hour at most had elapsed, I stored my book, and thought on what I had read. If there was anything peculiarly interesting or striking in the passage, I endeavored to recall it and lay it up in my memory, and commonly could effect my object."

Sir Edward Sugden explained to Sir Thomas Fowell Buxton the secret of his professional success in the following words: "I resolved when beginning to read law, to make everything I acquired perfectly my own, and never to go to a second thing till I had entirely accomplished the first. Many of my competitors read as much in a day as I read in a week, but at the end of the twelve months my knowledge was as fresh as on the day it was acquired, while theirs had glided away from their recollection." *Mem. of Sir T. F, Buxton, ch. xxiv*.

He who would read with attention must learn to be interested in what he reads. He must feel wants or learn to create wants which must be supplied. If it be history that he would read with attention, he must feel deficiencies that will not let him rest till they are supplied; he must be moved by a desire that will command its object. Is it poetry or fiction ? He must be excited by a restless appetite that longs to be amused with new pictures, or diverted by humorous scenes, or stirred by lofty ideals, or charmed by poetic melody, and that grows by what it feeds on. And the man must master, and not be mastered by, his increasing stock of knowledge and his treasured products of the imagination. He must exercise great and still greater energy in judging and applying the acquisitions he has made, making them accompany his musings, feed his memory, animate his principles, and guide his life.

CHAPTER IV.

HOW TO HEAD WITH INTEREST AND EFFECT.

"WE have seen that a book is the creation of a living man, and should be regarded and judged somewhat as a man himself is tried and estimated. A few books are indeed almost impersonal, and might have been written by one man as readily as by another. These are to be judged chiefly by their *value*, *i. e.*, by what they contain. But most books express more or less of the personality of their authors; and in reading them, we come in contact with living men. Good books, besides the value of what they contain and impart, have a positive *worth* in their effect on the principles, feelings and character.

If this is true, then in reading we are properly said to come into communication with a human being, who will either instruct and elevate, or mislead and degrade us. From these fundamental conceptions of **Books** and **Reading**, we have begun to derive our rules for the selection of the books which we read, and for our own behaviour in using them. We have also seen that, for success in reading, we must read with attention, and to read with attention, we must read with an awakened and sustained interest. Though this interest when awakened must be regulated by the rules of prudence and duty, yet it often needs to be enkindled and sustained, if we are to read with attention and profit. It becomes then a question of prime concern how we can so arouse, sustain and direct our interest in the books which we read as to make our reading most effective for good. In answer to this somewhat comprehensive inquiry, we reply:

1. If we are at a loss what to read, or if we can think of nothing which we desire especially to, read, it is well to ask ourselves what we care most to learn or to think of. No questions are more frequently pressed than these: "What shall I read? What shall I read next? With what books shall I begin a course of reading? What do you think will interest me?" Sometimes a person asks these questions of himself. More frequently he addresses them to another. The best answers which can be given to them are suggested by other questions like these: "What are you most interested to know? In what particulars does your ignorance most disturb or annoy you? With what class of facts and thoughts, principles or emotions would it please you best to be conversant?" If a person can answer these questions with any satisfaction to himself, he is in the way of knowing what books he ought first to read. For if he cannot without assistance find the book which he ought first to lay hold of, he can be more easily directed by another, when his adviser knows what he cares most to know or what excites his keenest appetite.

The great difficulty with the majority of readers is, that their sense is indefinite of any wants which books can supply, or their desire to supply these wants is feeble. Or, if they are aware of their deficiencies in the general, they have neither the courage nor the patience to know them in the detail, and manfully to * set about the work of removing them. To many persons the wants which books alone can supply are themselves either created or brought to light by the use of books. Many a man needs first to read and to read with interest, in order to have awakened in his soul a thirst for books and a taste for reading. There are however not a few who through a sense of ignorance, or shame when brought in contact with those better read than themselves, or through some other lucky though perhaps rude shock to their self-conceit and self-content, are suddenly fired with a desire for knowledge from books. Of history they begin to have some inkling, and feel the first desire to learn the story of their own township, their own family, their own nation or their own race. Of eloquence they have some idea, and they seek to be excited by written oratory. Poetry may have moved their ears with its rhythmic melody or charmed their souls with its wizard imagery. The drama or the novel may have startled and enchanted them by its pictured pages. Or perhaps the person who asks, "What shall I read?" or "With what shall I begin?" may have read and studied for years in a mechanical routine, and with a listless spirit; with scarcely an independent thought, with no plans of self-improvement, and few aspirations for self-culture. To all these classes the advice is full of meaning: "Read what will satisfy your wants and appease your desires, and you will comply with the first condition to reading with interest and profit." Hunger and thirst are better than manifold appliances and directions, in respect to other than the bodily wants, towards a good appetite and a healthy digestion. If a man has any self-knowledge or any power of self-direction, he is surely competent to ask himself, what is the subject or subjects, in respect to which he stands most in need of knowledge or excitement from books. If he can answer this question he has gone very far towards answering the question, "What book or books can I read with satisfaction and profit?"

2. It follows by a necessary inference that every man should aim first of all to read and master all the books which relate directly or indirectly to his profession or business in life. If a man is alive to any subject whatever, it is to his chosen occupation in life, and to whatever promises its easier working or more successful issue. If he dislikes his business, if he *frets* at and fights it, then God only can help him. On such a man human counsel and human aid must be thrown away; much more must books and reading, if they cannot bring him to acquiesce in his business or to change it. But if a man has something to do day by day in which he strives after the skill which leads to success, and if he can learn anything about it from books,

he cannot but read such books as will instruct him, with an excited and prolonged interest. No novelist is held to the charmed page of fiction, no rhapsodist reads and re-reads his favorite poet, with the keen and excited attention with which a man thoroughly aroused by some difficulty in his occupation or his circumstances, resorts to the treatise or the encyclopedia, the journal or the newspaper, which promises to answer the question which he is anxiously pondering. Let a farmer have brooded over the unac-countable loss of his wheat or potato crop, or have anxiously inquired what will restore the blight which is beginning to attack his favorite peach or pear tree, and he devours the printed pages that prescribe a remedy or promise relief. If a mechanic is at fault in his work, and finds his machinery fails to do the service for which it is designed, he feels no lack of interest and suffers under no failure of attention while he is consulting the books which promise to instruct him. Let either learn that by extensive reading he can gain an insight into the secret of certain and progressive success, and he will read widely in relation to his business with an ever-increasing and intensified enthusiasm. The madness of the so-called book-farmers and inventive enthusiasts, illustrates the truth which we assert, that if a man would learn to read with interest and attention, he should first of all read much in respect to his call-ing in life. If he is a farmer, he should read books of agriculture; if a mechanic, books on machinery; if a banker, books on banking and finance: whatever be his calling, he should make it the one subject upon which he will read, if he reads upon nothing else. In this way he will elevate his calling, from being a slavish and enslaving drudgery, into a rational discipline, not only for immediate profit but for manly cultivation. He will not only feed and cherish his body, and enlarge his comforts and luxuries by his better instructed toil, but he will discipline his intellect and elevate his soul by the thinking and reasoning which his reading will require. He will waken into life that within himself which is higher than his occupation or profession, and that is his thinking and feeling self. He will find in himself that which is more than the farmer, the trader, or the mechanic, and that is the manhood that he has and which he is bound to think of and care for. The wants and desires, the hopes and the aspirations which pertain to the man will be gradually awakened, and will connect him with the thoughts and feelings of other men as these are expressed in books, till it may be that books shall become one of the necessaries of his life, and reading, instead of being a listless and constrained employment, shall be his chosen occupation, his best society, his most delightful amusement, and perhaps his sweetest solace and comfort in dark and bitter hours.

3. In reading, we do well to propose to ourselves definite ends and purposes. The more distinctly we are aware of our own wants and desires in reading, the more definite and permanent will be our acquisitions. Hence it is a good rule to ask ourselves frequently, " Why am I reading this book, essay or poem; or why am I reading it at the present time rather than any other?" It may often be a satisfying answer, that it is convenient; that the book happens to be at hand; or that we read to pass away the time. Such reasons are often very good, but they ought not always to satisfy us. Yet the very habit of proposing these questions, however they may be answered, will involve the calling of ourselves to account for our reading, and the consideration of it in the light of wisdom and duty. The distinct consciousness of some object at present before us, imparts a manifold greater interest to the contents of any volume. It imparts to the reader an appropriative power, a force of affinity, by which he insensibly and unconsciously attracts to himself all that has a near or even a remote relation to the end for which he reads. Any one is conscious of this who reads a story with the purpose of repeating it to an absent friend; or an essay or a report with the design of using its facts or arguments in a debate; or a poem with the design of reviving its imagery, and reciting its finest passages. Indeed one never learns to read effectively until he learns to read in such a spirit—not always indeed for a definite end, yet always with a mind attent to appropriate and retain and turn to the uses of culture, if not to a more direct application. The private history of every self-educated man from Franklin onwards attests that they all were uniformly not only earnest but *select* in their reading, and that they selected their books with distinct reference to the purposes for which they used them. Indeed the reason why self-trained men so often surpass men who are trained by others in the effectiveness and success of their reading, is that they know for what they read and study, and have definite aims and wishes in all their dealings with books. The omnivorous and indiscriminate reader who is at the same time a listless and passive reader, however ardent is his curiosity, can never be a reader of the most effective sort.

4. Another good rule is suggested by the foregoing. Always have some solid

reading in hand, i. e. some work or author which we carry forward from one day to another, or one hour of leisure to the next, with persistence till we . have finished whatever we have undertaken. There are many great and successful readers who do not observe this rule, but it is a good rule notwithstanding. The writer once called upon one of the most extensive and persevering of modern travelers at an early hour of the day to attend him upon a walk to a distant village. It was after break-fast, and though he had but few minutes at command he was sitting with book in hand—a book of solid history, he was perusing day after day. He remarked: " This has been my habit for years in all my wanderings. It is the one habit which gives solidity to my intellectual activities and imparts tone to my life. It is only in this way that I can overcome and counteract the tendency to the dissipation of my powers and the distraction of my attention, as strange persons and strange scenes present themselves from day to day." To the rule already given—read with a definite aim—we could add the rule—make your aims to be definite by continuously holding them rigidly to a single book at all times, except when relaxation requires you to cease to work and to live for amusement and play. Always have at least one iron in the fire, and kindle the fire at least once every day.

5. It is implied in the preceding, that we should read upon definite subjects and with a certain method and proportion in the choice of our books. If we have a single object to accomplish in our reading for the present that object will of necessity direct the choice of what we read, and we shall arrange our reading with reference to this single end. This will be a nucleus around which our reading will for the moment naturally gather and arrange itself. If several subjects seem to us equally important and interesting, we should dispose of them in order, and give to each for the time our chief and perhaps our exclusive attention. That this is wise is so obvious as not to require illustration. " One thing at a time," is an accepted condition for all efficient activity, whether it is employed upon things or thoughts, upon men or books. If five or ten separate topics have equal claim upon our interest and attention, we shall do to each the amplest justice, if we make each in its turn the central subject of our reading. There is little danger of weariness or monotony from the workings of such a rule. Most single topics admit or require a considerable variety of books, each different from the other and each supplementing the other. Hence it

is one of the best of practices in prosecuting a course of reading, to read every author who can cast any light upon the subject which we have in hand. For example if we are reading the history of the Great rebellion in England, we should read if we can, not a single author only, as Clarendon, but a half-dozen or a half-score, each of whom writes from his own point of view, supplies what another omits, or corrects what he under or overstates. But, besides the formal histories of the period, there are the various novels, the scenes and characters of which are placed in those times, such as Scott's Woodstock; there are also- diaries, such as those by Evelyn, Pepys and Burton; and there are memoirs, such as those of Col. Hutchinson, while the last two have been imitated in scores of fictions. There are poems, such as those of Andrew Marvel,. Milton and Dryden. There are also shoals of political tracts and pamphlets, of hand-bills and caricatures. We name these various descriptions of works and classes of reading, not because we suppose all of them are accessible to those readers who live at a distance from large public libraries, or because we would advise every one who may have access to such libraries, to read all these books and classes of books as a matter of course, but because we would illustrate how great is the variety of books and reading matter that are grouped around a single topic and are embraced within a single period. Every person must judge for himself how long a time he can bestow upon any single subject, or how many and various are the books in respect to it which it is wise to read; but of this every one may be assured, that it is far easier, far more agreeable and far more economical of time and energy, to concentrate the attention upon a single subject at a time than to extend it to half a score, and that six books read in succession or together upon a single topic, are far more interesting and profitable than twice as many which treat of topics remotely related. A lady well known to the writer, of the least possible scholarly pretensions or literary notoriety, spent fifteen months of leisure snatched by fragments from onerous family cares and brilliant social engagements, in reading the history of Greece as written by a great variety of authors and as illustrated by many accessories of literature and art. Nor should it be argued that such rules as these or the habits which they enjoin are suitable for scholars only or for people who have much leisure for reading. It should rather be urged, that those who can read the fewest books and who have at command the scantiest time, should aim to read with the greatest concentration and method; should occupy all of their divided energy with single centres of interest, and husband the few hours which they can command, in reading whatever converges to a definite because to a single impression.

6. Special efforts should be made to *retain* what is gathered from reading, if any such efforts are required. Some persons read with an interest so wakeful and responsive, and an attention so fixed and energetic as to need no appliances and no efforts in order to retain what they read. They look upon a page and it is imprinted upon the memory. They follow the thoughts and trace the words and understand the sentences of their author and these remain with them as permanent possessions. Images, descriptions, eloquent passages, well sounding and rhythmic lines in poetry or prose, can all be spontaneously and accurately reproduced; or if words and illustrations are forgotten and lost, principles, truths and impressions will remain and cannot be effaced. Every book which such persons read enters into the structure of their being-it is taken up and assimilated into the very substance of their living selves. Every paragraph in a newspaper with every fact which it records or truth which it illustrates, is turned to some permanent account and remains as a lasting acquisition.

But there are others who read only to lose and to forget. Facts and truths, words. and thoughts are alike evanescent. We shall not attempt to explain here the nature of these differences- We are concerned only to devise the remedy: we insist that those who labor under these difficulties should use special appliances to avoid or overcome them. But that upon which we insist most of all, is that what we read we should seek to make our own, ***only in the manner and after the measure of which we are capable***. Each reader should follow the natural bent and aptitudes of his own individual nature. If we have not a good verbal memory, it is almost in vain that we seek to remember choice phrases and sentences, happy turns of expression, admirable bits of eloquent speech, or striking stanzas and lines of inspiring or moving poetry. We may read them again and again, we may admire them with increasing fervor, we may return to them with an ever augmented interest, but we shall make little progress in remembering them so as to be able to recite them. If we have a feeble capacity for the retention of dates and facts as such, unless they interest our feelings or illustrate principles, the utmost pains-taking will do little to help us to retain facts when isolated or uninteresting, or numbers when they signify nothing but so many figures. We do not advise a man laboring under these inaptitudes to fight against nature or to fall into a querulous, discouraged or fretful quarrel with himself, because, as he says, he cannot remember what he reads. nor when we enjoin upon him to use special efforts to remember, do we intend that he shall be more interested *in his efforts to remember* than he is interested *in what he is to remember*. We advise just the opposite. But we contend that when a man reads he should put himself into the most intimate intercourse with his author, so that all his energies of apprehension, judgment and feeling may be occupied with and aroused by what his author furnishes, whatever it may be. If repetition or review will aid him in this, as it often will, let him not disdain or neglect frequent reviews. If the use of the pen in brief or full notes, in catch-words or other symbols will aid him, let him not shrink from the drudgery of the pen and the common-place book. If he is aided to discern and retain the logical connections of an argument or a discourse by drawing them out in a complete skeleton or analysis, let him prosecute the dis-section without flinching. If a re-survey of the parts will give him a comprehensive view of the method of the whole let him complete his analyses with the utmost care and arrange their products in a new and symmetrical order. But there is no charm or efficacy in such mechanism by itself. It is only valuable as a means to an end, and that end is to quicken the intellectual energies by arousing and holding the attention. It is by awakening and energizing the reason—by concentrating and arousing the feelings that it can serve any very useful purpose. To remember what we read we must make it our own: we must think with the author, rethinking his thoughts, following his facts, assenting to or rejecting his reasonings, and entering into the very spirit of his emotions and purposes.

CHAPTER V.

THE RELATIONS OF THE READER TO HIS AUTHOR.

THE considerations presented already as well as the fun-damental conceptions of books and reading with which we set off in our search of rules and methods, enforce upon us the truth that effective reading depends most of all on the relations in which the reader finds himself, or into which he can bring himself, with respect to his author. If these relations are those of incongruity or of repellency, they will be more or less fatal to all profitable reading. The fault may be in the reader, or the fault may be in the author, or it may lie partly with the one and partly with the other, but if the fault exists, it will go far to defeat the best results which might otherwise follow. Accordingly, our interest in and our attention to what we read, and therefore our success in reading depend very largely on the authors whom we read. A book which is very suitable for one person may for this reason be entirely unfitted for another. The same book which is suitable at one time, or at a certain age, or with a certain degree of development or culture, may be entirely unsuitable to the same person in another mood, at another age, and after greater progress and culture. Thus the consideration of the manner in which we should read, in a certain sense depends upon *what we read*. The discussion of *how toe may read with effect*, depends largely upon *what we read*, and involves the consideration of the principles and rules by which we should select our authors. Upon this topic we observe:

1. That in order to read with interest and attention we should choose an author from whom we can gain some-thing. We do not say from whom we can learn something, for we do not hold that it is the duty of all authors to teach something in the way of fact or argument in order to be useful or interesting. Many books serve to amuse and impress as well as to inform and convince. Those authors are as useful who enforce and inspire, as those who en-lighten and instruct. The novel

that leaves us with a glow of contentment and thankfulness, that inspires us with a warm resolve to struggle with an unequal lot or to be con-tented and cheerful under adverse fortune, that confirms our faith in goodness and our trust in God, may be quite as useful as the treatise which enforces some new principle in finance, the history which clears up some disputed question of fact, or the argument which sets forever at rest some dispute upon a point of public policy, or even the sermon which proves or enforces some theological truth. A tale that fills an invalid with cheerful thoughts or whiles away a weary hour with pleasant pictures, is as useful as the most formal demonstration of a questioned proposition. A poem that elevates the soul, excites the imagination, kindles the emotions, and rouses the aspirations may be worth more to myriads of readers than scores of so-called books of fact and argument, or even of books of exhortation and edification.

But with this enlarged conception of the kind and variety of profit which we may expect from an author, we are more completely justified in requiring of every author who solicits our attention: whether he has anything to give us, *i. e.*, whether we shall gain anything by reading his book. If he can neither teach us anything which we do not know, nor convince us of anything of which we are in doubt, nor strengthen our faith in what we already receive, nor set old truths in new lights, nor warm our feelings into noble earnestness, nor entertain us with whole-some jokes nor excite us to honest laughter, then *he* is not the man and *his* is not the book for *us*. Whatever he and his book may be to others, they have no claims upon us, and we should be quite ready to show both the door. Stupid commonplace, pretentious twaddle, weak sentimentalism, feeble reasoning, confused narrative, silly novels, ambitious poetry, are not to be read except on compulsion, as in a desperately rainy day, in a lonesome cabin, when a last year's almanac or a thrice-conned newspaper have yielded up their last returns of nutriment and succulence. But in such a case the storm must forbid a walk, and there should be not even an intelligent spaniel or a playful kitten to furnish society. A stupid or senseless book is thrice as stupefying as a stupid man. A vain, ignorant and ambitious piece of writing has none of those redeeming features which a humane and charitable spirit will find in a vain, ignorant and ambitious person. If then I am to read anything with interest, I must be introduced to an author who can do me some good. If his book can teach or convince or ennoble or amuse me, then it may be reasonably expected that I should be aroused to an interested and wakeful attention. The *conditio sine qua non* of earnest interest in reading is to find something which is worth the reading. Said a youngster to a humorous old New England preacher, " I observe that your parishioners listen very attentively to your preaching." "I uniformly aim to give them something which is worth attending to," was the curt reply. "The man whom I like to converse with above all others," said Daniel "Webster, "is the man who can teach me something." If every reader would estimate, select and use his books by this rule, there would be far less listless, lazy and profitless reading than there is. What would befall large portions of many of our newspapers, and what use could possibly be applied to much of the time which many of their readers dawdle away over them, it is no concern of ours to determine.

2. It follows that we should read with a certain degree of deference and docility to our author. If we do an author the honor to confer with him through his book, for the supposed pleasure or advantage which his society will afford us, we ought to observe toward him the courtesies of polite intercourse. By the act of reading him we profess a respect for the thoughts and feelings which he expresses through the printed page, and we ought to maintain toward him that attitude of deference and courtesy which consistency requires. If we do not weigh his arguments with candor and accept his facts with confidence, if we do not yield our feelings to his control by that pliant sympathy which is requisite for the enjoyment of his enthusiasm, his wit or his eloquence; if instead of this deferential temper we are captious, critical -and hard to be convinced or moved, we had better dismiss the author from our presence by closing his book. It is far more civil to our author and more profitable to ourselves to dispose of him with a courteous bow than it is to detain him with a discontented air and a captious temper. It were better to be content with our own thinking than to treat the thoughts of another so unjustly and ill-naturedly. We had better even act after the rule quoted by Charles Lamb, "To mind the inside of a book is to entertain one's self with the forced product of another man's brain. Now I think a man of quality and breeding may be much amused with the natural sprouts of his own." As a general rule we had better not read an author from whom we cannot derive some important benefit and with whom we cannot sympathize at

least in some particulars. There may be special reasons for breaking this rule. Those who read for investigation, for criticism or for refutation, are often obliged to deviate from it. But such exceptions justify and enforce the rule in a gen eral way for all those who read chiefly to enrich their minds, to confirm their faith, to enlarge their knowledge and to elevate and kindle their aspirations. Mrs. Browning has said, and doubtless from her own experience,

> " We get no good
> By being ungenerous even to a book
> And calculating profits, so much help
> By so much reading. It is rather when
> We gloriously forget ourselves and plunge
> Soul-forward, headlong, into a book's profound
> Impassioned for its beauty and salt of truth—
> 'Tis then we get the right good from a book."

3. We add another rule, to correct any excess or abuse in the application of the foregoing, viz.: We should read with an independent judgment and a critical spirit. It does not follow, because we should treat an author with confidence and respect that we are to accept all his opinions and may not revise his conclusions and arguments by our own. Indeed we shall best evince our respect for his thoughts by subjecting them to our own revision. But it by no means follows because we re-judge his argument and opinions that we are not instructed by both. Milton, in the Paradise Regained, in connection with some important truth, puts a singular argument into the mouth of the Great Teacher.

> "Who reads
> Incessantly, and to his reading brings not
> A spirit and judgment equal or superior,
> (And what he brings what need he elsewhere seek ?)
> Uncertain and unsettled still remains.
> Deep versed in books, and shallow in himself."

The parenthetical line would imply that the capacity to judge and revise the opinions of an author renders a man independent of aid and incapable of instruction from and of his fellow-men. To a similar effect a saying of Charles Butler is quoted by one of Milton's editors, viz., "No man is the wiser for his books until he is above them." If this were true, the wisdom of another could not become our own except by the suspension or displacement of our individual activity of thought; instruction by books would be an assertion of simple dogmatism; and confidence and docility would only be other names for subservience and credulity. Still whatever is our deference for an author we cannot exalt his intellect into the place of our own; we cannot receive his facts without evidence, nor his arguments except so far as they produce conviction; nor should we profess to admire his eloquence, to love his poetry, or be delighted with his novels, because he is reputed to be a great genius or a splendid writer. Here we observe that:

4. *Favorite authors* often exert an excessive and occa-sionally a blinding and stupifying influence over their ad-mirers. We speak of such in connection with the duty of reserving to ourselves the rights of independent judgment and criticism, because it is rare that one human being ever gains a more complete possession of another than does a favorite author over his devoted readers. The most confiding friend and enraptured lover are rarely more completely taken captive in thought and' feeling, than are the readers of some fascinating writer, who is for the time being in the ascendant, whether over a small coterie of select worshipers or a whole generation which he sways by his genius. A special chapter might be written on the favorite authors of the present century; the secret of their influence; the explanation of their power—its rise, culmination and its sudden or gradual decline. The names of Scott, Southey, Byron, Coleridge, Wordsworth, Moore, Byron, Bulwer-Lytton, Carlyle, James, Dickens, Thackeray, " George Eliot," Mrs. Browning, Tennyson and many others in England, and of Irving, Longfellow, Mrs. Stowe, Beecher, Hawthorne, Emerson, Lowell, etc., in this country will occur to most persons as examples of writers who have more or less extensively exerted this peculiar influence. When it is salutary and elevating it cannot be estimated too highly as an influence for good. When it is equivocal or positively evil its disastrous power cannot be too greatly deplored. Of both we shall have abundant occasion to adduce illustrations

as we proceed. We hasten to observe:

5. That it is a good rule to read those authors whom we are competent both to understand and appreciate. This seems so true and obvious as to be a truism and a common-place. If a man is to sympathize with his author, much more if he is to criticise and judge him, he must certainly be able to understand his meaning. His thoughts and feelings if they do not produce answering thoughts and feelings, are nought to the reader. A complete and familiar mastery of both are necessary to instruction and pleasure in the recipient. We do not say an easy mastery nor a mastery which does not cost at times severe and patient labor; for he who has never struggled to comprehend a profound and subtle author has never had experience of the manliest of activities—but we do say that the struggle should be successful or it should be sooner or later abandoned. There is not a more silly spectacle often exhibited, than that of an untrained or an uninstructed person professing to follow and enjoy a writer to whom he is unequal, looking wise over his philosophy, interested in his narrative or enraptured by his eloquence and poetry, when they are all Greek or Chinese to him. The silliness is especially conspicuous if the author is at once popular, conceited and arrogant; if he understands and practises the arts of intellectual trickery and delights to set people agape with wonderment by sundry small artifices of high-sounding phraseology, far-fetched allusions, or any of the manifold impositions of word-play and imagery, or the more offensive attractions which are found in cool irreverence and audacious nonchalance with respect to the prevailing religion of the country in which he lives. The more real genius he has, the more provoking is the effrontery of the author who believes in and practises any kind of philosophical or poetical trickery, and so much the more conspicuous becomes the ridiculous plight into which his credulous but ignorant admirers bring themselves by trying to persuade themselves that they understand a writer who may not completely understand himself.

A reader should never be afraid to confess that he does not understand or enjoy an author. He ought indeed at times to say this with humility, and to feel that he thereby makes a confession of some kind of incapacity, but he ought to have the manliness to say it notwithstanding, if the truth requires it. It is a fundamental condition of all profitable study and thought, that a man should know his ignorance and frankly confess it to himself. If a reader does not appreciate a popular writer the fault may not be his own. It may perchance be in the author. But it can never be settled with whom it lies, unless the reader has the honesty to confess to himself his incapacity to understand or enjoy his writer. This bravery of an honest confession of one's incompetence to understand some things that are written, would be of especial service nowadays when so much brilliant guess-work and imposing dogmatism is put forth in the guise of all manner of philosophies -as the Philosophy of Religion, of Worship, of Art, of Literature, of Reform, of Education, of Voting, of Finance, of Woman's Rights and of Man's Duties, etc., etc.

The fable of Aristophanes concerning Socrates is literally fulfilled in our time, except that we have at least a score of sages of different schools hanging side by side each in his own basket, soaring and sinking between the heavens and the earth, swaying to and fro in peril of a sudden tilt from a capricious gust; each not rarely obscured by investing clouds, which betoken inspiration and add to the authority of the prophet, especially when, gilded by the sunlight of his genius. Beneath each basket stands a coterie of credulous listeners, each affecting to believe what they do not understand, or to understand what they ought not to believe—all charmed, rapt, persuaded and convinced at least of two things, of their own and their teachers' superiority; and all alike ready to reply to the question, *"Are you sure that you understand all the oracular sayings of your prophet " " Wa'd I hae the presumption"* The greater is the pity that many of them do not have the presumption to demand that their favorite teacher should write so that they can understand him ; and that much which they cannot but understand, they do not reject with frank and outspoken aversion! This duty of reading authors whom we can understand suggests another rule, viz.:

6. We should be contented to read that which is suitable to our present development of thought and feeling, or in plainer language, to our age and progress. Everything is appropriate and beautiful in its season. Eat strawberries in May or June, and wait for peaches and grapes till the Autumn. Let not the miss just entering upon her teens expect to appreciate the poetry or philosophy which her brother

of twenty-two is but just beginning to comprehend and enjoy. Above all do not meddle with philosophy of any sort, whether it comes in the form of history, of fiction, or grave discussion, until you can grapple with its problems and follow its subtle abstractions. Let your reading in every department follow somewhat the order of nature and of psychical growth, and the growth will be all the more rapid and easy. The transitions from that which is adapted to earlier and later youth and to dawning and developed manhood will be easily and gracefully accom-plished, and both intellect and feeling will find in the abundant variety of literary productions, suitable and satisfying nutriment for their newly-developed wants and tastes. Important aid in the selection of the right books according to this rule may be derived from advisers who know us well. But the rule furnishes in itself the means for its own enforcement, if we considerately apply it. As a general truth,,facts should come before philosophy; narrative before reflection; objective description before subject-ive meditation; poetry that is graphic, outward and picturesque before that which is meditative, learned and introverted; .and history that paints and describes before that which generalizes and interprets.

We have already intimated that we do not mean to say by either or both of these rules, that we should never read a book which is difficult to follow or comprehend, and which it may be, costs a severe effort to master. Books of this class are sometimes the most useful of all to read. The person, particularly the student, who has never wrestled manfully and perseveringly with a difficult book will be good for little in this world of wrestling and strife. But when you are convinced that a book is above your attainments, capacity or age, it is of little use for you, and it is wiser to leave it alone. It is both vexing and unprofitable to stand upon one's toes and strain one's self for hours in efforts to reach the fruit which you are not tall enough to gather. It is better to leave it till it can be reached more easily. When the grapes are both ripe and within easy reach for you, it is safe to conclude that they are ***not sour***.

7. The style of a writer should often determine whether we read or neglect him. But what is style and how shall we judge whether it is good or bad ? That depends upon our taste; i. e., whether it is healthy or vitiated, whether it is uncul-

tured or rightly trained. Savages and semi-barbarians are fond of stimulating and strongly contrasted colors, of violent and spasmodic gesticulations, of shrieking and dissonant sounds, of noisy and discordant music. So in literature, there are semi-barbarians who delight in the glaring and the grotesque, the extravagant and the spasmodic, the vulgar and sensational in diction and imagery. In the judgment of such, those books, journals and newspapers only are **up to the times** and produced by **live men**, which are distinguished by characteristics that belong to the barbaric age. That writer is trenchant and brilliant who is ill-mannered, coarse, personal and vituperative. That orator is magnificently eloquent who ranges through the classical dictionary for historic parallels to common men and common occasions, and always rides on the top-most wave of his tumid diction. Flippancy and audacity are taken for genius and power, and a perpetual straining after tawdry ornaments and effective diction, such as remind one of war paint and tattooing, is deemed the certain indication of intellectual power. People of more refined habits and a more perfectly developed civilization, require a somewhat different style in the writers whom they delight to read— as strength without roughness, elegance without affectation, ease without weakness, copiousness without verbosity and courtesy without loss of dignity. "We judge of style somewhat as we do of manners. Whatever in expression facilitates the easy apprehension and the pleasant reception of the thoughts and sentiments; whatever fits both like a glove and seems to have been their natural growth; whatever in form is the unstudied product of an earnest and refined nature is in general, good in style. On the other hand, whatever is awkward, indirect, involved and difficult to follow; whatever is factitious and affected; whatever is overloaded with obtrusive and gaudy decorations ; above all, whatever is swelling, declamatory, and overstrained in its illustration and diction, is bad in style. We may read **an** author whose style is defective or bad, for the worth of his matter, but a bad style ought never to please or attract us, and other things being equal, we cannot but prefer the well written to the badly written book.

Style, indeed, is not to be judged of as a thing of the su-premest consequence, but as chiefly valuable, as it renders easy and agreeable the communication of thought and feel-ing. " **The more sash the less light**," was a pithy saying in respect of diction, often uttered by a writer who illustrated the rule by his own example. It is slightly too pointed to be altogether true. A window may serve other ends than to let in the white light of winter or the dazzling glare of summer; and style may be allowed to color and warm intellectual clearness with the hues that express emotion, and to set off these hues by varying contrasts of beauty and shading; but when style is characterized by mere pomp and glitter, by artificial nicety or studied effect, it deserves the contempt of every person of sense, as truly when seen in a book as when displayed by man. But as in conversing with men, we are naturally pleased with an easy flow of language from the lips, so is it with language when it is written. There is a natural grace and order and beauty which lend a charm that cannot be described. There is a power in expression by which a word as used by one man will produce a stronger impression than a page composed by another. By one writer thought is thrust forth as dry as a withered branch; by another, through apt illustration, it is made fresh and blooming, like an orange bough just broken from the tree, in which bud, blossom and fruit mingle their fragrance and beauty. From one man truth falls as if wrung from unwilling lips; from another it leaps into form and action, with a resistless energy, warm and living, startling and overpowering.

It is of vital importance to our success and pleasure in reading, that the books which we read should be well written. It is also a prime necessity that our ideal of what good writing is should be just and elevated. Next to bad morals in writing, should be ranked bad manners in diction, or an infelicitous style. Awkwardness may be excused and even be accepted as an excellence when it betokens sincerity and directness of aim, but vulgarity, affectation, vituperation and bully ism, as well as "great swelling words of vanity" and lofty airs of pompous declamation, whether of the Asiatic and Oriental or the American and Occidental type—whether heard in the har-angue from the hustings, in the sermon from the pulpit, or in the speech to the universe in the legislature—whether written in the newspaper or the essay, are more nearly akin to moral defects than is usually believed or noticed. Indeed they rarely fail to indicate them. Vague declamation is a kind of conscious falsehood. Empty rhetoric is a certain sign, as well as an efficient promoter of insincerity and hollowness, of sham and pretence in the character.

The fearful slaughter of honest English that is committed so freely by sensation preachers and traveling politicians under the name of eloquence, and the more fearful depravation of popular taste and public honesty that follows the admiration of such tricks of empty rhetoric and factitious declamation, call for prosecution by the Grand Inquest as dangerous nuisances to the public conscience, no less than as open offences against rhetorical and grammatical propriety.

It is implied in these rules that no person should feel obliged to read everything that is published. Head everything that is published ! why should a man think of such a thing ? It were as reasonable to feel obliged to talk with every man whom you meet; and to talk with him as long as he chooses to hold you by the button, and this whether he talks sense or nonsense, or whether what he says concerns you little or much or not at all. And yet there are men who aspire to read everything that is printed—men who in order to keep abreast with " the literature of the day," as they phrase it, labor hard at the service and groan inwardly if not audibly, because the time fails them, amidst the multitude of books which every week brings out. But the attempt and the desire seem to us very unreasonable. Unless, indeed, all authors are equally able and honest, choice as well as necessity should direct to the opposite. For who would listen to an organ-grinder in the streets when he might hear from the noblest of instruments harmonies fit to be played in heaven ? Or who would stop to listen to a violin scraper while on his way to a series of solos by Ole Bull or Paganini ? Or who would read a blundering, confused or lying history when he might read one that is neat, orderly and trustworthy ? Or why read the one when you are satisfied from the other ? "Who would read a novel or poem that depicts disgusting or degrading scenes, or paints virtuously but feebly, when he might read those that present worthy themes and treat of them well ? Books are constantly issued, concerning which it is an honor to a man to say that he has not read them—books which repel a right-minded man on the very slightest acquaintance,—books of which such a man would say instinctively, that he knows enough of them, to wish to know nothing more.

But these thoughts bring us to a graver.aspect of books and reading, which we must reserve for another chapter.

CHAPTER VI.

THE INFLUENCE OF BOOKS AND READING ON THE OPINIONS AND PRINCIPLES.

WE have learned that the best ***books***, certainly those which are the most interesting, are the books which most distinctly express some individuality in their authors. We have also learned that ***that reading*** is ordinarily the most useful and invigorating which brings us most closely and consciously into contact with writers of marked and earnest personality.

We cannot resist the inference that ***books*** and ***reading*** must exert a powerful influence upon the ***opinions*** and ***principles***. This they do both directly and indirectly— directly, when they address well or ill-reasoned arguments to the understanding; indirectly, when their influence upon the principles is secondary and unnoticed. Hence the rule—and it is a rule of the first importance—that in reading we should make ourselves distinctly aware of the principles of a writer, so far as he consciously or unconsciously expresses them in his writings, so that if need be we may be on our guard against them. This rule is not so necessary in the case of books which are avowedly written for the purpose of defending a system of opinion, or establishing a political, scientific, or theological creed. In such cases the doctrines may be true or they may be false, the opinions may be salutary or pernicious; but the positions are distinctly avowed, and the reasons for them are urged directly and confessedly for the purposes of conviction. There may be serious exposure in such cases, but the exposure is one of which we are distinctly aware, and in which to be ***forewarned*** is to be ***forearmed***. In respect to these cases, we do not propose to write a homily on that most important and much abused direction, " Prove all things ; hold fast that which is good/' however useful and greatly needed such a homily might be. "We shall not stay to defend the utmost courage and freedom in the formation of our opinions, by the use of light and evidence, from whatever sources these may come. Nor shall we enlarge upon the important consideration that many, not to say most, inquirers after truth may often learn more from the antagonists than they can from the defenders of the opinions which they accept; nor shall we contend that every student and reader should honestly estimate and interpret the force of the arguments on both sides of every question, as they are in fact regarded and held by the defenders of each.

Considerations like these scarcely need to be urged upon thoughtful and earnest readers, in these days of free dis-cussion and large toleration; or, as we might say, these days when, among large classes of bookish and reading men, free discussion is but another name for universal doubt, or a free and easy vacillation of opinion; when free toleration is made both pretext and excuse for intellectual libertinism; when earnest and fixed convictions on many subjects are practically judged to be an affair of association or taste;—when jesting and sneering *litterateurs* so rarely think of asking what *is truth ?* or, if they ask, do not " *wait for an answer*"

Nor, on the other hand, do we care to insist on the dangers which lie in the opposite direction, from a premature agitation of opinions, before the mind is capable of a thorough and dispassionate examination of the reasons for or against them, although no abuse of the rule " *to read both sides* " is more serious in its consequences than that which is committed by persons as yet untrained to discriminating analysis or comprehensive speculation, when they attempt to judge of arguments which they can neither comprehend nor compare, or when they rush headlong into the study of controversies concerning opinions which they have good practical grounds for receiving. Admonitions of this sort, however needful or pertinent they might be for the selection of books and the direction of reading, would open too wide and indefinite a field of discourse.

We limit ourselves to the unconscious or the designed propagation of the principles of an individual writer, in an incidental way, by means of writings that have no direct relation to the truth or falsehood of these principles, and which, as works' of literature rather than of argument, profess to stand apart from the field *of* discussion and of doctrine. In writings of this kind no direct attack is made upon t,hose truths which are held sacred by right-minded men. The convictions which men are usually . taught to accept concerning self-restraint and self-denial— concerning the decent morals and the courteous manners, which are at once the bonds and ornaments of human life —are courteously recognized with outward homage. Conscience and duty, virtue and God, are named with respect, and the reader, it may be, is formally assured that no man holds them, when properly understood, in higher esteem than does the writer. And yet, in the tale or the history, the poem or the essay, such language is used, such insinuations are hinted, such associations are skillfully evoked, as to depress and chill the better aspirations and the nobler enthusiasms, and to leave the reader with a weakened faith in the nobleness of man and the goodness of God.

Notable examples of influences of this kind are furnished in the celebrated histories of Gibbon and of Hume. Gibbon has left behind him one of the most splendid monuments of human genius that modern literature can furnish. Inspired by the sublime and awful recollections that haunt the ruins of the Eternal City, he essayed to write the story of the " Decline and Fall" of that wonderful empire, of whose greatness that city in its ruins is at once the symbol and the sepulchre. This he accomplished with an industry that was equal to the herculean labor involved in the collection of his materials, and with a genius that overmastered and moulded his learning at its will. There are faults in Gibbon's style, and there may be defects in" his narrative; but no man can deny the genius that could attempt so great a task, and could execute it so well; and still less the value and splendor of the work which it has left as its memorial. But it happened that the decline and fall of Rome was coincident with the rise and growth of another Empire, mysterious in its beginnings and superhuman in its force—a kingdom which has survived the wrecks of many great empires, and which can be no better described than in the words of the prophet, as " the stone " which "became a great mountain and filled the whole earth," as the kingdom which "should break in pieces and consume all these kingdoms," and shall "stand for ever." Had Gibbon's genius been enlightened by Faith, so that he had been fired and elevated at the thought of the wondrous movements of this unseen empire—had he but conceived somewhat of the plan of God's providence in first subduing the world to the sway of one iron dominion, that he might provide and prepare a suitable arena upon which to introduce to the human race the most wonderful being that was ever born of that race; so that when this race was, as it were, taught to know one language, and gathered into one grand amphitheatre, it might hear God speak to man—he would have contemplated the growth and culmination of Rome under relations that were far higher and more elevating than any which he recognized. Had he also seen how, to further the purposes connected with the progress of the new kingdom, it must first be incorporated with the old Roman dominion, and even gain possession of the throne of the Caesars, so that when the empire should be broken in pieces, each shivered portion might become the nucleus of a new Christian state—had he written of Rome as thus falling, that a greater than Rome might rise, what a different book had Gibbon's history been in its plan and its principles, in its influence and its fame! Had Gibbon but seen, as it would require no great stretch of honesty or candor for a philosopher to see, that everything good which comes to man and dwells among men must be alloyed by human imperfection, and that, therefore, it was not wonderful that Christian priests and Christian teachers, in a barbarous age, should show much of human passion and human infirmity—and had he, instead of exaggerating and coloring these inconsistencies, set forth the virtues that shone the brighter because encompassed by such darkness, how much nobler and truer an impression had he made! Had he demonstrated to himself and to others, that the natural causes in the passions and prejudices of men, to which he ascribes the preservation and triumph of a system which was in deadly hostility with these agencies, did, in their presence and power, only serve to illustrate the over-mastering force of that vital principle which could work them out, throw them off, or live on in spite of "them, he would have done but justice to the truth as well as to the grandeur of his theme.

But Gibbon did no such thing, but rather made the History of Rome, with all its splendor as a theme for a Christian historian, to be an occasion for the insinuation of debasing unbelief, and the manifestation of the workings of an "impure imagination. Of the tens of thousands who have read this work as a history, and for historic purposes, few have been able wholly to escape the indirect influences which pervade it in every part, as the seeds of death will shake themselves from the gorgeous robes of damask and gold that have been worn by one smitten of the plague. We do

not wonder that the great and good Dr. Thomas Arnold was moved, by the thought
of this evil, to undertake to write a history of Rome, which should be animated by
a different spirit.

Hume had a theme only inferior to that of Gibbon; and that was the history of
an empire which is more wonderful in many of its relations to the world than Rome
ever was, or could be, even in the pride of its power. The one empire was honored
as the birth-place of Christianity. The other as the birth-place of that liberty of
which a developed and free Christianity could alone be the parent. For it was in the
struggles between the crown and the people of England, that the " good old cause
" of human rights and of human freedom was in fact made the issue, and it was
through many a hard-fought contest of debate and battle-field that liberty became
triumphant, and secured for herself a better abode and ampler room in her new-
found home beyond the ocean. How did Hume write this history, so inspiring in its
themes, so glorious in the heroic men and the splendid deeds of strife and suffering,
which emblazon its annals? What is the sympathy and what the spirit which he
breathed into his record of these men and their deeds ? With what judgments and
principles does he impregnate every line of his narrative? What impressions does
he leave upon the minds of his readers of that which is most valuable in political institutions and practical principles ? What faith does he awaken in the noble and the
heroic in character ? What feelings does he excite in his readers towards the dead
whom they ought to revere and the living who would emulate their example ? To
these questions we are compelled to answer, that he wrote with a continued sneer
at the religious faith and fervor which fired the souls who resisted the throne on
the one side, and with scarce spirit and soul enough to do justice to the chivalrous
loyalty that lent its grace to the mistakes and wrongs of tyranny on the other; and
the consequence was that he made out of the wondrous history of England, a work
fit only to be read by men who, having faith neither in God's truth, nor in man's
nobleness, are prepared to be skeptics, self-seekers, and slaves. And yet so easy is
his narrative, so plausible are his representations, and so specious are his arguments,
that thousands of readers have confided themselves to his direction, without sus-
pecting that the author was chilling their enthusiasm for private and public virtue,
or weakening their faith in self-forgetting devotion to freedom and to God.

The two well-known histories of the United States, by Bancroft and Hildreth, are pervaded by the political and practical philosophy of their respective authors. Their views of life, their estimates of character, as well as of the conditions of greatness in the individual and the state, are, in some respects, strikingly contrasted, and yet for different reasons the peculiar principles of each are open to exception. No man can study either of their histories without being either so consciously aware of their principles as to accept or reject them, or without being unconsciously moved to admiring sympathy, to unexplained antipathy, or to decided aversion. The sanguine and *naif* democracy of Bancroft sometimes becomes so emphatic and extreme as to remind us of the wretched rant which in the Reign of Terror thundered from the tribune in the daily assemblies of the Convention, and shrieked by night in the frenzied gatherings of the Hall of the Jacobins. His careful and exhausting research, and his painstaking compre-hensiveness, are an insufficient offset against the superficial philosophy that sometimes reminds us equally of the pedant and the demagogue. The pains-taking accuracy and the judicial severity of Hildreth, do not atone for his sardonic bitterness, his cynic misanthropy, and his inveterate dislikes; least of all for the chilling lesson of the *nil ad-mirari* with which he weakens our faith in and respect for self-sacrifice and self-denial.

The organs of great parties and interests, whether political or religious, do not merely defend by open and legitimate methods, the distinctive principles which they are set to represent, but their judgments of men and of books, of literature and philosophy, of tendencies and events—in a word their blame and their praise—are determined more or less completely by the political and religious opinions of their party and school. This influence is pervasive like the atmosphere, and it constitutes what is called the tone and spirit of the journal, of the presence and character of which the constant or occasional reader is not always so distinctly aware, as he must inevitably be more or less affected by it. We cite as examples, *Blackwood's Magazine and The Westminster Review*. In the conduct of the first, when at the height of its power, were employed genius the most splendid and various, as well as classical and historical learning both brilliant and profound. In the same number, and in the same paper, fun and frolic, carried to the extreme of bacchanalian revelry, mingle with sacred eloquence and poetry, and each of these incongruous elements is represented with unrivalled freshness and force. This magazine has been devoted from the first to the interests of the Tory party in Great Britain, and the influence of its wit and humor, of its poetry and phil-osophy, of its science and theology, has been to strengthen this interest in Church and State. Many an enthusi astic American youth has read it with admiration fot years, and, as the result, has found himself, without know-ing why or how, the bond slave or devotee to all its peculiar prejudices—has been made an English Tory on American soil, with all the comfortable self-complacence and the real awkwardness of such a position. The ***West-minster Review*** has stood at the other extreme. It has been critical and learned, acute and fearless, sharp and outspoken. The authority of tradition, the prestige of rank, the prerogative of office, the associations of the past, the pretension of the schools, have not deterred it from bold attacks on everything that is venerable and sacred in Church and State. Its principles stand out too distinctly to fail to be observed. No reader of this Review can fail to know what its principles are. We fear, however, that many who dislike and reject its doctrines are influenced by its spirit and philosophy more than they are aware or would be willing to acknowledge.

Thomas Carlyle never fails to impregnate whatever he writes with a large infusion of his opinions as the Prophet of Discontent and Antagonism towards whatever the age which he despises sees fit to honor. The sphere in which he rules is that of the " ***Everlasting No*** ;" his protest is a perpetual veto. That he never fails to utter this protest with brilliancy and power the multitude of his bewildered admirers testify with unwavering enthusiasm. That not a few of these admirers are affected by his supercilious misanthropy and his cynical discontent is confessed by all but themselves. Among American writers, the keen-minded ***Holmes***, the wide-minded ***Emerson***, the subtle-minded ***Hawthorne***, the cynical-minded ***Thoreau***, in whatever they write, proclaim each an Evangel, though it must be confessed that this Evangel, varies somewhat from that which has usually been received as the Christian Gospel.

It ought to be no matter of wonder that a book should be thus pervaded by the principles and even by the prejudices of its author. Every book comes from the mind of a man, and if he writes earnestly, as he must if he writes with effect, he will write as he thinks and feels, and even when he does not intend it, and his mind is intent on something besides, his thoughts and feelings cannot but make themselves manifest. We do not advise that a man should never read books that imply principles which he thinks to be false or dangerous. We only say that he should be aware of the fact that they are thus diffused; that they give character and tone to large classes of books; and most important of all, that they have no greater authority when insinuated by means of a book, whether it be history or tale, poem or book of travel, than when they are openly or insidiously uttered by the lips of a living man.

CHAPTER VII.

THE MORAL INFLUENCE OF BOOKS AND READING.— THE READING OF FICTION.

"WE are brought insensibly to a subject still more serious—the *Moral Influence of Books and Reading*. What is the question that presents itself? It cannot be whether books should be read of which the moral influence is evil. No man who seriously believes in right and wrong can give but one answer to this question. But the question is, What books are such ? how can they be distinguished, described and classified ? how can I be certain that a book which will be hurtful to another, will be injurious to myself? As a general answer to these inquiries, we can give no better rule than the following by Robert Southey: " Would you know whether the tendency of a book is good or evil, examine in what state of mind you lay it down. Has it induced you to suspect that that which you have been accustomed to think unlawful, may after all be innocent, and that that may be harmless, which you hitherto have been taught to think dangerous ? Has it tended to make you dissatisfied and impatient under the control of others ? and disposed you to relax in that self-government, without which both the laws of God and man tell us there can be no virtue and consequently no happiness ? Has it attempted to abate your admiration and reverence for what is great and good, and to diminish in you the love of your country and your fellow-creatures ? Has it addressed itself to your pride, your vanity, your selfishness, or any other of your evil propensities ? Has it defiled the imagination with what is loathsome, and shocked the heart with what is monstrous ? Has it disturbed the sense of right and wrong which the Creator has implanted in the human soul ? If so—if you are conscious of all or of any of these effects—or if, having escaped from all, you have felt that such were the effects it was intended to produce, throw the book into the fire, young man, though it should have been the gift of a friend! Young lady, away with the whole set, though it should be the prominent furniture of a rosewood book-case!"— ***The Doctor***.

These rules are uncompromising in their severity and strictness, but tolerant in their respect for individual freedom and discretion. They yield nothing to appetite and passion, however insidiously these may be addressed, or however tempting may be the allurements with which genius masks the temptations or palliates the consent to evil. They allow neither paltering nor parley with that which would mislead or offend. They stimulate the moral energies like a fresh and invigorating breeze. But they allow everyone to judge for himself what may expose him to harm, and permit no one besides to judge for him or to rejudge his judgments. No larger liberty for the individual can be conceived of than that which these rules allow.

"With such rules, or rules so phrased, a very large class of critics, are not at all content. They would be more definite. They must name not only the books, but the classes of books which are always and only evil. Some denounce all light literature so-called, with a condemnation that is by no means light in the matter or the manner. Others-reject everything that is fictitious, with a saving clause, that saves little or nothing that is worth preserving. Poetry, Novels, and the written Drama, and whatever addresses the imagination are labelled by such mentors as suspected or infected goods.

There is nothing which gives greater pleasure to the friends of that literature which is really demoralizing, than such wholesale and indiscriminate attacks upon works of the imagination, especially if they are made from the pulpit or in the name of religion. Such persons know, that as they are uttered they are not true, and cannot be successfully defended. They know, moreover, that the rejection of what is false and excessive in them will destroy the good influence of what is true—that those who make these attacks will be excluded from the field of literature in dishonor, and leave it free for their own exclusive oc-cupation. The false issue made in the attack gives the amplest opportunity for a false issue in the defence. This issue they thus present: ***They*** do not defend the per-version of the imagination, ***not they***! but only its inno-cent and healthy use; and thus under the name of the liberty of nature, they secure the sphere and influence of literature to the service of licentiousness. The motto prefixed to one of the most shameless poems of the present century, shows conclusively how an unfair attack suggests and justifies a skillful but unfair retort and defence: " Dost think because thou art virtuous that there shall be no more cakes and ale ? Yes, and ginger shall be hot in the mouth." After this defence of harmless " cakes and ale," spiced a little, but with nothing hotter than " ginger," what does the writer do, but under this label send out to the world a poisonous and disgusting mixture of arsenic and assafoetida, in a poem, parts of which are fit only to be read or heard in a brothel!

This being but too just an account of the manner in which the question in respect to the moral influence of fictitious and imaginative literature is argued on both sides, it seems desirable that one or two suggestions should be offered towards its right determination.

We assert then first of all, that a book is not of necessity demoralizing, because it is fictitious or imaginative. The imagination is an endowment from God, and as such is not to be dishonored or depreciated by the sneering or ignorant contempt of man. It is also one of the noblest human powers—the power which in some of its aspects is nearest to the divine, and as such is capable of the most exalted uses, and of an influence for good which cannot be computed. Of its products in literature Lord Bacon says: "The use of this feigned history has been to give some shadow of satisfaction to the mind of man in those points, wherein the nature of things doth deny it, the world being in proportion inferior to the soul. . . . Therefore because the acts or events of true history have not that magnitude which satisfieth the mind of man, poesy feigneth acts and events greater and more heroical, because true history pro-poundeth the successes and issues of actions not so agreeable to the merits of virtue and vice, therefore poesy feigns them more just in retribution, and more according to revealed providence: because true history representeth actions and events more ordinary and less interchanged, therefore poesy endueth them with more rareness and more unexpected and alternate variation: so it appeareth that poesy serveth and conferreth to ***magnanimity, morality***, and delectation. And, therefore, it was ever thought to bear some participation of ***divineness***, because it doth raise and erect the mind, by submitting the shows of things to the desires of the mind, whereas reason doth buckle and bow the mind unto the nature of things."— ***On the Advancement of Learning***. If Lord Bacon is right then there is nothing in the nature of a work as fictitious which makes it either immoral or of immoral tendency. It is no argument against a book, to say that it is a novel or poem, nor does the fact that it is a novel or poem show that it is less favorable to morality or even to religion, than to say that it is a collection of homilies or sermons. All appeals and indiscriminate assertions that are directed against the reading of novels or poetry as such, are like the guns of Trumbull's McFingal which,

> " well aimed at duck and plover,
> Bear wide and kick their owners over."

More than this is true. Not only is it clear that fiction and poetry may exert a good influence, but it is equally obvious that they do in fact exert an influence that is both healthful and elevating. Next to falling in love with one who is worthy of the first and best affections of the lover, should be ranked in its influence for good, the reading of the first really good novel or poem which takes a strong and perma-nent hold of the heart and character. There is a charm investing this ideal world for the first time unveiled to the view, and a superhuman elevation in the beings who live and move in *it*—a purity in their loves, a dignity in their acts, and a weight and sacredness in their words, which hold the young reader as by a spell, and lead him a delighted captive. "With what joy does the de-lighted pupil of Romance tread the common earth now glorified for the first time to his anointed eyes, or look out upon the transfigured sky now that heaven is seen to glow beyond it! With what delight does he greet the face of man and woman when he learns that they are capable of poetic idealization; what new views does he take of life? as soon as he awakes to the discovery that its common prose can be turned into romance and poetry ! It is not merely true that as young people *will* fall in love, so they *will* read poetry and novels, but we add, as it is *well* that they fall in love, if they love aright, so it is well that they read works of imagination, if they read them aright. Of many a young man has it been true, that the sentiments of his favorite poet, or of some ideal character in his favorite novel, have exerted a healthful and elevating influence over his whole being—have been made the standard of his own efforts, and have breathed the breath of life into his feeble aspirations. Were a wise man to have the complete control over the mind and heart of a young person of either sex, and to seek to form him or her after the ideal of a generous, affectionate, and heroic character which would be ready to labor, to suffer, and if need be, to die for man or for God, he would freely avail himself, at proper intervals and in a due proportion, of the writings of men of imaginative genius. He would teach his pupil not only to love and admire them, but to study them thoroughly, to enter fully into their spirit, that he might cherish purer thoughts, more disinterested affections, and better ideals than the actual contact with life can possibly furnish. The private history of the training of many of the noblest men and women whom the earth has ever seen, would amply justify the wisdom of this theory of moral culture. If we reflect upon the actual influence for good which proceeds from writers of this class, the argument gathers an uncomputed and a resistless force. We speak of good in the large and liberal sense of the word ;—not merely as it is obvious in writers who have consecrated their genius directly to the service of devotion, as Watts, Cowper, Young, and Milton in large measure; but of the good which has come from Shakspeare, Scott, Burns, and many others, by the introduction to the world of thought and feeling of ideals that are pure and elevating, when glowing with those golden hues with which genius transfigures the lowliest thing which she touches with her finger. What another place has this prosaic world become to every reader of the English language, since Milton, Shakspeare, Burns and Scott, have perpetuated in that language the visions which once met their imaginations? With what another atmosphere of thought and feeling is the intellect and heart of every reader elevated, invigorated, and refreshed ? The characters and scenes described and depicted by each have become to us as real and as permanent as are the sun and the stars, or the faces of our familiar friends. We never behold them but they quicken our thoughts and give new life to our feelings. They are a part, and not the least important, of the actual world, ever exerting upon our characters and lives a powerful and constant influence. Each new mind upon which open these wondrous pages, -gratefully owns their power. Their ideal but still intensely real scenes and characters henceforward control and possess his world of thought and feeling, and still they live on and will act on other generations with unexhausted energy. To these creations might be applied with eminent significance the remark of the old monk to "Wilkie concerning Titian's Last Supper: " I have sat daily in sight of that picture for now nearly threescore years; during that time my companions have dropped off, one after another, all who were my seniors, all who were my contemporaries, and many or most of those who were younger than myself; more than one generation has passed away, and there the figures on the picture have remained unchanged! I look at them till I sometimes think that they are the realities, and we but shadows." In Milton, the Paradise which was lost always blooms in virgin freshness. Satan, Moloch, and Belial are ever holding their perpetual council and uttering words of specious cunning or of inextinguishable hate. The mother of our race is always mourning the loss of her sinless home, or with heart-broken grief charges upon herself the guilt of the first transgression. In the Paradise Régained, the ancient world is still mapped out before the eye, which here beholds

> " Where on the AEgean shore a city stands,
> Built nobly, pure the air, and light the soil,
> Athens the eye of Greece, mother of arts and eloquence."

And there is described imperial Rome, along whose famous roads and through whose opened gates are, ever trooping her legions and tributaries, to and from the limits of her world-wide empire. Comus with his bacchanalian crew still tempts with artful cunning, and is still repelled by the pure-hearted lady who, strong in virtue, waits a certain rescue. The genius of mirth is always tripping by upon " the light fantastic toe," while her graver sister is ever moving forward with downcast eye and measured tread.

In Shakspeare, Hamlet is always the same, with senses half paralyzed at the wrong he has suffered, and with mind perplexed that the times should be so " out of joint," and he be called to set them right; the gentle Ophelia is always wailing; the wronged Desdemona is ever sobbing out the disappointment of her crushed and broken heart; the injured but uncomplaining Cordelia, wonders at, but does not reproach her cruel sisters, and comforts as best she can, the distracted father whom their cruelty has murdered ; Lady Macbeth stands in guilty horror pointing to the " damned spot" which will not "out" at her bidding; and ever as we gaze upon these forms, or hear the words of these creatures of the imagination, our flesh creeps with horror, our hearts are elated with joy, burn with indignation, or relax into weeping grief.

"What a world of living beings has Scott created, what personages has he called into life, what conversations do we hear from their lips, what stirring events are still wrought by their agency ! Nay, more; he has carried these all into the real world and given them a perpetual habitation there. Old castles, and moors, and mountain-tops, and battle-fields, each have received from him the new inhabitants evoked by his genius, so that when the traveler visits them it is not alone the ruined wall, nor the bare mountain, nor the unruffled lake that he sees; but here the royal retinue seems to group itself around the "maiden queen," within the ruined castle of Kenil worth; there Roderick's clan springs up, one by one, each from behind a concealing rock, and there the Lady Ellen pushes out her light canoe.

How has Burns by his wondrous touch turned the house of every Scottish peasant into an abode of content, and love and piety, and every simple Scottish lass into a fairy being, and as a reward for the glory which he gave to his beloved Scotia, has made for his poems in the actual homes of Scotland, a place next to the Bible, and a warm and thrilling remembrance in every living Scotchman's heart!

To hold intercourse with such creations, if the scenes be innocent and the transcripts are made from no vicious and degrading realities, cannot be unfavorable to pure and ele-vated moral feeling, even if there be no moral to the tale or poem and no religious enforcement of its lessons. It is at least an invigorating use of the powers to occupy them with such creations of the lofty or humorous imagination.

We are prepared to assert that not only is the so-called imaginative literature useful in its influence, but that all literature whatever finds its principal power to elevate, in the culture and stimulus which it furnishes to the imagination—that literature as such as distinguished from that use of letters which adds to scientific knowledge or aims at conviction, i. e. literature in the most of its forms, is chiefly valuable for what it does for the imagination by enlarging its range, elevating its ideals, stimulating its aims, and purifying and ennobling its associations. To decry the imaginative faculty and its products is to decry all literary culture if not to abrogate culture of every kind.

Let all this be granted says the objector or inquirer. But what if the scenes are vicious, the sentiments false, and the passions are sensual, malignant, and degrading? The answers to these and kindred questions must be reserved for further discussion.

CHAPTER VIII.

IMAGINATIVE LITERATURE: ITS REPRESENTATIONS OF MORAL EVIL.

IN our last we had reached the Moral Influence of Books and Reading, and in discussing this were brought to the questions so often mooted of the moral influence of the so-called works of the imagination. We attempted the defence of such works in the general, by citing examples from writers to whom all men pay a willing homage. Our discussion was arrested by the half-inquiry, half-objection: " What if the scenes are vicious, the sentiments are false, and the passions are sensual, malignant, or degrading ? Can it be morally healthful that one should be conversant with such pictures, thoughts, and feelings, especially if armed with double energy, and clothed with dangerous fascinations by the power of genius? Would you have your son or your daughter excited by the scenes, infatuated by the characters, or tempted by the words of byron, Moore, Bulwer, Goethe, or even of many that they find in Shakspeare, Milton, Burns, and Scott? In the works of every one of these writers, I can point you to many passages that should never be presented to a pure and virtuous mind. The very contact with them must involve some soil or taint, if it does not impart corruption. To entertain them in any form, to suffer them to confront the imagination, or to glide before the eye of the mind even for an instant, is to be debased and polluted, and towards them one should have no other feelings than aversion and disgust, however splendid or powerful is the genius that gilds or glorifies them" This is partly true and. partly false. "What is true is very true, and what is false is very false. The moral evil or danger in such cases, does not, however, arise from the fact that debasing scenes or wicked characters are made to stand or move before the imagination; nor again, that hateful passions are spoken out in venomous or malignant words ; nor that wickedness acts itself forth with complete and consistent energy. It still remains true that:

> There is some soul of goodness in things evil,
> Would men observingly distil it out."

The ground of moral exposure is not the fact that evil is painted, nor that it is painted boldly; but it is in the *manner* in which it is represented,—whether with fidelity to the ordinances of nature, or falsely to her eternal laws as written on the heart of man. This will be determined in a great measure by the man whose imagination reflects and recreates the evil, according as he writes like a Christian, or writes like a Turk—like a man. with a conscience and a moral nature, or like a man who makes his passions his conscience, and his will his God. Prof. F. "W". Newman, solidly observes, " In poetry, as in all other writings, the moral influence depends on its throwing our sympathies aright and leaving on the mind fit images and contemplations. Many darker passions may be portrayed: for the pathos which we seek has a two-fold character like the sublime and beautiful, viz: the terrible and the lovely. While we shudder at evil passion, it cannot make us worse. Demoralization begins, when we learn to sympathize with it, or to dwell upon things over which it is healthful to step lightly."— *Lectures on Poetry*, *i*. This difference between the two methods of depicting evil will be obvious by one or two examples.

Satan, as described by Milton, is well known to most readers. He is justly conceived and nobly painted. He is not a being who is low and offensive because degraded and brutish, but an archangel ruined, once possessed of the intellect and heart of a seraph, now blasted by bad ambition and consumed by unrelenting pride. Every feature is consistent with this conception. His will is as inexorable as that of Prometheus nailed to the Caucasian rock. The hatred is intense, steadying the powers by unrelenting determination, not distracting or weakening them by impotent rage. The cunning is masterly, yet dignified. The passion burns like a red-hot furnace, and the words speak out the inner soul with the energy of a fierce northwester. " Better reign in Hell than serve in Heaven," utters and describes his character and ruling principle. Had Milton painted Satan **thus and only** thus, he had given but half his being, as well as glorified him with splendors too attractive for the responsive tastes of many readers. But he did not leave him thus, for his truthful insight taught him, that thus described and only thus, he were no real fiend—no conceivable being of any species, but simply the half of an incomplete conception—a monster by defect. He therefore makes him confess his agony in such words as—

> " Me miserable! which way shall I fly
> Infinite wrath and infinite despair ?
> Which way I fly is hell—myself am Hell!
> And in the lowest deep, a lower deep,
> Still threatening to devour me, opens wide,
> To which the hell I suffer seems a heaven
> O then at last relent: is there no place
> Left for repentance, none for pardon left ?
> None left but by submission, and that word
> Disdain forbids me and my dread of shame."

In the presence of his old compeer, Zephon, severe in steadfast allegiance and white with unstained purity:—

" Abashed the Devil stood,
And felt how awful goodness is, and saw
Virtue in her shape how lovely: saw and pined
His loss; but chiefly to find here observed
His lustre impaired—yet seemed Undaunted."

He descends to the low and mean disguise of a filthy-reptile, placing himself at the ear of the sleeping Eve, " squat like a toad," from which disguise, when touched by the spear of Ithuriel, he cannot help himself but he must stand forth a treacherous tempter, " discovered and surprised." As he reports to his associates his success in the ruin of man, and waits with confidence for—

" Their universal shout and high applause
To fill his ear,"

there rushes in upon his enraged and disappointed soul

" On all sides, from innumerable tongues,
A dismal universal hiss, the sound
Of public scorn."

The completeness and truth of Milton's picture of Satan is in striking contrast with the Lucifer of Byron's Cain, who discourses atheism and blasphemy with such specious and passionate force that the trusting reader's faith in God and conscience is shaken and confounded, and it is well if, with heated brain and unbelieving heart, or passionate and despairing scorn, he does not plunge himself into some rash act of passion or crime; or, having done so, does not sullenly turn his back upon hope, and cast in his lot with those who curse God and die. In such a character there is but half the truth, and therefore truth itself is dishonored and belied. Passion is painted in sublime energy, in audacious daring, with impetuous and overbearing ferocity. So far there is truth. But the inward shame and agony are wanting; and most important of all, the conscious weakness of selfishness and sin that are self-confessed; the meanness of violating gratitude, fealty, and self-control; all of which should be present and made prominent to express and impress the truth, that this Lucifer, with all his sophistry and pride, with his boasting and his blasphemy, inwardly knows that he has sold himself to a falsehood.

Moreover, in the absence of this completing half-truth—so far as the poet's representations are concerned—God himself is, by these specious and passionate reasonings, made an almighty and malignant monster, injustice sits upon the eternal throne, and the universe itself is pervaded by a gigantic lie. A similar defect with similar evil consequences, is to be observed in the Devil of Goethe's Faust, except that the metaphysics are more profound and scholar-like, and the sneer is more consummately devilish at whatever is worthy in human pursuit, whatever is noble in human self-denial, and whatever is confiding in human affection.

We observe that by these three writers the same bad character is depicted, and so far as his badness is concerned, with feelings, words, and acts that are consistent; and so far, with more or less of aesthetic perfection. In Milton the evil is harmless; it is even morally healthful, because, with the attractions and force of evil, the weakness and self-reproach, the shame and agony are also represented. With Byron and Goethe, the diabolism that is dormant in man, is uppermost, and blasphemy, selfishness and lust rule in the universe, and sit upon the throne of the Eternal. [1]

We might also contrast the Hamlet of Shakspeare with the Manfred of Byron. Hamlet had been disappointed of his rightful crown, and wronged in his holiest confidence, by the frailty of his mother. Disturbed in his confidence in man and in God, he plots a murderous revenge, slays the father of Ophelia, and spurns and treads upon her

[1] We trust that none of our over-fastidious readers will sneer at our recognition of the " diabolism that is dormant in man." It was suggested by the words of Sir Thomas Browne: " The heart of man is the place the devils dwell in. I feel sometimes a hell within myself; Lucifer keeps his court in

my breast; Legion is revived in me." "In brief, we are all monsters—that is, a composition of man and beast; wherein we must endeavor to be as the poet's fancy that wise man Chiron, that is, to have the legion of man above that of beast, and sense to sit but at the feet of reason."—***Religio Medici.***

gentle and loving heart. Self-destruction is the readiest relief from his sufferings, and the speediest deliverance from a stage of existence in which everything is " out of joint." " To he or not to be," is the question which he debates with himself in thoughts and words which are forever true to the heart of man.

" To die;—to sleep,—
No more; and by a sleep, to say we end
The heart-ache, and the thousand natural shocks
That flesh is heir to,—'tis a consummation
Devoutly to be wished. To die;—to sleep;—
To sleep ! perchance to dream ;—ay, there's the rub;
For in that sleep of death what dreams may coma
When we have shuffled off this mortal coil, Must give us pause.
There's the respect That makes calamity of so long a life;
For who would bear the whips and scorns of time

But that the dread of something after death,—.
The undiscovered country, from whose bourn
No traveler returns,—puzzles the will;
And makes us rather bear those ills we have,
Than fly to others that we know not of.
Thus conscience does make cowards of us all."

Manfred by his own confession is far more guilty than Hamlet. His guilt he does not hide, he spreads it abroad for public gaze, but rather to incite the sympathy of lookers-on than in the spirit of confession and shame. Remorse he does not conceal, but he gives expression to it too often to leave the impression that it is either natural or sincere. In the struggle with conscience and avenging spirits, it is pride not conscience which prevails. In his exit it is the spirit of defiant bravado which dismisses him from life. The weakness and fear with which the guilty, and especially the confessed victim of remorse, looks over into the life beyond, are wholly wanting. Instead thereof, this mortal who by crime and remorse has made himself so wretched that he cares to live no longer stalks defiantly into the Unseen, a stupid atheist, successfully defiant of the earth-spirit that comes to fetch him away, yet without

a thought or prayer for that Greater Spirit whom he cannot avoid. There is little homage to conscience here—it is pride and self-will, not conscience and self-reproach, that win the day. The timorous weakness that comes from sin, the coward fear that looks forward to the undiscovered country, are not expressed. The self-centred though suffering criminal triumphs in his fiendish pride. Conscience is not the victor, but conscience is vanquished by unbroken and self-willed pride. [2]

We might also contrast at length Bulwer Lytton and Scott. We mean Bulwer Lytton in his earlier novels, the heroes of which are not only factitious men of high life, but they are very generally intellectual and sentimental adulterers and libertines, accomplished withal in the arts of life and the graces of society, who are deeply absorbed at times in the profoundest speculations concerning God and immortality, intermixed with the slang of high life at the club and the gambling-house. These all quietly terminate their career in the novelist's heaven of reform, wisdom, and wealth, without repentance and without shame. They are without a human conscience, and of course monsters—doubly monsters by the splendid accessories with which the writer's eloquence and power has contrived to set them forth.

The healthy and truthful mind of Scott could not depict, because it could not conceive, the possibility of such unnatural human creations. Though Scott does not write

[2] We find since writing the above that the Rev. F. D. Maurice, in his recently published " Lectures on Casuistry," refers to Manfred, as " that won-

derful play of the conscience," and couples it with Macbeth in this regard. But in our judgment, three words of Lady Macbeth express more, of both æsthctic effect and moral truth, than scores of lines of Manfred's ambitious self-flagellations. No reader would care to change places with the one; but there are many who sympathize with Manfred to the end, and suffer no recoil of horror.

in a professedly ethical spirit, or for- ethical aims, he always writes with ethical truth. Traditional and conventional prejudices may sometimes bias his judgments and representation of the historical characters and historic times which he depicts in his romances. The Cavalier and Tory writer may now and then be unjust to the Covenanter and the Whig of whom he writes, but the eternal distinctions of right and wrong are always honored, and the responsive emotions, which cannot be extinguished in the human soul, are recognized and honored with a woman's delicacy of sentiment. Scott may not always make the conscience sufficiently prominent as an element of human nature; he may not always give room and space enough to man's relations to the unseen, but he no more thinks of describing man without a conscience, than without a head, and he would as soon make him breathe without the air as live without a God.

Thackeray and Dickens both write with ethical truth so far as they go. The satirical tone of the one, and the comic humor of the other, may in a certain sense interfere with the most effective lessons'of either human sympathy or ethical earnestness. Much of the power of both writers, however, lies in the recognition by the one, of the flimsi-ness of shams, the vulgarity of snobs, and the emptiness of pretentious and uncultured fashion ; and by the other, of the meanness of avarice, the sweetness of a kindly spirit, the blessing of a sunny temper and the dignity of patient beneficence.

We cannot leave unnoticed the relations of literature, and especially of works of the imagination, to the virtue of purity, and to that sensitiveness and reserve which are at once the defence and ornament of the weaker sex. Many are offended at the freedom which writers like Shakspeare and Milton use in their portraitures of women, and at the boldness of speech with which they unveil the mysteries which the modesty of common conversation, or even of unimaginative writing rarely approaches. The young reader is appalled and shocked at his first acquaintance with not a few passages in both these writers. Perhaps he concludes that it is an offence against morality to have written or to read them. He cannot persuade himself that they do not offend against modesty, and if they offend against modesty, surely they must be condemned in the court of conscience. Scruples like these disquiet many older persons who feel a stain of impurity as a wound, and who would prefer to throw their Milton and Shakspeare into the fire than to offend their sense of right. To meet the scruples of such, the Family Shakspeare has been provided, and an expurgated Milton has very probably been thought of. The question is a fair one, Why are these scruples unfounded? why are these great writers not rejected as impure, when others perhaps less gross in speech are properly condemned? So far as these writers are concerned, we may say in answer, that the language of a writer may be free and seemingly gross, and yet the purity of nature may be observed; for nature is not a whit of a prude, and those who write with genius must follow nature wherever she leads. "But nature, though not a prude, is modest and chaste." True, yet still it is possible that in conformity with the freedom of the times of a writer, there should be much in language that is gross, and yet nothing be expressed that tends to inflame and excite lascivious passion. With all the freedoms of Shakspeare and Milton, there are few or no artful addresses to those desires that were made to be sternly controlled. There is little luscious and honeyed speech, like that of Moore or Byron, in which genius ministers directly at the altar of lust, and all the more effectively and shamelessly when her robe is studiously modest to excess, and her language *to the ear* is as pure as Diana's.

In the Scriptures both the Old Testament and the New, there are not a few passages which to the mind and ear seem and sound immodest, but there is nothing that is fitted to excite lascivious passion or to gratify prurient desire; nothing which is in the least akin to that which constitutes the chief interest of both plot and character in scores of modern novels in which adultery, jealousy, and lust are the prominent themes; in which the skill of the writer, often unhappily a woman, is expended in artfully suggesting pictures which he dares not paint, and stimulating curiosity by the suggestion of passions which it is indecent to name. A lawyer in a recent trial in which the question turned on the moral tendency of a novel represented to be impure, recited a long passage from Milton to show that nothing could be more indecent,—and that therefore no freedom of speech in a man of genius could be open to this charge. We are not forced, in order to justify or define what we consider the true criterion, to defend every passage of Milton, but we assert that he very rarely introduces any theme or dwells on it more broadly than the necessities of his subject require, and that he never gratuitously or directly, seeks to stimulate or excuse licentious passion. We cannot perhaps assert so much for Shakspeare. Some of his minor poems cannot be defended by the warmth of youth or the general freedom, even the grossness, of the times. But, in general, when we have bated from his plays, those passages which may have been interpolated by actors to please the groundlings of the pit, there is remarkable purity of tone—we may say chasteness of feeling, even in what to the ear is broad and free. In respect to the higher attributes of woman, nothing can surpass the delicacy of his conceptions, or the elevating purity, we might almost say the vestal chastity of his thought and feeling. If we compare him with the poets, and especially with the dramatists of his time, with Ben Jonson at their head—the most learned, who ought to have been the most civilized—he shines by the contrast with a radiance that surprises and delights the fair-minded critic. Dryden, the great leader of the next generation, with Shakspeare as an example to guide and elevate him, whom he both studied and criticized, deliberately wallows in a slough not only of grossness of speech, but of indecency and licentiousness in- sentiment and intent.

From these examples we think can be derived a canon which will enable even the most unpractised person to de-termine what is pure or impure in imaginative literature.

"A writer, from what we call the grossness or freedom of the times in which he lived, may be gross in language, and even in description and allusion, and yet not be impure. He may also introduce in writing, if his plot or character or theme requires it, both scenes and descriptions which it may not be pleasant to -recite or read in a drawing-room. Sometimes he must do this, or his picture would not be complete, or his character consistent. But he may never enact the part of the tempter to evil, either by soliciting or excusing passion. Whoever does this, is a licentious writer, whatever be the refinement of his allusions, or the euphemisms of his speech. Whoever goes beyond this, and makes the chief interest and excitement of his tale or character to depend on the attractiveness of sin, without its shame and sorrow, is often a more serious offender, just in proportion to the refinement of his *double entendres,* and the studied propriety of his descriptions. That modern literature, in both fiction and poetry, is often indecent, even when it seeks to be exquisitely refined, is too notorious to be denied or overlooked."

" It is very remarkable," says *F. W. Newman,* " that while the ancient theory concerning the relation of the sexes was at best deficient and at worst very base; while the abundance of slave women and freed women, and the unchallenged rightfulness of slavery, depressed the best men's notions of the rights of women; yet in their highest poets there is less than in our own that can minister to voluptuousness, even in Homer and Virgil than in Milton and Spenser. But here also Walter Scott is admirable. He has an unfailing sweetness of heart, full-charged with the morality of the future."— *Lecture i.*

A sharp humorist in Blackwood's Magazine is not at all too severe in the following, which purports to be an item in his last Will and Testament. " My sense of *Decency* and *Decorum,* my dislike to details of the Divorce Court and the general annals of prurient living—I leave to the lady-novelists, whose utter destitution in this respect moves pity and compassion; and I appeal to all those who have any qualities, even worn ones, of regard for cleanliness of life and decency of demeanor, not to forget creatures so utterly bereft of these gifts, and to whom even the rags of virtue would prove an unspeakable luxury."

A generation cannot be entirely pure which tolerates writers who, like Walt Whitman, commit, in writing, an offence like that indictable at common law of walking naked through the streets, and excuse it under the pretence that " Nature is always modest." Nor can such a writer as this be successfully defended, even by Emerson, if he regards one of his own maxims, that "Nature is severely chaste." That literary catholicity must be too broad for those who " can afford to keep a conscience," which accuses or applauds such lecherous priests of Venus as Algernon Swinburne, or would palliate not merely his enormous offences in the service of passion, but his more shameless defiance of the remonstrances of those whom he offends. Let the imagination of such writers be ever so brilliant and their diction ever so enchanting, the altar at which they serve is that of harlotry and pollution.

Lest it should be thought that these remarks are too sweeping, we would refer to one or two reasons why authors may sometimes be more refined in their tastes than their works would indicate, and why critics in literature and students of books are less sensitive than unpracticed readers in respect to certain freedoms of allusion and of treatment. , To critics and authors, the matter may be one of simple psychological development and study, while to the person whose sensitive imagination responds with vivid interest to every successful representation, the delineation of passion may be fraught with sophistical or seductive power. One who is fortified by the varied experiences of life, or whose passions are cooled by age, or controlled by habits of duty, may safely visit scenes and have to do with persons which would be dangerous to those younger and more inexperienced. The residents of a large city must of necessity come in sight of evil, to the attractions of which the stranger from the country has not become insensible. The physician, who is strong in health and hardened by custom, inhales with impunity the offensive and deadly air of contagion, without being even sensible of its nauseous and dangerous quality. The ***habitue*** of a dissecting-room, who in more than one respect may be likened to a literary critic, is so used in all his senses to every form of morbid anatomy, that he sometimes forgets that what is rightfully most offensive to others has ceased to be so to himself. Perhaps in this way we may explain why it is that certain imaginative writers, whose aims are usually pure and elevated, and whose tastes are sensitive and refined, sometimes introduce scenes and personages that offend right-minded and right-hearted readers, and why critics of the severest ethical tastes not infrequently tolerate what deserves reprobation. "We can understand why a writer who could handle such "extra-hazardous characters" as are introduced in "Peg Woffington" with such delicacy and even ethical truth, should excite offence by those in " Griffith Gaunt," and why in respect to the ethical influence of the latter work there should fail to be entire unanimity of dissatisfaction. The professional insensibility of a practiced *litterateur* is however scarcely an adequate explanation or excuse for the proclivities of such a writer as the author of " New America " and " Spiritual Wives." The pruriency of not a little modern literature is a sad sign of degeneracy of taste and of tone in certain circles which pride themselves upon their excessive refinement of taste and their secure elevation above the ordinary weaknesses and responsibilities of humanity as well as above the received maxims of propriety, not to say of decency in the relation of the sexes.

This variety of opinion and practice makes even more imperative the rule which we have laid down, that what offends one's moral tastes, or is condemned by one's moral judgment, should be uncompromisingly rejected. No freedom of practice or opinion on the part of others should be allowed, as against this law for the individual conduct. While there is force in the maxim, " To the pure all things are pure," there is truth in the proverb, "What is one man's meat is another man's poison;" and there is no poison so deadly, as there is none which is so insidious and tenacious, as the poison which denies the imagination by means of licentious litera- ture. That young man does a better thing than he knows of for his conscience, his character, and his manhood, who resolutely throws into the fire a book which he finds to be bad, even though it is bad only for him; and that young lady serves her conscience, and womanliness too, who does the same with any book which should cause her to blush to herself that she has not done it before.

Leaving this topic, we are prepared also to draw a still broader induction in respect to the general moral influence of imaginative writers. It certainly is not required that a writer be morally pure, and even morally elevating, that he should point—or rather blunt—every sentiment, tale, or poem with a moral. Nor is it nec- essary that the writer should at all times maintain a preaching tone, in order to be moral, or even in order to be Christian. All books ought not to preach at all times; no more should all men, even if preaching is their proper vocation. Too much preach- ing diminishes or mars the effect of good preaching, when preaching is required; much more is it to be avoided if the preaching is not of the best quality, as it rarely can be, in a story or poem.

The obtrusion of religious or ethical aims characterizes the so-called *Tendenz-roman* of the Germans, and the *Novel of purpose* or the *Doctrinal Novel* of the English. These are generally characterized by a single defect, and that is, that when the purpose or tendency is moral it is usually so obtrusive or embarrassing as to weaken the imaginative character of the work, and thus to hinder or destroy its power to be morally useful. A tale or poem that is constructed for the single aim of enforcing an ethical or religious truth, in nine cases out of ten, suffers materially as a tale or a poem. It is then by no means essential that the ethical aim of the writer should be apparent, nor even that he should write with an aim that is distinctively ethical at all, in order that he be both ethically useful and ethically pure.

NOR again, is it necessary in order that literature be in-tensely and in the best sense ethical, that bad scenes, bad characters, bad sentiments, and bad passions, should not be introduced, and, when represented, should not be consistently and forcibly described—giving to sin all the dignity and beauty and attractions which it may lawfully claim, else the mirror were not held up to nature. What we contend for is simply that the mirror should be held up to nature as it is, only with magnified proportions. Now nature, i. e., human nature, is intensely ethical; she recognizes conscience, not always in her actions indeed, but always in her convictions; she requires judgment and retribution too, at least within the domain where shame and self-reproach abide; she forgives indeed, but never without repentance, never to those who glory in wrong or hatred, in .selfishness or shame. It is just when, and just because, the mirror is not held up to nature, that there is moral danger, and often moral death; and the danger, is exactly in proportion to the power of genius to glorify or excuse the distorted and unnatural images which it reflects. It is when the magic mirror which genius has always at com-mand, is no longer a mirror of truth—reflecting the shame, the corruption, and the remorse of sin as well as its glory, its short-lived triumph and its joy—but the lying glass in which the harlot is set forth as a vestal, the fiend as a loving angel, and the atheist as an adoring seraph, that genius becomes one of the mightiest agents for evil, by bewildering the imagi-nation, confusing the judgment, and leading captive the passions of an admiring generation.

In discussing the ethical criteria of imaginative writers and their works, we have in fact considered the ethical characteristics of all sorts of literature. "We repeat the thought without hesitation, that literature as literature, invariably acts upon and addresses the imagination. In one word, all literature so far as it is literature proper is imaginative. Literature does indeed enlarge our store of facts, and in this way gives what is called information or knowledge ; but if what we learn does not excite us to recreate, either for delight to the feelings or for application to use, the facts and information which it imparts are as dry and barren as the tables of a book of logarithms or the rows of figures in an old ledger. Literature also reasons with us and convinces of truth, but if the truth is not recast and used to interpret nature or direct the life, wherein is its value ? But if used in either of these ways, it acts upon the imagination. It will be found moreover that all history, all reasoning, all eloquence, and all positive knowledge whatever, are more or less imaginative, and are fitted either to exercise and stimulate, and consequently to elevate or degrade the imagination. Literature in all these higher relations must therefore be ethically good or ethically bad. It cannot be morally indifferent. It must be healthful or injurious.

The imagination forms and controls the conscience so far as it forms and enforces the ideals of what we can and ought to become. The ideals which it actually forms and enforces must inevitably raise us upward or drag us downward. Literature in all its products, as history, essay, oration, or argument, modifies and energizes these ideals— entering into all by an unobserved but most potent influence. This influence is especially subtle and effective when the imaginative element gives character and name to the product, i. e., when, as poem, novel, or drama, it stimulates and directly addresses this controlling power. It follows that all those ethical criteria and rules by which we estimate and use confessedly imaginative writers, apply as properly to every department of literature.

There is a very abundant class of writings that are some-times denominated cheap literature, which, only by courtesy, deserve to be called literature at all. It is a class somewhat miscellaneous and comprehensive, consisting as it does of novels, novelettes, journals, and newspapers, in which so-called stories abound. Of many of these productions nothing worse can be said—though that is bad enough—than that they are utterly frivolous and vapid, that they while away the time, and interest the feelings, but neither elevate the tastes nor brighten the life. They are simply a reflex of the commonplace aims and the vulgar feelings of the mass of readers for whom they are written. They are made to *take* and made to *sell,* and they both *take* and *sell,* because they humor what their readers like, in respect to characters, incidents, illustrations, and style.

Much of this sort of literature is open to the more serious objection, that it stimulates and inflames the passions, ignores or misleads the conscience, and studiously presents views of life that are fundamentally false. The lower appetites are often directly addressed, or their indulgence is indirectly justified through the gravity that becomes a book, and the sophistical art which every writer must use to keep for himself and his reader the semblance of a becoming self-respect. Writings of this class lead men to believe that they can be rich without toil and saving; that they can be amiable and attractive, and yet be intensely hypocritical and selfish; that they can have exquisite moral sensibilities and lofty moral aspirations, and yet be debased by appetite and passion; that they can be profanely blasphemous, and yet fervently religious; in short, that they can be successful for the present and future life, without complying with a single condition of success for either.

And they find readers, too—scores, hundreds, thousands, myriads of readers. Yes, of myriads they constitute the sole reading. The man of business, whose tastes are low and whose aims are vulgar, reads them when he lays down his favorite newspaper—too often like them—and he becomes more intensely mean and animalized than before; the clerk reads them, and they furnish him with the slang of his loose conversation, or train him to rob his master's drawer, or tamper with his accounts, that he may visit the gambling-house and the brothel. The silly and unprotected girl reads them, and she is ripened by them to yield to the flatteries of her seducer. The neglected boy reads them, and they make him an incendiary or a pirate, a hater of law and a despiser of God. They are the Bible and the Primer to myriads of the rising generation at this very hour. One can never see a bale of books or papers of this sort without thinking, there goes a package of the seeds of robbery and lust. It were almost better to import living lecturers in behalf of sensualism and crime, and furnish them with pulpit and hall, for then we should have the disgusting facts of sin to give the lie to its flattering words. It were almost no worse that a procession of harlots should walk the streets of every city or village, for these would bear the brand of their own shame upon their foreheads.

But are not these books brilliant? Yes, brilliant as a rotten log, or a putrescent carcass, which shine because they are decayed, and are phosphorescent just in proportion as they are offensive. But do they not sparkle and delight? Yes, just as the will-o'-wisp, which is created of foul gases, and leads the silly pursuer through brush and brier, till it lands him in some miry swamp, or chokes him with the damps of death. No language can describe the influence of this so-called literature in degrading the tastes, in weakening or corrupting the principles, and in provoking the passions. No man can easily estimate the evil consequences that are to come of it, in a character at once frivolous, conceited, and vulgar, or sensual, ferocious, and atheistic.

It is grateful to turn from this painful picture to a higher and better kind of popular literature which we believe to be gaining a surer hold and a widening influence. While with one class of readers there is certain degradation, as there must be with forces so active as to carry them downwards, with another there is a steady and progressive elevation, as there are books to foster such an improvement.

Such are the histories which attract and instruct; the biographies which leave a glow in the minds of their readers; the poetry that is both popular and elevating; the criticism that discerns undiscovered beauties in our favorite authors; the travels that almost reconcile us to the necessity that forbids us to wander; and the tales that sparkle without corrupting, and that let us laugh and still be wise.

It is still more grateful to imagine the time when Books and Reading for the people shall become altogether good in their influence; when their agency, which is to the health of the mind what the atmosphere is to that of the body, shall be like a fine June or October morning; invigorating, exciting, inspiring—an atmosphere in whose breath is no poison, detected or concealed; no seeds of plague, neither the rank and offensive nor the delightful but deadly.

Such a literature would be both flower and fruit of a perfected Christian civilization, and in that sense a truly Christian literature. But what is the just conception of a Christian literature has been a matter of some question. The conception itself is also not easy in all respects to define ; we must therefore defer the consideration of it to a separate discussion.

CHAPTER IX.

THE RELIGIOUS CHARACTER AND INFLUENCE OF BOOKS AND READING.

FROM the moral, we proceed to the religious relations of books and reading. The two are very nearly allied, and yet each requires to be discussed apart from the other.

Their affinity suggests similar criteria in judging of books, and similar rules in using them. As the law of duty is in its very nature supreme, so the sanctions of religion are, by their very sacredness, inviolable. As what we obey from conscience should be obeyed without reserve, so what we reverence as divine must be worshiped without a rival. Duty gives law in all relations and to every kind of action, and religion asserts attractions which outshine and exclude rivals of every sort, even in the forms of culture, art, or literature.

We have seen that whatever in books or reading weakens the conscience or corrupts the moral feelings, should be rejected as evil. By the same rule, it follows that whatever in either hinders or depresses the religious life should be scrupulously avoided. The religious nature, though it is sanctioned and controlled by the conscience, is more sensitive than the conscience itself. It feels a stain like a wound, not merely as doing violence to the most sensitive emotions, but as involving dishonor to the objects and persons hallowed for its worship and trust. If, then, we converse with any book, or practice any reading which consciously interfere with our religious faith or fervor, we should dismiss the one and desist from the other without hesitation or compromise.

This rule applies both to faith and feeling, the two elements of the religious life. Whatever in literature disturbs or weakens ***our faith,*** injures us in a vital point, inasmuch as it cuts off or dries up the fountain of life. Whatever disturbs or shocks the religious ***emotions,*** introduces discord into the harmony of the highest and best sensibilities. This rule is very general, and, so to speak, is entirely formal. It neither provides for nor regulates its own application. Whether or not the effect or the tendency of a particular book, or the reading of an author or a class of writings, is good, evil, or indifferent in these respects, must be decided by every man for himself. Books that are harmless or useful to one man, may be injurious to another. Reading which is useful to the religious life of one, may be worse than useless to that of another. Every reader who is capable of independent judgment must decide for himself. Those whose judgments are immature, or whose tastes are unformed, should ask advice of those whom they have learned to trust.

We cannot overlook or deny the fact that the religious faith of some men is perversely narrow, bigoted, and positive ; while that of others is broad, lax, and uncertain. The religious feelings of one are gloomy and depressing; those of another are irreverent and presumptuous. But whatever the faith and feelings are, they constitute the religious life of the individual; and this life is, for him, sacred and supreme, whether it is strong or weak, whether it is well or ill controlled. The effect of books and reading upon each individual can be measured and estimated best by himself.

We must also assume and concede that the faith of every man should be founded upon reason, after weighing the arguments for and against its conclusions. The duty to read books of argument or evidence for or against our creed, it falls not within our plan to discuss or to en-force. This subject belongs obviously to the debatable and vexed department of polemics, and tends so directly to awaken special jealousies as properly to be excluded from consideration. It would be nothing less than discourteous, if indeed it were nothing more, to assume or imply that the faith and worship of any *one* of our readers were not the products of thought and reflection—were not commended to his conscience and justified by his reason.

All these things being assumed and conceded, we re-assert with greater emphasis, that whatever in books and reading, whatever in literary enjoyment or culture, hinders the religious activity or lowers the tone of religious faith and feeling, should be abandoned at the cost of any pain or sacrifice. We assert with equal confidence, that every man must judge for himself what in fact hinders or helps him in this regard. We insist also, that in many cases a book may seriously hinder the religious life by lowering the tone of faith and feeling, even if it does not lead to avowed unbelief, to hesitating skepticism, or bold irreverence. If we may not safely yield ourselves to the personal influence of an unbelieving or irreverent man, we should for the same or still stronger reasons, hesitate to expose ourselves to the sophistries or scoffings of a fascinating writer who is atheistic or profane. Indeed, the fascinations of a bad man are less ensnaring than those of a bad book which is written with brilliancy and power. A man who is atheistic and profane may, it is true, be dangerously attractive from the force and fascinations of his very presence and the charms of his conversation; but he must also be repellent to sensitive natures, from the defiant hardness which usually attends upon wilful unbelief, and the selfish heartlessness which commonly lurks behind irreverent feeling, however refined may be the culture or polished the manners. But in a book these defects and repellencies are not so obvious, and hence the poison to the soul may be the more readily conveyed, for the very reason that it is not so obtrusive to the perceptions. The powerful or brilliant genius that knows how to heighten those ideal attractions which altogether surpass any impersonated charms, is equally skilful in suppressing that offensiveness which cleaves to evil when personated in a man. For these and manifold reasons, a bad book, though its energy may not be so intense and striking, may, by its subtle and insidious influences, be far more dangerous in a religious regard than a bad man, however plausible and attractive are his manners or conversation.

The inquiry will here be interposed: Do we not associate freely and often intimately, with living men whose religious faith,—or no faith,—we reject, and with whose feelings we cannot sympathize ? Should we not count it folly to do otherwise ? Why, then, should not we do the same with those books which are openly anti-religious, or which are divergent from our own faith and feelings ? We answer, We may do the one and also the other. The rule is not that we may never read nor even study books of the class described, but it is that whenever the reading or the study does us positive harm, or tends to a conscious evil, then such books should be abandoned and proscribed for our individual use. The Great Master of the faiths of Christendom, and In a sense even of its no-faiths, has laid down the rule, ' If thine eye causes thee to offend, pluck it out' Is a book, a favorite author, or a course of reading, worth more to us than the eye or the hand? Or may we say or think that because we have become great readers we have outgrown the authority of Christ's teachings ? Surely not those which concern our duty and allegiance to Himself. Shall we count Him too severe when He comes into our libraries to scrutinize our reading and to judge our literature? Not surely if we remember that this censor and judge, who is seemingly so severe upon some of our books and reading, has done more than all the writers and all the culture of all the ages, to excite the imagination, to elevate the emotions, to give power and breadth, tone and pathos to what we call modern, but should call Christian lit-erature ; that he has given themes and inspiration to Dante and Milton, to Tasso and Shakspeare, to Wordsworth and Coleridge, to Schiller and Tennyson, to Scott and the Brownings, to Dickens and Hawthorne— has not only ***subdued*** modern thought and feeling by his authority, but in so doing, has ***elevated*** and ***transfigured*** modern thought and feeling to the enlargement and the aspirations of which modern literature is the splendid product.

But here it will be insisted, and with great apparent truth, that literature is in its very nature free, and the imagination in order to be creative must for the time be freed from those restraints which the actual and the practical both acknowledge. " Literature," it will be urged, " has always in its influence been catholic and liberalizing, for the simple reason that it has embodied in its products the results of every form of thought and opinion, and every shade of sentiment and emotion, without respect to the exactest orthodoxy of opinion, or the precise quality or intensity of the religious feelings. It has served as the one liberalizing agency in the world of controversy and intolerance by providing a common arena where the professors of all faiths have met on the footing of courteous toleration, have had access to each other's views, and learned rightly to appreciate and judge emotions with which they have not sympathized. Had it not been for this fusing and liberalizing influence, it is urged, theology would have been hopelessly bigoted and unreformed, every sect and party would have shut itself up within its own narrow pale, and those humane and charitable sentiments which are acknowledged as the genuine products of true religion would scarcely have found expression or influence. It is to a free and catholic literature that theology owes thanks for its most important advancements, and it is from such a literature that religion has learned to be charitable and humane. From the days of those Athenian bigots, who caused the martyrdom of Socrates in the interest of an established religion, down to the latest mitigation of the ferocity of Christian theologians, literature has been most efficient in improving theology, while the culture fostered by literature, when untrammeled by religion, has in its turn humanized religious sentiment, as well as refined the means and methods of expressing it. Above all, literature in its freedom has refined and elevated that prime instrument of both culture and religion—the human imagination. But literature has only been able to accomplish these changes by acting on an independent footing, and by maintaining a position aloof from and above all current crude and narrow controversies; especially the intense and exclusive emotions that belong to the zealot and devotee. It is only as men of genius have compelled the religionist to allow them an exemption from his narrow sympathies that they have made for literature a sphere of its own, a refuge and a home for all noble and ennobling emotions, a veritable Delectable Ground where the imagination may disport itself freely and be refreshed."

This is true and important. But on the other hand the commands of the Master are definite and uncompromising, if we could only ascertain what they signify. Moreover, it is in the world of thought and imagination that He claims especial control, because it is here that the principles are formed and the affections find their nurture. It is because the imagination is so nearly allied to faith that her power to hinder or to help is so unlimited, and that literature itself becomes to religion either the deadliest foe or the most potent ally. There are not a few who say, " Leave to religion and literature independent spheres. As of science so of literary activity, their maxim is, l Render to Caesar the things which are Caesar's, and to God the things which are God's' Allow to each untrammeled activity. As religionists we must maintain our creed, as worshipers we must perform our devotions. These should satisfy the demands of religion, but in the sphere of literature we may claim and use the utmost freedom. As readers and critics we need not care whether what we read is in opinion The-istic and Christian, on the one hand, or atheistic and Christless on the other; whether in sentiment it is devout and thankful, or Godless and despairing; whether it is reverent and trustful, or scoffing and profane." This device is accepted by some and practiced by more. The sermon on Sunday and the Scripture on the week-day are dutifully attended to; the prayers are said and the songs are sung morning and evening with earnest devoutness; and so religion has her rights. Religion having received its dues literature asserts its claims. Forthwith our favorite authors plunge us into an atmosphere of thought and feeling in which there is neither God, nor Christ, nor thankfulness, nor hope; or perhaps into an atmosphere which is " earthly, sensual, devilish." Such a compromise as it would seem, is a hollow truce, an armed neutrality, giving the amplest opportunity for disguised treachery on the one hand and a compliant surrender on the other. It can satisfy no religionist whose belief is any thing more than a tradition to accept or a symbol to swear by, or whose worship is aught, beyond a superstition or a spectacular display. The man whose religion does not show itself in forming and regulating his taste for books and reading, or which allows a practical libertinism in this regard, might as well dispense with it altogether. He can hardly be said to have any religion " worth the speaking of."

It is in these forms that the question of the religious relations of books and reading presents itself at the present clay. Religion on the one hand urges its authority, and this authority knows no compromise. On the other hand, literature rightfully asserts its freedom, shows that this freedom has the sanction of Christianity itself, and has most efficiently served Christianity by making it tolerant and humane. " I would not read Shelley's Queen Mab, because it is atheistic," said one college friend to another. " Why not read Shelley," replied the other, " as soon as Lucretius, who is far more deliberately and consistently atheistic; or as soon as Homer or Virgil, those hoary old assertors of ' lords many and gods many ?' And yet you not only allow yourself to read these inveterate sinners, but you would steep the minds of the young in the literature of antiquity, pervaded as it is with the exploded orthodoxies of the past." Again, it is asked, " Why not read the modern Emerson, because some say that he teaches a subtle Pantheism, as freely as you read the ancient Plotinus, to whom he refers so often, and with a deference so profound ; or as you read those Indian sages, from whom he quotes a striking line now and then, with the intimation that should he tell us all they have written, Jesus and His teachings might be greatly cast into the shade, and perhaps lose much of that public confidence with which they have hitherto been favored ?" " Or why is it worse for a Christian family to be amused by the clever caricatures of Holmes than it is to read and laugh at the lampoons of Lucian, -inasmuch as both are directed against the same object, the current Christian orthodoxies of the nineteenth and second centuries ?"

Questions like these are not unfrequently asked, and it is not always easy to answer them. It is safe to say, that who-ever the author may be, whether he be Shelley or Lucretius, Emerson or Plotinus, Holmes or Lucian, if he shakes your well-established confidence in God, or leads you to disown the name that is above every name; or if he disturbs the serenity or fervor of your Christian devotions, then he is not an author whom you should read. If he does not exercise this influence over you, if he casts upon you no spell or blight of evil, you may admire his genius and rejoice in its products, while you are amazed at his presumption and pity his blindness to the light which to you is so cheerful and satisfying. As between the ancient and modern Pantheists and anti-Christians, one difference, however, deserves to be noticed. The older writers represent principles and modes of thinking that are more or less effete. Their arguments and images have little force with the present generation, occupied as it is with modern thought and animated by the modern spirit. Their modern followers invest their opinions with the dignity of present science, and make them glow with the interest of current thought, as well as breathe the warmth of men who have the ear and the sympathy of the present generation. The philosopher of ancient times protests against degrading and childish superstitions, and, by contrast, finds an advantage for his deification of nature and his serene and self-relying resignation to fate. The modern rejects the personal care and scorns the personal sympathy of an Infinite Father. The ancient stands with his eye to the east peering—sometimes wistfully—after the faint indications of the dawning twilight; himself a dark and cold shadow against the breaking light of the, as yet, unrisen sun. The modern looks westward with his back proudly turned on its risen splendor, amid a world that from every object reflects its pervading light; himself suffused with that light and glowing with the attractions which it gives, but denying that it proceeds from the sun or that the sun is risen and shines. The Atheist or Pantheist of antiquity is a cold spectre, shivering in the chill morning. His imitator of the nineteenth century, rejoices in the strength and glows with the beauty of the high noon of the Christian day. While his power to attract and move the men of his time gives plausibility and currency to the little argument which he employs, these very attractions are its most efficient refutation, because they are all derived from the Christian Faith or the civilization which has flowered from its roots.

CHAPTER X.

A CHRISTIAN LITERATURE—HOW CONCEIVED AND DE-FINED.

THESE several inquiries and arguments—these marchings and counter-marchings of thought which we have taken,—force upon us the more general inquiry : Is there anything which can properly be called a Christian literature ? If so, what is it ? How can it be deined so as to secure, on the one hand, the essential freedom which literature imperatively requires, and on the other, the deference to Christianity which Christianity uncompromisingly exacts? How far can we be tolerant of every variety of sentiment and opinion and yet be just to our allegiance to the great Master of our faith, and indeed, of modern literature ?

These questions are very much vexed in modern thinking, and the answers to them are also vexatious to many who strive to adjust the claims of culture and of Christian feeling. They cannot be answered without considering what is the correct conception of literature, as well as what must be taken as essential to Christianity so far as it should be recognized in literature. In respect to both these points, the views of many are diverse and unsettled. Hence the term Christian literature is used by different men in senses which are exceedingly vague, and often plainly contradictory. We shall best explain our own meaning by asking first, What a Christian literature is not, and second, What it is ?

A Christian literature is not necessarily *Theological* in its matter or form. Theological treatises, however able and convincing, are not therefore works of literature. They may be convincing and exhaustive in argument, and erudite in history, without that perfection of style, that attractiveness of imagery, or that eloquence of feeling which are the requisites of whatever is dignified as literature. While in one sense we include in literature all the products of human thinking which are made permanent in books or pamphlets—and in this sense everything that is printed belongs to the literature of the day, of the week, or of the century—we usually require certain characteristics of form and illustration for that which we call literature in the eminent sense. Theology is not of course included in Christian literature because it is Christian, if it does not possess these special features; nor, again, should it be ex-cluded from its sphere because its themes are both religious and Christian. Some of the finest contributions to modern literature have been works of theology. The writings of Bossuet, Massillon, Hooker, Taylor, Howe, Robert Hall, Mason, Edward Irving, Channing, Coleridge, Robertson, and many others, hold the highest rank as literary compositions.

Not every *devotional or practical* treatise is a contribu-tion to Christian literature. By the rule already given, many devotional works fall within, but many more fall without this sphere. The Hebrew Psalms; many Christian hymns, as of Milton, Watts, Wesley, Heber, Keble, Faber and J. H. Newman ; to say nothing of the Latin and German Lyrists, all give grace and beauty to Christian literature. With them are ranked a few devotional and practical works, such as the *De Imitatione Christi, The Holy Living and Dying, The Pilgrim's Progress, etc.* But it is no dishonor to say of numerous products of devotional rhyming and meditation, that they belong to literature in no tolerable sense of the word, and therefore not to

Christian literature at all. They may be useful in their sphere, and therefore deserve to be tolerated and even en-couraged, but they are not literature. They may be honestly thought and earnestly written, and withal be very useful for the circle of readers for whom they are designed. Perhaps from their plainness and want of formal attractions they are fitted to be more useful than works of greater ability and genius. The man who requires the highest perfection in form and diction may be content with them for their Christian excellence, but he is not therefore obliged to be pleased with what is uncultured in language, mean in illustration, and commonplace in thought. That which is positively offensive in both form and conception may be a positive injury to the cause which it professes to serve. The claim is sometimes set up that Christianity is to be held responsible for the mass of wretched doggerel and drivelling that has been written by its earnest but uncultured disciples, and that every reverent Christian is obliged to treat it with respect and read it with deference. The claim is preposterous, and to seem to allow it by those whose taste it offends or whose intellect it does not instruct, is to sin against both taste and Christianity. Such stuff may be tolerated when it is useful, but is only to be endured as a useful evil. To recommend or to circulate all sorts of goodish writing because of its Christian aims, or to encourage the reading and printing of it, under the title of a Christian literature, is to commit nothing less than a pious fraud, which is as weak as it is dishonest.

A Christian literature is not usually written in the interest or with the spirit *of a Christian sect or denomination.* While it is the impulse and the duty of every such division of Christian confessors to set forth and to defend its distinctive tenets, and while the champions of each are often most eloquent and able in such vindications, it is to be observed that the themes which most readily challenge the intellect to its noblest achievements, and inspire the imagination to its loftiest flights, are the truths which the Christian Church holds in common. Those religious and Christian writers whose works have been received as the permanent glories of literature, if they have written for their own communion, have usually addressed what was

Christian in it, and by this means have found a response in the Christian sentiment of all believers.

Again: A work need not be ***religious,*** either in matter or form—it need neither avow Christian doctrines nor express Christian feelings—to deserve a place in Christian literature. A history, a novel, a poem, a tale, an essay, a drama may be eminently Christian without uttering the name of Christ or recognizing directly a faith in His person or teachings, and without even expressing those emotions which are distinctively religious. No disavowal or denial of Christian truths can be allowed, no dishonor may be put upon the sentiments of Christian faith, hope, and worship, but the obtrusion of either for the purpose of expressing the creed of the writer, or of confirming that of the reader, may be forbidden by the proprieties of the occasion, and be so manifestly an offense against good taste as to hinder rather than help the good cause. All that may properly be required is, that the work should be such as a Christian writer might be supposed to produce without inconsistency, and such as a devout Christian reader might be conceived as reading, without offense to his opinions and feelings. This leads us to consider positively what a Christian literature is or ought to be. If it need not be theological, devotional, practical, or even religious, in order to be Christian, pray how can it be characterized and judged ? We reply: First,

A Christian literature must be controlled and pervaded by those ***ethical faiths and emotions*** that are distinctively Christian. Many of these have become so completely the property of Christendom that it is often forgotten that they are the products of Christianity. They have been accepted more or less intelligently and consistently as constituting the right standard of the true and the good for the human race, and the measure of what is ideally noble in human attainment and desirable for human aspiration. They in-fluence communities which would scarcely call themselves Christian. Not a few individuals who are ambitious to show that they think very slightly of the claims of Christ's person, or of the influence of the Christian church, are foremost to pay homage to the eternal truth and the unquestioned excellence of those ethical faiths and feelings which we claim are distinctively Christian, and which we assert should characterize any literature which is in any sense Christian. The faith in the moral order of the universe as supreme and beneficent, because directed by a holy and sympathizing Father, the belief in the ultimate triumph of the good and the right, the conviction that love to God and love to man comprehend all goodness—are some of these prominent *ethical faiths.* Hope in adversity, resignation under affliction, penitence for transgression, forgiveness under wrong, the desire to recover and reform the vicious, charity in judging of the motives of other men —these and many kindred feelings are distinctively *Christian feelings.* Just in the measure in which these faiths and feelings give spirit and tone to the productions of any writer, just in that proportion is he a Christian writer. Just in the measure in which any one or all of these emotions and convictions, fail to show their presence and power when required, does the writer of any work depart from the Christian and fall back into the Pagan spirit. We do not speak of the obtrusive or pharisaical lip-service of an essayist or poet, but of the homage of the convictions and the heart. We do not require ill-placed or obtrusive moralizing, or wearisome cant. These are sometimes as eminently unchristian in fact as they are pretentiously Christian in form. But we insist that any writer who does not accept the faiths, and sympathize with the emotions which are Christian, is not a Christian writer, in whatever year of grace he may write or whatever may be the charm or the power of his thinking or his style. Let those who write in the faith of Stoicism and with the feelings to which it schools the heart, receive all the honor which they deserve for their gifts or genius, but let them not ask to be called Christian writers. Nor let their genial self-complacence be ruffled by the slightest ripple of contemptuous disdain if critics or readers who receive a *more humane,* —i. e. a less "advanced" (or retrograde)— *practical* creed than themselves, shall fear or avoid their influence as ethically defective or injurious.

But Christianity, even as it influences literature, is more than an ethical system. It would be easy to show that the faiths and emotions which have been enumerated, have all been matured by the power of a belief in the personal and historic Christ. Whatever value or dignity they may have in the judgment of the race which has been trained to accept and approve them—whatever hold they may have gained upon the sentiment and the literature of Christendom, is owing to the energy with which this faith in the person of Christ has wrought upon the minds of His believing disciples. This positive faith has not wholly died out. However confidently it may be claimed that all the "advanced thinkers" of the times reject the historic traditions of the gospels and the church, it remains true that a large number of thinking and cultured men still retain this faith, and recognize this faith in the varied literature which they produce and delight in. Whatever they write, whether it be poem, novel, essay, or history, is written in the spirit of a fervent faith in Christ as their Master and Saviour, and as the destined Judge and King of the whole human race— as the master of the world's future thinking and the central inspirer of its future literature. There are others who do not attach this importance to His person or to faith in it, who find in Christ nothing more than a genius remarkable for ethical discernment and religious tenderness, for whom all claims to special homage or confidence must be abandoned, with the progress of knowledge and of insight. In this spirit they write not works of grave theology alone, nor treatises of sagacious and learned philosophy, but works of literature, essays, poems, histories, and fictions.

In respect to writings of this class we are required to ask and to answer the questions, Are they Christian writings? Is the literature which they compose Christian literature ? If they are not Christian for defect of faith in the person of Christ, how precise must that faith be made and what one of the manifold shades of alleged orthodoxy upon this subject must it assume in order to be accepted as Christian? To this we reply, and in doing so develop the second distinctive mark of a Christian literature:

That literature alone is Christian which ***recognizes Christ as the object of trust and reverence.*** Christ's own language is here most pertinent. " Ye call me Master and Lord; and ye do well, for so I am." This test is reasonable, for the reason that so far as literature as such can be affected by the faith of a writer, it must be chiefly affected by his faith or his want of faith in the personal authority and position of Him from whom Christianity takes its name. We cannot agree with Emerson that " by the irresistible maturing of the general mind, the Christian traditions have lost their hold. The dogma of the.mystic offices of Christ being dropped, and He standing on His genius as a moral teacher, 'tis impossible to maintain the old emphasis of His personality; and it recedes, as all persons must, before the sublimity of the moral laws." "We believe that all the movements of thought and feeling must be affected by the presence or absence of this faith in Christ's personality. Mr. Emerson would be the last to deny that up to a very recent period the intellect and heart of Christendom have been swayed by this faith in Christ's person as a ruling principle, and that much of the manhood and more of the womanhood which is reflected in modern literature, is represented as formed by its influence. The two not un-common prints from Ary Scheffer, the **Christus Consolator** and **Christus Remunerator,** forcibly depict what have been the central forces of the Christian literature of the past, as well as symbolize its distinctive criteria in all time.

The criterion we propose, is **reasonable and just.** If a man does not believe in the reality or significance of Christ's person, his disbelief must modify his judgments of the characters and the sentiments which are formed by this faith. He may respect these for their sincerity, but he cannot honor them for their reasonableness. The emotions to which they prompt, the style of character which they form, the hopes and fears which they inspire, the principles of action which they create, in a word, the manhood and the womanhood which they produce, cannot receive his full and hearty sympathy. Let a writer have a marvellous power of passing into the character which he depicts, and of feeling for the time the very emotions which the character he impersonates should express; still the capacity of truly and adequately rendering the emotions of a Christian soul can scarcely be reached by him, if they do not awaken his believing sympathy. Goethe's delineation of the **Confessions of a Beautiful Soul** in **Wil-helm Meister,** George Eliot's Dinah in **Adam Bede,** might be cited as instances against this position. Both these writers, it will be generally conceded, do not accept the faith which controlled the feelings of the characters whom they depict. Shall we call these delineations failures ? Goethe succeeds in most respects in hiding his own face beneath the mask and robes which he assumes, but the voice of Jacob at times betrays the half-sympathizing, half-mocking skeptic, even in the most plaintive tones of confession and of hope. Of **Dinah** we scarcely can trust ourselves to speak. The character is so eminently and heartily Christian, even in the most of its finer shades, that we do not care to point out the particulars in which it betrays the want of the entirest sympathy on the part of the author.

Surely it was written from the fresh remembrances of days of warm and confiding Christian faith, now perhaps under the chill of an honest, and, a temporary eclipse.

To use this criterion is also ***historically just.*** "We do not call Plato, Plotinus, or Epictetus, Christian writers, however noble be their faith, or lofty their ethics, for the reason that neither the one nor the other are Christian in the historic sense of the word. We do not call Julian a Christian because he would exalt the Christ whom he disowned among the sages and gods of the ancient mythology; nor do we call Spinoza a Christian writer, because his ethics are so lofty and his resignations are so saint-like. Pray, what should we call Emerson, or Thoreau, or the hosts of "advanced thinkers" who in their writings obtrusively announce their absence of faith in the received import of the Christian history, and in the lowest possible significance of the central personage in that history; who quietly assume that it is now beyond dispute, among all those whose opinions are entitled to respect, that this history is an effete mythology, and that Christ as a personage to be trusted and adored, is an exploded imposture ? Or what shall we call those literary critics who in their judgments of history or philosophy, of poetry or fiction, tacitly assume or confidently assert that the results of what is significantly called "negative criticism," in respect to a belief in the miraculous and the supernatural, are now accepted by all enlightened and well-read thinkers ? "We make a difference, it is true, between those whose intellects are oppressed with perplexities, while their hearts are thoroughly Christian, and the confident and contemptuous anti-Christian; between those who long to believe, but who cannot fully accept the Christian record and the truths which it contains, who are yet devout worshipers of the as yet unknown God and the unfathomed Christ, and those who desire no God but " the beneficent laws," and no Christ but some idealized human genius. There is an important sense in which it is true that

" There lives more faith in honest doubt Believe me, than in half the creeds."

To call this literature and these writers a-Christian, um-Christian, or anfi-Christian, is not ***intolerant.*** We do not desire to suppress either by law or by the force of public opinion. We will defend the right of those who hold their opinions to propagate them to the utmost of their ability, by all those means which are recognized as proper by the laws of the country and the courtesies of literary freedom. Not only would we tolerate them in the propagation of their theologies and philosophies, but we hold ourselves ready to study their reasons, to weigh their arguments, and ponder their facts, with the utmost attention and care. We will even welcome them to the arena of public criticism and discussion, as those who are likely to render an important service to the cause of truth and Christianity, just so far as they present facts for our con-sideration, or arguments for our scrutiny. But we claim from them a like toleration in turn. They may not regard questions as settled to the disadvantage of Christianity, which we consider as open for its vindication. Least of all may they seek to transfer the discussions which are appropriate to the fields of philosophy and theology—the recognized fields of lawful strife—into the arena of literature, where the rights of the flag of truce prevail. A truly knightly soul would scorn under such a flag to ask for any one-sided courtesy. We welcome these writers to the arena of discussion when they present themselves as theologians and philosophers, and concede to them all the rights of toleration which we ask for ourselves; but when they claim the one-sided privilege of proclaiming at our fire-sides, with cold-blooded assurance or sardonic scorn, that the victory is with them, over our cherished faiths, our hallowed worships, and our immortal hopes, we deny that the question is any longer a question of tolerance.

Nor is our position ***discourteous.*** It is not discourteous to call certain writers, rejecters of Christ as an object of love and confidence, or to say of them that they make literature a medium by which to express and propagate their private opinions. Whether it is altogether courteous ***on their part*** to obtrude these opinions in ways so manifold and unnecessary, is a question which we will not discuss. If it is true, as they insist so often as at least to persuade themselves, that those who adhere to the old faith in Christ's personality, are blind to argument and ignorant of history, that they know nothing of criticism, and are unacquainted with philosophy, it would be a matter of humanity at least to leave such to the quiet enjoyment of their own ignorance and want of thought. If it is not discourteous to dishonor what they revere, and satirize what they respect, it is at least inhuman to make them uncomfortable. If it is not indictable under the statutes of dis-courtesy, it may at least be condemned under the laws against cruelty to the ignorant and imbecile.

Our position is not ***proscriptive.*** We do not contend that these anti-Christian writers are never to be read, admired, arid enjoyed by a person who rejects their version of the New Testament history; but only that if they weaken his faith and disturb his peace by an indirect suggestion of sentiments and opinions that are incongruous with his own, he had better leave them alone, or have to do with them only so far as his taste and conscience will allow. We do not disuse the literature of the old Pagans, nor need we forego the use and enjoyment of the new, provided we recognise them as Pagans.

" No one who acknowledges Christ," writes Dr. Thomas Arnold, " can be indifferent to Him, but stands in such re-lations to Him that the highest reverence must be pre-dominant in His mind when thinking or writing of Him"

"If I think that Christ was no more than Socrates (I do not mean in degree but in kind,) I can, of course, speak of Him impartially;" that is, I assume at once that there are faults and imperfections in His character and on these pass my judgment, but if I believe in Him, I am not His judge, but His servant and creature, and He claims the devotion of my whole nature, because He is identified with goodness, wisdom and holiness."

We admire all that this literature presents for our admiration of truth in morals and philosophy, and of beauty in imagery and diction; even though we are«disturbed at the poverty of its argumentation, the recklessness of its assertions, and the undisguised effrontery of its self-satisfied illumination. But we are not prepared to substitute, at its bidding, the worship of Genius for the worship of a higher Master, least of all, the worship of a genius that in some respects is so superficial, even though in others it is so admirable.

The influence of this anti-Christian literature is far more prevalent in this country, than it is in England. With us the majority of the cultivated men are not authors and critics, but theologians, lawyers, physicians, politicians, and projectors of all types. Of the few who have been the most distinguished in fiction, poetry, and criticism, not a small party sympathize with a very much smaller party in England in holding what is called a negative or uncertain position in respect to the very grave questions which are now so earnestly agitated concerning Theism and Supernatural Christianity. The readers and students of literature technically so-called, among us, are more impressible in any direction to which their favorite authors and critics may lead them, than are those of a similar class in any other country. Confident assertion in imposing phraseology and under attractive imagery, passes for more with us than with any other cultivated people. The critical journal, whether it be quarterly, monthly, weekly, or daily, insinuates most successfully what it believes, or rather what it fails to believe. While there is no country in which the Christian faith has a stronger hold upon the convictions of earnest and sober thinkers, or upon the feelings of the true-hearted, it cannot be denied that among the cultivated classes as such, that is, the classes devoted to literature as a passion and an employment, there prevails a practical, if not an avowed Paganism, in one of the two forms of a philanthropic Stoicism or a refined Epicureanism. *We* call it Paganism, because, though it accepts the ethical spirit which Christianity has created, it is as far removed from the Christian worship of a personal God and the Christian trust in Christ, as was the cultured but comfortless Philosophy of Athens, which ostentatiously erected manifold altars to the Unknown God—which was always eager to run after any novelty in speculation, but conld make nothing of the teachings of Paul the Apostle.

This literary Paganism with its culture and its confidence, with its positive and not always courteous assertions that science and history are entirely upon its side, has no need to ask for toleration. It has little occasion to complain of social persecution. It is far enough from being in danger of reproach or ostracism, while it has the hearty sympathy of multitudes who are so ambitious of culture as to be ready to accept any novelty in the form of speculative suggestions or brilliant improvisation.

We do not propose to discuss the influence or the prospects of this Pagan tendency in American or in modern literature. Had we no higher assurance that its influence must be short-lived, history would teach us that its vagueness and barrenness must soon dry up its life. That a vigorous literature cannot be long sustained in an atmosphere of no-faith is demonstrably certain. The creative and fervent periods of English literature have been closely connected with the prevalence of a positive Christian belief, and a fervent Christian feeling. Among the writers of eminent genius now living who are influenced by the Pagan spirit, there is not one who does not give tokens of the blight and depression which the cheerfulness and fervor of a better hope would remove.

But we need not pursue our theme in these new directions. Its practical aspects have already detained us too long.

CHAPTER XL

HISTORY AND HISTORICAL READING.

WE propose to leave the discussion of books and reading in general, and to proceed to some more particular observations upon different classes of books and different kinds of reading. Perhaps in so doing our thoughts may be less general than they have been; we cannot promise that they will be anything more than useful.

We begin with History. It seems natural to begin at this point, as history is the favorite and the common field of all industrious readers. The bright-minded boy, who is withal a little solid and thoughtful, if he is known among his companions as a great reader, usually takes a special delight in History. If he is merely bright-minded, he may be satisfied with novels or plays, childish or otherwise ; but if he is also intelligent and curious, he uniformly takes to History. He usually does this very early, and not rarely he follows this taste so passionately as to seem more at home in the old and the distant than in the new and the near. Such a boy often, in the first gush of his historic enthusiasm, thinks and talks more of Athens and Pericles, of Rome and Julius Cæsar, of Moscow and Napoleon, than he does of the places and the men that are present to his senses. This taste is also conspicuous in the earnest and thoughtful among so-called well-informed men, as the steady and sturdy mechanic or farmer who thinks for himself, who expresses opinions on public affairs to which other men listen in a debating-club or a town-meeting, or when occupied in earnest talk at a shop or grocery.

Now and then we meet with a thoughtful old lady or an intelligent old gentle-man, to whom history has all their life been both instruction and pastime, and the result is seen and felt in the mellowed and comprehensive views which they utter upon every subject of which they chance to speak. They are rightly revered as the oracles of their circle.

History has also a kind of precedence .from having been the first form of writing. Books of history are the oldest written productions. This was both natural and necessary. The child of modern times sits on the father's knee, to listen to the stories of what happened in his childhood to himself and his play-mates—how they hunt-ed in the forest and sported on the holidays. And so, as we may believe, was it in the earlier times. In the morning of the race, the reverent family and the deferential tribe gathered often about their patriarch to hear the story many times repeated, of those whom he had known—brave warriors, great hunters, sagacious inventors and skilful artists. As soon as language was framed into connected phrases, history began to be recited. The story-teller, as he wrote or read upon the monument of stone or wood the names of great men or the dates of great events, would expound at length the tales of which these names and numbers were only the suggestive texts. Now and then, if he had a rhythmic tongue and a vivid imagination he would frame history into a ballad—like the song of Chevy Chase, or the ballads collected by Scott in " The Minstrelsy of the Scottish Border," or by Percy in " The Eeliques of English Poetry," or " Frithiof 's Saga "—which he would recite to his family or clan, in the long twilight, or under the bright starlight, or in the deep arctic nights. Others would recite to crowds on festive occasions—as at the feast of Tabernacles among the Jews; or at the Olympic games among the Greeks when the poems of Homer were chanted in recitative ; or as in the middle ages the wandering bard made himself welcome by his impassioned histories in verse. In many of these ear-lier histories, not only the power of description was brought into requisition, but the imagination was allowed the freest play. Literal truth was not always so much cared for as an effective story, especially one in favor of the heroes or penates of a family or tribe. Such stories would grow most rapidly in transmission, and what was at first a somewhat faithful narration, would soon become more or less of a poetic exaggeration. When History begins to be written for the sober ends of truth, as by Herodotus, its so-called Father, there is manifest abundant credulity and play of fancy. This spirited and cheerful narrator, with much that was true and well-attested, gathered together somewhat loosely much that he had picked up in his travels of the traditions that had come down from preceding generations in their narratives and songs, their epics and fictions. These being currently reported, when they were once written down and read, would obtain a sort of credit and footing in the faith of the world. People are so eager to know something of other times and of distant countries, that if anything passes current as a story it is soon accepted as a fact.

This is the first stage of historical writing—the period of simple and *naif* narration, largely intermixed with what is purely imaginative and fictitious. It confines itself to recording such facts as strike the imagination and interest the feelings, especially of admiration and reverence; following the method of simple narration, with large credulity, few critical attempts to distinguish between truth and falsehood, and absolutely no philosophy. As writers and readers reach a . more sober and less childish age, history becomes more grave and dignified in its manner, and events are recorded with a more careful exactness. To the imagination and feelings far less freedom is allowed. Facts and dates are copied with care from monuments and records. But history is still very credulous and undis-criminating; its writers set down without sifting the most of what they find recorded or hear reported without weighing authorities or adjusting conflicting testimonies. It is to be noticed also, that only the so-called great personages and great events, are deemed worthy to be recorded. Great battles, decisive victories, the deeds of heroes, the lives of kings and princes, of nobles and statesmen; the events which make one people the conqueror and another the subject; these stand conspicuously forth from the ordinary level of human affairs and are alone thought deserving of preservation. The fortunes of the common people, the condition of those who do not belong to the court or the aristocratic classes, the ways in which they lived, tilled the soil, built houses, sat at their tables, slept in their beds, navigated rivers and the sea or traveled by land, their customs and rites, their manners and feelings, their thoughts and their faiths, these are overlooked as beneath the so-called ***dignity of history.*** The great events judged worthy of notice are set forth in an exaggerated style, such as impresses the imagination and excites the wonder of the commonalty. Partly from the natural operation of reverence and the nobler sentiments of respect, and partly from the exalted imagination of the narrator, the great men of the past are set forth in gigantic outline and intensified coloring as something superhuman. All men were giants in the ancestral days, as the writer describes and as the reader conceives them. Many of the classic historians write in this vein, as Livy and Plutarch; and almost all of the modern writers of ancient history, till a comparatively recent period, have imitated very closely their style and spirit. As we read Plutarch's Lives, or Rollin's Ancient History, we seem to be lifted above the actual solid earth of every day life, and to fly or float in a sort of cloud or enchanted land. Lofty forms stalk before us, stately and long-robed personages, always in attitudes of superhuman dignity or grace, never speaking except as they utter short orations or weighty apothegms, enacting no deeds except deeds of staid and awe-inspiring solemnity. The events with which we are confronted are all more weighty and significant than those to which we are accustomed in our daily, or even in our modern life. They cannot be compared with these. To conceive of them or to measure them by the common men and the common things of our time and of modern days, would be to degrade the events and to dishonor ourselves. The whole impression is solemn, stage-like and magnificently imposing, as when a familiar scene is viewed by the weird moonlight—half elevating, half bewildering, but always impressive and disposing to admiration and reverence. We may say, indeed, of the impression received by the readers of the great men of antiquity as described by Plutarch, that it is not unlike that made by the statuary in the Vatican, or at the Louvre, as exhibited by torch-light, when the effect of every object is exalted and made mysterious by the unnatural lights and shadows that play upon them, and the witchery of the scene is heightened by the back-ground of impenetrable darkness beyond. Many of the histories of the ancients by the moderns, were in a certain sense little more than transcripts from such ancient originals. The early legends were all faithfully copied by most of these historians, some of them being recognized as exaggerations or myths with a slender basis of fact, and others as being of uncertain import; but no serious, certainly no successful attempt was made to discover what was true or certain. Many of the extravagant stories and improbable events were set down as true, and all the judgments of both men and events were in the highest degree credulous and timid. The surprising deeds of the heroic ages and the superhuman virtues of the ancient republics —the simplicity, fidelity and patriotism reported—were all confided in, and it was scarcely even suspected that any of the traditions of the ancients themselves might require a careful scrutiny and a critical revision.

The modern histories of modern events have been too often written in the. same exaggerated and undiscriminating manner. The common stock histories of England and the United States are almost universally in this vein, beginning with the well known older histories and coming down to the declamatory laudations of Bancroft, and the curt and biting sentences of Hildreth.

The names of Hildreth and Bancroft as well as those of Mitford and Gibbon, Hume and Burnet, Lingard and Neal,. suggest the remark that history in all its forms, whether ancient or modern, is liable to be written *in a partisan spirit.* The ancient writers have long been recognized even to the uncritical and trusting eyes of their admirers, as not altogether unbiassed in their sympathies and antipathies. Even honest old Homer tells the largest and the most favorable stories of his favorite Greeks and makes the gods sympathize a little unfairly with Achilles, while the gossiping Herodotus uniformly flatters his favor-ite nations. As we come down into the region of history that is more sober and accurate, we find that almost every author writes in the interest of some political party, some social caste, or some favorite hero. Even those grave and judicial old narrators, whO look and write in such a solemn and stately way, are not always so disinterested as they seem, but contrive to set off their impressions concerning men and things to the advantage or disadvantage of those whom they like or dislike. They do not write in the manner of special pleaders or retained advocates so obviously as some of the moderns, for it was inconsistent with the dignity of ancient manners to do so; but it is almost as easy to be solemnly one-sided and unfair with the air of a judge, as to be violently partisan with the gesticulations of an attorney. Modern History is too extensively and notoriously partisan, to require any special comment. Especially has the history of England, which is that with which we have the nearest concern, been written in the in-terest and by advocates of almost every shade of political opinion and religious belief. There have also been special histories of almost every party and sect, written with more or less of partisan partiality.

History, as we have reviewed it, has had two distinct stages of development: First, the narrative, which is abundantly imaginative and largely credulous ; next, that of the sober and accurate narrator, but only of such facts as are stately and dignified, with a more or less indiscriminate admiration of what is recognized as superhumanly great and good; which in turn has readily and almost uniformly degenerated into a blind or willful partisanship.

Within the last fifty years, there has been a decided reaction from these excessive and mischievous tendencies. This reaction has led to a new method of writing history; which involves new methods of studying and reading it. History both ancient and modern has been written in what is properly called the *critical* spirit. This has well-nigh involved a revolution in the scrutiny of historical documents, and in the judgment of historical facts, as well as .in the spirit and aims in which history is written and read. Under its influence it has become almost necessary that all history, both ancient and modern, should be rewritten. Many of the old standard histories and historical series have been discarded and displaced. Long series of uncritical narratives like "(The Ancient and the Modern Universal History," of some fifty volumes, have become almost so much rubbish. History also is read as it were with new eyes. This reaction, and the application of the critical method, took a distinct and recognized form under the shaping genius of *Niebuhr,* though eminent critics and scholars had prepared the way by the method and spirit in which they had studied antiquity before his time. It was reserved for Niebuhr, however, to accomplish a revolution in the prevailing ideas in respect to the early history of Rome, and in so doing to establish and vindicate a new method for the treatment of all History. He not only suggested but vindicated the position that a large portion of what is recorded by Livy as historical truth is little better than a series of mythical and exaggerated legends with a slender basis of fact. Much of the history of the seven kings went the same way with the story of the miraculous she-wolf who suckled Romulus and Remus, the reputed founders of the Eternal City. The subsequent, and, till then, the universally accepted narratives of the gravest and the most trustworthy historians, were also revised with rigid care; being carefully tested by close comparison with one another, with the allusions of contemporaneous literature, with permanent monuments, with well known and newly discovered or newly interpreted inscriptions, and last not least, with the testimony of languages and dialects; which, strange as it may seem, serve as the means of correcting many errors and confirming many conjectures. Other writers, following the example of Niebuhr and catching his spirit, have traversed the same and other fields of ancient history. Of histories well known to English readers, Arnold's History of Rome, and G rote's History of Greece, are eminent examples of the superiority of the new over the old method. As the result of Niebuhr's example and influence, not only have the fabulous and legendary elements been eliminated from the histories of the older nations, but the overstrained and exaggerated conceptions of the men and events which had come to us from the ancient Plutarch and the modern Rollin, have been toned down to the modesty of a probable and rational judgment. The tendency to see heroes in both virtue and vice beyond the possible attainments of human nature, which had free indulgence, has given way to a juster estimate of what was possible and is therefore credible. '

The old times, which were ignorantly admired and ex-travagantly lauded, have been carefully measured by what we know of the workings of the human nature of to-day. The institutions, the principles, the passions, the aims and the achievements, of such men as Pericles and Alcibiades, of Cicero and Seneca, of Catiline and the Cesars, have been examined, not under the colored lights of blind admiration, nor by the weird lights of myth-making credulity, nor the false lights of blind or lying partisanship, but by the dry and white light, which is reflected from the aims, principles and passions of men in similar circumstances in modern times—the good men not being **over** good for human nature, and the bad not so much, and so desperately, worse than the very bad of later times. In short, the historian has learned to measure the ancient world by the modern world, instead of by an extravagant and distorted creation of his own bewildered admiration and his excitecl fancy; because the modern is known to be the actual world, and as such illustrates those permanent laws and forces of humanity, by which alone all history, whether old or recent, can be rationally estimated and judged. But while this critical tendency has dissipated what is false and extravagant in the pictures and conceptions of ancient life, it has established more firmly and set in bolder relief whatever is true, though it be peculiar and even supernatural. While it has explained the myths and legends of superstition and credulity in the false religions that cloud the morning of the historic period, it has justified and confirmed the miracles that are so appropriate to simpler times, which have so fitly signalized the presence of One who is higher than nature, and introduced those manifestations of his moral character and his loving care which have been required in the world's moral history. The same criticism which has proved so destructive to the myths of Grecian and the legends of Roman story, has proved itself most positive and constructive when applied to the miraculous and supernatural which are alone adequate to explain the rise and development of the Mosaic and Christian economies. This has been the actual result of the most careful and critical investigation of the two by some of the most eminent students of the new historical school. Niebuhr himself, after some sharp experienees of misgiving lest the miraculous in the Old and New Testaments should, under the ritical method, go the same way with the mythological in the Roman and Greek History, writes thus concerning the education of his son: u While I shall repeat and read the old poets to him in such a way that he will undoubtedly take the gods and heroes for historical beings, I shall tell him at the same time that the ancients had only an imperfect knowledge of the true God, and that these gods were overthrown when Christ came into the world. He shall believe in the letter of the Old and New Testaments, and I shall nurture in him, from his infancy, a firm faith in all that I have lost or feel uncertain about." His biographer records further, that "The Word made Flesh—the Divine brought into visible contact with the Human, and finding an historical embodiment in an individual—was a doctrine that found a warm response in a mind so full of earnest aspiration towards heaven, and at the same time so thoroughly historical in its views of the world. His personal reverence for Christ was a sentiment that deepened with the progress of his life ... He once exclaimed, in the course of an argument with the present [former] King of Prussia, 'I would lay my head on the block for the divinity of Jesus!'" *Life and Letters, etc.* Arnold observes: "The miracles of the Gospel and those of later history, do not stand upon the same ground. I do not think that they stand on the same ground of external evidence; I cannot think that the unbelieving spirit of the Roman world, in the first centuy, was equally favorable to the origination and admission of stories of miracles, with the credulous tendencies of the middle ages. But the difference goes deeper than this to all those who can appreciate the other evidences of Christianity, and who, therefore, feel that what we call miracles were but the natural accompaniments of the Christian revelation—accompaniments, the absence of which would have been more wonderful than their presence. This, as I may almost call it, á 'priori probability in favor of the miracles of the Gospel cannot be said to exist in favor of those of later history."— *Lectures on the Study of Modem History, ii.* Again, "Strauss writes about history and myths, without appearing to have studied the question, but having heard that some pretended stories are mythical, he borrows this notion as an engine to help him out of Christianity. But the idea of men writing mythic histories between the time of Livy and Tacitus, and of St. Paul mistaking such for realities!"— *Memoirs, etc.*

If we pass to the modern histories of modern times, which have been written with the true historic spirit, we find that they have been as truly improved by the new method as the histories of the ancient world. The tone of blind admiration and of exaggerated laudation has been sensibly lowered, the intense and bigoted partisanship has been exposed and answered by counter-criticism, or has quietly given way before the more judicial spirit of a cooler judgment.

One improvement is especially noticeable in modern his-tory, if it be not almost a revolution. This is the fact, that much less is made of the so-called great events of history now than formerly. As history has learned new notions of its own dignity, it attaches less importance to the fortunes of princes, the movements of generals, and the issues of campaigns, and occupies itself far more earnestly and busily with the condition of the middling and lower classes, with their progress in civilization, in political freedom, in wise laws, general education, and the security of property, as well as in general thrift, prevailing frugality, courteous manners, moral principle, and religious faith. History has become more humane and democratic as it has become more critical and just. It looks beneath the surface of events for the springs of action. It searches under facts for principles. It strives to discover the great laws of progress and stability in the world's evolution. It regards moral interests as higher than physical, the faith and heroism of a people and a period as of greater consequence than the external and physical events which distinguished either. Hence it tends to be more ethical, more reverent, and more religious, while it is also more candid and tolerant.

Two characteristics are especially worthy of notice in the tendencies of modern history. It is at once more *ima-ginative* and more *philosophical.*

The new history employs the *imagination* more liberally and yet more wisely than did the old. While it does not yield indiscriminately to its direction so as to be misled by its vagaries, it avails itself freely of its guidance and aid that it may more perfectly and vividly reproduce the past. The historian no longer conceives the past to have been so utterly unlike the present as to allow him to credit all the fantastic creations of the mythological and the credulous school, but rather conceives it to have been so nearly like the present as to justify him in freely using the present that he may more vividly picture and reproduce the past as it was. Hence it is the persistent effort of the modern historian to revive the past by means of every possible appliance of which he can avail himself. He continually asks himself, How did men live in the earlier times, what sort of houses did they build, how did they light and warm them, at what sort of tables did they eat, and of what food, and how was this cooked and served, on what seats did they sit, in what beds did they sleep, how were they dressed, of what material was their clothing made, and into what sort of garments was it shaped, how did they travel and visit, in what fashion did they greet one another ? So minute have been these inquiries, and so successfully have they been answered by the aid of the paintings, and mummies of Egyptian tombs, by bas-reliefs on Assyrian monuments, by Greek and Roman statues and inscriptions, as also by the exhumations of Pompeii and Herculaneum, that it seems now almost possible to build again a Grecian and Roman house, to provide it with implements and furniture, and to reproduce in detail all the particulars of ancient life. In the same way the historian of Old or New England of two hundred years ago, concerns himself with thousands of details, which enable his reader vividly to imagine how the people actually lived, what was the daily aspect and history of a street in London or in Boston, what was the method of spending a day or a week by a merchant or a farmer, a laborer or a professional man.

What is of far greater consequence, the historian asks and can answer, How did the men of other times think and feel in regard to the great and small things which interest the human race in all times ? What was the measnre of their knowledge and of their intellectual power ? What were their loves and hatreds toward God and man? He seeks to place himself within their very souls, so as to gaze on the visible creation with their eyes, to meet his fellows with their loves and hatreds, to scan the firmament with their infinite longings or their shivering terror, to seek after God with their awe or their longings. In all such efforts of history the imagination must be largely employed ; but it is employed in the service and for the ends of truth. It does not dress up its ideals of past generations with impossible and there-fore fantastic perfections, nor does it make them stalk forth in robes of gorgeous stateliness, nor does it bring them in fantastic conflicts like the spectred hosts of departed warriors such as are seen by a belated shepherd far off in cloud-land above some real battle-field, but it seeks to conceive these generations as they actually lived and acted, thought and felt. The power, when trained and used in the search after historic truth, becomes what is called *The Historic Imagination,* which by long practice becomes so discriminating and so trustworthy as to be termed *The Historic Sense.* It is not till the imagination is thus matured that a man is able to appreciate adequately the literature of other nations and other times than his own. He must, first understand the times in which its speeches and essays, its poems and its plays, its novels and its sermons were composed, in order to judge of them by their relations to the men by whom and for whom they were written. When thus heard and read they are received as far more real and living, and are judged with a far more sensitive and just appreciation than they possibly could be if read or judged apart from the forces which produced them or the conditions under which they came into being. "What is more important still, the actions of the men of another age are studied in the light of the knowledge which they actually attained, the aims which they proposed, and the motives by which they were impelled. What would be inexplicable if .done in our times can be accounted for if allowed in other days.

What in our day would be a work of cruelty and revenge is excused, palliated, or even justified, when traced to the motives and feelings, which occasioned it. What seems laughable and grotesque, formal and superstitious, when looked at with our eyes, is grave and proper, natural and rational, when looked at through the eyes of the men of other times, as we are enabled to do, by the cultured *his-toric sense* when this is quickened and guided by the *historic imagination.*

As the result of this liberal and wise use of the imagination, history has become more true and more just in its judgments as well as more elevating in its lessons and influence than formerly. The more vividly and fully we represent the men and the scenes of other times, the more entirely shall we do justice to them. The more thoroughly we understand events in their motives and principles, the more truthfully shall we estimate and weigh, them. The new method educates and elevates the imagination, as well as employs it as an auxiliary to truth. We read and study history somewhat as we read and study the drama, viewing it as a grand spectacle of the past that is vividly reproduced in scenery, personages, and events; that fixes our attention, excites our curiosity, and kindles our sympathies. As the actual drama is fitted to ennoble the ima-gination and purify the passions, so does dramatized his-tory act with even greater energy in these directions, when it is fitly rendered by-the writer and justly conceived by the reader. These thoughts lead us to,

The second characteristic .stated, viz., that the New His-tory is more *philo-sophical* than the old. It recognizes more distinctly the truth that all historic events are to be explained by certain causal influences or agencies, which are furnished in man's own nature, in the circumstances of his condition, and in the purposes of the living God. Different historians differ in the variety of the agencies which they recognize, in the importance which is to be attached to each, and in the power of harmonizing one with another; but all agree that to some agencies or principles, acting after fixed methods or rules, all great historical events are to be ascribed, and that the problem of history and the duty of the historian is to discover what these principles are. The historian nowadays is not content to entertain his readers with striking descriptions of the startling events which give to history its dramatic in-terest, nor to paint to the life the story of those great personages who illustrate the pathos and power, the tenderness and energy of human passion, but he seeks also to explain historic phenomena both the greater and the less—by their principles and laws.

To determine what are the principles and what tire laws which underlie all these events is the aim of what is technically called *The Philosophy of History.* Much is made of this phrase in our times. To many persons it suggests something very profound, attractive, and incomprehensible. To others it is big with high-sounding verbiage, transcendental pretension, attenuated Pantheism, or depressing Fatalism. But there ought to be no special mystery in the phrase. If a philosophy of the universe of spirit and matter, is possible in its present manifestations, then a philosophy is possible of the past history of man, from which lessons of instruction may be derived, and if need be of monition for the future. As there is a variety of theories of the present, each one of which may be incompatible with the other, so there may be an equal variety of philosophies of the past. A Mohammedan, a Mormon, a Brahmin, and a Christian, would necessarily have each a peculiar philosophy of history. It need not be a mystery or a wonder that a materialist and a spiritualist, a necessitarian and a believer in freedom, should each interpret the history of man after a fashion of his own. One who studies man as an animal only, and recognizes no other forces and laws than those which are vital, will of necessity, like *Draper,* make physiology the basis of his Philosophy of History, or rather, he will resolve all his-torical into physiological phenomena, whether they are material, vital, or spiritual. Temperature and moisture, of a certain degree and quantity, acting on certain chemical combinations of nitrogen, carbon, phosphorus, etc., are the formulae by which historical phenomena can all be explained. Napoleon and Waterloo, Abraham Lincoln and Bull Run, General Lee and Appomatox Court-House, are satisfactorily accounted for by various formulae, of which the terms are H, O, C, N, etc., in various combinations. A writer who recognizes a somewhat wider range of forces, some of which are spiritual, but all, whether material or spiritual, obey mechanical laws and act by a necessitating force, will, like Buckle, evolve and explain all possible occurrences and phenomena according to an á priori *necessity, from whose iron embrace there is no release.' Those who, like* Froude, *believe in the caprices and energy of human passions and. individual freedom, or who, like* Niebuhr,

Arnold, Goldwin Smith, and hosts of other Christian historians, distinctly recognize a Divine Providence fulfilling merciful plans of human progress and redemption, will have another and a nobler philosophy of history, because they accept a nobler philosophy of the universe and of human life.

It ought to be added that to serve more effectually the philosophical explanation of the Past, the great movements of historic progress in separate lines and the several agencies on which they depend have been treated of in distinct works. Thus we have not a few generalized histories, as of ***Commerce, Geographical Discovery, Emigration, Philosophy, Morals, Literature, Poetry, Fiction, Criticism, and*** even of Civilization itself. The treatment of these topics of historic research separately has this great advantage, that it limits the attention more effectually to single classes of phenomena, and to the workings of single forces. It withdraws the mind from the more palpable and material effects and causes, to the more refined and spiritual. It enables each student to look at the history of man from that point of view which most interests his own feelings, or bears upon his own studies, and it saves the general reader an immense amount of special research and laborious investigation.

But the impatient reader, who may have followed us thus far, will be likely here to interrupt us with the inquiry ; " But what has all this to do with a course of historical reading ? These general disquisitions on the writing of history may have some interest for those who have history to write, but they can have no possible application to those who have history to read. The progress and development of history, from poetic narration to philosophical interpretation, may be instructive to learned students but not to general readers." To which we reply: Have patience; " History is a vast jungle, an impenetrable morass to the reader who undertakes to find his way through it without a guide, and even to him who reads the first book which is recommended to him, and having finished that seizes upon another. To read history with any profit or even with much satisfaction whether alone or under the advice of a sagacious friend, one should know something of what history is, and how it is written, in what various forms, with what diversity of honesty, truth, and trustworthiness." To furnish this information, preliminary to special advice respecting the selection of books and the manner of reading them, has been the aim of this chapter.

CHAPTER XII.

HOW TO READ HISTORY.

IT is not easy to prescribe a course of Historical Reading for a single individual, even though he is an intimate friend, whose character and culture, whose aims and habits, whose leisure and opportunities are all supposed to be familiarly known to his adviser. It is more difficult to do it for many persons, every one of whom may differ from the other in every one of these particulars. An extended or general course which might be equally suitable for all readers, is idle to think of. To attempt even a selection of the best authors, without knowing somewhat intimately the person for whom they are chosen, would be foolish and futile. All that we propose to do is to lay down a few principles which will enable a reader to begin wisely and to proceed with satisfaction in selecting books for himself; and also to illustrate these principles by referring to a few authors of marked peculiarities and of unquestioned excellence.

We observe, *first* of all, that a thorough mastery of the field of history must be the work of many years; in some sort, of a lifetime. To fix in the mind the dates of the most important events, to impress the events themselves upon the memory so that they shall be permanent and familiar, to settle the great questions which are in dispute in respect to facts and principles, to be able to summon at call the great pictures which make up the diorama of the world's past, can be achieved only by the few students to whom historical research is the exclusive occupation of their life. For such we do not write. They would not need our assistance, could we give it; for it is the prerogative of every such student to find his path opening naturally and easily before him as he proceeds. To such the author immediately in hand introduces many others whom he will wish to read. The subject which at present occupies the attention inevitably suggests numerous kindred topics. In part this is true for the class of persons for whom we write—who are supposed to be comparatively igno-rant of booKs and unpractised in reading. Even such readers ought not to expect to finish in a year or two the brief and imperfect course of history which they may immediately require. We grant, one may learn a compend of events or a table of dates within a few months. He may commit to memory an outline history of Greece and Rome, of Europe in the middle ages, of Great Britain and the United States. But to do this is simply to lay the foundation and to erect the scaffolding. To master the history of these countries, so as intelligently to enjoy it and be instructed by it, requires a far longer period, and must be, at the shortest, the work of several years of earnest and awakened attention. Moreover, it would not be desirable, were it practicable, to finish such a course of reading more speedily. To read history should be proposed by every thoughtful person as the learning and pastime of his entire life; as capable of perpetually opening new views of re-gions unseen before, and of bringing before the same eye fresh aspects of scenes that are none the less interest-ing be-cause they have been often revisited. Indeed, there is an important sense in which it is true that a man must wait till he is somewhat advanced in life before he can read history with full advantage and enjoyment, because such a person only can bring to it the observation and interest furnished by actual experience. If " old ex-perience " alone, as Milton suggests, can attain " to something like prophetic strain " in its forecast of the future, it is almost equally necessary that one may intelligently appreciate the history of the past. History to the eye of the young has the interest of an exciting spectacle; to the old it is as inspiring as the counsel of a life-long friend. The youth gazes with excited and breathless curiosity upon the shifting panorama of great empires rising mysteriously like overhanging clouds, of vast cities thronged with representatives from a hundred nations, of endless caravans of barbaric emi-grants; of the confusion of battle, the pomp of victory, and the splendor of pageants. All these are to his eye brilliant, imposing, and exciting. But when the same eye has seen more of living men and of actual life, when the man has interpreted the causes and meditated upon the lessons of the events which have occurred within his per-sonal experience, then and then only is he prepared to gather instruction from the story of the past, because in the men and the events which this story records he sees the counterpart of what has passed beneath his personal observation. To the young, history must be an exciting drama or a painful task; to the old, it is as fresh as a fairy tale, and as instructive as the lessons of a patriarch.

Those persons who are impatient to acquire in a twelve-month a satisfactory knowledge of history, or who expect or wish to finish up their reading in order that it may be done with and laid aside, might almost as well not begin at all, for by such history can be read only for convenience or show, and to them it can bring little instruction and less enjoyment. There are not a few who, having just left school or college, say to themselves, " A man must know something of history, in order to pass respectably with intelligent people; Without having read history, one cannot understand the newspapers, or take part in conversation, or shine in a debating-club, or make speeches ; there-fore I will take a course in history—what is the best, be-cause the shortest and the soonest over ?" To such persons we would say: " Study a table of chronology as you would take a dose of medicine, or buy the best and briefest com-pend of universal history which you can hear of, and master it because you must; but do not call such occupa-tion the reading of history." This sort of read-ing should, of all others, be regarded as the constant occupation and pastime of the life of any one who reads at all; and it is well to begin history as it is to begin our reading life, with this view of it—to form our plans, and to select our authors with these expectations distinctly in mind.

There is the greater need of cautions of this sort, for the reason that so many persons, under mistaken impressions, or by the direction of stupid or thoughtless advisers, commence reading a course of history with such authors or after such a plan as to be very soon disgusted and disappointed. We recall very distinctly a friend who, on finishing his college-life, gave himself up for a year to what he fondly an-ticipated would be " the still air of delightful studies," with glowing expectations of what he should accomplish and enjoy in a year of general reading. To master an ample course of history was his first ambition and his most attractive ideal. He seated himself at his desk with the expectation of finishing this course in a twelve-month, and in order to begin at the beginning, he opened one of the dreariest and most matter-of-fact books that ever was written, viz.: ***The Old and New Testament Connected, by Humphrey Prideaux.*** It was a part of his plan to follow this work with another, which, if possible, is more dreary and forbidding, ***viz.: Shuckford's***

Sacred and Profane History Connected. But he never got so far as Shuckford, for the reason that, after a few weeks' trial with Prideaux—so many hours a day, and so many pages of the wooden volumes read in a mechanical way—he became dispirited and discouraged, and the course of historical reading " never did run smooth " with him, after such an inauspicious beginning.

Second. This instance may give meaning and interest to our next suggestion, which is, that history, to be wisely begun, should be commenced by every person at what is the right starting-point for him. We have already insisted that the book on which every man should first lay his hands is the book which will instruct, amuse, or elevate him most in any direction in which his needs are the most imperative, whatever the subject-matter may be. This rule is pre-eminently good in historical reading. If we assume that the entire field is to any one unoccupied and unknown, there are yet certain countries, personages or events—one or all—of which every man has some immediate interest to know something. Whether his interest arises from the curiosity of the inquirer or the useful-ness of that which is to be known, is unimportant. At this very point should he begin. The author who best meets this impending want, whether he can do this by his ease of style, clearness of arrangement, copiousness of infor-mation or elevation and truthfulness of aim, is the author with whom he should begin. But suppose a person . has few historic needs, at least few of which he is conscious, and little or no curiosity, what shall be said to him? Should there be such a person, we have only to say, that it may be the time has not come for him—and it may be it ought never to come—to read history at all. It would be safer, however, to deny that a person ever existed who is without any historic curiosity or historic needs, if it could only be discovered in what direction they lie. With some these wishes and wants may turn upon that which is nearest their senses,—the local history of the town or county in which they live, of the family to which they belong, or the state or country in which they are born; or perhaps their imagination may be excited to ask questions concerning some prominent personage whom they have seen or of whom they have heard, as some great lawyer, physician, clergyman, banker, merchant, sea-captain, or general. If they are interested in any trade or employment, the history of their own occupation, or of the objects with which it is concerned, may be the history which will take the strongest hold of their feelings.

When, then, a man comes to us with the question, " What history shall I read first ?" we reply, as we have already suggested, with the questions: " What history do you care to know the most about ? Of what country, or of what people—of what events or what personages do you wish or need to be informed accurately and fully ? Concerning what great interest, as of trade or commerce, tariff or business, of shipbuilding, or invention in art or literature, do you at present feel disposed to ask the most numerous questions of a friend or acquaintance ?" If you can answer to yourself these questions, then you will be able to decide what history you should begin to read.

Third. History should be read after the laws and habits of the kind of memory with which the reader is naturally endowed, without any violent efforts to resist or reform these laws or habits. For example, there are a few persons who have a natural memory for dates. They can scan with the eye or hear with the ear the dates of the principal events of a war, a reign, or a century, and can fix them with exactness so as to recall them when they are wanted. But the majority, even of young persons—in whom the spontaneous memory is most active—find it somewhat difficult to imprint a table of simple dates upon the memory. Those who labor under this defect are soon discouraged in the reading of history. They complain that before they have finished a single volume most of the dates of the events which it records have escaped from their possession. Of what possible use, say they, can it be to read the next, if even the times and the order of the great events which it recounts are in like manner to slide from our recollection ? Of what use, if this is continually to happen, will it be for us to read history at all ? To relieve the minds of those who feel these difficulties, two considerations are pertinent. The *first* is, that history may inscribe many most valuable lessons upon the memory of those who can remember the dates of but few of the great events which it records. It is with reading history very much as it is with seeing people and observing the course of nature. A thousand lessons may have been impressed upon the understanding, a thousand most important relations may have been discerned, a thousand inferences or principles may have been suggested or confirmed, a thousand movements of feeling or will may have been evolved in connection with a thousand persons and events observed, of which very few, and perhaps none at all, can be recalled singly and in their individual relations. To be profited by history in almost every way conceivable, it is by no means essential that we retain a distinct remembrance of the individual facts which history records and recites. We would not intimate that a knowledge of dates and events is unimportant, nor again that strenuous and persevering efforts should not be made to fix and hold them. We would only preclude the inference that great exactness or facility in this respect is essential to the most important uses of this study. We would also insist that any range, exactness, or readiness in the memory of historical facts is only important so far as it is attended with the capacity to discern and connect these facts by means of their higher relations. Simple memory is so very convenient that it is often greatly over-valued. School-teachers and school-children, pedants and paragons of memory, who can promptly tell you the precise date of every event in history, plume themselves very often upon what is merely a great intellectual convenience. Those unfortunates, on the other hand, who are always at a loss when called on to furnish such details for themselves or others, are often mortified and discouraged at their constantly recurring failures. For this reason it needs often to be repeated that a knowledge of dates is chiefly to be valued because of the higher relations to which it constantly ministers. This suggests the second consideration to which we referred, viz; That when the dates of history are habitually contemplated in these higher relations, the study of chronology becomes fascinating and easy to many who are deficient in the mechanical memory. It may seem of little importance to know, and therefore, it may appear difficult to recall, the precise number of months or years by which the American preceded the French Revolution, or to recount the exact order of the several events which ushered in the bloody catastrophe, and the inevitable reaction of the Directory, the Consulate, and the Empire. But viewed in another light the exactest knowledge of these time-periods and time-epochs may be of the greatest service. It may even be absolutely essential to enable the reader to estimate the force and to compute the laws of the agencies which produced these stirring and frightful phenomena. At first view, that would seem to be the most trivial coincidence which connects two events together by the relation of time —as a discovery, an invention, a bold and beneficent enterprise achieved by two or three minds in the same month thousands of miles distant.

But coincidences of this sort observed and remembered, illustrate how the thinking of the race proceeds with an even step, and may bring out the exact occasion or condition which has evolved in many minds a similar intellectual or moral result. The exact date of the first emigration of miners to San Francisco, or of the first large shipment of gold from California to New York or London, might be of the first importance to illustrate the beginning of some new movement of commerce, or a new tendency in the money markets of the world. The exact date, to the day of the month, of the proclamation of the Queen of England concerning the belligerency of the parties in our late civil war, is esteemed by many as of the greatest significance in determining what were the feelings and what the position of the English Government with respect to the two parties.

We have cited these examples to illustrate the truths, that to any person who reads history with a moderate degree of intelligence and reflection, the chronology of history may be invested with a high intellectual, and even a high moral interest, and that those who study dates and time relations under these higher lights can by degrees learn to remember them. This is but a special inference and application of the general rule already laid down, that every man should read history after the methods and connections of his own memory. If a reader has little force of that spontaneous power which reproduces dates and facts by a mechanical method, let him learn to elevate these dates and facts by the dignity and interest which belong to higher relations and deeper principles. If, on the other hand, he remembers isolated facts and incidents with ease, let him not be content with the convenient service or the doubtful reputation of an intellectual instrument that passively depicts everything that has been presented to the mind.

It is interesting to notice how the driest of all books,—a table of dates, may to the enlightened eye become radiant with instruction and interest; and especially how a table of comparative chronology, like the Oxford Tables, or those prepared primarily for the study of Church History by Dr. Henry B. Smith, and many others may become a most attractive manual.

Against passive reading of every kind we would enter our repeated protest as an idling of time and an enfeebling of the powers. History tempts not a few to such habits. Many read history as they read a novel or a drama, moved only by the excitement of the story, permitting scarcely re-flection enough to assent to the story as a recital of actual events,—dreaming over its pictures rather than believing its realities; neither measuring its facts by principles, nor deriving principles from its facts. Others, of an opposite habit of mind, bestow so much reflection upon the facts, that they often forget the facts which have suggested their reflections. They read history very much as an absent-minded man listens to a concert or an opera, or as under a lecture or a sermon he surrenders himself so completely to the thoughts which the speaker suggests, that he forgets very much of what the speaker has said. Such persons bring away everything which history can teach them except its facts, viz., the truth and reflections which it suggests. A little faithful and persevering self-discipline would enable such persons to remember both the incidents and the dates, which their own reflections should make permanent by ennobling them. These thoughts inculcate a consideration, which it will not be wise to forget or overlook, and that is, that the reading of history must be prosecuted somewhat as a study, in order to be permanently pleasant or profitable. History need not be learned as a lesson to be repeated to another, but the reading of it should be prosecuted with a special wakefulness of attention, with constant and deliberate reflection, and with frequent and wisely arranged reviews. Particularly should history be read with some sort of system at the outset, it being always remembered that it should never be regarded as an enforced task-work.

While, then, we should begin to read history by using the kind of memory which we have at command, we should not despair of cultivating our memory by the very act and effort of reading. Surprising achievements have been accomplished by trifling acts of painstaking, when these have been reduced to fixed and pleasant habits.

Fourth. History should always be read with the aid of Geography. If the dates of the events of History are important and instructive, so - are the places in which they occur. Indeed we may say without reserve, that it is impossible to read history with intelligence, without bringing distinctly before the eye of the mind the place-relations of the scenes in which these events occur. Nor does it suffice that one should be able to fix these as presented by a map if one cannot interpret the lines of the map into pictures of boundary and surface. Not only should the ordinary map and atlas be kept constantly within reach, but what are called *historical maps* should be freely and constantly employed by every reader of history who can procure them. These are constructed for the special purpose of representing to the eye the various changes and divisions of a country which have occurred in great historic periods, as the result of conquest or colonization. These changes are represented to the eye by a series of maps of the whole or a part of a continent drawn to the same scale and with the same completeness of physical features; the growth, diminution, or absorption of its subordinate divisions being indicated by changes in their variously colored boundary lines, and by the presence or absence of its marts, fortresses and capitols. The several changes in Western Europe which took place after the French Revolution and during the career of Napoleon, are most impressively depicted to the eye by a series of such maps, each one of which tells its own story of rapid conquest and humiliating defeat, of sudden and surprising growth, and of contractions and retreats as unlooked for. The decisions of the Congress of Vienna made it necessary to reconstruct the map of Europe. No sooner had Prussia achieved the one victory of Sadowa after a seven weeks' campaign, than the maps of Germany were all altered, and new maps of the new Prussia were sold in Berlin before her troops had returned in triumph to the capital. A series of good historical maps of the Rise and Fall of the Roman Empire suggests volumes of Ancient History. The moral and political lessons which a few moments' inspection of a series of such maps is fitted to enforce, cannot fail to be noticed by any thoughtful mind. The career of the great Napoleon is full of admonitory wisdom as it is illustrated to the eye that follows his unbounded ambitions and his astounding achievements,—in the expanding and still expanding lines of the Empire which centred in Paris,—to that crisis, which contracted them in a day by the victory of Waterloo, and sent him to the distant rock of St. Helena. Historical maps of the great empires of the ancient world are like the successive pictures of a prophet's vision. Historical atlasses have hitherto been almost inaccessible to ordinary English readers, and have been scarcely known except by historical scholars. "With a few exceptions, they have been prepared by German editors, and are not easily used by a person who is ignorant of the German language. The simple inspection of one of the atlasses of **Carl von Spruner** cannot fail to impress even such a reader with the great utility of such maps as an aid to the reading of history. It cannot be long before appliances so useful and almost indispensable will be freely furnished to English and American readers.

We name another use of Geography in the reading of history, which is of far higher interest and of nobler appli-cation—its use in the Philosophy of History. As the dates of events are often of the greatest significance in explaining them, so also is their scene and place. The physical features of every country—as its mountains, coasts, and rivers—should be carefully studied, not merely as they have furnished the s *Jiow-place* upon which, and the limits or framing within which, the great transactions have occurred that have made the country famous, but as they have had a large influence in determining what the history of the country should be. As *the* material has not a little to do in determining what the *spiritual and moral* shall be in the development and career of the individual man, so the study of the physical geography of a country is the best interpreter of its history. It often furnishes the only clue by which the student and the reader can explain its most striking peculiarities. For example, if we would understand the peculiar and wonderful history of England, it is not merely convenient, and in many senses necessary, to know that the island is moored alongside the Continent, at a convenient and yet a safe distance from France, Spain, Holland and Germany ; but it is entirely essential to keep this fact continually in mind, and to refer to it again and again, as the one condition which England required for the development of her unique and marvellous history, and for the attainment of her boasted imperial power. Had the English channel been only a little less formidable than it is in its rock-lined walls, its storms, its fogs, and its tides, England, might in a half-score of instances, have been possessed and overrun by foreign invaders after she had become great enough to tempt as a prize, or defiant enough to invite as a conquest. Dutch Fleets, Spanish Armadas and French Expeditions, in conjunction with Irish Rebellions, Scotch Risings and Romish Intrigues, would, but for this single physical feature of England, have figured very differently in the changed history of the kingdom, and in the story of Protestant Christianity and of general political liberty. Indeed, had the

English channel been a little narrower and its currents a little less fearful, Protestantism and freedom might neither of them have had a permanent foothold on the earth—assuredly not upon English soil. The free spirit of the English people would have wanted the insular protection within which to find its free development, that gave it a home and a fortress as against foreign assailants, and a convenient city of refuge for many a noble exile. The seafaring tastes and the adventurous spirit of the English navigators and traders owe to this circumstance their early and marvellous growth—from which originated the naval supremacy, the colonial extension, and the enormous wealth of this sometimes unscrupulous and always imperious people, which so long rejoiced in the exclusive title to the dominion of the seas. But the high tides and stormy passages along the coasts of this island would themselves have accomplished little for England's power and wealth had it not been for the coal and tin and iron which were also provided beneath her rocks, as the means of developing her manufacturing skill, and of fabricating the metallic and textile products with which for so long a period she has tempted and controlled the markets of the world. Here, again, the proximity of England to the Continent, with her insular independence of it, were most important, as they enabled her government in repeated instances to introduce skilled labor from Flanders and from France, on critical occasions, when it was not only convenient for manufacturers and artisans to leave their homes, but when this became necessary if they would save their consciences and their lives. Thus did England, by its physical features, become not only an asylum for many of the noblest exiles, but she also made of this asylum a treasure-house for her future wealth and a work-shop for the supply of the world, which in this way became her tributary.

The example of England is one of many which might be adduced to illustrate the relation of physical geography to history. The honor of discerning and setting forth this relation in its adequate and manifold importance belongs to ***Professor Carl Ritter,*** one of the most eminent men of the present century, who was alike distinguished for his vast learning, his historical sagacity, and his modest and Christian humility. His views were given to English readers some years ago by one of his most eminent disciples, ***Professor Arnold Guyot,*** in " *The Earth and Man* " and more recently in translations from a few of his works. The intelligent reader, however, needs only to seize upon the clue which Ritter's speculative wisdom has furnished, to be able to read history by a new light and with a new interest, as he finds the physical features as well as the geographical situation of every country to be essential to the understanding of its political and moral growth, and of the part which it has enacted in the world's drama.

The thought is kindred, but not unimportant, that to understand and appreciate either history or geography with the highest profit, and especially to understand the two as mutually related, traveling with an intelligent eye is an important auxiliary. We would not be understood to assert or intimate that a person who cannot travel cannot do justice to the reading of history. The fact is notorious, that some of the most intelligent and appreciative students of history have traveled but little; while hundreds, if not thousands, yearly look upon Rome and Jerusalem and the Nile with unanointed eyes, who neither bring to these exciting places nor carry away from them a single historic association.

Nor, again, is it needful to travel long distances, or to visit many of the seats of ancient or modern commerce and empire, in order to learn the most important and the most substantial lessons which travel is fitted to impart. A journey of a hundred miles can be turned by one person to uses that are far more abundant and instructive than a journey of a thousand miles by another. The sagacious eye needs but few hints or motives to be able to judge of the remote by the near, of the long by the short, and of the great by the small. Gibbon found in the study of tactics which he made as captain of the Hants militia a sufficient preparation to enable him to understand the movements of the great military leaders of the Roman em-pire. " The discipline and evolutions of a modern battalion," he says, " gave me a clearer notion of the phalanx and the legion; and the captain of the Hampshire grenadiers (the reader may smile) has not been useless to the historian of the Roman empire." On the other hand, no intellect can be so acute, and no imagination can be so active, as not to be stimulated and instructed by the excitements of the eye and the ear. The traveler who has crossed the Alps in person and on foot will be far more likely to do justice to the difficulties which impeded Hannibal ; and he who has traversed Palestine with the Scriptures in his hand cannot but make more .real to himself and more intelligible the Old and the New Testament history. It is worth noticing that the best historical writers have almost uniformly been fond of traveling. At least, they have had " the topographical eye," and that interest in natural scenery which seems to be essential to the vivid representation to the mind of historic scenes, events, and personages.

This suggests our *fifth* point, viz., the use of the ima-gination in the reading of history. Whately pertinently observes, in his annotations upon *Lord Bacon's Essay on Studies:* " In reference to the study of history, I have elsewhere remarked upon the importance, among the in-tellectual qualifications for such a study, of a vivid ima-gination—a faculty which, consequently, a skilful narrator must himself possess, and to which he must be able to furnish excitement in others. Some may, perhaps, be startled at this remark who have been accustomed to consider imagination as having no other office than *to feign* and to falsify. Every faculty is liable to abuse and misdirection, and imagination among the rest; but it is a mistake to suppose that it necessarily tends to pervert the truth of history, and to mislead the judgment. On the contrary, our view of any transaction, especially one that is remote in time and place, will necessarily be imperfect, generally incorrect, unless it embrace something more than the bare outline of the occurrences; unless we have before the mind a lively idea of the scenes in which the events took place, the habits of thought and of feeling of the actors, and all the circumstances connected with the transaction ; unless, in short, we can in a considerable degree transport ourselves out of our own age, and country, and persons, and imagine ourselves the agents or spectators. It is from consideration of all these circumstances that we are enabled to form a right judgment as to the facts which history records, and to derive instruction from it. To say that the imagination, if not regulated by sound judgment and sufficient knowledge, may chance to convey to us false impressions of past events, is only to say that man is fallible. But such false impressions are even *much the more* likely to take possession of those whose imagination is feeble or uncultivated. They are apt to imagine the things, persons, times, countries, etc., which they read of, as much less different from what they see around them than is really the case. The practical importance of such an exercise of imagination to a full and clear, and consequently profitable, view of the transactions related in history can hardly be over-estimated."

To stimulate and aid the imagination in its efforts to re-produce the past, historical plays and poems, and more recently historical novels, have been abundantly employed. Their usefulness has been the subject of frequent discussion and of various opinions. It has been forcibly, and perhaps not untruly said, that the majority of the present generation of English readers have learned more of English history from Shakspeare and Walter Scott than from the entire library of professed historians. Of course no man would contend that either Shakspeare or Scott can be substituted for the usual historical authorities, but only that they may supplement them in certain important particulars. Many other historical plays and novels are invaluable, as enabling the reader to enter more fully into the spirit of past times. They are of especial service in helping him to appreciate the feelings and motives of prominent personages, and vividly to reproduce the manners and institutions of another age. It is not often that an historical writer is endowed with the painstaking zeal of the antiquarian and the creative power of the poet. If we cannot have the two gifts in a single writer, we must seek for them apart, in the historian and the novelist.

Thackeray's Henry Esmond is an admirable example of a good historical novel, when carefully and conscientiously written by a man of rare gifts, and of a rarer honesty. no reader of this tale of the times of Queen Anne could fail to derive from it such impressions of the state of manners and of morals in the higher circles, as well as of the political jealousies and the religious feuds which divided men of all classes, as no formal history could possibly convey—such as even the most abundant and painstaking research into the less accessible sources of historical knowledge would fail to impart to a man of feeble capacity to picture and re-combine. The service is not a slight one which is rendered to the world, when a painstaking explorer of historic truth like Thackeray gathers his materials with faithful and laborious research, and weaves them together into so fascinating and instructive a story. But this tale, marvellous as it is for its elaborated truthfulness and picturesque effects, strikingly illustrates the possible dangers and disadvantages to which the historical novel may be abused. Thackeray was not without his prejudices in certain directions. These, with his desire for producing striking effects, are manifest in the occasional *overdrawing* of this generally well balanced representation of one of the most interesting periods of English history. It is notorious that **Walter Scott** gave very serious offence to multitudes of his admiring readers by some of his portraitures of the representative characters of the great historical parties of Scotland and England. With all the good sense and candor which he had at command, his sympathies were too intense and his prejudices too tenacious to allow him to write otherwise than he did, though he knew he should excite the indignation of thousands of his fervid countrymen. *Mrs. H. B. Stowe,* says in the preface to her recent historical romance, Old-town Folks:—" I have tried to make my mind as still and passive as a looking-glass or a mountain lake, and thus to give you merely the images reflected therein." But a fervid and sympathetic nature like hers can no more free itself from a theological or personal bias, in representing the New England of the past, over which she has laughed, and wept, and speculated, and struggled all her life, than "the mountain lake" can hold itself in glassy smoothness against the gusts and breezes that sweep upon it from the heights above. Writers less conscientious and trustworthy than the three we have named would very easily make the historical novel to be the vehicle of partisan prejudice, dishonest misrepresentation, and virulent vituperation. It is also so easy to exaggerate for the simple purpose of effective representation, that many such novels have been written with no conscious bias, and yet have been no better than coarse exaggerations and extravagant caricatures of the simple truth. Some of the novels of *"Mrs. Muhlbacli"* (Clara Mundt) are sad and humiliating examples of this sort, doing equal violence to historic truth, to correct taste, and to dramatic propriety. Others are written with greater fidelity to both dramatic and historic truth. The very wide-spread popularity of these tales illustrates the fitness of this kind of writing to meet an important craving of human nature. The volumes of the **Schonberg-Cotta** and the **Erckman-Chairian** series will readily occur to many of our readers as exemplifying the same truth. *George Eliot's Romola* is if possible a still more surprising achievement than any which we have named; as the period was more remote and the materials more scanty, and the actors and scenery more strange to a native of England.

The fact deserves notice in this connection that, of late, professed historians have indulged somewhat freely in ro-mancing, and so in a sense turned their histories into quasi-historical novels; especially when they attempt to give elaborate and eloquent portraitures of their leading person-ages, in which the most lavish use is made of effective epithets and of pointed antitheses. *Macaulay,* among the recent historians, has set the fashion very decidedly in this direction. In his efforts to make history minute, vivid, and effective, he has often described like an impassioned advocate, and painted like a retained attorney, with the most unsparing expenditure of contrasts and epithets. *Carlyle* gives sketches alternately in chalk and charcoal, that exhibit his saints and demons, now in ghastliest white, and then in the most appalling blackness. But though he draws caricatures he draws them with the hand of an artist, and if his outlines are often bold and grotesque there are many of which Michael Angelo would not have been ashamed. *Froude,* by research, eloquence, and audacity combined, attempts to reverse the settled historic judgments of all mankind in respect to the characters that had been " damned to everlasting fame." *Bancroft* and *Motley* abound in examples of this tendency to paint historical characters so much to the life, that the impression is made that the result is only a painting to which there never was reality. The ghost of the miserable Philip II. would suffer more than the purgatorial tortures which he dreaded and deserved so long, were he made to writhe under the unsparing pertinacity of Motley's invective, from which there is no release, and to which there is no termination : while the spirit of William the Silent would be more reserved and reticent than ever were he forced to listen to the perhaps not undeserved, but the certainly unqualified laudations of his admiring narrator. The elaborate portraits of Bancroft, if they do nothing more, do most effectively illustrate the historian's own conceptions of what sets off a man well in description, so intense is the coloring and so abundant are the adornments which he employs. The disposition to use two colors certainly allows striking contrasts, if it does nothing more. The hero in black is drawn with deep shadows, if they are few. The hero in white is as white as is practicable, and allow him to be distinctly visible. Gradations in color as well as flowing outlines, if less effective in the excitement with which they shock and excite the nerves, are more pleasing to the taste that is truly refined, as well as ordinarily more true to nature, and just to the reality of things.

To satisfy the imagination history must be individual and minute. Hence it is that *biography* supplements history so happily by imparting an individual interest to the events which concern a larger number of men, by giving minuteness of detail in place of general and vague descriptions, and by awakening our personal and human sympathies in what would otherwise be conceived as indefinite and impersonal. The life of a great ruler or a distinguished commander becomes for these reasons the most satisfactory medium for recounting the history of a great nation or a critical war. We need only cite as examples the lives of Frederick, Napoleon, and Abraham Lincoln. A single human being takes the central place in the picture, and his personal feelings and interests awaken active interest and sympathy. The recital of the events of which he had personal knowledge stands out in bold relief from the hazy back-ground of general descriptions and the dry details of dates, numbers, and results. Hence a snatch from the diary of a soldier on a march, a brief letter after a battle, a personal narrative of what he saw and felt in a charge or repulse, is often more attractive and even more instructive than scores of official summaries and despatches. The few diaries which were faithfully kept in the stirring times of England, as those of Evelyn and Pepys, the personal recol-lections of Mrs. Lucy Hutchinson, and the stately recordings of Burton in his Cromwellian diary, are not only valued above all price for the distinctness with which they bring again to life those exciting times, but they have given suggestions for scores of imitations in manifold fictitious autobiographies and diaries. A few series of letters from an active, correspondent to his intimate friend like those of Horace Walpole, are sometimes of great interest and service. Indeed a bundle of old letters, freshly gathered from some forgotten chest or dusty closet may aid the imagination and move the heart more than a score of elaborate volumes. The zealous student of history is moved by the true historic spirit, to fill his library with books and collections of this sort, and is never weary with ruminating over the past which he ever anew recreates to the eye of his mind out of these fragmentary hints, and these tat-tered, seared, and dusty memorials. An old letter reveals a new world; an old account-book recalls a past generation, with its ways of getting and spending, of buying and selling, of marrying and burying, of clothing and furnishing. We have read a manuscript correspondence of sixty years from a friend in England to a friend in the United States that seemed to introduce us to much that was most important of the inner life of England during the interesting and exciting period which it covered. An old musket or a soldier's outfit represents a battle-field of another time ; and an old diary unrolls a pictured procession of deaths and burials, of weddings and funerals, of famines and pestilences, in which the long dead reappear upon the earth, inhabit their old houses, and walk the once-frequented streets. The imagination of many a **Dr. Dry-asdust** is pictured all over with unwritten romances; and his heart, which seems as desolate and forbidding as his dusty and disorderly den, is brimming over with the ten-derest recollections. Peace to his ashes, for in them slumber the glowing embers of the loved and therefore the un-forgotten past!

CHAPTER XIII.

A COURSE OF HISTORICAL READING.

WE proceed next to give an outline of a course of Historical Reading. It will be remembered that we do not propose to furnish a list of books for the student, but only for the general reader. We begin with the earliest period, and follow the order of time.

The best and most readily accessible general history of the earliest nations is Philip Smith's **History of the World, from the Earliest Records to the Present Time,** of which the history of the nations of antiquity is complete, and comprises three volumes. This History has the very great advantage of using the results of the latest researches and explorations in literary and monumental remains, and is written and compiled with a distinct recognition of the **critical method** which we have already noticed. It suffers, as was unavoidable, under the disadvantage of being a compilation. It is of necessity not written with the enthusiasm and earnestness which those writers only attain who have limited their investigations to a single country or a single period, and are not constrained by the necessity of condensation. It is especially serviceable as an introduction to more special and particular histories. This work cannot be recommended too earnestly as compared with Roll in, Prideaux, Shuckford, and numerous writers like them, whose usefulness and authority have been superseded, and whose occupation ought by this time to be gone. It is to be feared that notwithstanding the progress of civilization, shoals of their works will continue to be multiplied by the zeal of interested publishers, and that book-agents will still sell them as standard histories. Niebuhr's ***Lectures on Ancient History***, etc., in three volumes, treat of special topics with learning and freshness. They are of a general character, and are in striking contrast with those excessively minute and learned investigations which were given to the world in the first volumes of his History of Rome, and which have occasioned the impression that Niebuhr in all his writings is unintelligible to those readers who are not scholars. C. L. Brace's ***Races of the Old World*** is an excellent companion in all historical studies.

A. H. L. Heeren, in his ***Polities, Intercourse and Trade of Ancient Asiatic Nations*** and his ***Politics, Intercourse and Trade of the Carthaginians, Ethiopians, and Egyptians***, treats of these special topics with great freshness, and has the great merit of continually confronting and comparing the past with the present, making the ancient world to seem a real world to the modern reader, and its life to be reproduced as an actual and present reality. He writes for the historic imagination as well as for the historic judgment. Rawlin-son's ***History of the Five Great Monarchies of the Ancient Eastern World*** is a recent work, which is at once original, drawn from direct research, critical, and reverent of things and truths which are sacred. Rawlinson's ***Herodotus*** ought to be named in this connection. Le Normant and Cheval-lier's ***History of The Oriental Nations of Antiquity***, 2 vols. partially satisfies a long-felt want. A. H. Layard's ***Discourses on Nineveh*** and ***Nineveh and its Remains*** would naturally be consulted here.

In the history and antiquities of Egypt, Sir J. G. "Wilkinson is the highest authority, and he may be read either in his larger work, ***Manners and Customs of the Ancient Egyptians,*** 3 vols. 8vo., or in the more popular and abridged ***Popular Accounts of the Ancient Egyptians,*** 2 vols. 12mo. Uhlemann's ***Three Days in Memphis*** is as successful an attempt at reviving the Egyptian world to the imagination of the moderns as could be expected. Osburn's ***Monumental History of Egypt*** is a work of interest and authority. ***Egypt Ancient and Modern,*** by M. Russell, is a brief com-pend of Egyptian history. ***Egypt and the Boolcs of Moses*** is an elaborate work, by E. W. Hengstenberg. ***Egypt Past and Present***, by Dr. J. P. Thompson, is carefully prepared. ***Egypt, its Place in the World's History***, by Baron Bunsen, has the characteristic excellencies and defects of its well-known author.

If we pass from Egypt to Palestine, we have for the general reader the well-known and the well-written ***History of the Jews***, by the eloquent and scholarly H. H. Milman. This work is not as frequently and faithfully read as it deserves to be. It is written with the critical spirit of a thorough scholar, with the candor of an enlightened Biblical student, with the imagination of a poet, and the faith of a believing Christian. Jahn's ***History of the Hebrew Commonwealth***, from the German, is solid and trustworthy, but heavy in style. Ewald's ***History of the People of Israel, from the German, translated in part, is masterly for its learning and originality, but abundant in capricious and not always well-sustained suggestions. M. T. Raphall's*** Post Biblical History of the Jews *is a faithful and painstaking History by a well-known learned Rabbi. For the understanding of the Hebrew institutions in their relation to the Hebrew literature, Herder's* Spirit of Hebrew Poetry, *from the German, is invaluable. No intelligent and thoughtful reader can fail to be delighted and instructed by its eloquent pages. Isaac Taylor* On Hebrew Poetry, *and Robert Lowth on* the Sacred Poetry of the Hebrews *are both excellent adjuncts.* Helm's Pilgrimage, *an historical novel, from the German of F. Strauss, published more recently also under the title of* The Glory of the House of Israel, *is a very successful attempt to reproduce in a tale the life of the Jewish people in the century preceding the advent of Christ. It was prepared with great care, with competent learning, and as an aid* to the study of the Jewish history and institutions, as well as a successful interpreter of the Jewish faith and worship, is worth a score of professed and formal commentaries. Its merits are far superior to many extemporized and superficial imitations purporting to be reproductions of the times of the Old Testament and the Jews, that seek to supply what they lack in historic accuracy, by exaggerated diction, ill-conceived illustrations, and extravagant portraiture.

No thorough student of Jewish history would be willing to overlook the works of Josephus, the only, but not always to be trusted authority upon many points. The ordinary reader cannot but find great advantage in reading portions of these works, if for no other reason than that they so effectually transport him back into the past, and enable him to understand and to sympathize with the spirit of the enlightened political Jews of the times. The Geography of Palestine has been treated in an exhaustive and critical way by the eminent Professor Robinson in his ***Biblical Researches,*** and his ***Geography of Palestine***. The ***Sinai and Palestine, in connection with their History***, by Arthur P. Stanley, is more popular in its form, and is better adapted to the use of the general reader. The ***Maps of Palestine*** that were edited by Dr. Robinson are very carefully corrected, and the ***Map of the Holy Land***, by C. "W. M. Van de Velde, is in every respect deserving the highest confidence. Raas? ***Map of Palestine***, an imitation of maps in relief, is at once ornamental and instructive, and should be in the hands of every student of Biblical History. The Dictionaries of the Bible and the Encyclopedias of Religious Literature which we shall notice in the Chapter on Religious Reading are indispensable auxiliarics.

From Palestine to Greece is but a short distance, and the transition is not unnatural from the Hebraic to the Greek history. C. Wordsworth's ***Greece, Pictorial, Descriptive and Historical, and a History of Greek Art***, is an admirable introduction to the study of the geography, history and literature of that wonderful country. The extended and carefully written ***History of Greece*** by George Grote has superseded almost every other, and no objection can be urged against it, except its excessive minuteness and its length. A good abridgement of it for schools and beginners has been prepared by William Smith. ***W. Mitford's History of Greece*** is written with great spirit and with masterly vigor; but it is excessively partisan in its character, the writer being a desperate enemy to popular institutions of every kind, and finding in the convulsions and changes of the states of Greece abundant confirmations for his political sympathies. C. Thirl wall's ***History of Greece*** is carefully written, but it wants the spirit of Mitford, and the critical research and masterly insight of Grote. E. Curtius' ***Manual History***, from the German, from the reputation of the author, must be accepted as of high authority. ***Ana-charsis' Travels***, by J. J. Barthelemy, from the French, is an attempt to recall the Greece that was, in a series of imagined travels taken in the palmy days of the Grecian States. Pausanias's **Greece**, an itinerary from a careful traveler and antiquary of the second century, is invaluable as a record of places, buildings, and works of art .as seen by Greek eyes and judged by a Greek mind. W. A. Becker's **Charicles** is a brief and formal, but for its purposes, an admirable historical novel, the design of which is to reproduce Greek life as it has been re-created and interpreted by the thorough critical researches of modern scholarship. It is fortified and illustrated by abundant notes, which refer to the classical writers. C. J. Felton's **Greece Ancient and Modern**, is learned and spirited. **Athens, its Rise and Fall**, by Sir Edward Lytton Bulwer, is cloqucntly written, and serves to quicken and aid the **historic imagination, while** Attica and Athens by C. O. Müller and others is at once learned and interesting, and A. Boechh's **Public Economy of Athens** is full of solid and satisfactory information in respect to the political organization of the State.

The later history of Greece has been carefully and labo-riously written by George Finlay in the following works, which are above the taste and the wants, as they are beyond the reach of the ordinary reader: Greece under the Romans, Mediæval History of Greece, History of the By-zantine and Greek Empire,

The history of Rome may be said to be well represented in English literature by Thomas Arnold's **History of Rome** and his **Later Roman Commonwealth**, and by Charles Merivale's **Rome under the Emperors**. These works may be recommended as of the very highest authority in respect to research and thoroughness. They are all written in a clear and fluent style. H. G. Liddell's History is a scholarly manual compiled from the best sources. J. C Eustace's **Classical Tour through Italy** is a useful book of reference. Theodore Mommsen's **History of Rome**, from the German, is now accessible to English readers, and cannot be too highly praised for its brilliant generalizations and its success in comparing ancient with modern events and institutions. "W. A. Becker's **Gallus** does the same for Roman which his **Charicles** does for Greek life. "W". Forsyth's **Life of Cicero**, though a little stiff and ponderous in its movement, is valuable to the reader who desires to understand something of the individual life of one of the most distinguished of Roman writers and statesmen, and who also would learn somewhat of the domestic and social life of the country, as reflected in the personal record of the feelings and the fortunes of so great a man. This biography, like the most interesting of modern lives, is in the main drawn from Cicero's private letters. The whole correspondence of Cicero with Atticus is accessible by translations to English readers. *Plutarch's Lives* have been read with enthusiasm by thousands of youths, and have at least imbued their readers with vivid impressions of ancient thought and feeling. They are lauded by R. "W. Emerson as one of the books which every man should read and re-read. *A. H. Clough's* revised edition is the best.

This suggests the thought that the reader of Greek and Roman history who is not a proficient in the Greek and Latin languages,—as well as many who are,—cannot be said to master the history of these countries unless he knows something of their literature and of its history.

There are now accessible many good translations of the works of the leading writers in prose and poetry, as also good critical and popular histories of these literatures. The great poems of Homer have been rendered into English with various ability and success, from the quaint and graphic Chapman down to the Earl of Derby and two or three after him, of whom our own Bryant is the last, but not the least successful. The history of Herodotus has been translated and commented upon by Rawlinson. W. E. Gladstone's *Juventus Mundi* is intensely interesting in its reproduction of the Greek life from the representations of Homer. In this connexion we name G. W. Cox's *Manual of Mythology, Tales of the Gods and Heroes, Tales of Thebes and Argos,* C. O. Müller's *Scientific System of Mythology*. Several of the *Dialogues of Plato* have been translated into fluent English with annotations by the eminent philosopher W. Whewell. George Grote has written an elaborate treatise upon the writings of Plato, in the form of a careful analysis of each of his Dialogues. Aristotle's *Ethics, Rhetoric,* and *Treatise on Poetry* have been well translated and published in Bohn's Classical Library. *The Tragedies of Sophocles* have been translated by E. H. Plumptre, and some of the *Comedies of Aristophanes* have been admirably rendered by J. Hookham Frere. Conington's *Virgil* is interesting even to a school-boy. The well-known translations of the leading Latin writers need not be enumerated. William Morris's *Life and Death of Jason*, imitated from the Greek, is admirably fitted to awaken the feeling for ancient life and to carry the reader back to the earlier centuries. Of the histories of Greek and Roman literature we may name W. Mure's *History of the Language and Literature of Ancient Greece*, also C. O. Müller's *History of the Literature of Ancient Greece*, published by the Society for the Diffusion of Useful Knowledge, and Dun-lop's History of Roman Literature. William Smith's Dictionaries of Ancient Geography, 2 vols.; *of Antiquities*, 1 vol., and of Biography and Mythology, 3 vols., are an encyclopedia of reference upon all points and questions which relate to Greek and Roman history, literature, and biography. Rollin's *History of the Arts and Sciences of the Ancients* is a much better book than the much better known Ancient Universal History.

As we come from ancient to modern times, the introduction of Christianity and the rise and growth of the Christian Church attract our attention. They cannot be left out of view, for they are entwined with the rise and growth of all the modern States, and in great part constitute as well as in greater measure explain our modern history. We may speak hereafter more at length of books upon these topics under the title of Religious Reading, but at present we shall confine ourselves to the notice which they deserve from the reader of general history. H. Milman's *History of Christianity in the First Three Centuries* is perhaps the best single work of the general character which is required by such a reader. This work is neither ecclesiastical nor religious. It professes to treat of Christianity chiefly as it affected the secular, political, and social relations of the Roman empire and the Roman world. C. Merivale's *Conversion of the Roman Empire* is a work of the same general scope. *Helena's Household*, an unpretending story by J. De Mille recently issued, gives an interesting and faithful picture of the workings of Christianity in a Roman household, and interweaves also much of the history of a part of the first and second centuries. *Zenobia, Aurelian and Julian,* by the Rev. "William Ware, Salathiel, by Rev. George Croly, and *Valerius*, by J. G. Lockhart, are all excellent examples of good historical tales of the earlier Christian centuries. Neander's *General History of the Christian Religion and of the Christian Church* is not un-worthy the attention of the general reader, although it is professedly written from a religious as well as a secular standpoint. The great work upon this transition-period which meets and satisfies the wants of the general reader most completely is the masterly history of Gibbon of the ***Decline and Fall of the Roman Empire***. It still remains the treasure-house of digested learning and of critical judgment for all other historians. We have already taken exception to the moral spirit in which it was written, and to the antagonistic attitude which it assumes towards Christianity. While we ought not to insist that every historical writer should write in a believing or devout spirit, we may reasonably require that he should treat with respect the opinions of believers in Christianity, and that he should not dishonor by contemptuous and indirect depreciation that religious system which is universally conceded to be the noblest which the world has ever witnessed. To counteract the influence of these arguments and insinuations of Gibbon, both Milman and Guizot have edited special editions of this History, with abundant notes. ***The Student's Gibbon***, prepared by W. Smith, in a similar spirit, is an edition greatly abridged, which is designed for school and college use, and may serve as a convenient manual for review and reference. J. Sismondi has also written an excellent brief ***History of the Decline and Fall of the Roman Empire***. Milman's ***History of Latin Chris-tianity*** is of the highest value, and is universally accepted as one of our best standard histories.

Gibbon's celebrated history is the connecting bridge by which we pass from ancient to what we are accustomed to call Modern History. A dark chasm intervenes between the two, in which barbarism and disorder struggle with the tendencies to civilization and order, which during a long series of centuries are furnished first and almost exclusively by the Christian Church, itself greatly unenlightened and corrupt. Others sprung from the literature, art, and free spirit that were introduced and inspired by the revival of classical study, and both at last struck their own roots and developed an independent life in what we call modern Europe. It is not yet given to special students of history to understand this period perfectly, and the results of what has been satisfactorily established are not accessible in general histories that are adapted to the ordinary reader. Koch's ***Revolutions of Europe*** is an expanded chronological table, convenient for reference and instruction to those who have patience to use it. A. F. Tytler's **Modern History** was once used in schools and colleges, but has now been generally disused. **W**. C. Taylor's **Manual of Modern History** is to be preferred to this. Rus-sell's well-known and much used **History of Modern Europe** may perhaps be set aside by the compilation of Philip Smith. A few manuals translated from the German, as those of J. Von Müller, Schlosser, Weber, furnish the principal facts, with little or no expansion, illustration, or philosophy.

Rev. James White's **Eighteen Christian Centuries** is written with spirit, and furnishes a very convenient and interesting general view of the prominent events of modern history. It is, however, and professes to be, nothing more than a sketch of these events. A sketch of an entirely different character is found in Guizot's **History of Civilization in Europe.** This work treats of the great moving influences and agencies which brought order and light into the chaos and darkness consequent upon the breaking up of the ancient civilization. Hallam's **State of Europe during the Middle Ages** is a work of the highest authority. Though exceedingly dry and condensed in its matter and manner, it is indispensable even to a general reader. In this connection we may properly refer to Hallam's **Introduction to the Literature of Europe**, as giving the best ac-count which is accessible of the beginnings and progress of literature from the period of its revival and onward. Froissart's **Chronicles** carry us back to the fourteenth century, and give us vivid impressions of the stir and romance of chivalry. Professor G. W. Greene's **Lectures on the Middle Ages** is a useful and trustworthy manual. Leopold Ranke's **History of the Popes** and **History of the Reformation** should also be read as supplementary to the exclusively secular histories of those times. It is, of course, written from a Protestant point of view, but is generally accepted as candid and trustworthy. No man can understand the history of Europe who does not make himself intimately acquainted with the manifold phases and-the powerful agency of the Romish Church, and with the re-lation of the Protestant Reformation to the political action of the Protestant pow-ers. An historical essay by James Bryce, **On the Holy Roman Empire**, treats very ably of the fancied successor to the old Roman dominion, which at times embraced within its supremacy many of the separate European States, and had the most im-portant influence over the whole field of European history. D'Aubigne's **History** *of the Reformation*, which is-decided-ly Protestant and positively and earnestly religious, is drawn from original sources and largely biographical. The *History of the Crusades* by Michaud, from the French, and C. Mills' History of the Crusades, should be read here, with Tasso's *Jerusalem Delivered* and Walter Scott's *Ivanhoe* and *The Talisman*.

If we leave the general history of Europe and consider its separate States and countries, we naturally turn first to Italy. In this field the supply for English readers is unfortunately very meagre. Frederick von Raumer's *History of Italy and the Italians*, from the German, and J. C. L. S. de Sismondi's *History of the Italian Republics*, from the French, are works of deservedly high reputation. "William Roscoe's *Life and Pontificate of Leo X.* and *Life of Lorenzo de Medici* are elegantly and carefully written. Sir Edward Lytton Bulwer's *Rienzi, or the Last of the Tribunes*, and *Romola*, by " George Eliot" (Mrs. Lewes) are historical novels of great excellence, the last deserving all the high encomiums which it has received. Sismondi's History of the Literature of the South *of* Europe is very full upon the literature of Italy. Dante's great poem should be studied in connection with Italian history.

It is with Spain as with Italy. There is no general history of Spain of very high authority. This is perhaps the less to be regretted, as this history is covered to a considerable extent by the histories of the Empire, and by those of special periods and personages. Mrs. Calcott's *Popular History* is said by a competent critic to be as successful as the materials and the nature of the subject would allow. Ticknor's *History of Spanish Literature* is of the highest authority, and is very readable. Robertson's well-known *History of Charles V.* , Watson's *Philip II, Pres-cott's History of Ferdinand and Isabella*, Washington Irving's *Life and Voyages of Columbus*, J. L. Motley's Histories of the *United Netherlands* and of the *Rise of the Hutch Republic*, supply in a good measure the deficiency of a single general history of this splendid but ill-fated country. Napier's Peninsular War is one of the ablest and most interesting of all military histories.

Spain naturally suggests Holland, inasmuch as the fortunes of the two countries for many memorable years were closely connected. Grattan's ***History of the Netherlands*** is a good manual history. Motley's histories, just named, are nearly all that could be desired for the periods of time which they cover. For the periods subsequent to those, the history of Holland and Belgium is treated pretty fully, as it necessarily would be, in the special histories. of the great States which are adjacent, and in the general history of Europe, and especially in all histories of the French Revolution.

For Germany, the English reader must content himself with Kohlrausch's ***General History*** and Menzel's ***History of Germany and the Germans***; both translated from the German. Coxe's ***History of the House of Austria, and Carlyle's Frederick the Great***, are books of the highest authority, the last being deformed by the author's worst faults, which are redeemed by striking excellencies. No book can be compared with this to enable the reader to understand the rise and growth of the now great Prussian power. Schiller's ***History of the Thirty Years' War*** is full of striking and eloquent passages. J. S. C. Abbott's ***Austria*** is a mere compilation, as it professes to be, but is faithfully executed.

For the history of Russia we are dependent upon a few manuals—among which Abbott's takes a respectable rank. The more scholarly reader must resort to works in French and German.

Geijer's ***History of the Swedes*** as translated, is unfortu-nately not complete.

France is a country of which the history is most closely intertwined with that of England and America. It excites the warmest and deepest interest in almost every reader, and deserves careful study. Rev. James White's brief history of this country, and Parke Godwin's as yet incomplete manual, are both good. Michelet's eloquent sketches are excellent, and Martin's elaborate volumes, translated (as yet in part only) from the French, are admirable. ***The Student's History of France*** is dependent on Martin, and is an excellent compend. Parke Godwin's ***History of France*** cannot but be solid and brilliant. Guizot's ***History of Civilization in France***, Sir James Stephens's ***Lectures on the History of France***, Smedley's ***History of the Reformed Church in France***, Smiles's ***Huguenots, The Memoirs of the Duke of Sully*** and of the ***Cardinal de Retz***, Miss Pardoe's ***Louis XIV.***, come in as representatives of a great number of monographs on special topics and periods. Bungener's ***Preacher and King*** and ***Priest and Huguenot***, are effective and eloquent portraitures of the reigns of Louis XIV. and XV., which attract all classes of readers. G. P. R. James' ***The Huguenot*** is trustworthy and useful. The French Revolution, as was natural, has been a very fertile theme for a great number of special histories. Mignet gives a brief and trustworthy narrative of the principal facts. Carlyle presents the chief incidents and personages in a series of brilliant and impressive pictures. Thiers has wrought up the abundant material at his command into elaborate and effective representations in his Histories of ***The French Revo-lution*** and of ***The Consulate and Empire***. Alison's ***History of Europe*** from 1789 to 1815 gives the English aristocratic view of those convulsions in Europe. The novels of the Erckmann-Chatrian series illustrate the same period. Not a few tracts and treatises on the French Revolution of a general character have been written by writers of the first ability, which it is worth while to read in connection with its history proper—as for example Edmund Burke's ***Reflections on the French Revolution***, Sir James Mackintosh's ***Vindicice Gallicce***, Madame de Stael's ***Events of the French Revolution***, Paine's ***Rights of Man***, Lamartine's ***Histories***, and William Smyth's ***Lectures***.

The history of England is the history above all others which is important and interesting to the man of English origin, not merely because it is the history of his own nation and lineage, but because it records the development of the liberty and the institutions, of the literature and the commerce which have already exerted the most widespread influence upon the human family, and which are destined to exercise a still more extensive influence on future generations. The history of many of the countries of Europe, as of Holland, France, and Prussia, may present many single passages of dramatic interest; they are ennobled by the character and deeds of many heroes in arts and arms; they have added many single products to human civilization of lasting value and splendid renown. But none of these have achieved so much for man, by as uniform and steady progress in a noble direction, as have England and America. We say England and America, for to the historic student both these countries are one. No other countries have embodied their achievements in political institutions so free, in laws so beneficent and humane, in a public sentiment so efficient, so just, and so wide-reaching, and in a literature so various and so ennobling. The Englishman who is not proud of the history of his own country is degenerate and low-minded. The American who does not study it with filial delight and gratitude is narrow-minded and barbarous. Whatever temporary alienations may have disturbed our sympathy with the old homestead, or whatever wrongs we may have suffered from the haughty and unnatural jealousy of the old mother, they should not abate in the least from the interest which we feel in that part of the history of England which is our history as truly as it is hers, or make us content to alienate from ourselves the least item of our share in its achievements and its renown. Indeed, were the American disposed to do so, he cannot avoid reading the history of England, if he would understand his own. Her history is a part of the history of his own country. It is essential as an introduction to this history. What we most value in our ancestral spirit was first developed on English soil and in the conflicts which are recorded in English annals. The habits, the principles, and the faith which have moulded this country are English in their origin. The literature which has both formed and expressed our public sentiment has much of it been composed on English soil, and all of it flows in a common stream of sentiment that has been derived from English hearths and English altars, from English tribunals and English customs. The contributions which we have made to this stream do not discolor its purity or disturb its flow. The early English history is in some respects even more important to the American reader than it is to the resident upon English soil, for the reason that to the home-born and home-bred the traditions and customs, the names of places, the associations that cleave to the very soil, that haunt every common and gather about every church-yard in the old country may in some sense and to a certain degree take the place of written history. The American must find all these, or their substitutes, in books and descriptions. To him books must supply the place of tradition, and it is in books only that he can interpret the origin of the laws, the government, the church; the opinions, and manners, which make his country to be what it is. The resident of old England smiles at the enthusiasm with which the

American visits the old churches and churchyards to which he has been wonted from his infancy. He wonders at the delight with which the stranger explores the rickety houses and the rambling old streets of many a city or village which to him are only squalid and offensive. Bat the same enthusiasm which sends the intelligent American to England to explore the home of his fathers, should lead him to study with care and zeal the records of what his ancestors did and suffered in the same old home. The best History of England for the general reader is Knight's ***Popular History*** in 8 vols. 8vo. It comes down to the death of Prince Albert, and is a history of the peo-ple as well as of courts and the cultivated classes. It is a history of manners and of literature, of the arts and of commerce, as truly as of the politics and the wars of the empire. It is not written with the spirit and the power which we find in such writers as Macaulay and Froude. This would not be expected from a writer who acts rather as the gatherer of the results and the conclusions which have been reached by a judicial survey of the movements and strifes of political and religious parties than as the representative and advocate of any. Its tone is quiet and cool. Its summings up are deliberate and dispassionate. It is written, indeed, in the interest of freedom, of progress, and of toleration. It sympathizes with the people rather than with their rulers, and with free principles and free institutions, as against the defenders of prerogative and of tradition, but it aims to be neither violent nor one-sided. We think, therefore, that for a single history which may serve for constant use and reference in the library, or for frequent reading, it is to be preferred to every other. The ***Pictorial History of England***, in 8 vols. 4to. by the same editor, was prepared earlier, and with less skill in respect to style and form. It is also more over-loaded with matter, and is so heavy in style as to be less readable. It terminates with the death of George III. We have already given our opinion of Hume's History as delightful in style and most readable in manner, but as open to grave objection for its intensely partisan character, as well as for the flippant though graceful insinuations with which it abounds to the disadvantage of freedom and Christianity. No diligent and zealous reader of English history, however, would be contented not to be familiar with Hume. Among the special historians who treat of separate portions or periods of history, we name the brilliant and spirited Macaulay, who always sustains and excites the reader, even if offended by his style, or forced to reject his conclusions; Lingard, who is universally acknowledged to be eloquent and able, although he writes as the avowed defender of the Catholic Church against the representations of Protestant historians; Lord Mahon, now Earl Stanhope, who always writes with dignity and elegance, and inspires confidence in his candor if he does not transport the reader with enthusiasm for his brilliancy; Froude, whose merits as a writer are universally acknowledged, and who has certainly set forth in a bold relief, an important class of facts concerning the people of England and the state of the times, even though his opinions in regard to Henry VIII., rather astonish than convince his readers. Godwin's **History of England** during the Commonwealth and Catharine Macau-lay's **History of England** have not been read so generally in England as they deserved, because of their pronounced Republican sympathies. Sir James Mackintosh's brief and unfinished history is pronounced by all who have read it to be brilliant and philosophical, though its style is better suited to philosophical generalization than it is to flowing narrative. Clarendon's **History of the Rebellion** is written with warm sympathies for the cause of Charles I., but it has the interest which pertains to a narrative composed by one who was personally present during many of the stirring scenes of the most memorable movement by which England was ever agitated, and was personally acquainted with many of the leading spirits of those times. **The Life of Colonel Hutchinson,** by his widow, herself the fairest and the most cultivated of Puritanesses, and **the Narrative of his own Life and Times** by Richard Baxter, have a similar fresh and personal interest. Both these works are written under sympathies and a bias in a direction opposed to those of Clarendon. Carlyle's. **life and Letters of Oliver Cromwell** is fraught with interest to every honest inquirer for historic truth. It has made the name of Cromwell respected in circles that for generations had named it with contemptuous scorn, and came near to give Cromwell a statue among the rulers of England in the corridor of the Houses of Parliament. The **Diary of John Evelyn** was written by a devoted Royalist of accomplished culture and earnest religious character. It stretches through the times of the Commonwealth into those of the Restoration. Pepys's **Diary** records most fully many of the events which occurred after the Restoration, and presents a living picture of those frivolous and shameless times, which is all the more trustworthy and life-like because the writer seems unconscious of the severity of the sentence with which he condemns what he often seems to palliate. If any person has the desire or is laid under the necessity to learn more of the grossness of the shameless court of Charles II., he may peruse the **Memoirs of Count de Grammont**. Butler's **Hudibras** should be read by all means in connection with the history of the Rebellion and the Commonwealth. Burnet's **History of his own Time is** gossiping and garrulous, but honest. No reader can doubt that the author might easily have been misled by his own prejudices and the misrepresentations of others. As little would it be denied by any one that this history is in the main a faithful picture of the men and scenes which it portrays. Baxter and Burnet write from opposite points of view. Their histories cover very nearly the same period. They were both credulous and one-sided; but he must be a bold partisan who would deny the honesty of either. Lord John Hervey's **Me-moirs of the Reign of George II**, Horace Walpole's letters (several series,) and his **Journal of the Reign of George III**, are instructive and entertaining.

Guizot's History of the Revolution of 1848, as also **Cromwell'; Monk, or the Fall of the Republic,** are of espe-cial value as giving the opinions upon critical questions of a candid and well-informed Frenchman.

Mackintosh's **History of the Revolution of** 1688, and Fox's **Life of James II.**, are both written by earnest Whigs and pronounced partisans of the Revolution, and are esteemed of the highest authority. If one reads Ma-caulay, however, it would seem that he might be satisfied in this direction. There is one political history of England which no intelligent reader, especially no intelligent American, can possibly dispense with, and that is **The Constitutional History of England** by the judicious and fair-minded Hallam. This history, with the supplement of the same by **T. E. May**, from 1760 to 1860, is of priceless worth. We would almost say to any reader, if you can read but a single history of England, peruse this above all others, for the light that it sheds upon what is most important to us in respect to the heritage which we have received and derived from our English ancestors. It should never be forgotten that what has made our country what it is was but the development of the free spirit, the principles, the rights, and the institutions which our fathers brought with them across the seas; and that the story of the origin and growth of all these is more interesting and instructive to us than it can be to the Englishman at home. The beginnings of this history of Hallam are to be found in his work on the Middle Ages. Br. Robert Vaughan's **Revolutions of English History** are excellent examples of instructive and trustworthy historical essays. Vaughan's **History of England under the Stuarts** is worth consulting. Goldwin Smith's little works on **Ireland** and **The Umpire** are of surpassing interest and value.

There are not a few readers who are especially attracted to the history of the stirring times of the Commonwealth. Such readers should not overlook Mr. John Forster's **Statesmen of the Commonwealth**, his history of The Debates on the G-rand Remonstrance, and his **Life of Sir John Eliot**. Goldwin Smith's **Three English Statesmen** will satisfy the most ardent champion of the cause of the Parliament. Burton's **Cromwellian Diary** will attract the patient delver into the sources from which history is derived. The comparative freedom of the press which was so long allowed in England has given birth to a multitude of political pamphlets, tracts, handbills, lampoons, caricatures, which are invaluable for any zealous and patient student of any of the later periods of English history. Some of these have been collected and reprinted in series, like **The Somers Tracts** and **The Harleian Miscellany**. Many others have been gathered by book-collectors, and are found in the largest and best furnished libraries in this country. It is quite aside from our aims to give any titles or references for matter of this kind. Those who have the capacity or taste for such researches usually know what they need and where to find it. we only observe that Hansard's Debates, Dodsley's **Annual** Register, and the **Celebrated State Trials** can be readily found and referred to. The collected speeches of the great orators who have been distinguished at the bar and in Parliament, and the biographies of the great political leaders, are the most interesting commentaries and illustrations of the political history of the country. A very convenient and comprehensive work of American authorship, Goodrich's **British Eloquence**, contains a good selection of the best speeches of the leading British orators, from Sir John Eliot to Lord Brougham, with carefully prepared sketches of the life and times of each, and many excellent explanatory foot-notes. This book has been highly commended in England, which has produced no manual which deserves to be compared with it for comprehensiveness and careful preparation.

The history of the British Empire can scarcely be con-sidered as in any sense completed if Martin's **History of the Colonies** and Mill's **British India** are not consulted.

Miss Martineau's **History of England since the Peace**, in 4 vols. 8vo., is very full upon many points of very recent interest, and is a very useful compilation.

The earlier history of England may attract the special attention of a limited class of readers. The works of J. M. Kemble are of the highest authority in Anglo-Saxon history, but Sharon Turner's **History of the Anglo-Saxons** will meet the wants of most readers, and is easily accessible. Sir Francis Palgrave's **England during the Anglo-Saxon Period** is also one of the few classical books in this department. John Thrupp's **Anglo-Saxon Home** is a monograph of no little interest. Our English Home: its **Early History and Progress**, is a work of similar character. Thierry's **History of the Norman Conquest**, from the French, is brilliantly written, though probably in many points more eloquent and highly colored than solidly true. Freeman's **History of the Norman Conquest** is likely to supersede all other books on this subject. T. Wright's **History of Dress, Manners, and Sentiments in England during the Middle Ages** is a work of some interest, though not superior to the chapters in the **Pictorial History** upon these topics.

A few among many historical novels may be named which illustrate different periods of English history. E. L. Bulwer's **Last of the Barons**; Scott's **Ivanhoe, Kenil-worth, Woodstock, Fortunes of Nigel, Peveril of the Peak, Old Mortality**, etc., etc.; Kingsley's **Hereward** and Westward Ho! Thackeray's Henry Esmond; The Youth of Shakespeare; W. Shakespeare, His Life and Times**; Mrs. Charles'** The Draytons and The Davenants**, and** On Both Sides of the Sea**, are a few of the many tales which are fitted to throw no little light and interest upon different periods and passages of English history. To the same class of works belong** The Diary of Lady Willoughby, **The Maiden and Married Life of Mary Powell**, and others.

We have already recognized the important truth that the literature of every country must be freely and familiarly consulted in order to master its history. This is true in a pre-eminent sense of English history. The freedom of thought and speech which the English people have asserted for themselves from very early times has expressed itself in an endless variety of productions more or less worthy to be called its literature, the study of which enables us to understand the temper of the times. The more we read the great writers of each generation, the more completely can we understand the spirit of the age in which they lived. The more various our reading is, especially of all sorts of ephemeral and miscellaneous publications, the greater will be our satisfaction. Much of the most lively and most effective English writing has been composed upon political themes and occasions. Much of it has been inspired by the noblest patriotism, in the double form of chivalrous loyalty on the one side, and of stern devotion to the Parliament and the people on the other. Not a little of the most spirited thought and the most effective writing have been incited by party virulence. John Milton", Andrew Marvel, John Dryden, Daniel Defoe, Roger L'Estrange, Jonathan Swift, Samuel Johnson, Edmund Burke, Sir James Mackintosh, Richard Price, Lord Brougham, Samuel Romilly, Sydney Smith, Robert Southey, William Cobbett, S. T. Coleridge, John Wilson, T. B. Macaulay, Richard Cobden, and hosts of others, have been distinguished as political writers, and every reader of their writings of necessity makes new additions to his knowledge of the events of English history. What we have said in general of the significance of pamphlets and newspapers as interpreters of history, is in a special sense true of the history of England and America. For the American who has visited England and who would understand the country in many of its most interesting features both physical and social the following may be named, H. Colman's ***European Life and Manners***, ¥m. Howitt's ***Rural Life in England***, J. M. Hoppin's ***Old England***,

"We hardly need add, that much of the best and most permanent knowledge of the history of England is to be acquired by the study of the lives of its eminent men. Many of these lives have been written with special care by their personal and familiar friends, or those devoted to the cause or interest in which they were conspicuous. Individual men in England have always been prominent in the eye of the public, and have impressed themselves strongly upon every great cause. The lives of John Knox, John Wesley, Johnson, Goldsmith, Burke, Garrick, Reynolds, Chatham, Pitt, Buxton, Walter Scott, Chalmers, Arnold, Keble, of Romilly, Robert Hall, and Henry Crabb Robinson, are not less valuable as contributions to the general history of the times in which these individuals lived, than as additions to our personal knowledge of individual character.

The history of America is limited especially to that of the United States, for reasons which are so obvious as not to require enumeration. Bancroft is very full, and generally very accurate, on the Colonial history of the States, and his history generally is indispensable as a work of reference. It is unfortunately written in an ambitious style, which sometimes excessively crowds the information which it seeks to give, and not infrequently distracts the attention by affected turns of thought and exaggerated declamation. It is foolishly demagogical at times, and betrays also somewhat of the want of earnest faith in the very truths and principles which it ostentatiously parades before the reader. In one word, it is very deficient in the sterling qualities of simplicity of matter and of manner. Hildreth lacks neither earnestness nor directness. Unfortunately, this very able writer, though wholesome and whole-souled in his strong attachments to the Federal party, is so obviously bitter in his spirit, and intolerant in his judgments, as to weaken the confidence of his readers in his candor and trustworthiness in respect to all subjects. His history terminates with the close of Washington's administration. He has no sympathy with religious faith or fervor in any form; least of all with the religious aims of the New-England settlers, and no tolerance for their political systems. He does them scant justice in many other particulars. Palfrey's ***History of New England*** is eminently fair, truthful, and trustworthy in its representations of its themes, as well as a model for classical condensation and elegance. Burke's ***History of European Settlements in America*** is written with spirit and philosophic insight, and Parkman's well known volumes need only be referred to in passing. The history of almost every State in the Union has been written by some well-known writer. Many of these States have also an historical society which has published collections of old pamphlets and other important documents. The histories of many Counties, towns, and churches have been written with more or less fidelity and success. These particular and local histories should receive especial attention from every person who reads history at all. These local fields are within the reader's own observation. The events and personages are those of which he can form, in some sort, a personal judgment. Human nature is very nearly the same on a large and on a limited scale. A town-meeting is a Congress or Parliament in miniature. A village or church quarrel represents a national war or an ecclesiastical schism. A traditional jealousy between the north and south end, or the east and west side of a township, is the type of a great sectional controversy that has endured for generations. A dispute over a mill privilege or a town-line represents many a border war. A sharp discussion between the supervisors of two towns is a school in which to study diplomacy, and its skill to conceal intentions and to use ambiguous language. If we become familiar with the history of what is within our reach; if we learn to know what history means by reading it when written of the persons, events, and scenes which are in a certain sense personally known to ourselves, we shall be able to understand it when it treats of objects that are distant in place, remote in time, and grand in their proportions. We do not include in our list any titles of books or collections of this sort, for the most obvious reasons.

The study of the government and institutions of this country, and of the origins and transformations of its great political parties cannot be too earnestly recommended. The best works on these subjects are *The Federalist*, which has been edited with great care and published in two rival editions; *The Madison Papers*, and the lives of Washington by John Marshall and Washington Irving. A very able work, with Federalist sympathies, entitled Sullivan's *Letters on Public Characters*, is invaluable—as is also Theodore Dwight's *History of the Hartford Convention*. For the illustration and defence of the Jeffcrsonian principles no better authority can be found than Jefferson's collected writings, and the laudatory memoir of his life by Randall. G. T. Curtis' *History of- the Origin, etc., of the U. S. Constitution*, with the *Commentaries* on the constitution, by the eminent jurists Kent and Story, are classical works on this subject. Benton's *Thirty Tears' View, or History of the Government from* 1810 *to* 1850, with Martin Van Buren's *History of Political Parties*, and Buchanan's *History of his Administration* coupled with the *Speeches* of Clay, Calhoun, Webster, Seward, and Sumner, will enable the reader to understand our political history. Benton's ***Abridgement of Debates in Congress*** may be found and consulted in many public and some private libraries. Frank Moore's ***American Eloquence, a Collection of Speeches by the most eminent Orators of America***, will always be useful.

For the American Revolution, Botta may be read in ad-dition to what Bancroft and Hildreth furnish. B. J. Los-sing's ***Pictorial Field-book of the Revolution as also of The War of*** 1812, gives the picturesque and striking incidents of both, and G. W. Greene, an admirable generalized statement of the leading facts and lessons of the first. Trumbull's Hudibrastic poem, ***McFingal***, should by no means be omitted. For the history of the civil war, ***The Rebellion Record*** is a great storehouse of documents, and Greeley's ***American Conflict*** a condensed view of its memorable events. Lossing's ***Pictorial History*** has the same charm which belong to the other works of the same author. The lives of Lincoln, by Raymond, Holland, and others, and separate sketches of the campaigns of Sherman, Grant, etc., will occur to every one.

"What has been said of the relation of the biography of Englishmen to the history of England applies to that of the biography of Americans to our history with equal pertinence.

As the reader makes progress in the knowledge of history he will naturally desire to read some works upon the study and philosophy of history itself; in order to learn something of the sources from which it is derived, of the evidence by which its assertions are supported, and the lessons which it inculcates. In some works of this kind particular directions are given in respect to the authors and parts of authors which should be read upon particular countries and periods. Bolingbroke on ***The Use and Study of History*** was formerly much read and referred to. Priestly's ***Lectures on the Study of History*** is a useful book. Dr. Thomas Arnold's ***Lectures on Modern History***, and Gold win Smith's ***Lectures on the Study of History*** are good books for the general reader. G. C. Lewis' ***Credibility of early Roman History***, and W. O. Taylor ***On the Natural History of Society*** are standard works. Prof.

Henry Reed is the author of some very elevating and suggestive lectures on English history. Prof. William Smyth's ***Lectures on Modern History***, edited by Sparks, is at once an extended directory for study and a manual of the best books and parts of books which should be read. Frederick Schlegel's ***Modem History***, and A. W. Schlegel's ***Philosophy of History***, are well worth attention as good specimens of German generalization and philosophizing. The philosophy of Buckle's ***History of Civilization in England*** we have already characterized. W. Draper's ***The Intellectual Development of Europe***, is written after the manner of Buckle. Some of the ablest contributions upon this subject are in'the form of essays or reviews upon history in general or upon some historical writer. We name as examples Macaulay's well-known article on ***History in the Edinburgh*** Review, and an article on ***Hume as an Historian*** in No. 73 of the ***London Quarterly***. The indexes of modern periodical literature abound in the titles of such papers.

It is safe to say that much which is written on the Phil-osophy of History is the product of conjecture, pretension, or an atheistic theory of the universe, and much more is mere philosophical romancing.

The list of books which we have furnished may seem to many very meagre, and to others much too extensive. The titles of many works have doubtless been omitted which should have been included in a list constructed for the ends and according to the theory which we have proposed. We have endeavored to indicate the books which should be preferred by the place which they occupy in the several heads of the catalogue, or by the comments which we have made upon them; but in selections of this sort much liberty should be allowed to individual taste and judgment. Advice ought not to be urged beyond certain general suggestions and information. We can only say that the list has been prepared with some care and painstaking, and is doubtless capable of being enlarged and improved.

CHAPTER XIV.

BIOGRAPHY AND BIOGRAPHICAL READING.

BIOGRAPHY is closely allied to History. We have observed, that it is only by reading the lives of distinguished personages, that we can most satisfactorily acquaint ourselves with much that is valuable in History. It has been forcibly said that " History is the essence of innumerable biographies."

There is an important distinction, however, between biography as the interpreter and representative of other times, and biography as the record of an individual life and the exponent of individual character. It is with biography in the last sense that we have now to do. The ˜ written lives of individual men are as various as the men who are described, and the writers who describe them, Their interest and worth depend upon two circumstances— the significance of the events and characters recorded, and the skill and fidelity of their narrators. It is also true and worthy of notice, that the interest with which any biography is read—its value and usefulness indeed—may depend nearly as much upon the tastes and culture of the reader as upon either the worth and interest of the character which is recorded, or the genius of the biographer. This, in a sense, is true of all books, but it is especially true of books of lives.

To many readers biography is especially uninteresting and unattractive. Not a few persons have been heard to say, " I hate biography—to me it is the stupidest of all reading." It would seem at first to be a general fact that the taste for biography must be acquired, like the taste for tomatoes or olives. On a second thought, however, the suggestion might occur that the fact is capable of some sort of explanation. The first solution would probably be, that biography must always put the reader upon a course of analysis and reflection which is unnatural to most men. As the majority of readers do not care to examine their own motives and springs of action, much less do they concern themselves with those of other persons. Very many, again, do not like soberly to estimate themselves by any very high standard, whether it be of public opinion, of conscience, or of God, and for a similar reason prefer not to judge the being and doing of their fellows. To this should be added, that the capacity for this sort of analysis is not developed, if ever, till late in life, and hence is especially unsuited to the tastes of youth.

In view of these facts, we propose to consider the different sorts of biographies and the different methods after which biography is written, in order that we may explain why it is that the taste for this kind of writing is so various,—and also furnish a general directory for this department of reading. We aim here, as elsewhere, to establish principles by which to select and judge of books of this class, rather than to furnish a complete and annotated catalogue, to be implicitly followed.

The first class of biographies which we name are those *of incident and adventure*. The subjects of such lives are always heroes, and the life, whether true or exaggerated, is more or less of a romance. In biographies of this kind, two things are conspicuous : the striking events and uncommon positions by which the life of the hero is distinguished, and the spirit, skill, and courage with which he meets and overcomes them. Books of this sort are favorites with the young, especially with boys. It cannot be said that such biographies are stupid or uninteresting to that usually very fastidious class of readers. Very few boys are indifferent to such lives as those of General Francis Marion, Commodore Paul Jones, Charles XII., Admiral Nelson, General Andrew Jackson, Napoleon Buonaparte, General Sherman or Stonewall Jackson, Baron Trenck, Frederic Douglass, Mungo Park, Captain Parry or Dr. E. K. Kane. It matters little in what particular field of adventure the hero may be engaged, it is all the same to the boyish and often to the older reader; provided the adventures are sufficiently stirring and hazardous, and the spirit and resources of the hero are equal to the occasions. Whether it be on the battle-field or in a prison, in a storm or a shipwreck, whether the conflicts be with bad men or good, with villains or policemen, if the adventures and the heroism move the sympathies and excite the admiration, the life is always interesting, even to boys. Upon this principle we explain the strong hold which *Plutarch's Lives* have had upon the minds of so many boys and so many men for so many generations. The grandiose attitudes in which the great men of antiquity stand out to view—not so much men, as moving and walking statues—and the grand lights in which their biographer displays them, both contribute to this impressiveness, and have stamped their influence upon all the generations which have read them. The lives of great criminals especially when narrated by themselves, the confessions of famous murderers, pirates, and forgers, derive much of their interest from the same sources. By these we explain the potent and often dangerous fascination which attracts so many to stories of lives which were stained by daring crime and dishonored by gross excesses of cruelty and violence. The excitement of the incidents and the pluck of the hero are more than a match for any horror of cruelty or aversion to crime in the youthful reader. It cannot, we think, be said, that any of the biographies of the class to which we have referred are especially unattractive, or that the reading of such lives is especially stupid.

To the same class we refer the lives ***of great generals and 'captains***, which have fascinated so many young readers with the thought of a military or naval career, and have so long been the favorite reading of multitudes of older people. Who has not delighted to read the story of Alexander of Macedon and Julius Caesar, of Prince Eugene and Gustavus Adolphus, of the Duke of Marlborough and Frederick the Great, of Napoleon and Wellington, of the Napiers and Lord Clive, of General Havelock and Captain Hedley Vicars, of Generals Grant and Sherman, and last, not least, of the many youthful heroes who fell in our recent civil war? No books are more popular than the lives of old or young soldiers, with both young and old. The ***Harvard Memorial Biographies*** has largely this element of interest, as well as many that are far higher.

Akin to the interest with which military biographies are studied and read, is that which is attached to distinguished ***historical personages***. Such characters are indeed often military heroes; but whether they are or are not, their career is of that public and heroic sort which attracts the attention of those readers who require startling scenes and splendid actions. The lives of kings and queens, of courtiers and court favorites, have always been noticeably popular; the more minute and detailed are their descriptions of the scenes in which they figure, so much the better.

Whether the scene be public or private; whether it be a pageant or a ball, whether a frivolous or a criminal intrigue, is altogether indifferent. The elevation of the station, the splendor of the surroundings and the wide-reaching character of the results will always invest the life of the central personage with a real or a factitious importance. The biographies of Alexander and the Cæsars, of Charlemagne and Alfred the Great, of Henry IV. of France and Henry VIII. of England, of Charles V. and Francis I., of Philip II. and William the Silent, of Frederick the Great and George III., of Charles I. and Oliver Cromwell, of James II. and William III., of Elizabeth and Mary Stuart, of all the Queens of England down to Victoria, are read with breathless interest in many a log-hut and thatched cottage, simply because the personages were kingly or great. The reading of kings and courts introduces to the imagination brilliant pageants, splendid dresses, imposing state, thrones, crowns, gorgeous robes, and long processions of personages magnificently grand. Indeed, as we have already noticed, much of our pleasure in reading history arises from our sympathy with the fortunes and the story of the great historical personages who have figured prominently in its scenes of splendor and depression, of victory or defeat.

Closely allied to these are great ***statesmen and political leaders***, diplomatists and orators, who have helped and hindered sovereigns and nations, whose intellect and skill have sustained or thwarted the plans of kings, have inspired the achievements or marred the fortunes of great nations. The interest in the events and the heroes is in these cases of a more elevated description. The arena is intellectual, the struggles are of sagacity, eloquence, or craft. The issues are the progress or regress, the triumph or downfall of a great party or a great empire. The reader who has intelligence enough to comprehend the nature of such struggles, and the courage and skill which are required for success, always follows with interest the personal career of this class of great men. The lives of Wolsey, Sir Thomas More, and Cranmer, interest us as deeply as the life of Henry VIII. The personal character and history of Burleigh, Leicester, Essex, Raleigh, and Bacon, we follow with as keen an interest as the career of the imperious but capricious Elizabeth, and the pedantic and conceited James. The lives of Laud and Strafford are, if possible, more exciting than those of the ill-fated sovereign whom their counsels so fatally misled. Sir John Eliot, John

Hampden, Lord Falkland, William Pym, Sir Harry Vane, and Colonel Hutchinson have left lives as fraught with exciting interest as that of Cromwell himself. We follow the lives of Algernon Sidney and of Lord Russell with far more breathless attention than we do the stupid and senseless course of the bigoted monarch who sent them both to the scaffold. Richelieu, Mazarin, Sully, and De Retz, each had a personal character and a personal career which has an interest separate from the character and career of the great monarchs whom they served. Lord Somers and the great Whig leaders of the Revolution of 1688 interest us by the adroitness and personal courage with which they planned and achieved a bloodless victory for the rights of the English people and the establishment of constitutional restraints upon the crown. The lives of Chatham, Fox, and Burke are as exciting as a drama to one who knows what were the forces against which their lives were a perpetual struggle, and what were the weapons of argument and oratory, of sagacity and leadership, with which they strove. Pitt presents in his life a history as interesting as that of the great soldier against whom he subsidized the armies of Europe with the wealth of England.

We follow in the career of Brougham and Romilly, Mackintosh and Horner, of Macaulay and Cobden, the great thoughts, the courageous daring, and the persevering tenacity which have overturned the traditional policy of England and rooted up the prejudices of centuries, though backed by the wealth and prestige of the crown and aristocracy.

If we think of our own country we find the interest of a drama in the more or less complete and satisfactory Biog-raphies which we have of the lives of James Otis and Samuel Adams, of Joseph Warren and Patrick Henry, of Benjamin Franklin and Alexander Hamilton, of Thomas Jefferson and Aaron Burr, of John Jay and Timothy Pickering, of John Randolph and De-Witt Clinton, of John C. Calhoun and Henry Clay, of Daniel Webster and Martin Van Buren, of Thomas H. Benton and William H. Seward. The life of each of these statesmen and orators must be intensely exciting to every one who can comprehend the great objects for which each one of them lived, and the energy and skill which each displayed in bringing over the nation to his own opinions and policy. It may be questioned whether the great men of history are not the objects of the most intense personal feelings of like and dislike, chiefly because we view them as struggling for or against some great cause or party which we ourselves accept or reject. It is certain that every one follows the career of his favorite orators and statesmen with somewhat of the same excited suspense with which he watches the course of a living party leader in a present or impending conflict. In England and America, where so many intelligent persons take so warm and active an interest in political questions and party leaders, it is not strange that the most positive and excited interest should be. felt in the personal history and personal character of the great men who have organized or led those political parties in other generations, whose traditions and passions are still active in the present.

Those readers who rise above party sympathies and con-siderations, and are interested in the conflicts and struggles which result in great reforms, whether they are distinctively religious or political, moral or social, find the most abundant excitement in the life of any great **Reformer**. The incidents and the heroism kindle the imagination and stir the blood. In any soul in which the sense of public justice is wakeful, and the sympathy with human suffering is glowing, and the courage to contend against popular opposition is determined, there is the capacity to be stirred by the life-history of any man who has dared to brave power and faction and public opinion in favor of suppressed truth, an oppressed class, or a much-needed but long-delayed reform.

The lives of Savonarola, of Luther, of Ignatius Loyola, of George Fox, of John Wesley, of William Wilberforce, of Thomas Fowell Buxton, of John Brown, and of multitudes more, never want for sympathizing readers, even among men who do not sympathize with the principles or the spirit of their heroes. In the interest which is aroused by such lives, fanaticism and imprudence are overlooked and forgiven, and bold words and bolder deeds are admired and applauded. The dramatic interest of the shifting positions of the contest, and the imposing attitudes of the central figure, often fighting single-handed with myriads of foes, engross the attention and carry off the admiring sympathy. We admire and sometimes adore the heroes of a cause which we cannot but detest.

The biographies of *self-made men* are almost universally attractive. No man of any generosity or spirit can avoid being excited by the determination and perseverance which these exemplify. Only a snob or a tuft-hunter, or a toady to the rich or great is ashamed of a strong interest in the men who have risen from humble beginnings. They are especially fascinating and instructive to those young men of limited means who aspire to make something of their own lives. Smiles' *Self-Help* abounds in brief sketches of, and allusions to, a great number of men of this class, and one is surprised in reading such a book to find how large a number of those who have been eminent in every condition in life have risen from lowly conditions at the start.

The interest in such records is felt alike by those who have already risen in life and those who are just beginning to rise—pre-eminently by the latter.

This leads us to observe that those who are earnestly devoted to any art or profession are especially attracted to the lives of those persons who have attained special eminence in a similar profession or employment. Especially is this the case if their own career is as yet incomplete—if their aspirations are high and their difficulties are manifold—if the goal is bright but distant, and the path to it seems long and steep. The ever-present consciousness of the difficulties under which we labor leads us to compare our own condition with that of another like ourselves. The desire to overcome these difficulties and to attain eminence speedily, leads us to consult the experience of those who have, succeeded, and to inquire minutely what was the secret of their success. We are never tired of studying their devices, of hearing of their discouragements, of fighting over their battles, and of triumphing in their victories. The young advocate who is looking impatiently for his first brief, or who is forced to wait for days for the welcome step of a new client, reads with intense excitement the story of Erskine's speedy and brilliant entrance into a crowded practice. The young lawyer who proposes for himself a successful professional career, which shall be adorned and elevated by noble aspirations and liberal culture, can find few books which are so inspiriting as the lives of Sir Samuel Romilly and Francis Horner, of Patrick Henry and William Wirt, of Daniel Webster and Rufus Choate. The physician who wonders whence his patients are to come, and whether he can ever win his way into a lucrative practice, reads and re-reads with fresh interest the life and experience of any city or country doctor which he may chance to encounter. The lives of John Hunter and Sir Charles Bell are fraught with inspiration to him.

Many a journeyman printer has been inspired and, as it were, remade, by the records which Franklin has left of his own experiences at the press. Many a young writer has read and re-read the story of Franklin's patient attempts to attain a good English style. The popularity of Franklin's life in America and England is a complete refutation of the assertion that biography is to the mass of readers essentially stupid and uninviting. The life of the Learned Blacksmith has encouraged not a few laborers at the anvil. The lives of "Watt and Arkwright, of Fulton and Whitney, of Stephenson and Goodyear, have stimulated many an inventor to renewed patience and courage. No romance can excite a more kindled interest and excited enthusiasm in any generous mind than Hugh Miller's *My Schools and Schoolmasters*, as no book can possibly be more instructive to the working-man who will follow its guidance and yield to its inspiration. Horace Greeley is nowhere more interesting and wise as a guide to readers who have their own fortunes to make than in his *Recollections of a Busy Life*. The young physicists and scientists, who are so numerous at the present day, can find no reading which will please and reward them so well as the lives of Franklin and Ferguson, of Davy and Faraday, of New-ton and Dalton, of George Wilson and Edward Forbes. Artists never tire of reading the lives of the unhappy devotees of their craft, like Haydon, and the more fortunate, like Reynolds and Turner, Gainsborough and Wilkie, West and Allston. Literary men of all classes gather fresh inspiration and instruction from the biographies of literary men—an ample and most valuable class of lives, to which we shall again return.

The partial review which we have taken of these few classes of biographies and the grounds of their attractiveness for their several classes of readers, enable us to gain a more satisfactory view in regard to biography and biographical reading in general. We have seen that biography is attractive for the incidents which it records and the sympathy which it arouses with prominent actors. Biography is interesting to this or that reader just so far as he cares for and comprehends the incidents, the feelings, or the characters which biography describes. The lives of some men present pictures and emotions into which all, even the youngest and the most unreflecting, easily enter. In all cases, however, the interest must depend very largely upon the skill and success with which the scenes and characters are depicted. If the incidents are beyond the capacity of the reader to comprehend, through defect of age, culture, or reflection; if the feelings and character are such as he cannot or does not care to study or interpret —then the life cannot be interesting; it may be positively distasteful. We cannot expect the life of a metaphysician, a philologist, or scientist, to be intelligible or interesting to a child, or to a full-grown man whose knowledge and culture are limited. William Wordsworth was known to his neighbors only as a kind-hearted and frugal neighbor. Sir Walter Scott was esteemed by a large class of well-to-do acquaintances not as the magician of the North, but simply as the Sheriff who gave glorious suppers and was great in his talk of dogs and horses. Burns had a jolly set of associates, who cared more for the good fellowship than for the poetry of his songs. What could any of these friends of Wordsworth, Scott, or Burns know, or what should they care for the events or the characters which make the record of their lives so intensely interesting to the student of literature and the student of man ? That which made their lives so famous, and the story of them so exciting to a certain class of readers, lay entirely beyond the range of their comprehension and their sympathy.

While then, as we have seen, there are not a few bio-graphies which are within the range and comprehension of all classes of readers, there are many others which are reserved for men whose culture takes a special direction, or is of a higher order than is accorded to the many.

The first of these which we name are those which are eminently *psychological, i. e.*} those which involve an analysis and record of the inner processes or growth of the soul. There are not a few biographies of which the chief interest arises from and turns upon the changes in the inner life which they record. The external incidents of the life may be unexciting, the career of the man may have been very uneventful or very humble; but the record of the progress of the man, of his varied experiences of feeling, of the development of his intellect, and the changes in his opinions, of his new views of life, his strengthened faith, his refined culture, and his intellectual or moral achievements, lend an indescribable charm to the narrative, and gather around it a circle of excited readers.

It is obvious, however, that no man can be interested in such a biography who has never given attention to the pro-gress of his own inner life, or watched the several steps by which such progress has been made. Those who recognize the improvement of one's position in life as the great end of living, and who measure progress by the vulgar tests of gain in wealth or power, cannot be expected to understand or care for the inner life of a man who esteems the culture of the intellect, the refinement of the tastes, the victory over the selfish and sensual passions, and the enlargement and confirmation of all right and noble principles, as the most elevated ends to which any life can be devoted. Those who never look within but always look without, must find the biography of that which is within to be necessarily stupid and uninteresting. But those who care for their own improvement in good habits and noble achievements, and who are accustomed closely to watch and carefully to judge of their progress or failure in these particulars, may naturally be expected to study with intense and wakeful interest the inner record of any noble life, pro-vided the story be told with requisite skill. Those who include moral culture and religious growth in their conception of true progress, will follow with a lively interest any-such record which is sincere, provided the subject of it be otherwise so gifted as to attract the attention, or the story be told in such a way as to satisfy a pure and simple taste. Even the absence of any special gifts of nature or attainments of culture will often be abundantly compensated by pure aspirations and honest endeavors. The record of an honest and unlettered mind, if unskillfully made, like the life of John Woolman, the Quaker, can be so elevated by simple purity of heart, or like the life of John Bunyan, can be so irradiated by flashes of seraphic fire, as successfully to vindicate the essential superiority of moral and religious greatness over greatness of every other sort. But no gifts of genius in the subject or skill of portraiture in the writer can or ought to compensate for the absence of moral earnestness in a professedly ethical biography, or for the presence of the debasing alloy of Pharisaism and cant in a professedly religious life. Hypocrisy is always hollow; Pharisa-ism and affectation are invariably offensive, in proportion to the elevation of the ideals to which they pretend to rise, and the purity of the saintliness which they profess to imitate. Hence, while a good biography of a truly good man is the best and often the most inspiring of all biographies, if it be written with tolerable skill; an inflated, overstrained and laudatory life of a man who was very imperfectly or defectively good, is often one of the most offensive and depressing of books.

The temptation to error in the form of overdoing in the quantity and quality of moral and religious biography is ex-ceedingly strong. The religious public is frightfully inundated with the lives of persons whose lives had better not have been written, or if written, would better have been privately printed. It is the dictate of friendship to magnify the virtues of the departed, and to fail to notice their defects, when we look at either through the tears which we weep at their graves; but no man is, for such a reason, justified in setting forth the life of a person of merely commonplace goodness, simply because he was good. While every good life is far more eloquent and winning in the circle which it illumines than any book can be, those lives only deserve to be brought before the public in a book, which had characteristics sufficiently uncommon to make the goodness specially attractive when it is portrayed.

Second.—The lives which we have called psychological are usually most successfully written in greater or less part by the persons themselves who were the subjects of them— in part by their recorded conversations, their diaries and letters, or wholly in formal autobiographies. Hence the most satisfactory lives of really superior men are made up of their reported sayings, their private journals, and extracts from their correspondence, set in a framework of explanatory history. ***Boswell's Life of Dr. Johnson*** is, for two reasons, the best example of a life made up of sayings and conversations. The sayings of Johnson were well worth reporting for their intrinsic interest and value, or for the manner in which they were expressed, and Johnson had an admiring Boswell always at hand to report them. It has of late become much the fashion to make up the lives of significant men very largely from their journals and their letters. Some of the most instructive and delightful biographies of modern times are of this class; such as those of Robert Burns, Charles Lamb, Robert Southey, John Sterling, Walter Scott, John Wilson, Thomas Chalmers, Samuel Romilly, John Foster, Dr. Thomas Arnold; of Charlotte Bronte, J. Blanco White, Thomas Fowell

Buxton, Edward Irving, Richard Whately, B. G. Niebuhr, Frederick Perthes, John Keble, Frederick W. Robertson, Henry Crabb Robinson, Baron Bunsen, Theodore Parker, Margaret Fuller, Horace Mann, and Lyman Beecher.

In all these instances the persons named were more or less distinguished for public and literary activity. This fact suggests the remark that the lives of this class of persons are generally more instructive and interesting than those of any other. The reason certainly cannot be that their intellects were superior, or their principles were more elevated; that their feelings and tastes were more refined, or their influence was more commanding than were those of others whose lives remain wholly unwritten. It is rather that such men more frequently leave behind them copious materials of this sort. But even this is not universally the case. It is only men who write easily, and of such men only here and there one who leaves behind him a journal or diary in which he notes events as they occur, or records his views in regard to them, or his own principles, feelings, and aims. Many journals which are extended and copious are chiefly objective, and fail to express the individuality of the man, and to manifest his inmost feelings and the springs of his character. very many really able and communicative men fail to write letters with that fullness and freedom which should satisfy a biographer. But when all these conditions are present, when the character or career is worth describing, and the character and aims are copiously expressed by the individual himself, then we have the conditions of such a life as Lockhart's Life of Scott, or Stanley's Life of Arnold, or the Lives of B. G. Niebuhr and Frederick Perthes, of Thomas Fowell Buxton, and the Rev. F. W. Robertson.

The lives of men devoted to ***science or letters*** are spe-cially interesting for another reason. Such men reflect the sentiments of their times more completely and vividly than men of any other class. In great part they form these sentiments, or are the central points around which they gather. They give to these sentiments a concrete and personal interest, and cause the times to revive and live before the eyes of the reader. They are very often symbolic and representative men—men who either originate or impersonate some striking tendency of thought or feeling. At all events, they record in their own diaries and letters more or less fully, by allusion or formal discussion, the phases of thought and feeling which prevail in the community, and so preserve fresh and living pictures of transient and momentary events. These pictures are usually colored with the hues of their own personal feelings. They are warm with love, clouded by displeasure, or disturbed by anxiety or terror. English literature has of late been greatly enriched with many biographies of this class, of the choicest description—biographies interesting from the excellence of the character which they record, from the variety of incidents which they narrate, from the exciting phases of prevailing thought and feeling which they reflect, and from the insight which they open into the inner springs and motives of the persons described.

Autobiographies have for many, not to say for most persons, a peculiar charm. They do not always give so com-plete a picture of the inner life as we desire, nor do they reveal so fully what was characteristic of the man as we hope to discover when we begin to read; but they almost uniformly delight the student of human nature, by their honest and *naif* detail of what we are more or less curious to know. They are usually brief, almost every writer of his own life being apparently overcome with irresistible modesty when he attempts to introduce to the great public his comparatively humble self. They are often unfinished, the writer getting on very comfortably with the recollections of his childhood and the experiences and feelings of his early days, but growing suddenly timid as he is obliged to look in the face the follies, and perhaps the sins, of his later life, and not liking always to speak so freely of others, whether dead or living, as would be necessary should he speak freely of himself. It is worthy of notice how many brief sketches of this sort are suddenly broken off, as if the writer had become disgusted with thinking and talking about himself, and had left for his children a mere fragment, where they expected and longed for a full and detailed narrative of his entire life. We have, however, a few autobiographies that are tolerably complete, and they are all in their way fraught with interest. The life of Franklin is attractive for many reasons; but pre-eminently because it was written by himself, and because he tells a story which of itself is fitted to interest every poor boy who is beginning life, with a simplicity and directness which enlists the sympathies and holds the attention of every reader. No book has been more popular in our country than this. None has exerted a more powerful influence, not always of unmixed good. Tried by the more elevated standard of either pagan or Christian morality, it is often defective. The persistent self-seeking which crops out so offensively now and then, and the absence of faith in the more generous sentiments, as well as the sarcastic condescension with which Franklin treats revealed religion, are not always healthful. They have lowered the tone and weakened the faith and the principles of not a few. But with all these abatements its attractions are at this moment as fresh as at the first. It has in these days the additional merit of giving a vivid picture of simple times forever gone by, as well as of unfolding the inner movements of a very unique personality. For the same reason that the apprentice and clerk read Franklin with special interest, the scholar never tires of reading Gibson's ***Memoirs of his own Life and Writings***, or the brief autobiographies of ***Hume, Voltaire***, and ***Lord Herbert of Cherbury***. The lovers of excitement and adventure will return again and again to the autobiographies of ***Cellini, Vidocq, Wolfe Tone***, and ***Madame du Barri***. These autobiographies, with many others, are found in what professes to be a ***Collection of the most Interesting and Amusing Lives ever published, written by the parties themselves. London***: 1826-1832. This collection certainly contains a very great variety of very amusing and instructive reading. The fragments of autobiography which often precede the more elaborate lives of prominent men are almost invariably read and re-read with careful attention.

We cannot think that biography is especially uninteresting and unattractive. On the other hand, we believe that the want of interest in any life or class of lives must arise from one or more of three prominent causes—a want of capacity to comprehend the character described—a want of sympathy with his aims and principles, or some defect of skill in the biographer. "While, as we have seen, there are some biographies which interest both the young and the old, the uncultured and the refined, there is a very great number which, from the nature of the case, can only interest a few—according as they understand or care for the style of man which the life describes. It is therefore impossible to furnish any but the most general rules for the selection of this class of books—and it is, for this reason, less easy to select any list which may be called the best. What are the best for one age, or one degree and kind of culture, may be wholly unsuited for another.

There is no class of reading which is ***ethically*** more profitable than this. "When I am sick of the world in church and state, in solitude and in society," says a sharp and stern thinker, "I turn for relief to the portraits of two saintly heroes which hang in my library, and say to myself, These two were honest and noble men, and they teach me never to despair of mankind or of myself." In like manner there is nothing so quickening and elevating to the generous and high-minded as to read a few pages in the biography of one who has been a prince among men for greatness and goodness combined, especially if his life and character are largely interpreted by himself. "No young man can rise from the perusal of such lives as those of Buxton and Arnold without feeling his mind and heart made better, and his best resolves invigorated." " Horner says of the life of Sir Matthew Hale, that it filled him with enthusiasm; and of Condorcet's ***Eloge of Holler 'l*** never rise from the account of such men without a thrilling palpitation about me, which I know not whether I should call admiration, ambition, or despair " A snatch of such reading is like the injection of fresh and generous blood into the veins, or the drinking a generous and refreshing draught to one who is thirsty and faint, or the breathing copiously of a highly oxygenated atmosphere. That young man or young lady is to be congratulated who has his or her favorite biographies to which he or she habitually turns and returns—if, indeed, they present noble ideals. The lives of Dr. Arnold and of F. "W. Robertson have done more for the quickening and encouragement of Christian culture and of Christian nobleness in the present generation, than the personal influence of the two men when living—inspiring as were the teaching and intercourse of the one, and the preaching and conversation of the other. In no sense is it so eminently true, that the good which men do lives after them, as when the spirit and essence of their lives are embalmed in a worthy biography.

"More sweet than odors caught by him who sail3 Near spicy shores of Araby the blest, A thousand times more exquisitely sweet, The freights of holy feeling which we meet In thoughtful moments, wafted by the gales From fields where good men walk or bowers wherein they rest"

But how is it with the evil which bad men do ? Is not this equally powerful to ensnare and corrupt ? To this we reply, such evil is not often so frankly and fully exposed, and never by themselves; and herein is very strikingly illustrated the homage which vice pays to virtue. It is rare that a bad man confesses to the world in his letters how bad he is, unless he does it with repentance and shame. It is rarer even that a man writes down in his diary, as an eminent scholar was once in the habit of doing, " This day read the Antigone of Sophocles, after which I was desperately drunk." Or if a man occasionally forgets decency in his letters, and self-respect in his diary, it is rare that his biographer will spread out such revolting details for the perusal of the public. If he is forced to allude to the sins or the foibles of his hero, he usually endeavors to palliate and excuse them. No libertine or drunkard, no unbeliever in duty or denier of God, ever shines attractively in an honestly written life, or inspires his readers with a desire to be like him. But while the lives of bad or imperfect men do not attract, they very often warn. In the realm of biography the saying is emphatically fulfilled, " The name of the wicked shall rot." The memory of the wicked does rot, either in the withering neglect of succeeding gen-erations, to which it is so often doomed, or in the putrescent phosphorescence at whose lurid light posterity stares and shudders.

In view of these considerations, we advise for all those who have leisure and opportunity a large and liberal reading of biography. We advise that the taste for this description of reading should be fostered. If fostered, it certainly will grow more active and intense. The study of biography is the study of man. A generous familiarity with the lives of men of all sorts of opinions tends to liberalize the feelings and to enlarge the understanding. Its influence in this regard is like that of a very extended and varied acquaintanceship with living men. Nor need we fear to study the lives or to converse with the characters of men from whom we differ very widely in opinions, or diverge very materially in our sympathies. If our own principles are fixed, we shall find sufficient strength and inspiration from the lives of the, men with whom we agree in opinions and character to enable us to withstand, as far as we ought to desire, any counter-influence from the lives of those with whose opinions we do not entirely sympathize. No man of liberal culture can afford to be without —no such person ought to desire to be wholly without— the liberalizing influence which comes from a study of the lives of men of the greatest variety of opinions and characters. On the other hand, no man whose opinions are fixed or whose principles are earnest can fail to have his favorite biographies, his lives of men most loved and honored, to which he continually resorts—it may be to enjoy with them a few moments' converse in their most elevated moods, or perhaps to rise by their aid to those noble positions which the soul is more competent to gain for an hour than to keep for a day.

Of biographical reading we may say, that the man who has no heroes among the truly noble of the earth, must have either a sordid or a conceited spirit. He must be too ignoble to admire that which is really above himself, or must be too satisfied with himself to care to concern himself with the characters or the claims of others. He who reverences and admires no one of the great and good of other times, is likely to reverence and admire the man who is least worthy of honor and admiration, and that is himself,—and to bring to his altar an unshared and solitary worship.

Two rules may serve in the selection and judgment of biographies. The first is, " see that the man whose life you would read had a marked and distinctive character." The second is, " see that this character be set forth with truthfulness and skill." A man with small individuality, either of gifts or of goodness, is not entitled to have his life written, and certainly has no claim that his life should be read. The circumstance that he held a high position in life, or attracted honor or attention from his wealth or rank or office, is of the slightest possible significance to those who come after him, provided there was nothing in his genius, his industry, or his goodness which entitles him to the consideration of others. Mere goodness which is commonplace, however useful and honorable in the living, cannot shine as an example through a written life, unless there was something distinctive enough to attract the attention and to impress the feelings of lookers-on. The number of stupid biographies which encumber our libraries, of lords and generals and bishops, and of clergymen and physicians and lawyers who were simply significant from their position, is something frightful to contemplate. Now and then they fill several bulky volumes. They are glanced at by a limited circle, and stand upon the shelves of our libraries, to be consulted by an antiquarian or a genealogist, and this is all the service which they render.

It is not enough, however, that the subject of the life should have had something in his character that was so distinctive as to be worth recording. The life should be skilfully set forth by his biographer. The power of seizing the individual characteristics by nice analysis, or of interpreting them by sagacious generalizations, does not " come by nature " to all biographers. The gift of selecting from conversations and correspondence what is worth preserving is not possessed—certainly it is not exercised, by all. To narrate with method and clearness, and also with spirit and life, is not so easy to a writer as it is pleasant to the reader.

The following protest, directed against the indiscriminate publication of an author's remains, is equally appropriate to those lumbering biographies in which little wise selection rules:—

" The imperfect thing or thought,
The fervid yeastiness of youth,
The dubious doubt, the twilight truth, The work that for the passing day was wrought, The schemes that came to naught,

" The sketch half-way 'twixt verse and prose,
That mocks the finished picture true,
The splinters whence the statue grew, The scaffolding 'neath which the palace rose, The vague, abortive throes,

"And crudities of joy or gloom:—
In kind oblivion let them be!
Nor has the dead worse foe than he Who rakes these sweepings of the artist's room, And piles them on his tomb."

"Whether a particular biography will meet the conditions prescribed must be left, in most cases, to the judgment of the reader himself. To attempt to make a selection from the very rich and copious library of works of this class with which English literature abounds, would be difficult, if not impracticable, within our limits. We must ask the reader to accept in its place the classification which we have made, and the illustrative examples which we have cited under its several heads.

CHAPTER XV.

NOVELS AND NOVEL-READING.

FROM History and Biography to Fiction and Poetry the transition is natural and easy. It is none other than from true to what Lord Bacon calls " feigned history" —the one being the narration of events which have actually occurred, the other the narration of events which are only supposed to have taken place. The form of the two is the same; the matter is different. The story which the novelist and poet narrate would be history if what is narrated had actually taken place. But the end in both cases always is or always should be the same—*i. e.*y the communication of truth ; not always what we call real truth in the sense of actual or literal occurrences, but always real truth in the sense of those relations and impressions which are real in that import which is most comprehensive and profound. Whenever the imagination, by its creations of incidents and drapery, can assert or impress truth of this kind more effectually than the memory by its transcripts from reality, then is it at liberty to do so, provided it does not disturb the relations of truth to veracity. There are other ends for which the truth is conveyed than the ends of instruction and science. It may often be largely for ends of amusement; but it is truth nevertheless. The mirror of the imagination must always reflect nature, though with enlarged and altered proportions. The criterion of every good work of imagination is well expressed by the description of the *Arcadia* of Sir Philip Sidney as a work of which " the invention is wholly spun out of the phansie, but conformable to the possibilitie of truth in all particulars."

We have already defended works of imagination from ignorant and prejudiced objections. We have also sought to show that the highest advantage which can come of literature and reading of all kinds is the .service which they render to the imagination, as they enrich it with multiform and varied images of beauty, elevate it by noble associations, and inspire it with pure emotions. We shall neither repeat nor expand our argument in vindication of Fiction and Poetry. If anything needs to be added, it will naturally present itself in our suggestions concerning the wise and profitable use of both.

Prose Fiction is of comparatively recent growth in English literature. It is within the present century that it has attained its gigantic proportions. Our grandmothers read ***Rasselas, The Vicar of Wakefield, Sir Charles Grandison***, ***The Castle of Otranto***, and a few other tales. Some of our grandfathers allowed themselves now and then the entertainment of ***Tom Jones, Humphrey Clinker***, and ***Tristram Shandy***. There are thousands of their grandchildren who would be puzzled to tell what novels they have read, or to recite the names of their authors— both are so numerous. Two novels a week is the smallest number that is produced as an average from the British Press, if we say nothing of the novels translated from the French and German; and the names of all the leading popular novelists it would be difficult for even the most desperate and practised novel-reader to recount. The year 1814, in which ***Waverley*** was published, ushered in the new period of English, and, we may say, of modern fiction, and since that time the number and variety of novels has been steadily increasing. The writing of Fiction has been widened and enriched as an art, and the reading of Fiction has been more distinctly recognized and worthily appreciated as a means of culture and a source of enjoyment. Juvenile Fiction has of late been increased to well nigh enormous dimensions. The writing of novels has become one of the regular professions; the reading of novels is the chief occupation of a certain class of persons who are exempt from the ordinary claims of business or study, and even the criticism of novels has become a specialty—almost as much as the criticism of art or music. The world of Fiction in many minds overbears and outweighs the world of reality. To not a few, the creations of the imagination are more interesting and absorbing than those of real life. With many persons the successful conduct of a plot excites more interest and elicits a more active criticism than the direction of a campaign, and the de-velopment of a fictitious character is watched with as keen an interest as the life and fortunes of a great general or an eminent statesman. The issue of a tangled story is followed more anxiously than the result of an exciting criminal trial, or a closely contested political canvass.

Prof. David Masson, in his very able and readable work on ***British Novelists***, divides British novels, since Scott's appearance in the field, into thirteen classes, as follows : 1. The Novel of Scottish Life and Manners; 2. The Novel of Irish Life and Manners; 3. The Novel of English Life and Manners; 4. The Fashionable Novel; 5. The Illustrious Criminal Novel; 6. The Traveler's Novel; 7. The Novel of American Manners and Society; 8. The Novel of Eastern Manners and Society ; 9 and 10. The Military and Naval Novel; 11. The Novel of Supernatural Phantasy; 12. The Art and Culture Novel; 13. The Historical Novel.

This classification cannot be accepted as exhaustive, but it may serve to impress the reader with the variety of topics that are treated in modern novels, as well as be convenient for reference and illustration. A broader and simpler classification is that which divides all novels into two groups, according as they are more or less conspicuously Novels of Incident or Novels of Character, *i. e.*, according as they are more or less occupied with pictures to the objective phantasy, or as they present strongly marked and strikingly individualized characters. There are no novels of incident in which various personages do not figure largely, but there is only now and then one in which these personages have the relief and reality of living men and women, with a distinct personal existence and a strongly marked individuality. On the other hand, there are no novels of character in which there is not more or less of a story or plot. But the interest in all novels which deserve to be so-called, turns invariably upon the illustration or the development of character. Novels of incident are especially fitted for the young, because their tastes are eminently objective. They like an exciting and picturesque story, no matter how grotesque and improbable it may be. Persons are as real and objective to them as incidents and events. It is what these do and suffer for which their readers care, not what they are, or how their characters are impeded or made known. With the analysis of their motives, their inner conflicts of feeling, and the developments or changes of their character, their readers have little concern. The excitement of the story is the chief attraction, and if the story is exciting, they neither care nor inquire whether the events are probable or possible, or whether the characters are natural or true. Nor are they fastidious in respect to either imagery or style. Indeed, provided the imagery is bold, they do not care if it be coarse and highly-colored; and provided the language be strong and passionate, they do not mind if it be declamatory and raving. The taste of young people in respect to novels is very like their taste for food. They do not totally reject the more delicate fruits and dishes,, but they swallow them without discrimi-nation, and without appreciating their exquisite flavor. But the stronger and coarser edibles they devour not only with no offence, but often with an astonishing relish, as unripe apples, squash-like melons, rank soups, and ranker meats. They are not insensible to Robinson Crusoe and the Pilgrim's Progress, and the manifold *delicatesses* of modern fiction; but they do not see the difference between these and the *Pirate's Own Book, Jack Sheppard Beadle s Dime Novels*, and the sensational stories which inflate the English language till it almost bursts with the expansion, and whose heroes scream out all the possible varieties of hysterical passion. There is nothing which is more amazing to a refined and cultured mother than the favorite stories of her obstreperous boy. But all this is in the course of nature, and will be outgrown in the progress of time. There is hope that the boy will grow up to his mother's tastes, if her tastes in reading are cultured and re-fined. But what hope is there for him if her favorite novels are, in point of culture, not higher than his coarse and sensational stories ? As long as the savage sees lines and shades of beauty in the tattooing or the war-paint that makes the face hideous, and the wild African grins with ecstacy at the flaunting colors which shame the noon, so long will sensation novels of the vulgar sort be read with eagerness, and be written, lauded, and sold. It is well to remember that the acquisition of wealth does not necessarily bring refinement in the intellectual tastes, and that much which is called culture of the superficial sort, and which enables a person to be self-possessed and at ease in society, does not of course involve culture of the imagination or the intellectual judgment. Fashionable people, and people who aspire to give tone to society, may delight in low and vulgar novels. Even persons who are morally pure and right-hearted may want the capacity to discriminate between what is high and low toned in fiction. It now and then happens that a family rises suddenly to wealth from abjeet poverty. Its members pass in a month from rags to satins, and from squalor to diamonds, and assume the airs of their new position with what success they may. Usually, however, some defect in their new appointments betrays that their culture is not complete. Sometimes *their shoes* or their lace or their jewelry reveal their essential vulgarity; sometimes it is the low and vulgar character of the fiction in which they delight. In cases that are not so extreme there are people whose aristocracy is unquestioned, and whose manners have the unmistakable confidence that bespeaks a well-established social position, who by the novels which they habitually read, betray the essential vulgarity of their intellectual tastes, and the low grade of their aesthetic culture. Few things are more properly offensive to the traveler than to see a second or third rate novel in the hands of a well-dressed and well-mannered lady, or an intelligent and otherwise well-cultured youth. Few indications are more depressing than to enter a house in which wealth and comfort abound, in which taste and refinement are everywhere manifest, and perhaps a high tone of moral and religious feeling is maintained, and yet to find that the library of the family is made up of a score or two of third-rate novels, with perhaps a few books of devotion.

If we suppose the taste for different kinds of fiction to be developed in a normal way from youth to age, from rudeness to culture, the novel of mere incident will gradually give way to the novel of character. The personage with a name and nothing more, who figures in so many stories for children, and in so many sensational novels for grown people, will be required to give some indications of individual personality. The reader will learn to look for men, and men of definite and unmistakable individuality, in the leading characters of any novel which he tolerates or delights in. He will by and by learn to notice that character cannot be made known with skill or success, by mere description, but must be expressed in the words or deeds of the personages portrayed—that a long-winded and elaborate setting forth of what sort of a man this or that person is, attended perhaps with a commentary upon the characteristics of his class, is not nearly so satisfactory to the reader as the brief or pithy sayings which are put into his mouth, or his characteristic actions when brought into a critical position. The *second step* of progress in the taste for fiction may be said to be attained when the reader has learned to prefer the novel of character to the novel of incident, and can distinguish the one from the other.

The *third stage* is reached when the reader learns to study and analyze the characters which he finds in fiction; when they not only enlist his sympathies by assuming distinct and personal being, but he can study them in their motives, trace out their springs and discover their leading traits, and illustrate them to his own judgment by examples from real life. This interest is greatly heightened if the characters are complex, perplexing, and apparently contradictory; and if the real secret is veiled and withheld till the development of the plot is complete. Novels of character must of course differ greatly in the style of character which they furnish, and their adaptation to the power of the reader to comprehend them, or his capacity to enjoy them. The perplexities of a hero or heroine may arise from speculative studies or religious difficulties, or from social inequalities, or a morbid mood induced by a childhood of wealth and luxury, or by some reverse of fortune. Whatever may be the occasion, if the kind of human being is not such as should be looked for in the ordinary experience of human life, and can only be developed from an exceptional nature or a very rare conjunction of circumstances, the power to understand the character will be possessed by few. Or again, if the principal interest in the hero arises out of the peculiarities of his profession, (as of a musician or artist, like **Charles Auchester**,) the idiosyncrasies of his nature can only be fully appreciated by a few. Then, if the habits of the novelist be scientific or philosophical, and he wishes to exhibit a hero occupied with his specialty, or exemplifying certain limited habits, or if he sets forth the character by technical or scholastic terminology, or a professional or philosophical dialect, he can expect no more than a limited class of readers. All the so-called novels of **purpose** or, as they might be termed, propagandist or doctrinal novels, whether they be Christian or Infidel, Romanist or Neological, High Church or Evangelical, Episcopal or Presbyterian, Royalist or Republican, Conservative or Radical, Slavery or Anti-slavery, Poor Law or Anti-poor Law, Protectionist or Free Trade, so far as they involve any properly theoretic discussions, as distinguished from pictures of personal or social life or public and individual tendencies, —can strongly attract those readers only who have some special knowledge of or interest in the subjects discussed, whatever may be the interest of the plot or the individuality of the characters. In general, novels that are in any way specialized, whether because the topics handled are necessarily limited, or because the mode of handling is not adapted to the habits and tastes of men of ordinary culture, must necessarily be reserved for a limited class of readers.

No man in his senses would aspire to read all the novels, or even the majority of the novels that are written and published. It is within the limits of possibility that a person who should restrict himself to this kind of reading, and should devote to it say six or eight hours a day, and allow himself no respite for sickness or holidays, might, in a certain sense, read the most of the novels that are now published in the English language. But who would desire to do this ? Who would not refuse the task with disgust and revulsion if it should, be imposed upon him ? Most persons would rebel for higher reasons than because the occupation would be a task. The task itself would be most ungrateful. To be forced to occupy one's mind with feeble or extravagant portraitures of scenes and incidents, with inadequate or distorted delineations of character, with false and repulsive conceptions of honor, duty, and life; to give one's self up for the waking hours of every day to the control of the depraved or frivolous taste or the prurient imagination of now a weak and then a strong but corrupt nature, should be esteemed an intolerable bondage. No man with a moderate endowment of human feeling or manly spirit could endure it long. There is a show of reason why the reader of history should feel obliged to read many histories which he would prefer to leave unread, or why a philosopher or critic must read many weak and illogical treatises that give very poor returns of thought. But a poor novel is very poor and un-satisfying. It is not -only so weak as to sicken, but it is so offensive as to disgust the man who has any positive tastes which he cherishes, or who sets much value upon his time. "We might add in the case of many, by any man who has any regard for his reputation; for the man or the woman who systematically dawdles away his or her time over a succession of third or fourth rate novels, weak in imagination and doubtful in morality, deserves a very low place in the estimate of people whose good opinion is worth regarding. There is no description of filth that is so filthy or so tenacious as that which comes from handling an equivocal or obscene novel. A white-gloved hand is for ever soiled by a smutch that cannot be drawn off with the glove, if seen to hold a low-lived and trashy tale, such as many a fashionable miss and pretentious coxcomb are known to handle.

If we cannot and would not read all the novels that are published, we should read the best. What the best are, it is not always easy to decide. The novel which is the best for the child is not the best for the youth; the best for the youth is not the best for the man; the best for one man is not the best for another. The child and the youth, as we have seen, delight in the objective novel—the novel of incident—above the novel of character. By the same rule, the man of introverted and reflective tastes not only prefers the novel of character, but requires that the characters delineated should themselves be of the speculative and introverted cast, and that the plot and dialogue should turn upon some recondite theme, or illustrate some important speculative truth. The tastes of men in respect to the novels which they prefer are as various as their tastes in dress, in manners, and in companions. The only limits under which this rule can be safely and wisely applied, are that every man should have tastes which he can safely follow, and that he should know what his tastes actually are; and that, having tastes that are not evil, and knowing them well, he should have the courage to consult and follow them, despite the rigors of conventionality and fashion.

Every man has his moods as well as his tastes. The novel that is fitted for one mood is not suited for another. If simple amusement or relaxation is required, a novel may be just the book for a man who would not care to read it at a time when his aims were higher and more severe. If instruction is required, the novel may be tolerated which would not satisfy if it were required to amuse, elevate, or enrich the imagination. A novel may be good for traveling, which it is scarcely worth while for a busy or earnest person to read at home. A reader of independent and liberal spirit would also carefully avoid giving himself up to the control of any single novelist. While every reader ought, on the one hand to be select in his reading of fiction, he should shun being so select as to limit his reading to a single writer, even though by general consent the writer should be pronounced the best. At least it should be required that the author be the best for him, by his fitness to his individual habits and tastes, and even to his prevailing moods. The reasons for this rule are two. No class of writers, except perhaps the poet, can diffuse himself so completely into his writings as the novelist, and can do it so insensibly to the reader. The reader may seem to find nothing but a description of scenery, or a picture of domestic life, or a delineation of a person, or the record of conversations or the development of a plot. All these elements may be so skillfully woven together, and may stand out so prominently from the canvass, as to give the impression of objective reality. The whole may be finished with the careful minuteness of Gerard Dow, or with the defiant boldness of Rubens, and still the picture, whether of nature, man, or human life, will be the picture as seen by the novelist's eyes and reflected in the novelist's mind, and it is through his eyes and his mind that we must look at it, if we see it at all. Or he seems to open to our inspection the workings of a highly individualized character in extraordinary circumstances of trial and perplexity, like Morton in **Old Mortality**, or Becky Sharp in **Vanity Fair**, or Oliver Twist as described by Dickens, or Jane Eyre by Charlotte Bronte, or Mary Barton by Mrs. Gaskell, or Dinah in **Adam Bede**, or the preacher of Salem Chapel by Mrs. Olyphant. All that we seem at first view to see is the individual skillfully described; at the second view we discern, perhaps, that this seeming individual is also a representative human being, combined and created by the dexterous hand of the artist, working after the nice observation of the artist's eye. It is not often that we take a third observation, and discern that it is some representative man, not merely as discerned by the dispassionate eye, but as judged by the principles and colored by the feelings, and distorted, it may be, by the prejudices of the writer.

Thackeray, and Dickens, and Miss Bronte, and George Eliot have each a private practical philosophy of their own, even though it is unconsciously held, according to which they must construct all the types of human nature which they draw. It would have been morally impossible that either should conceive or portray the characters depicted by the other. This practical philosophy of life, this creed concerning the ends of human excellence, and the ideal of human perfection, is that which sweetens or sours many superior novels, and causes them to emit the aroma of health and life or the poison of disease and death.

Again, second—no class of writers exercises so complete control over their readers as novelists do. This control reaches, to their opinions and prejudices, if it does not insensibly control and reshape their entire philosophy of duty and of life. The fascination which they exercise becomes of itself a spell. No enchantment is so entire and delightful as that with which they invest the story which they recite. It is a very glamour which they pour not only over the scenes which they depict, but over the senses of the beholder. With this enchantment and fascination come the ready and even the forward acceptance of their practical philosophy, and even of their accidental prejudices. A favorite novelist becomes, for the time being, often more to his enamored and enchanted reader than preacher, teacher, or friend, and indeed than the whole world besides, casting a spell over his judgments, moulding his principles, forming his associations, and recasting his prejudices. The entranced and admiring reader runs to his favorite when he can snatch an hour from labor, society, or sleep. He broods over his scenes and characters when alone, he quotes from him as often as he dare, he cites proverbs and favorite phrases from his leading personages. He even aspires to be familiar with his slang and his cant. He warms with incensed ardor if his reputation is attacked. He defends linn if he is criticised or unfavorably judged. He is impatient if another is preferred to him. The partisan of Thackeray and Dickens is always ready to couch a lance for his favorite.

Indeed we may go further, and say that the devoted reader of a favorite novelist often becomes for the time an unconscious imitator or a passive reflex of his author. Like the chameleon, he takes the color of the bough and leaf from which he feeds. He is more likely to absorb and reproduce his defects than his excellences. The admiring and passionate devotee of Dickens is in danger of copying his broad caricature, his not very elevated or elevating slang, and the free and easy swing of the society in which Mr. Dickens delights. On the other hand, the intellectual and high-toned devotee of Thackeray is likely to be not a little satirical, suspicious, and dissatisfied; to affect the ***nil admi-rari*** and the air of one who is compelled to live in a world of which he has already seen the hollo wness, and for which he is a little too good. The admiring students of George Eliot take a pensive view of our human life, sympathize hopelessly with its sorrows and its tragedies, and above all, with its moral enigmas, seeing for it no redemption and no hope. "They are as sad as night only for wantonness." Their burden is, the times are out of joint—oh cursed spite, that we were ever born to set them right Charles Kings-ley's readers, on the other hand, are ready to set everything right by the force of muscle and pluck, of bravado and faith. The admirer of the witty O. W. Holmes is crisp, Voltairish, and satirical. The devotee of Hawthorne is unrelenting in certain moody prejudices, Epicurean in his tastes and aspirations, and dreamy and uncertain in his theory of this life and the next. The admirer of Mrs. Stowe is generous, rash, one-sided and positive, and given to a variety of over-doing. So complete a subjection to a single novelist, even for a limited time, is not desirable, because its tendency is to make us one-sided and unnatural. For the same reason we should not confine ourselves entirely to current and contemporary novels. Strong as is the temptation to do this, by reason of the greater freshness of the novel for our own times, this temptation should sometimes be overcome, if for no other reason than to give the reader a wide range of vision, and to bring him back to his favorites of the passing hour with a fresher eye and a less partial judgment.

Nor should novels constitute our sole reading. The temptation is strong to make them so, especially with young persons, and those who are responsible only to themselves for the use or abuse of their time. It is not easy to turn to a history or scientific essay when an attractive novel is lying by its side, particularly for one to whom novel-reading is new. There is no fascination connected with reading to be compared with that experienced in youth from the first few novels. The spell-bound reader soon discovers, however, that this appetite, like that for confection-ery and other sweets, is the soonest cloyed, and that if pampered too long it en-feebles the appetite for all other food. The reader of novels only, especially if he reads many, becomes very soon an intellectual voluptuary, with feeble judgment, a vague memory, and an incessant craving for some new excitement. It is rare that a reader of this class studies the novels which he seems to read. He knows and cares little for the novel of character as contrasted with the novel of incident. He reads for the story as he says, and it usually happens that the sensational and extravagant, the piquant and equivocal stories are those which please him best. Exclusive and excessive novel reading is to the mind as a kind of intellectual opium eating, in its stimulant effects upon the phantasy and its stupifying and bewildering influence on the judgment. An inveterate novel-reader speedily becomes a literary *roue*, and this is possible at a very early period of life. It now and then happens that a youth of seventeen becomes almost an intellectual idiot or an effeminate weak-ling by living exclusively upon the enfeebling swash or the poisoned stimulants that are sold so readily under the title of tales and novels. An apprenticeship at a reform school in literature, with a spare diet of statistics, and a hard bed of mathematical problems, and the simple beverage of plain narrative, is much needed for the recovery of such inane and half-demented mortals.

Why, then, it may be asked, should we read novels at all ? Why not set them aside altogether, especially as the quantity of light literature of other descriptions is so great, and the quality of it is constantly improving ? These questions are certainly fair questions, and merit answers as explicit and as fair. We have to answer first: The reading of fiction furnishes a kind of amusement and relaxation which no other reading can give. There can be no question that this description of "feigned history serveth and confcrreth to *delectation*." No intellectual enjoyment is so delightful as this. No withdrawment from one's customary occupations and associations is so complete as that which a good novel effects; no breaking up of the .cares and the sorrows, of the weariness and the fears of the ordinary life is so entire as that which an absorption in its scenes and an interest in its personages so easily accomplishes. That this indulgence is attended with special dangers and peculiar temptations we cannot deny; but that the amusement and relaxation are innocent and desirable, every rational man will acknowledge. Many of the bravest workers for God and man have found this sort of relaxation to be the most complete, and have used it with the happiest results. Why it should be so is not difficult to discern. Do we delight in a vacant hour to survey a quiet nook, a placid river, a luxuriant valley, or an ample and varied panorama ? We open a novel, and one scene after another rises before the mental vision more rapidly and in quicker succession than any which nature can present. Does it rest the brain because it amuses the mind to gaze upon a crowded street, and to watch the motley and brilliant succession of the passers-by? But over the pictured page of animated fiction, one group follows after another of men and women, of children and youth, in country and town, crushing and jostling in the alleys and thoroughfares of the city, lounging upon the open lawn, or sauntering along the shaded lanes of the country. Tournaments, races, hunting courses, fishing parties, rushing cavalry, marching infantry, gangs of robbers, stealthy assassins, a cavalcade of knights, a tribe of Bedouins, a gang of gipsies, a band of pirates, pass and repass in swift suc-cession before the mind's eye. Does it refresh because it excites us in a new direction to tell and hear the news of our neighbors, or of the last fire, shipwreck, or battle? But it refreshes us more, because it excites us less painfully, to follow the fortunes of a few imaginary beings with whom the novelist acquaints us completely, and in whom he contrives to interest us profoundly,—as they pass from sunlight to shade, and from shade to sunlight, till, in our anxious or our curious sympathy for them, we lose for the hour all thought and care even for our personal joys and sorrows.

The novel *instructs* as well as amuses the reader, and it instructs him by methods and in directions in which no other reading can. It instructs him in **History**, as has already been explained in our remarks upon the historical novel. It instructs him in respect to *scenery* as no traveler ever does, and as few travelers would dare to attempt. The pictures of the oriental plain, jungle, and forest; of the Irish bog, pass, and shieling; of the Scottish heath, loch, and manse, and of the English lawn, cottage, and rectory; of hedge-rows and oak vistas, of clumps of yew and game preserves; of the American prairie, forest, and the settler's clearing and log cabin ; of the Southern negro quarters, rich fields, and hunting grounds, which we find in countless novels, are invaluable as substitutes for views of those scenes which we cannot receive by the eye, and as reminders of those which we have actually seen. No man with a moderate amount of curiosity can well afford to dispense with such pictures. The cultivated person whose curiosity has not yet been awakened, may need, most of all, that this curiosity should be excited in ways which, and for ends in respect to which, there can be no substitute for the novel.

The novel instructs in respect to the ***domestic and social life*** of other countries, or grades of life in our own country to which few readers can have direct access, and fewer, if they have such access, can observe and judge of fully. The reader of Scott and "Wilson, of Hogg and Macdonald, learns to understand and to sympathize with Scottish life and manners, and to appreciate the Scottish character, as he could not possibly do in any other method. In a similar way Lever and Lover have made it possible for us to understand Ireland and the Irish, in their blunders and their genius; their frugality and their improvidence; their wit and their folly; their beauty and their squalor, on manifold more sides of their character than any personal observation or reports of fact or history could qualify us to know and love them. Bulwer and George Eliot, Mrs. Gaskell and Trollope, Dickens and Thackeray, enable the foreigner to understand somewhat of the secret of English society, with its singular contradictions of conventionality and independence, of suspicion and confidence, of blandness and gruffness. They even introduce us to the sacred privacy of the English home, without the doubtful experiment of letters of introduction, or the more questionable impudence of thrusting open the door. Does not every English reader of the tales of Miss Bremer and Miss Carlin feel that he owes to them obligations of gratitude which he cannot repay for the fresh and delightful pictures of Swedish manners and Swedish life with which their tales abound? Have not Freytag, Tautphæus, and Auerbach and Spielhagen, done the same for German life ? and have not Balzac, Paul de Kock, George Sand, Eugene Sue, Alexander Dumas, and Victor Hugo taught these readers more of the worst side of life in Paris and in France than it is desirable or healthful for many of these readers to learn ? Of Italian life and manners, Manzoni and Ruffini give us delightful pictures.

That the wise reading of novels is fitted to ***enlarge our acquaintance with human nature***, and in this way to give the most valuable instruction, is sufficiently obvious. It invites, and often compels us to enter into the thoughts and feelings, and to share in the experiences of men and women most remote from our personal observation or our possible acquaintance. It opens to us the heart of the skeptic in his torments of doubt and his gropings after certainty. It makes us watch the tempted man as he maintains his doubtful step along the narrow and swaying bridge that overhangs the fearful gulf, or to recoil with horror as he makes the desperate plunge. It opens to our inspection the inner being of the condemned. It enables us to overhear the fearful soliloquies of the cell, and the procession that leads to the scaffold. In manifold methods does it enlarge our knowledge, enlighten our personal experience, and widen and make yielding our sympathies. In short, it lets us into a wide range of human experiences, under the greatest possible variety of conditions, of excitements, and of issues. It places at our service the results of the sharp observation, the subtle analysis, the earnest sympathies, and the skilful interpretations of many of the most gifted students of humanity, who present the products of their observation and their skill in a form best fitted to attract the attention of the unreflecting, and to excite the curiosity of the listless—the form of an exciting and artistic tale. If the representations are often too extreme and too highly-colored to correspond to the observations and experiences of fact, and if it may reasonably be objected that for this reason they are actually misleading as representations of human nature as it is, it cannot be charged that they mis-represent the ideal possibilities of human nature; that they either overpaint human nature as it is desirable it should be in its good, or degrade its evil lower than it is conceivable it should sink. If either happen, it does not follow that the most important results of substantial truths are not attained. If stronger impressions concerning the evil or the good of human nature are thereby achieved than could possibly be reached in any other way, then the mind is taught the most essential truth, while the imagination is enriched in respect to the range and variety of conceivable or ideal human experiences.

The objection may sometimes hold good against novels of incident, that they excite mischievous expectations of ex-traordinary turns of fortune, and beget, even in sober and sensible people, a romantic and dreamy habit of mind in respect to the chances of success in life, and the conditions by which it is to be achieved. Nothing too severe can be said against the mischievous influence of a certain class of so-called romantic stories upon uncertain, shuffling, indolent, and brooding sort of people, with feeble energies and strong self-indulgence. It is not such novels that we commend, but novels of character. A similar objection might be urged against the influence of novels of the latter class —that they encourage extravagant views of what a person may become in character, or of what he may demand of his associates or expect from his fellow-men. If such a tendency should now and then be observed, we may set off against it the very desirable and elevating influence in the other direction, which comes from elevated ideals of character in ourselves and in others. If our conceptions of character be correct as to their principles or elements, they cannot be too elevated or noble in the scale after which they are adjusted. They should be human and practical and ethical and Christian, but they cannot be too unselfishar aspiring.The sordid, the mean, and the prosaic; the selfish, the trickish,and the bullying; the uncultivated, the sensual, and the vile, are already so rampant and unblushing in our religion, our politics, our literature, and our society, that there is little danger from excess in literature in the direction of the nobly romantic and the ideal. Whatever fiction can contribute to quicken and elevate the imagination, so far as its ideals and estimates of character are concerned, is only actual and positive gain to the sum of good influences; and it is a gain of a kind which cannot easily be spared.

It is not a trivial advantage of the novel reading of our day that it suggests elevated and quickening ***topics for con-versation***. This advantage is not a trivial one, when we reflect that conversation too readily degenerates into gossiping personalities or unmeaning twaddle about the weather, or the last insignificant occurrence that happens to interest any person present. For young persons especially it is of no little service to have topics at hand that are fruitful of thought, that awaken .a warm interest and call out positive opinions. The last new novel is suggestive in all these directions. It stimulates to the analysis of its characters and the criticism of its plot, and calls out likings and dislikings, which the holders of either are forward to assert and defend. These opinions, and the rea-sons by which they are defended, invariably turn upon the observations of actual life, characters and manner which the parties may have made, and in this way stimulate to activity of thought and independence of judgment. Even if the novel is second-rate, the incidents unnatural, and the characters extravagant, the effect of discussing these is usually good. Novel-reading is a powerful educating influence in whatever aspect it is regarded, and though it may often educate to evil, its power to stimulate from barrenness and frivolity should never be overlooked.

Having already answered the two questions, ***what*** novels we should read, and ***why***, it may not be amiss to inquire how we should read them. "What we have already said upon the general topic of how we ought to read all books, will apply with pre-eminent propriety to the reading of novels, because there is no description of reading in which there is greater exposure to the worst of habits. Coleridge has pungently enough described these habits: " As to the devotees of circulating libraries, I dare not compliment their ***pass-time***, or rather ***kill-time***, with the name of ***reading***. Call it rather a sort of beggarly day-dreaming, during which the mind of the dreamer furnishes for itself nothing but laziness and a little mawkish sensibility, while the whole ***materiel*** and imagery of the dose is supplied ***ab extra*** by a sort of mental ***camera obscura*** mannfactured at the printing-office, which ***pro tempore*** fixes, reflects, and transmits the moving phantasms of one's own delirium, so as to people the barrenness of an hundred other brains afflicted with the same trance or suspension of all common sense and all definite purpose. We should, therefore, transfer this species of amusement .... from the genus *reading* to that comprehensive class characterized by the power of contrary, yet coexisting, propensities of human nature, namely, indulgence of sloth and hatred of vacancy. In addition to novels and tales of chivalry in prose or rhyme (by which last I mean neither rhythm nor metre) this genus comprises as its species, gaming, swinging or swaying on a chain or gate, spitting over a bridge, smoking, snuff-taking, tête-à-tête quarrels after dinner between husband and wife, conning, word by word, all the advertisements of the daily advertiser in a public-house on a rainy day, etc., etc."

These remarks are pointed and explicit as to *how not to read novels*, and the reader can very easily infer by the rule of contraries how to read them.

They also forcibly suggest the inquiries—" What is the method after which children read the majority of the books called tales and stories, which make up so large a share of juvenile and Sunday-school libraries? What is the average value of the great mass of 'juvenile'books which are prepared by the score every month to quicken the intellect and elevate the imaginations of the rising generation? Are not the most of these books *eminently juvenile* in the greenness and crudeness of their authors as well as of their work?"

CHAPTER XVI.

POETRY AND POETS.

"WHAT is Poetry ? We ask this question, because in order wisely to select the poetry which we read, as well as to read with intelligence and sympathy that which we select, we need to know what poetry is; so far at least as to be able to discriminate the real from the factitious and the counterfeit. But to answer our question we do not need to construct or defend an elaborate theory of poetry. Nor need we study and criticise the several theories which have been proposed, from Aristotle and Horace, down to Matthew Arnold and F. W. Newman. We may be satisfied to adhere to the definition of Lord Bacon, that poetry *is a species of feigned history*. Every description of poetry may with no" great violence be brought under this comprehensive definition. *Narrative* poetry of every sort, from the stately epic of the ancients down to the familiar tale of the modern bard—from the **Iliad** to **Aurora Leigh**—will easily be classed as history. This feigned history must indeed also have a human interest. Every descriptive poem, even if it set forth some objective scene, supposes this human interest; even though it only concerns the single human being who is the looker-on, and out of whose experience have sprung the feelings with which he colors, and the ends for which he constructs the picture, of which nature furnishes the materials. Beneath every sonnet of Wordsworth, and every description of Browning, there lies a chapter of human history. The **Lyric** in every one of its varied forms, from the loftiest ode to the most trivial love-song, is the breaking forth in verse—suited to song—of the feelings of some human soul, under the circumstances of some real or supposed personal history; and these must be known or supplied by the reader, to enable him to understand and appreciate the ode or the song. The *meditative* and the *moralizing*, the *didactic* and the *satirical*, cease to be poetry and become prosaic and heavy, the moment that there falls out of either some form of human life, enacted or conceived.

Every *drama* is eminently a story—a story acted and not alone described; *dramatica poesis ist veluti spectdbilis*— a story in which the parties are made to live again before the eyes of the reader or hearer, to speak their own thoughts and to pour forth their impassioned utterances, as they seem to be freshly excited by the deeds and words that are produced upon the pictured stage, or upon the written page which the imagination-dresses up as a mimic theatre.

But not every feigned history is poetry, else every novel were a poem. Poetry is *feigned history in verse*. The feigned story whether it is narrated or suggested, must be told in verse; *i. e.*, in measured and rhythmical language. "We are accustomed to call verse an artificial structure; in contrast with prose, as more natural and obvious. If it has become artificial in our less excited and more critical modes of existence and action, it certainly was not so originally, in the earliest times, when the most literal truth was framed into a poem under the excitement of love and admiration, and was set forth with measure and cadence from the lips of sages and bards. Then the prophet, the lawgiver, and the historian were also poets. Admonitions to duty, and rules of living, and the records of the past, were all committed to some rude or measured form of verse, out of which now and then the flashing war-song would gleam as the lightning, or along which the pean would thunder in triumph. Whether this preference of verse in the earlier days is owing to the predominance of imagination and feeling, or to the greater convenience which verse affords to the memory when its effect depends not upon what is written for the eye, but upon what is heard by the ear, the fact is unquestioned, that the earliest compositions take the form of verse. We know also that to the individual man in the dawn of intelligence, verse is far more pleasing and easy to be retained than prose. The ditty with its readily recurring refrain, the song that suits the simplest air, are forms of composition which are most pleasing to infancy. Whether it be more natural in the earlier ages to compose in verse than in prose, we will not inquire. Whether with the poetical modes of conception which are natural at that period, in the forms of affluent imagery and elevated feeling, there springs up for man's use a fit medium of expression in " the gift of numerous verse," we need not ask. We are forced to confess that this gift is not universal when literary culture is refined and matured. As, in this condition, man finds it less easy to write in verse than in prose, so he reserves for this form of writing his choicest thoughts and his best emotions. The constraints of verse also compel a selection in the words employed and a special nicety in their arrangement and combinations. Hence he is insensibly led to require as fit for verse, sentiments that are rare—usually that are rare for their nobleness— and emotions that are uncommon for their elevation, strength, and purity. So far Matthew Arnold is in the right when he insists that there must be something of the grand style in every com-position that is truly poetic. This leads the reader or critic almost instinctively to reject the trivial and the low, or even the familiar and the homely, as beneath the dignity of poetry. it was an exaggeration of this feeling that led so many of the poets of the last century to adopt a peculiar stilted and factitious poetic dialect as alone suited to the elevated uses of poetic writing. This diction became by its traditionary character not only empty of meaning, but was followed by the double evil of repressing that freshness and individuality of language which are indispensable to poetic power and freedom, and of appearing as a substitute for thoughts and feelings which were in no sense poetic. Against this Thomson and Cowper entered their practical protest, by refusing to conform to the rule and example of their times, and Wordsworth set up the theory of poetic diction which gave so much offence and aroused so warm a controversy. Moreover, the oft-recurring pauses and turns of verse do not admit protracted or complicated arguments, refined abstractions, or a philosophical terminology. Hence there grows up the sentiment and the demand that everything which is fit for verse should be simple in phrase, should be lively with imagery, and be readily followed by the common mind.

For this reason offence is taken at metaphysical discus-sions, protracted reflections, labored conversations, and even elaborate descriptions, as unsuited to poetry. Hence the reasonableness of those criticisms and complaints which are often unreasonably urged against Milton, Wordsworth, Tennyson, and the Brownings, that they are abstract, metaphysical, over-refined, and difficult to read.

Simplicity, however, is neither silliness nor common-place ; it does not exclude the extremest subtlety of thought nor the most delicate refinement of feeling, but its rule demands that the poetic diction should be direct, brief, and easily followed. In this way, out of the very exigencies which the use of verse prescribes, do we derive the usually-accepted characteristics of poetic thought and expression. These characteristics we often find abundant and conspicuous in prose-writing. In such cases we say truly, and with an intelligible meaning, this or that passage is highly poetic. We call Jeremy Taylor the Shakspeare of Divinity. We say that Milton in his prose writings surpasses himself as a poet. We are amazed at the bewildering beauty of many a magnificent passage in Coleridge's prose. We say of this or that person of our acquaintance, he has a highly poetic mind, simply because his thoughts and emotions are intensely ideal and imaginative, even though he may never have written a line of verse, or even may be unpractised in any form of written composition.

We ought also to add, as pertaining solely to the matter of poetry, that it deals chiefly with those thoughts and sentiments which are universal to the race, as distinguished from those which are in any sense limited or conventional. The poet speaks to the heart of man as man; and he must, therefore, speak from his own heart as that of a man ; uttering only those thoughts and sentiments to which all other men will respond, and leaving unexpressed much that is peculiar to his race, his time, his civilization, or even his religion, except so far as this answers to what is common to the race, the time, the civilization, and the religion of another, and thus addresses the intelligence and enlists the sympathies of all human kind. The truth with which the poet deals is common and universal, in the sense -of being accessible to all men who have attained that degree of culture and of thought which is supposed in the use of the simple diction that poetry requires. It is, moreover, truth in an attractive form,—that truth which is worthy to be draped with the " singing robes" of poesy. Pleasure as truly as reflection, delight as truly as impression, are ends which poetry may never lose sight of. The measured cadences which soothe or excite the ear, the flowing diction which is rippled with sparkling imagery, are all unsuited to any truth but that which pleases by its in-telligibleness, its weight, its liveliness, and its emotional attractions. " Poetry," says Wordsworth, "is the breath and finer spirit of all knowledge; it is the impassioned expression which is in the countenance of all science ; emphatically may it be said of the poet, as Shakspeare hath said of man, ' he looks before and after.' He is the rock of defence for human nature ; an upholder and preserver, car-rying everywhere with him relationship and love. In spite of difference of soil and climate, of language and manners, of laws and customs; in spite of things silently gone out of mind, and things violently destroyed, the poet binds together by passion and knowledge the vast empire of human society, as it is spread over the whole earth and over all time." " Poetry," says Matthew Arnold, in memorable words, " is simply the most beautiful, impressive and widely effective mode of saying things and hence its importance."

But while the poet must invariably be universal in the spheres of thought and feeling, he is none the less emphati-cally an individual in both. Indeed his power and genius depend entirely upon that intense individuality, which can set forth that which commands universal intelligence and sympathy in the form and coloring of individualized thoughts and emotions. Not only must the local coloring of his own race, nationality, and civilization tinge every stroke of his pencil, but the private thoughts and feelings of his individual self must impress themselves upon every sentiment which he utters and should give direction to every turn of his language and imagery. Homer is a Greek in every fibre of his being, and none the less because his pages move alike the stately Latin, the fierce and moody Scandinavian, the sentimental German, the reserved Englishman and the talkative Gaul. Isaiah and David are none the less Hebrew in thought and imagery because their odes are the fit vehicles to express the praises and prayers of men of all races and of all times. Shakspeare was English of Elizabeth's time, and Milton a Puritan of the times of the Commonwealth, and Dryden a wit of the days of Charles and William, and yet they speak to the heart of every nationality. While the universality of the poet requires that he should use a language which all can understand, his genius impels him to employ a dialect of his own which no man can imitate.

The poet, especially the poet of modern times, must reflect the culture of his own generation, and in that form and degree in which it has affected himself personally ; his own individuality determining very largely the use which he makes of it. Neither Tennyson nor George Eliot nor Kobert Browning could have written what or as they have done, in any other than the present generation. The *In Memoriam*, the *Spanish Gypsy*, the *Ring and the Book*, all treat of themes and follow trains of thought which their authors did not wholly create. Nor could they have imagined these had they not found them existing already in the minds of multitudes of their countrymen. The so-called Poets of the Lake School—Wordsworth, Coleridge, Southey and Wilson—found already existing, a readiness to be moved in the direction in which they thought and wrote, much as they accomplished in giving that direction permanence and force. They could scarcely have gained a hearing in the generation previous, however earnestly or boldly they might have striven. On the other hand, Tennyson, Browning, and Eliot are no more closely united by sharing in the thought and feeling of their times, than they are severed by the pronounced individuality for which each is distinguished. However closely the Lake Poets resemble one another in certain common aims, each individual poet is distinguished by features which are un-mistakably his own.

It by no means follows, however, because every poet must deal with those thoughts and feelings which are common to human nature, and are as universal as the race, that every poet should be popular in the sense of being easily understood and passionately loved by men of every type of thought and every shade or degree of emotion. There are and there ought to be poets for the multitude and poets for the people, as well as poets who, while they move the multitude to a certain degree of appreciation and pleasure in single poems or passages, move the few far more profoundly in every line which they write. Even those who are called poets for the multitude—the poets in whom all men delight—delight the few far more intensely whose taste has been ripened by culture and has become more appreciative by critical training. As culture advances and thought becomes more just and profound, as society is in a certain sense more artificial and yet comes nearer to. the simplicity of nature and the frankness of honesty tempered by love, we may anticipate that poetry will follow in the line of culture, wherever it can find " an audience fit though few." " If the time should ever come when what is now called science, thus familiarized to man, should put on, as it were, a form of flesh and blood, the poet will lend his divine spirit to aid the transfiguration, and will welcome the being thus produced, as a dear and genuine inmate of the household of man."

It follows that a taste for poetry, especially that of the highest order, is to a great extent the product of special culture. It is true, as we have observed, that an ear for verse and an eye for bold and brilliant imagery are natural to all men, and that children even in their earliest years are charmed with any measured refrain that sets forth a stirring or plaintive story. The "drum and trumpet" lyrics of Macaulay suit the martial bravado of the storming boy. By and by the pictured tales of Scott will enchant his fancy while his ready ear responds to the rapid lines that hurry the attention along by the simple rush of their own movement. Gentler ballads of olden times, of deserted children and ladies sore oppressed or captured and immured by giant or robber,—plaintive tales of the Edwins and Angelinas of later days, delight the ear and move the heart of the little maiden, in whom the poetic sense begins to stir and futter. This is the period for reading and for learning verses of all sorts, both ballads and hymns, provided the ballads and hymns are fraught with poetic feeling and imagery. Much of the stuff which passes for poetry with young folks, and their parents also, should be carefully shunned. Its rhythm is jingle, its words are strained, its pictures are hazy, its sentiment is silly. But if the imagery be sharp and bold, the diction concise and strong, the measure be smooth and sweet, and the sentiments manly, tender and correct, then the more that is learned the better. It were not amiss if books of ancient ballads were studiously sought for and learned by heart, and by this means the leading scenes and personages of English history were permanently fixed in the mind. There are not a few boys who are capable of enjoying the *Iliad* in a translation, and scarcely one who might not be trained to delight in Scott long before it is dreamed that they can relish poetry. Certainly such reading is greatly to be preferred to the rubbish of the sensation novels, whether moral or otherwise, with which now-a-days the appetites of so many are weakened or debauched.

But this early relish for poetic tales scarcely deserves to be called a taste for poetry. That which is really such, supposes a nicety of eye, a reflecting habit, and, above all, a delicacy of feeling which are not native to impetuous and objective childhood—least of all to boyhood, after the gentleness of infancy has entirely given way to the storming and outward life of school and the play-ground. It is not unfrequently observed that the sister who is younger by many years than her older brother has developed a taste for poetry long before he has dreamed of such an experience. Perhaps she is forced to endure his ill-suppressed contempt that she is growing sentimental, because she begins to delight in Cowper or Milton while as yet he finds no interest in either. The reason is obvious. The girl begins to reflect sooner than the boy, and sooner finds in the poet whose verse detains her ear some transcript of an observation of nature without, or of the heart of man within,—such as she herself may have made, only the poet has expressed them so much more fully and successfully than she could have dreamed were possible. Or, it may be, some romantic preference may have called into life the latent poesy of her nature, and to her girlish enthusiasm nature has suddenly become flushed with a roseate light, and man himself transfigured with idealized perfections. However it may come, and whether sooner or later, the day is memorable to boy or maid when he or she begins to read genuine poetry with interest, not for the tale, nor the verse, but for the transcript which he finds of what he himself has seen, or felt, or thought. Should perchance a sensitive and thoughtful boy find a volume of Cowper opened at the Winter Evening, or the Winter Walk at Noon, and, caught by some striking line, read on till what he has seen in nature or observed in life should seem imaged as in a mirror, there is awakened within him a new sense, and he has found a treasure of enjoyment of which he had never dreamed. Or let Whittier's **Snow Bound** be effectively read of an evening to a family circle. The listless boy or romping girl sits impatiently and wishes the hateful task were over which defers a promised sport, when all at once some striking scene from life starts into view, and the recognition is waked as in a moment, ' that I have seen and felt myself.' Such a sense may be gradually quickened and developed under the readings of the school in a well-selected class-book, or be suddenly called forth by some impressive recitation of descriptive or impassioned poesy.

Such a taste is not, of course, matured because it has sprung into being. It is simply an awakened capacity of feeling which needs the direction of the judgment. Its very freshness and strength may be the more misleading, if its impulses alone are consulted. It may, through perverseness an4 conceit, remain what it was at the outset, crude, coarse, and confident, or weak, silly, and sentimental. It may even be degenerate in its judgments, and teach it-self to prefer rant to inspiration, or weak bombast to solid brilliancy, provided it refuses to defer to the guidance of others or blindly gives itself up to the influence of the single author who first waked its poetic feeling into life. Poetic sensibility is not poetic taste, however frequently the one is mistaken for the other. The capacity to be pleasantly affected by poetic composition, and even the capacity for a high degree of excitement under its influence, may coexist with a perverted taste and a misguided judgment in respect to the comparative merits of an author, and an almost entire absence of any just conception of what constitutes poetry. It is a rash conclusion which not a few admit, that because the end of poetry is pleasure, therefore all writing in verse which pleases must of course be poetry; or, this or that composition does not please, and therefore it is not poetry. Yielding to this hasty inference, not a few young persons, never rise above the first favorite author; who was well enough fitted to awaken the earliest romance of youthful feeling, but should long ago have given place to writers of a higher tone in sentiment and diction. Or, not pursuing poetic studies, they judge of poetry by the depreciating estimate which in later years they form of the authors that once enraptured but now disappoint or disgust them. Or if asked to read a poet of superior grade, and they fail to find the excitement of their youthful readings, they conclude either that there are no poets like their early favorites, or that poetry itself has become one of the lost arts, and is fast dying out from the world.

We may not then judge of poetry by our earliest likings or our first impressions. It were as reasonable to judge of color and form in nature and art, by the crudest impressions of childhood. The coarsest tints, the most flaunting hues, as well as hideous forms and violent contrasts should be approved, because they attract and please the uninstructed eye. This is so far from being true, that " an accurate taste in poetry, and in all the other arts, as Sir Joshua Reynolds has observed, is an acquired talent which can only be produced by thought and a long-continued intercourse with the best models of composition." We should therefore begin our reading of poetry, or should direct the reading of others, just as we should begin the cultivation of the eye or the ear in drawing or in music, with the distinct expectation that our capacity to feel and to judge is to grow more correct and become more refined by what it feeds on. We should indeed not disdain what pleases us at first by idly imagining that we ought to enjoy something higher. As for the pretence that we enjoy and comprehend what we neither understand nor love, we should shun it as a paltry affectation, if not as a mean dishonesty. But we should expect that our taste is to be elevated and refined, as we exercise it wisely and lovingly upon what the advice of others may recommend, and as we strive at times to see beauty and finish in writers who at first neither excite nor overwhelm us. No spirit is so hostile to progress in any of the finer studies or the nobler arts as the spirit of satisfaction and conceit with present ideals of perfection, or as an obstinate unreadiness to open the mind to those which are higher and nobler. With this precaution, we may use the liberty of selecting our poets according to our present tastes, and, if we select for others, according to their prevailing tastes and capacities. We should not force upon ourselves, least of all should we force upon others, the works of poets whom we or they do not fancy, and whom we or they by any effort cannot learn to enjoy. This is especially true of poetic reading, because enjoyment and sympathy and heartiness are its very atmosphere and life. The miss who delights in Mrs. Hemans or Miss Landon, and can find neither meaning nor music in Coleridge, Jean Ingelow, or Tennyson, may be let alone for a while, in the hope that perhaps her taste may ripen, and in becoming mature may be changed. The objective youth, whose ear is captivated with the ring of Byron's verse and the boldness of his passion, should not be crammed with Wordsworth or Tennyson. Whittier and Longfellow are better for many a reader, at a certain stage of their culture and taste, than Bryant or Dana. As age advances and reflection matures, as the ear becomes more delicate, the sensibility to choice and pure words is more refined, and the choice of imagery is more wisely and honestly more fastidious, the old and familiar poets will disclose new beauties, and poets before unappreciated will be understood and enjoyed. With this progress in the tastes, there will be some change in our favorite poets, or at least in the reasons why our favorite poets are loved.

We have already sought to illustrate the truth, that although the poet should recognize that which is common to the race, and which in a certain sense attracts the sympathies of all men, he may also reflect the thoughts and feelings which are distinctly recognized by men in peculiar circumstances or of special experiences. Tennyson's **In Memoriam** speaks to the heart of man as man; yet it is only the man of the present century, who is acquainted with the speculations of the time and has been staggered by its doubts and misgivings, who can fully appreciate thousands of its masterly strokes and its delicate suggestions. **The Princess** of the same author, and the **Aurora Leigh** of Mrs. Browning, can be adequately enjoyed only by one who has read much and thought deeply on the social problems of the time. But it is none the less true that the poetry is genuine and excellent for all. Shakspeare and Milton, and even Burns and Cowper, contain many passages of which only the man of much reading and of grave reflection can adequately estimate the meaning or enjoy the subtle flavor. It is most unjust to say of the works of Words-worth and Tennyson, of Browning and Eliot, or of the passages of Shakspeare and Milton referred to, that they are not poetry, because they are not understood by men of all classes and in all stages of culture and thought. The mature and refined thought of an age of daring speculation, and the subtle emotions which spring out of its life of doubt and faith, of fear and hope, may properly be reflected in its poetry. Poetry should never be technical or select, in the sense of using the language of a coterie or a school, but it may express the feelings and thoughts that are produced by an age or a generation of special culture and special conflicts.

It is implied in all these hints and rules that poetry, to be fully appreciated and enjoyed, must be earnestly and perseveringly studied. This may seem to many like an obvious and a startling paradox. How can that which is chiefly designed for pleasure require study, which is universally associated with painful effort ? We reply: a poem must be studied for the same reasons and in the same way that a painting, an engraving, or a drawing must be studied, in order that the refinement of its perfection may be revealed. If the poet has a soul that is " finely touched " it is " to fine issues;" and in order that he should be adequately estimated and judged, he requires a soul akin to his own, a soul in some sense *as fine* to receive as his is *fine* to give. How shall one sing joyous songs to him who is of a heavy heart ? By this same rule, let the poet's imagination be ever so fertile and refined, how can it create for the reader who cannot ecreate after him at his suggesting words ? "What are the words that speak his thoughts or feelings if the reader does not translate them into meaning by his own answering thoughts and feelings ? To require that the poet should inject his thoughts into a lazy intellect, or kindle emotions in a torpid or stupid heart, is to insult his very name and office. If the priest should not be allowed to approach the altar except with unspotted robes, and after many lustrations, let not the worshiper enter the sanctuary with soiled feet and careless tread. When it is* fit to inspect a choice engraving with careless eye and divided attention, or to handle a Sevres vase or an exquisite chasing with a rough hand and a heedless grasp, then shall it be seemly to read the choicest works of a poet's inspiration and a poet's ear with a dawdling nonchalance, or to answer to his thoughts and feelings with energies half aroused or an attention that is slack or divided. Many of the poet's best productions are so subtle as to escape the notice of any other than a close and fixed attention. His felicities of thought can only be appreciated by a mind that concentrates its eye for subtle differences. His images and allusions, his pictures and emotions, are often the more beautiful because they do not spring into the eyes of the reader, whether he will or no. Beauties that are modest and even shy are often specially attractive in poetry as they are in life. It is to be remembered, also, that great writers, and especially poets who are great, are usually wiser than their readers. They know more of the art in which they excel than many of their readers or critics. They are often too proud ostentatiously to display or set off their wares by rhetorical *tours de force*.

If the genuine poet often require, he will always bear study and repay it. That man has a most dishonorable and unjust conception of poetry and the poet who regards poetry as valuable only to while away a lazy or listless hour. If poetry, to be appreciated and enjoyed, must be studied, much more does it require to be studied in order that it may be intelligently criticised. But the study is not painful, though it must be faithful; it brings its abundant and exquisite enjoyments, though it requires faithful and persevering effort. No luxury of literature is so exquisite as that which comes of a really superior poem, of which the diction is finished and smooth, the imagery is bold and brilliant, the sentiments are inspiriting and elevating, the pathos is tender and sweet, and the faith is reverent yet bold.

It follows that it is well, at least for the time, to have a favorite poet, who engrosses our chief attention, and whose best works are read, and read again, till they become alto-gether familiar. It may expose to a certain narrowness and bigotry when our taste is crude and unformed, but it is wise after this taste has become catholic and self-reliant, because in this way we really master the works which we have in hand. A poem, of all literary products, deserves to be often read if it has superior excellence. It cannot be appreciated without; neither the diction, nor the imagery, nor the allusions, nor the feeling, nor the truth. If we give ourselves up for a little while to a single writer, we live in his atmosphere, and form with his mind and heart the sympathy of almost a personal friendship. There are not a few men who make a single poet the favorite of their lives, for some conspicuous fitness of his to their own tastes and needs. Thus Shakspeare is cherished for his many-sided fullness; or Milton for his majestic music and his stately and solemn truth ; or Dryden for his comprehensive common sense and ready wit; or Cowper for his domestic sympathies and habits, or his religious tenderness; or Scott for his romantic spirit; or Wordsworth for his sympathy with nature as a peace-giving and elevating friend; or Tennyson for his struggling faith in goodness and in God; or Whittier for his love of simple men and simple manners, combined with a fiery enthusiasm for the right; or Long fellow for the clearness, the music, and the pathos of his rhymes; or Lowell for the ***abandon*** of his affluent and quick moving genius. It would not be difficult to show that the familiar study of one of the great poets of England brings an education of wider reach and higher elevation than that which is often attained at the most pretentious and costly schools. We have seen men and women of the olden time, trained in the old-fashioned schools of " plain living and high thinking," of rugged face and form, of manners unstudied yet most refined, with whom Milton, or Cowper, or Shakspeare, or Burns had been a life-long study, and who had gained thereby a power of thought, a refinement of feeling, and a sagacious insight of which many a flippant Bohemian can have no conception, whose mind has been inundated by the sewerage of modern poetry, made up of the good, the indifferent, and the bad. We have been told of a wrathful farmer, with whom Miltonic studies were always fresh, who, when selling a basket of eggs and talking politics, in the same breath vented his indignant impatience at the inevitable law by which bad politicians unite and honest ones divide, in the words—

Devil and devil damned
Firm concord hold. Men only disagree.

The farmer's family, in a secluded valley in New England, or on the remote prairie, in which the girls can effectively and lovingly read, and the boys can intelligently and responsively appreciate Milton, or Shakspeare, or Coleridge, or Whittier, may boast of a better culture than many a saloon in the most pretentious avenues of the wealthiest and most luxurious cities. Many a Scottish cottage draws from its well-thumbed copy of Burns more refinement of thought and feeling than is attained by the cultivated coxcomb or the accomplished miss, whose manners and accomplishments are consummate in everything but the nobleness and refinement of sincere and elevated feeling.

Better still than to confine ourselves too long to a single favorite poet, is it to read very frequently from a choice selection of the best poems of a variety of authors. Very busy men, who in their youthful and less occupied days nave become familiar with the circle of the best English poets, may refresh their recollections, and deepen and strengthen their best lessons, by having always *at hand*, and frequently *in hand*, a good selection of the best brief poems and parts of poems, in which English poetry is so abundant. We know more than one such person, who often takes Palgrave's **Golden Treasury** as a traveling companion, and never tires—as who could possibly—of reading again and again one of its many gems in the vacancy of the crowded rail-car, or the ennui of the steamboat trip, or the prolonged delays of the waiting-room. Such a resource is worth not a little if it enables one under such .depressions to rise in a moment by the withdrawments of the imagination,

Above *the smoke and stir* of this dim spot
Which men call earth, and with low thoughted care
Confined and pestered in this pinfold here,
Strive to keep up a frail and feverish being.

Such a snatch of reading is more than refreshment; it elevates and purifies the imagination, and gives new spring and tension to our nobler nature. It is reasonable to hope that many may thus

"by due steps aspire
To lay their just hands on that golden key
Which opes the palace of eternity."

Dana's *Household Book of Poetry* is indeed a *Hausschatz*, as similar collections are called in Germany, from which may readily be drawn the beguilement of many a weary hour, rest from eating cares, and deliverance from petty irritations.

We have already anticipated in part the answer to the question, " Why should we make much of the reading and study of poetry?" We may be more explicit and add: They are valuable for the peculiar and elevated pleasure which they give. Poetry pleases the ear. The charm of rhythmical verse is universally confessed. There is nothing in well-turned prose, however choice in words, or weighty in thought, or eloquent in emotion or appeal, which can be compared with a consummate passage of superior poetry, whether it be graphic in description, or passionate, intense, and elevating in lyric effect, or suggestive in reflection, or life-like in the action and emotion of the drama; provided only the diction answers to the sentiment. The limitations and the demands of verse require something in language which cannot be enforced of prose writing. The satisfaction of these demands is gratifying to the well-trained ear, not with a merely sensuous effect, but with the effect of sound as expressive of, and corresponding to the soul of sense and meaning. The practised student of poetry may augment this pleasure if he will train his ear by the hearing of poetry well read. Few accomplishments are more satisfactory in the use than the skill to read with effect and feeling, the poetry which we or others admire and love. The gift of song may be more admired because it is more rare, but the gift of reading musically and well, is " an excellent thing " in man, and pre-eminently in woman. To hear good poetry well read is always pleasing, and even to imagine we heard it read as we follow the rhythm in appreciative and critical judgment gives no trivial pleasure.

The study and reading of poetry exercises and cultivates the imagination, and in this way imparts intellectual power. It is impossible to read the product of any poet's imagination without using our own. To read what he creates is to recreate in our own minds the images and pictures which he first conceived and then expressed in language. The unimaginative soul cannot enjoy poetry; he cannot understand it, because he cannot interpret its words by re-sponsive pictures of his own creating. On the other hand, the man who does read poetry, and with effect and appreciation, must use his imagination, and by use make it more dexterous in its power to create, and more refined in its capacity to judge. We do not intend that such a training involves the power of expression either in prose or verse; for the reason that this gift, and pre-eminently the gift of expression in verse, is the product of another and an entirely different species of training. But that poetry strengthens and refines the imagination is evident from the fact that it trains the mind to view nature and the human life under poetic aspects. The student of Thomson, Cow-per, of Wordsworth and Tennyson, cannot read them with success without forming the habit of seeing nature under poetic aspects and with poetic eyes. He cannot be taught by these writers to muse upon the human life which they describe in its ideal and imaginative relations, without reflecting himself upon the human life which he sees, under similar lights and shades. He must inevitably view its darker shades as transfigured with poetic beauty, and its brighter aspects as tinged with graver shadows. Whatever he sees, however common-place or 'prosaic, he learns to look into a picture. Whatever he thinks of he must invest with ideal beauty and refinement. That these habits are favorable to purity and nobleness of feeling, and to magnanimity and morality of word or deed, we shall not argue over again. We are contented to cite a second time the words of Bacon, that " Poesy serveth and conferreth to magnanimity, morality, and to delectation. And therefore it was ever thought to have some participation of divineness."

What Coleridge says of the writing of poetry must be true of the reading of it. " Poetry has been to me its own exceeding great reward; it has soothed my afflictions, it has multiplied and refined my enjoyments, and it has given me the habit of wishing to discover the good and the beautiful in all that meets and surrounds me." Wordsworth's lines recur to us in this connection—

" Blessings be with them—and eternal praise,
Who gave us nobler loves and nobler cares—
The Poets, who on earth have made us heirs
Of truth and pure delight by heavenly lays."

The habitual reading and study of poetry, especially of the loftier types, is eminently useful as a preparation for the writer or speaker, who is required to compose in moving discourse on grave and elevated themes. It was the counsel of a very eminent Christian preacher to one who was just entering upon his profession : "Always have some fine poem in hand—dramatic is to be preferred—if you would keep yourself in tone for the successful composition of sermons;" and the advice is pertinent to every species of elevated prose composition.

That the poetry which elevates and excites the imagination is also favorable to religious aspiration and religious faith need not be argued. It is evident from the single fact, that however grievously the highest gifts of imagination have been occasionally abused, no great poet has ever failed to express at times the semblance of high religious aspiration. Every poet of the higher type has often fired his imagination at the altar of religious worship. Whether the aspirations and worship which he has offered are inconsistent or not with fixed principles and high moral purposes, or whether they are the passing flush of the excited phantasy, makes little difference with our argument, that the imagination cannot soar without flying upward towards God, and in seeking God must approve that which is holy and pure, as well as unselfish and self-controlled. The imagination, in order to rise and soar, must at least feign that she believes and worships. Shelley and Byron and Goethe are memorable witnesses to this important truth.

But what poets shall we read, and in what order ? and why should we select certain poets above others ? Upon this topic we have sought to furnish principles rather than rules; to enable the reader to select for himself rather than rely on the authority of another. But we may for a moment glance at a few of the leading names in the long list of English poets. Chaucer leads the way—the morning star of English poesy—fit leader of a host so brilliant; for we may say, without conscious exaggeration or fear of dispute, that the poetry of England is the richest, the most varied, and the most brilliant of any which the world has ever seen; as it should be, reflecting as it does a manhood which has been developed most variously and most nobly, and a life the most heroic, the most fervent, the most affectionate, that has marked the world's history. Chaucer must be studied in order to be read ; but when Chaucer has been studied so as to be easily followed, he confronts you with the dawn of a brilliant day—dewy, fresh, transparent, and invigorating. He gives you the Odyssey of the English poetry, and reveals the spring-time of English life. Next comes Spenser, wearisome for his meandering verse laden with its wealth of bewildering imagery, but affluent to excess with pictures that are clear and bright, and always noble, chivalrous, pure and Christian. He gives English feeling in its knightly aspect, as it was exemplified in the life of Sidney and others of the selecter spirits of " great Eliza's golden time." Then comes Shakspeare, the myriad-minded indeed, reflecting in the manifoldness of his products and the power with which he lives and feels in all, the fervent and manifold life of England's population in his times ; the admiration of the modern world in its height of culture and its depth of philosophy; the challenger of critics, before whose mysterious power to think and express they confess themselves abashed, and by the unsolved enigmas of many of whose characters and whose truths they continue to be dazed and overcome. Milton follows, representing another type of poets, and another aspect of English life; learned, grave, and stern, bearing the impress of one who had indeed been " caught up into Paradise and heard unspeakable words ;" but still human in his unmatched love of nature, his tender sympathy with human life, and his delight in music, whether

> He hears the pealing organ blow
> To the full-voiced choir below,
> In service high and anthems clear,

or rejoices in the sweet rising of the earliest morn with " charm of earliest birds." Milton gives us the life of the English people, when believing in God as the greatest of kings, they dared in his name to vindicate the rights of human subjects, and showed the virtues of that stern knighthood which had received such a fiery consecration. We name Dryden next, the best and the manliest poet of English thought and feeling at the beginning of a sad degeneracy—the man of the world, frank, brave, outspoken, with a brilliant genius, but often untrue to his better self through the corruption of manners and the degradation of the higher imagination. Pope follows next, sententious, acute, brilliant, and felicitous, the servant of an age which he was content to flatter and to please, but never attempted to elevate, who fixed for English poetry that factitious and stilted poetic diction which was echoed and re-echoed by imitators till it became ashamed and vexed at its own empty re-iterations.

Against this excess of factitious emptiness there came an inevitable reaction. Thomson dared to follow his own luxuriant fancy, and rose to occasional flights that remind us of the earlier and better times of Milton and Spenser. Cowper with no suspicion of his own genius, and often homely and uncultured in his diction, was by the very unconsciousness of his power left more free from the trammels of allegiance to poets or critics, to follow the promptings of his love of nature, humanity, and God. Crabbe, more homely even than Cowper, was also more literal than he in his transcripts of the humble life with which he was familiar. Burns, having no impulse and little guidance except from within, sung from his own heart songs of penetrating sense and wondrous tenderness. Campbell, Scott, and Joanna Baillie represent types that are unique, but each gave an impulse to the better spirit. Byron was stirred by pride and wrath to use the genius which he could not repress; breaking other of the traditions of the past besides the poetic, which he fancied he kept as against his rivals, the Lake Poets. "With Byron, Shelley may properly be connected, though in many respects more spiritual, refined and noble. Meanwhile the Lake School had been gathering strength, and began to act as a redeeming force. Wordsworth, with his cool defiance of the prevailing fashion, promulgated an extreme theory, with a practice still more extreme. Coleridge, Southey, "Wilson, Landor, and Lamb were agreed, not in adopting the theory or following the practice of Wordsworth, but in their emancipation from any fashion of poetic diction, and in their fresh and liberal imitation of, or rather inspiration by, the elder poets. From their triumph commences the new era of English poetry in England and America. Milman, Tennyson, Barry Cornwall, Henry Taylor, the Brownings, Hood, Ingelow, Arthur Clough, and Matthew Arnold, in England; Dana, Pierpont, Percival, Bryant, Longfel-low, Lowell, Whittier, and Emerson in America, follow in great or less measure the impulses of the modern school, which we need not characterize. Last of all comes William Morris, with his antique and objective spirit, as a healthful and needed counterpoise to the excessively subjective tendencies of the same recent school.

In religious poetry English literature is rich. Milton, George Herbert, Watts, Doddridge, the Wesleys, Keble, and Faber are examples of its different types. In poetic translators from the ancient bards we have of Homer, Chapman, Pope, Cowper, Lord Derby, Sotheby, Newman, Bryant and others; of Virgil, Dryden, and Conington; of Horace, Lytton Bulwer and Conington; of Dante, Cary and Longfellow; of Tasso, Fairfax; and of various works of the modern German, Coleridge, Scott, Lytton Bulwer, and others.

But it is time we had ended. The golden roll of English poetry is embarrassing from its wealth and tempting suggestions.

CHAPTER XVII.

THE CRITICISM AND HISTORY OF LITERATURE.

WITHIN the present century, there has come into being a new description of Books and Reading, viz.: those which are ***devoted to the criticism and history of literature itself***. Our libraries and book-shops are furnished with many books which consist of criticisms of other books. Not only is there a countless number of essays devoted to the criticism and interpretation of single authors and even of single works, but entire volumes are occupied with commentaries on great authors or some one of their writings. We have more than one series of essays, and even whole libraries, occupied solely with critiques upon single writers, as Homer, Goethe, and Shakspeare. Active controversies have arisen between the partisans of opposing theories. Indeed, critiques and counter critiques are so abundant, that it almost seems as though this was the age of nothing but criticism, and literature were nothing if not critical. It is certain there now exists a special department of literature which is employed in the interpretation and judgment of literature itself, and that it has enlisted the services of many of the ablest writers of their time, some of whom have not only been distinguished as critics of the productions of men of surpassing genius, but have themselves been known as foremost writers of their own generation. We need name only ***Goethe***, the ***Schlegels, Coleridge, Wordsworth, Made. de Stael, St. Beuve, Professor John Wilson***, and ***Matthew Arnold***. Criticism itself has become a department of literature, and is justified in its claims by being also historical, philosophical, and almost creative of itself.

This new criticism, in the eminent sense of the phrase, may be said to be of German origin, though it has attained a vigorous growth on English soil. That it should first have taken form in Germany was natural. It is the natural outgrowth of extensive reading, joined with an appreciative imagination and reflective sagacity. It must necessarily have been somewhat late in its development. As men must act poems before they write them,—as one or many must act the hero, before others can recount their exploits or celebrate their praises, so literature must be created before it can be criticised. There must be brought into being a considerable number of productions, in the forms of poetry, fiction, the drama, history, biography, and eloquence, before the materials are prepared with which the critic can begin. When we assert that the species of criticism which we have in mind is comparatively of recent origin, we do not say that criticism of every kind is recent in its growth, nor indeed that before the present century there were no profound and genial critics, who took historic and philosophical estimates of the great writers who had gone before them, but only that criticism as it now exists has come into organized being, with distinctly recognised functions and fixed principles and laws for its direction. Dryden and Johnson were both penetrating, and to a certain degree large-minded critics, but neither Dryden nor Johnson rose above very narrow traditions, or personal prejudices. We speak of the old and the new generally when we say, that formerly, criticism confined itself almost exclusively to the forms of literature, as the choice of words, the rhythm of verse, the proportion of parts, the order of development, the effectiveness of the introduction the argument and the peroration, and these, with the illustration and explanation of the meaning of a work or a writer, constituted its principal aims. Now, while it does not neglect the form, it thinks more of the matter, i. e. the weightiness and truth of the thoughts, the energy and nobleness of the sentiments, the splendor and power of the imagery, and the heroic manhood or the refined womanhood of the writer as expressed in his or her works. Formerly it judged of the form by the fashion of the day in respect of style and diction, and pronounced everything barbarous which was not after the newest type, very much as the dress or hat which are most becoming in themselves are declared to be dowdy and frightful, if worn a year or a season too early or too late. Now the form is regarded as that which in some re-spects must be transient and changeable, according to the shaping power of the matter itself, the temper of the writer, and the temper of the times in which he lived and in which he wrote. Formerly the critic was regarded by others and too often regarded himself as the natural enemy of the author. Now it is exacted of him that he "should be the expounder of the author's thoughts and the sharer of his feelings; that he should almost see with his eyes, hear with his ears, and judge with his mind. But this estimate of the characteristic features of the new criticism is general and superficial. A closer and more careful examination, gives the following results:

First: the new criticism starts with a ***more enlarged and profound conception of literature itself.*** The word literature, etymologically considered, is necessarily somewhat loose and general in its import, signifying whatever is committed to a permanent form by writing. When this import is somewhat narrowed, it signifies whatever survives a merely ephemeral existence, and attracts the notice of a second generation. In this sense, any book or tract would come under this designation, if it be worth retaining in a library, or if it happens to be so preserved. "With the older critics, literature included only those works which were eminent and attractive from perfection in style, beauty and fitness of imagery, or elevation of sentiment; those being preeminent which combined all these excellencies in one. By a practice that was almost universal, the word was restricted to those works whose prime object was to address the imagination or to please the taste. Under this usage literature was confined to poetry, fiction, and the drama, also to various lighter effusions, but they all must have the common characteristic of being designed to amuse rather than instruct, to gratify some aesthetic interest rather than to convince or to arouse to action. If a work had any higher end than these, it was by general consent excluded from literature and deemed unworthy of the notice of the critic, as it was exempt from his censure. The poetry of Milton was literature, but his ***Areopagitica*** with its magnificent prose, and his ***Defensio Populi Angli-cani*** with its splendid invective were not, because they were political tracts. The poems of Donne and Cowley were literature, but the sermons of Jeremy Taylor though luxuriant with the wealth of an oriental imagination, were not literature, because they were composed with an earnest Christian purpose. A work * profound in thought, if it was designed to convince of truth; impassioned in eloquence, if it was written to persuade; bright with humor, if it was intended for practical effect; was ex-cluded from the roll of the literature of the period, as too severe and earnest, however finished it might be in style, rich in imagery, or elevated in sentiment. A conception of literature so narrow must, of necessity, be belittling and trivial to author and critic. It could not but make the writer trifling and heartless, and his censor fastidious and flippant.

Now-a-days literature is restricted within no such narrow limits, and, as the result, both literature and criticism have been elevated. While it is required that every work which aspires to be called a work of literature should have a certain perfection of finish and of form, none are excluded by reason of their solidity of matter, or earnestness of aim. A history or a sermon, an oration or a political tract, even a scientific essay if excellent in method and style, in eloquence and imagery, takes the place as a contribution to the literature of a period or of a nation, to which its merits entitle it. As a consequence, the conception of literature itself is greatly elevated and ennobled. Instead of being regarded as one of the accessories of culture and luxury, it is viewed as the best and noblest expression of the best powers of the ablest men of an age. Instead of being judged by the mere accidents of form, and according to the capriciousness of a changing taste, it is both studied and tested according to its perfect ideal. It follows,—

Second: that while the older was narrow and conventional in its standards, the new criticism is ***catholic and liberal in its spirit***. The tendency of the earlier criticism was to set up a single author who was supposed to be nearest the ideal perfection, as the standard by which to try every other. Every other author, and the literature of every other period, were measured by him and the literature of which he set the fashion. Thus, in the days of Queen Anne, Dryden, Addison, or Swift furnished the norm of actual and almost of possible perfection. A generation later, Johnson and his imitators imposed, if they did not constitute, the rule of measurement. The earlier and nobler writers of the days of Elizabeth and James were now depreciated for their latinized and lumbering sentences and then counted half barbarians for that individual freedom which inspired their genius and constituted their real strength and glory.

In a generation still later, literature was still more or less conventional, because criticism kept it in bonds to the factitious standards which were derived from Addison, Pope and Johnson; inconsistent with one another as were the examples and the teachings of the masters from which she received her laws. In vain did Thomson give range to the impulses of his creative imagination, and Cowper plead the exemption from rule of one who claimed to be a rhymester and did not aspire to be called a poet. In vain did Burke give vent to the eloquence and imagery which his fiery imagination could not restrain, and Scott followed the bent of a romantic spirit which was inbreathed from his infancy. Criticism was still inexorable, till the more catholic spirit of Coleridge, Wordsworth, and others whom they incited and inspired, awakened the English mind to the personal and admiring study of the older writers, and encouraged the young ***litterateurs*** to dare to use all the resources of their own affluent language with the freedom of the elder days, and to give utterance to their thoughts in a more copious and untrammeled diction. The cumbrous phraseology of the old writers, their involved sentences, their learned pedantry, their disregard of neatness, directness, simplicity, and taste, had previously made them outcasts from polite society, or if they were admitted they were wondered at, rather than admired on account of " the barbaric pearl and gold " with which they were so richly clad, because their ornaments were not in the mode and their garments were out of fashion. But now these defects are little thought of in comparison with the greater copiousness and variety of their diction, the individuality impressed upon their style, and the shaping of the diction to the thought and feeling of the writer. To the victory, thus achieved by this more catholic criticism, do we owe it, that, in the last two generations, ***the*** range of thought in our leading writers has been so greatly enlarged, the depth of their researches has been proportionately increased, their philosophy has been more profound, their strength and intensity of emotion have been augmented, their imaginative power has been more unrestrained and more creative, and their diction has been more varied and powerful.

The modern criticism has not only been more catholic in its tastes and judgments of native literature, but also in its ca-pacity to judge fairly and to appreciate adequately the lite-rature of other countries and of remote ages. In this respect the earlier criticism was eminently bigoted and narrow. In looking upon its own narrow domain as the celestial empire and the flowery land, it regarded all foreign writers as in a certain sense outside barbarians, who might indeed be worthy of consideration for certain excellencies of style or imagery, or for the purposes of grammar and philology, but were thought to have no special claim to attention as varied expressions of that common human life which makes the whole world kin.

The new criticism, in rising above such narrow prejudices, has not only done justice to its neighbor, but it has gained more than an equivalent for itself—reaping the double benison of charity, which always blesses him that gives as well as him that takes. In this, it has sympathized with the general movement of our times. While many of the sciences, both physical and humanistic, have become liberal by becoming *comparative*, as anatomy, physiology, and philology; criticism has also learned to compare the literatures of different ages and different nations, and to estimate them by certain fundamental principles. Critics now bring to the same bar of judgment Goethe, Shakspeare and Moliere, and try them all in respect of their common adaptation to express and please the same human nature. Criticism concludes its examinations and allots its sentences without respect of persons. What is different in each writer, in language or nationality, serves to set in bolder relief what is common; and the various methods by which writers of different countries ac-complish the same effect, impress the reader with the varied resources of human genius. National peculiarities, whether of matter or form, are relished with a special zest, and the reader's attention is quickened as he turns from one to the other with a freshened interest. This leads us to observe— Third: The new criticism is more *philosophical* than the old in its methods, and is therefore more just in its conclusions. Indeed it calls itself, by eminence, *philosophical* criticism. This claim is not extravagant, if the criticism is at once really elevated and catholic, inasmuch as these terms are almost interchangeable with profound and comprehensive. In aspiring to be philosophical, it seeks to find those principles which explain and justify everything that is excellent, and to expose and reject whatever proves to be defective or bad. In respect of style or diction, it seeks for the permanent and common characteristics of good writing, in those endless and manifold peculiarities of an individual writer, which spring from the constraints of language, from the genius of his nation, from the temper and culture of his period, and from his own individual habits or circumstances. In respect of thought, it measures each writer by the circumstances of his people and his time, as well as by the special aims which he has in view, and the capacity or attainments which the workings of his imagination may have showed.. If it estimates a poet or novelist it judges his genius by all the local and temporary influences, which made him what he was, as well as by his acceptableness to the private taste of the critic or the critic's special coterie. It does not try Goethe by Molière, or either by Shakspeare, or each and all by a living English dramatist or poet, but according to a just standard for each. It does not claim from Auerbach and Freitag, what it exacts from George Eliot and Anthony Trollope. In the same way among English writers, it does not measure Scott by Dickens or Dickens by Thackeray, or Thackeray by George Eliot, or George Eliot by Hawthorne. It does not test the subjective Tennyson by the objective William Morris, nor Robert Browning by the simple William Barnes of Dorsetshire, nor *The Spanish Gypsy by The Ring and the Book*, nor Whittier by Longfellow. It finds what is good in each, and judges the good of each, by the individuality of the author, the ends for which he writes, the audience to whom he writes, the times in which he writes, and the language through which he writes, as well as the people whose genius inspires what he writes. While it receives, as the rule of its judgments, the nature of man, it recognizes the truth that this nature exists and manifests itself under an indefinite variety of conditions, without ceasing to be the same.

We add next, and—

Fourth: that this criticism, in being more just, is necessarily more generous and genial. It cannot well be other-. wise. For its cardinal maxim is, the critic cannot be just to an author unless he puts himself in the author's place. Its comprehensive rule is, if you would understand an author's meaning you must learn to think as the author thinks, to feel as he feels, to look at nature and man through his eyes, to respond to both with his soul, to estimate his audience as he knew them, to measure the instruments of language and imagery which he had at command, in their several limitations, as well as their capacities. You must do all these things before you can even begin to judge him. This is only a special application of the principle which is expressed in the golden rule, " Whatsoever ye would that men should do to you, do ye even so to them." In putting in practice this rule of simple justice to any author who deserves our attentive study, there is wakened toward him an appreciative sympathy. It is only by seeking fairly and fully to understand a writer, that we are enabled to enter fully into his feelings, to catch his spirit, and to weigh his reasonings if we are not convinced by them. So complete, at times, is this sympathy with a writer whom we desire to understand, that as we give ourselves up to his influence, we seem to be his other self; we seem with him to create, and, borne on the rushing stream of his thick coming fancies, to revel in the joy of exercising the gift which we have newly acquired. Criticism thus applied wakens enthusiasm rather than represses it. It teaches us to look for excellences rather than to search for defects— and when it has taught us to find them, it prompts to our unrepressed enjoyment of them. It wakens in the mind a generous, because an intelligent delight in the beauties it reveals. It bids the reader be lenient to inadvertencies and defects in a writer of positive merit, because it teaches him how they are to be accounted for.

Fifth: The philosophic critic, in the very.best sense of the term, ***interprets*** the author to the reader. Thomas Carlyle says, in his peculiar way, of Heyne, the editor of Virgil, " I can remember it was quite a revolution in my mind when I got hold of that man's book on Virgil. I found that for the first time I had understood him—that he had introduced me for th'e first time into an insight of Roman life, and pointed out the circumstances in which the poems were written—and here was interpretation." This is indeed interpretation, and such interpretation is needed in a far wider and deeper sense than is commonly appreciated, and of a multitude of authors whose meaning seems obvious to a man of common understanding, while yet it may be imperfectly understood. What Carlyle calls the circumstances in which a work was written, are very comprehensive in their significance. They include almost everything which may be known about an author; not the accidents of his external life— the day of his birth and death, or the number of years that he lived,—but the sort of a man he was in character and the sort of people with-whom he had to do; and this, not so much in their manners and habits as in their conceptions of life, their moving principles, including their prejudices and superstitions— what they were willing to fight for and die for, what they loved most heartily and hated most bitterly; how they kept their holidays, how they spent their work-days, and all else that may give a complete picture of the life out of which sprung the poems or sermons or tracts which the writer composed, and for which he wrote them. Matthew Arnold says, very pertinently, that " creative literary genius does not principally show itself in discovering new ideas," but " its gift lies in the faculty of being happily inspired by a certain intellectual and spiritual atmosphere, which finds itself in them." "This is the reason why creative epochs in literature are so rare," " because, for the creation of a master-work of literature, two powers must concur, the power of the moment and the power of the man, and the man is not enough without the moment." To understand the atmosphere on which a great writer depends for the development of his genius, is not always easy. It requires much study and sagacity to find it out, much honesty and zeal to appreciate it, and often great skill to represent it for the ready apprehension of another, This is the reason why the greatest gifts of genius can be so severely tasked as well as worthily employed in this service of interpretation, and also why when this service is successfully performed, it invests the author with manifold greater attractions for the reader, and binds him to his in-terpreter by heavy obligations.

There is also another sense, perhaps a higher, in which the critic interprets his author, especially if he be a great dramatic writer who must outline his characters by a few bold and masterly strokes, and manifest their inner life by means of a few significant words and actions. The reader, without the aid of the critic, may be astonished by bold deeds and be excited by passionate words, and yet be una ble except with this aid to penetrate their significance or to fill out what the poet has only suggested. We select Hamlet as a striking example of what we mean. As we study this character, it seems to require some age and thought to interpret its obvious import. Let us concede, however, that an intelligent person however young can scarcely follow the fortunes of the unlucky prince, without feeling a saddened sympathy stealing over his soul, even while he is more and more perplexed by the enigmatical character of much that he says and does. But let the reader study the analysis of the ideal Hamlet which Goethe has given in two or three pages of Wilhelm Meister, and return to the play; he will find it invested with a new interest, as well as enriched with a deeper significance. If we suppose Goethe's conception of Hamlet to be correct, it not only explains the play as a whole, but it also gives significance to incidents and sayings that would otherwise be unintelligible, if not offensive. The difficulty in fully understanding Hamlet without such a guide is, in part, as we have already intimated, that his character is rather sketched than completed—that it is suggested rather than developed ; and also that many readers lack the experience of human life, and the sagacity to interpret what they observe, which are requisite to comprehend a character so complicated and strange. Goethe interprets Hamlet when he teaches the reader to imagine some one of his own circle who has had an experience similar to his, and to conceive what would be his conflicting emotions, under a calamity so sudden and so sad. He goes even further and teaches us to understand the almost superhuman sagacity of the poet in making a word or an act, perhaps of irony or bitter scorn, to express or suggest so much. For Goethe to have interpreted Hamlet may not be so signal a proof of genius as it was for Shakspeare to create him, but no man who could not also create could have interpreted the character so well, if he could have interpreted it "at all. The acceptable service which Goethe has rendered to the readers of the great Dramatist is one of the most important which modern criticism has achieved. "While it illustrates the need which the reader may feel of the critic's assistance, it exalts the service to which the critic is called. "What Goethe did for Hamlet, has been done by other critics for many of the other characters of Shakspeare. We know it is often said that some of the most distinguished of these critics have found more in many of his characters than ever Shakspeare dreamed, and that by the extravagance of their fancies and the boldness of their suggestions, they have displaced the originals which Shakspeare conceived. This may be conceded, and the fact still be unquestioned that even where critics err by overdoing, they stimulate to healthful inquiry and to wakeful earnestness. Certainly, the modern world would lose much of stimulating and instructive reading, if it should lose what Coleridge, and Hazlitt, and Mrs. Jameson; what Ulrici, Schlegel, and Gervinus; what Henry Reed, H. N. Hudson, and Richard Grant White have written upon the great English Dramatist.

If the gifted critic sometimes errs or overdoes by substi-tuting his own fancies for the thoughts of his author, he more than compensates for this, by making the suggestions of the author a text for brilliant thoughts of his own. As there is nothing more stimulating to a man of genius than the works of another man of genius, so it should not be surprising that the criticisms upon a great write'r of such thinkers as Coleridge, Goethe, and St. Beuve, may contain the most valuable and inspiring original contributions. The thoughts need be none the less original because they are excited by the thoughts of another, any more than the thoughts of two persons who are brilliant in conversation, are less original or less weighty because the one stimulates or arouses the other. The encounter, when the critic meets his author, may not be unlike that which the witty Thomas Fuller records of Shakspeare and Ben Jonson, in the words which, though familiar, will bear repeating: " Many were the wit-combats between him and Ben Jon-son, which two I beheld like a Spanish great galleon and an English man-of-war. Master Jonson, like the former, was built far higher in learning; solid but slow in his performances. Shakspeare, like an English man-of-war, lesser in bulk, but lighter in sailing, could turn with all tides, and take advantage of all winds, by the quickness of his wit and invention."

Sixth: Philosophical criticism not only interprets an author by means of his times, *but it interprets the times of an author by means of his writings*. In other words, modern criticism is a most important adjunct to history, and for that reason eminently deserves to be called *historical* criticism. Not only *must* we know something of the history of an author's surroundings,—his atmosphere, as Matthew Arnold calls them,—in order to appreciate more justly either the man or his works, but we can also learn very much of these surroundings by means of his writings. The literature of a period is one of the most important adjuncts to the story of its history. It supplies certain descriptions of information which no other sources of knowledge can yield. It stamps and fixes impressions of much besides, such as no secondary or indirect information can possibly imprint, giving those vivid and life-like images of the men and scenes of the past which are the best substitutes for having actually lived among them.

The Odyssey of Homer is a fresh and detailed picture of the Greek life in its golden age. As we follow the story of the wanderings of its hero, we see and feel how the Greeks must have lived in the times when Homer actually wrote,—what they thought, how they felt, how they furnished their houses, how they supplied their tables, how they entertained their guests, how they regarded their wives and children, and in what esteem they held their horses and dogs. "We learn with what thoughts they looked up to the stars, with what longing and admiring eyes they looked out on the neighboring azure sea as it lay along their sharp horizon, ever glittering with its rippling laughter, and with what a shuddering awe they thought of the mysterious and unexplored ocean which extended Beyond, how far and whither they knew not. We are made to know how the Greeks viewed the present life in its wealth and friendship, its prizes and honors, its love of country and of glory, its comforts of home and its delights of love, and how they sought to penetrate into the life unseen, filling it with the shapes of beauty and of terror with which their brilliant mythology also peopled the earth and the air. We visit Greece with longing expectations. We rejoice in its transparent atmosphere and delight in its beautiful islands and azure sea. We admire the few remnants of its temples and shrines. But we are appalled at the misery and degradation of its present inhabitants, and cannot find the lively and polished Greek whom we look for among the loungers in the market places of Athens or the attendants upon its university. We can only find him as we study the comedies of Aristophanes. We look for Socrates in the scanty and starveling groves which we fancy may be haunted by his shade, but we can only find Socrates where we find Alcibiades and Plato, in the dialogues written by Plato himself, and in Xenophon's sketches from the life. We go to the Pnyx to hear Demosthenes, and to the Areopagus to listen to Paul, but it is only in the recorded words of each that we can either hear the orators or see their audiences.

We visit Damascus, Syria, and Palestine. Simple history, even when it is the best constructed, and the most faithful, can only give us imperfect impressions of the people which once inhabited the now half deserted plains and mountains. The brief, but graphic, annals of Jewish patriarchs and kings supply us only with the facts concerning the external life of the tribes that once made these deserts blossom as the rose. But in these records we can neither find the people as they were, nor can we imagine how they felt and lived. We must go to Job to find the devout man of the desert, the counterpart of Abraham, the father of his people; but with Job and the Odyssey together, we begin to understand the monotheistic patriarch of the East. "When we study the code of laws which Moses enacted, and the solemn counsels with which he en-forced these laws, we learn more of who the Hebrew people were. If we proceed to study those matchless Psalms, in which God was praised for the glory of the heavens, the beauty of the stars, the tumult of the storm and the noise of the ocean over which He thundered with His awful voice; the Psalms in which His holiness was extolled, the victories of His leadership were recounted, the nation's feasts of thanksgiving and sacrifice were solemnized, and the glory of Jerusalem was fitly set forth ; in which also the prayer and praise, the penitence and thankfulness of the individual worshiper were expressed in words which have never been surpassed; then, and not till then, do we learn, in the spirit of Hebrew poetry, the spirit of the Hebrew people. If we follow on through the sad lamenta-tions of their prophets, their fierce rebukes, their faithful admonitions, and their glorious predictions, we learn to know this people more perfectly in their evil as well as their good, in their sad perverseness, as well as their many repentings and frequent returns to God. Moreover it is only in all these treasures of poetic and prophetic literature, that we trace the rising of the star of promise, till it stood at last over Bethlehem, and heralded the angelic shouts of glad tidings of great joy.

We wander lingering from Bethlehem to Calvary,

—in those holy fields, Over whose acres walked those blessed feet, Which, eighteen hundred years ago, were nailed For our advantage to the bitter cross,

studying the path in which those footsteps lie, if perhaps we may catch some vision of the present Jesus. But both in Bethlehem and at the Sepulchre, we hear the answer to our longings, He is not here, He is risen. As we read the history which records His deeds, we cannot bring Him back to the desolate land which He once inhabited. But as we read His own words in the most precious legacy which human literature has preserved, we seem to see Him living—and while we worship at His feet, we rejoice in His benediction.

When we go to Rome and Italy we cannot find the old Romans, however ear- nestly we search for them in their sepulchres, in the Forum, or the Coliseum, or however sanguinely we look to see them repeated in the population which now in- habits the Eternal city. We cannot revive them to our imaginations by the unaided force of all the suggestions which haunt the Tiber or the Appian way. We find them only as we consult the letters of Cicero and of Pliny, and the poems of Virgil, of Lucan, and of Lucretius, or study the treatises of Seneca and Antoninus. The old Ro- man life re-appears in the incidental records of their thoughts and feelings, which we find in these and similar writers, and in the incidental glimpses which they give of the life of the people with whom they had to do. As we compare ancient literature with modern, we reach the confident conclusion, that the virtues of the ancients were patriotism, hospitality, friendship, and honor, all restricted in their sphere, however noble in kind, and limited to ccrtain external duties and elevated sentiments. We, miss entirely the self-denying love of man as man, which Christianity sanctioned by the most characteristic act of its great founder. The Christian love to enemies, the Christian forgiveness of injuries, its sweet and contented submission to adversity, its patience under undeserved wrong, the overcoming evil with good—all being special virtues of the temper, springing from charity as the bond of their perfectness—were not known, we do not say in the practice of the ancients, but they were not honored as elements of their ideal. All this we know from their literature when it is critically studied as a trustworthy re-presentation of the people's inner life. From the literature of the ancients we learn with satisfactory certainty the place which woman held in the house and in society. We know that in the esteem and affections of the best and the purest, she did not hold the place, with the rarest exceptions, which she now holds in the confidence and love of myriads of households and of hearts. The ideal man of the noblest ancient schools, was immeasurably inferior to the ideal man of multitudes of humble and uncultured Christian communities. We learn all this from what is plainly manifest in the literatures of the ancient and modern worlds.

The importance of the critical study of literature as an aid to the interpretation of modern history is equally manifest. It is even more so, because the appliances which literature furnishes for the exposition of many periods of modern history are so much more varied than those which illustrate the best known of any of the ancient generations. The reign of Queen Elizabeth is reflected, as in a magic mirror, in *the* plays and letters, in the sermons and diaries of her time. The times of the memorable conflict between Puritan and Cavalier can be almost literally reproduced from the direct and indirect sketches which were made of its various characters and scenes, in the manifold forms of literature which were photographed from the life by unconscious artists. The writings of Swift and his compeers, the plays and songs of the hour, libels and street placards, sermons and letters—all these were materials which enabled Thackeray, with the rarest critical discernment to reconstruct his admirable historical tale of the days of Queen Anne. It was out of the literature of their several periods that Scott was able almost to recreate these periods.

The service of the critical study of literature is as great to the reader of history as it is to the writer. No one can fully appreciate the history of any people or of any period by relying on the descriptions and judgments of others. He must, in a certain sense, construct this history for himself, even when he reads it as constructed by others; at least he must reinforce the assertions, and verify the conclusions of his authorities, by looking for himself, so far as he may, upon the people and events described, and doing this face to face. This he can in no way do so effectually as by studying their literature. But in order to do this with the most eminent success, most readers require the aid of the philosophical critic, to explain the relations of literature to history.

Seventh. The critical study of literature is of service to **biography** as well as to history. If we can read the times of an author by the pictures of them which he reflects in his writings, much more can we learn the character of the author himself by the sentiments and feelings with which he reproduces his times, as they are seen in the shadings and colors with which he represents them. If a man's private letters are often the best materials out of which to construct his biography, it should be remembered that much of what he publishes as his works are in some sense his public letters, his epistles to the world and to posterity, as these convey, not alone what he professedly aims to produce and record, but often much more of what he unconsciously reveals. Some books from their very nature, reveal very little of their author's feelings and character. But very many books communicate much more, at times, than he designs or desires. The sonnets of Shakspeare, the poems of Milton, the playful and serious essays of Cowper, the meditations of Wordsworth, the passionate outbreaks of Byron, the vague aspirations of Shelley, and the prolonged lament of Tennyson, when skillfully interpreted, enable us to penetrate into the secrets of their hearts, and open to us the hidden springs of their character. It is the office of the critic to discriminate between what does and what does not express the man, and thus to interpret the man by many of his works; and the service which he renders to the reader is often of surpassing interest.

CHAPTER XVIII.

THE CRITICISM OF ENGLISH LITERATURE.

THE features of modern criticism which have been enu-merated, may suffice. We may perhaps more profitably, as well as more practically, proceed to consider our own literature as a field for its exercise. We may aver with confidence, that English literature furnishes the amplest, the most varied, and the most interesting materials for the critic, of any whether ancient or modern. It ought not to surprise us that it should. The compound structure of the language gives an advantage to the writer as well as to the philologist, furnishing often a richer choice of terms, a greater variety of phrases, and a wider range of structure, than is possible for any other modern tongue. That this structure pertains to its form alone is true, but the form in. this instance happens to furnish large capacities for the embodiment and expressions of a rich and manifold material. This material is rich and manifold, chiefly, because its people have been free, have been bold in thought, and earnest in feeling. They have been moved and stirred by the largest spirit of adventure in commerce, in war, in coloniz-ing, and in self-government. They have had an intense religious spirit, manifested in a sufficient variety of forms, and inspiring to fervent faith, to martyr-like boldness, and to consistent and heroic self-denial. They have had earnest political struggles *for* the crown and *against* the crown —*for* the liberty of the commons, and the traditional rights of the people, and *for* the divine right of kings, and the dignity of the royal prerogative. They have had sacred and happy homes,—fireside enjoyments hallowed by domestic love, and made doubly sacred and dear by ancestral recollections. They have had exhaustless and irrepressible humor—an inborn love of noisy hilarity, an infinitude of original characters to provoke this humor, and inspire the songs of a people ever ready to be excited to uproarious merriment. They have had a free press—a free pulpit, and free newspapers, in spite of occasional censorship, packed juries, and venal judges.

If we trace the history and characteristics of this literature we may well be amazed at its varied riches, and be excited to avail ourselves of its inviting stores by a more earnest as well as a more critical use of its ample resources.

We begin with Chaucer. In the Canterbury Tales we have a worthy counterpart to the Odyssey, giving as they do, a graphic and varied picture of the many-sided life, and the strongly marked characteristics which, even at this very early period, were manifest among the English people. Indeed we could not desire a more satisfactory illustration of the truth and justice of all that we have said of literature as a field for the study of history, than is furnished in these tales of Chaucer. The attentive reader cannot fail to observe how eminently true it is that the times illustrate the author and the author illustrates his times; how, through these tales, we have a direct insight into the manners and the sentiments, the customs and the philosophy of our ancestors, as they were, and as they lived some five hundred years ago. We have only to look through this magic show glass, and we are transported back to the very scenes which were then transacted, and those early times live again before our eyes. It is not a lifeless chronicle which we read, it is not a grave description, not a careful analysis, not a logical generalization, such as the annalist and the historian furnish. It is not even an historical novel in which a writer of a later period has endeavored to recreate the times as he conceived them, but it is an unconscious painter of the men and the manners with which he was conversant. How strong and bold-hearted were those men, how natural their manners,—how brave and sincere, how humorous and tender-hearted, how beneficent and devout were the sentiments which they express. After a long and somewhat dreary interval, we come to the age of Shakspeare, and not to the age of Shakspeare alone, but to that of Spencer and Sidney, and Raleigh, and Hooker, and Bacon, and Ben Jonson, and the train of dramatists of whom Jonson was the representative and the head. We call this truly the golden age of English literature, and we ask what agencies could have produced such writers as these ? We find our answer—first in the original force of the English stock, that under all the burdens of royal and churchly oppression, had never been corrupted or crushed, but had held its own in the halls of the gentry, the farm-houses of the yeomen, and the cottages of the laborers. This vital force was marvellously aroused by the Protestant Reformation, and when after many struggles, a Protestant Queen had come to the throne, it experienced, as it were, a thrill of newly created energy. Foreign wars, commercial adventures, romantic discoveries, all united to keep this young life excited to its utmost tension, and to move it by an inward ferment. The thoughts of men were great in those times; their hopes were unbounded; their feelings were fervent, their self-confidence was untram-meled; their power of expression was untamed. They had at their command the language not as yet shaped by critics or developed into any normal structure,—a fit instrument for the young giants, rejoicing in their strength, who were ready to use it, each as he would. Could the reader desire a study more inviting than that to which the literature of those active and hopeful days invites him ? Whether he would study the authors or their times, or both together, whether he would study the matter or the form of literature,—thought, sentiment, and imagery, on the one hand, or diction, rhythm, and periodic power on the other,—he could ask for nothing more exciting or more rewarding than what is furnished here.

The age of Milton follows, and not of Milton only, but of Taylor and Sir Thomas Browne, of Baxter and Bunyan, of Hobbes and Fuller. Here the English life—and with it English literature—appears in other forms, more fixed, and serious, and grave,-but with not a whit of its force abated, nor aught of its fiery energy repressed. Imagination is still as soaring as ever, and the manifold and seeming exhaustless varieties of diction illustrate the resources and the plastic capacities of the English language. This period was marked for its political struggles and its religious strifes, for its intense feeling and its strong thinking; for its ardent longings and its patient endurance, and above all, for its faith in God and in man; and all these influences shaped the literature, as the literature helped to form the period.

The age of Dryden followed, and not of Dry den only, but of South, and Locke, and Boyle, and Newton. It was a tamer period, in which accuracy of thought, and exactness of language, and symmetry and conciseness of style, and repression of feeling, and caution in imagery, were all con-spicuous. It was an age of repression and of criticism, as was natural after the real and imagined excesses of principle and feeling which had characterized the times of the Commonwealth,—an age in which religion declined and im-morality was less restrained—an age of free thinking and unbelief which were scarcely held in check by the efforts of Locke and

Boyle. With an age thus characterized by the life of the people, the literature of the period sympathized. First of all, it was the period in which the modern and the better English style was developed and fixed—pertinently by Dryden. Next criticism itself was first applied with systematic aims and definite results. In this Dryden was also conspicuous. With more accurate thinking and careful writing, there were not wholly lost the fire of feeling and the splendor of imagination which had distinguished the earlier periods.

Then followed the age of Pope, and not of Pope alone, but also of Addison, Swift and Shaftesbury, and these were closely followed by Bishops Butler, Berkeley and Warbur-ton, by De Foe, Richardson, Fielding and Smollett. It was an age in no wise distinguished for earnestness or for faith, an age of conventionalities, gaiety, and frivolity, an age of free living, and of free thinking, an age in which satire and sneering criticism would be likely to flourish, and in which both were abundant. As was the life, such was the literature of the period, with here and there an exception. For the ease and felicity of its prose diction, and for the correctness and smoothness of its verse to the ear—it has been called the Augustan age of English literature, but the perfection of form to which it brought this literature scantily compensated for the loss of those higher qualities by which the earlier periods had been distinguished.

In the latter half of the same century there was a change for the better. This was the period of Johnson, and of Burke, of Thomson, Goldsmith, and Cowper. The national life grew more serious. The lower classes had been moved to greater religious earnestness by Wesley, White-field, and others. The higher were tired by the emptiness and dissoluteness, by the heartlessness and frivolity of the generations before them,—there was a longing after better things, and to this longing the literature of the period gave expression in manifold signs.

Then came the French Eevolution, filling many hopeful and sanguine spirits with ardent enthusiasm, and stirring their minds with inquiries which led to profounder studies of the principles of moral, political, and theological truth—then the inevitable reaction, involving strong repressive measures, and dividing society into angry sections,—then the long and costly wars of the allies, and the exciting career of the first Napoleon. All these movements in English thought, attended, as they were, by the corrupt demoralization of the court and example of the last of the Georges, were reflected in English literature as it presents itself in the first thirty years of the present century. This is the period of Scott and Burns, of Byron and Shelley, of Coleridge and Southey, of Wordsworth and Wilson, of Macaulay and Hallam, of Jeffrey and Mackintosh. Literature is sharply divided into opposing schools —expressing the divided sentiment and opinion of the English nation. Foremost among them is that catholic and comprehensive school which dared to free itself from the fashion of the day in both thought and diction, and to go back to the English writers of the earlier periods, and to vindicate Shakspeare, and Milton, and Hooker, and Bacon, from the neglect into which they had fallen. More than all, this school dared to vindicate for itself the liberty to use all the resources of the English language, as well as to sound all the depths of English thought and feeling after the ancient ways. While in one direction, as with Byron, literature is passionate and Satanic, and in another, as with Shelley, it is blasphemous and atheistic; while in Scott it is brilliantly romantic; while with Hallam and Mackintosh it is solidly earnest; with Coleridge, Wordsworth, Southey, and Wilson, it is more thoughtful and affectionate, it is mindful of nature and of God, and above all it dares to be true to whatever is best in human character and aspiration. With this school and its awakened interest in all the older literature, there arose also the spirit of historical and philosophical criticism, which has very largely contributed to the many-sided, and in general, the elevated literature of the present generation. Of this recent literature we need not write, for to attempt to characterize it would lead us beyond our limits.

This English literature is our heritage, and to study it should be our delight and occupation. That it may be a delight, it must be, in some sense, an occupation. If we are to judge of it in a truly critical spirit,—if we are to understand historically its authors and the times in which they lived—if we are to judge of it philosophically, and to read intelligently its graver writers of the past, or the more novel and fresher of the present,—we must read it earnestly and comprehensively; we must make it our study—not a study that is painful or repulsive—but one that is patient, systematic, and earnest.

English literature when once it has become a familiar field of intelligent study, brings this advantage, that it is a field which the student will never be able and never will desire to desert. To him who has learned to read aright, every week will bring some fresh tale, or poem, or essay, or history; every season will introduce some fresh author, summoning the reader to a new feast of delight, which will be none the less keenly enjoyed, because it is enjoyed with a chastened taste, and is judged with critical appreciation. All the life-long, amid its cares and its sorrows, its employments and its leisure, there will be at hand a capacity and a taste for those satisfying and elevating pleasures,—which instruct while they delight,—which lead us upwards to heaven, while they make us content with the earth. No class of habits that are purely intellectual can possibly enter so largely into our happiness for life, as those habits of reading with discrimination and with ardor, which are formed by abundant studies in the history and criticism of English literature.

The appliances for such studies are ample and accessible, and they are likely constantly to increase. "We have R,. Chambers' *Cyclopedia of English Literature*, which is furnished with separate biographical sketches of the leading English authors, and sufficiently copious extracts from their works. This may serve as a convenient guide and reference book, after which to mark and map out one's journey. Dr. G. L. Craik's compendious *History of English Literature and of the English Language from the Norman Conquest, is* more learned and critical, while it is unequal in its character, some portions being skillfully and carefully written, and others being hastily and superficially sketched. Its estimates of authors and its tone are in general very candid and judicious. Abraham Mills' *Literature and Literary Men of Great Britain and Ireland* is a well con-sidered and trustworthy book. H. Morley's two volumes, *English Writers before Chaucer, From Chaucer to Dun-bar*, are far more learned, and the work when complete bids fair to be an encyclopedia of learned criticism in the literature of England. S. A. Allibone's *Critical Dictionary of English Literature and British and American Authors* is at once the most extensive and complete reference book for facts and dates and critical estimates, that can be found in any language. Special editions of the earlier poets, as Chaucer and Spencer, are ROW accessible; also of single poems and plays of the earlier writers, which are designed for school purposes, and for the general reader. Cheap reprints of the best single works of the older writers, as *Arber's Reprints and The Bayard Series* promise to dif-fuse more extensively a taste for reading of this kind, by making it possible for every one to gratify it. The publi-cations of the earlier English Text Society are doing the same service for scholars. B. Tauchnitz's Five Centuries of *English Literature* is a very instructive selection. J. P. Collier's *Early English Literature* is critical and able. E. A. and S. L. Duykinck's *Cyclopedia of American Litemture* is carefully and faithfully prepared, and is a classical work of reference and authority. 0. D. Cleveland's Manuals, entitled *A Compendium of English Literature, English Literature of the 19th Century, and A Compendium of American Literature*, as well as his edition of Milton's Poetical Works with a verbal index, are very convenient and useful books, which are wisely used in many seminaries, and are good substitutes for the more bulky works of reference which we have cited. Thomas B. Shaw's Complete *Manual of English Literature*, with a volume of selections from English authors, may be confidently recommended as compact and well prepared volumes; also Wm. Spalding's *History of English Literature*. The same is true of *Angus's Hand-book of English Literature*, and *Specimens of English Literature*. Prof. Henry N. Day's *Introduction to English Literature* may be safely trusted as scholarly and ingenious. Thomas Arnold's *Manual of English Literature Historical and Critical*, is a solid and judicious history, such as we should expect from a son of the genial and loving critic who was once master of Rugby. H. Hallam's *Introduction to the Literature of Europe* is always judicious and often full in its notices of English authors. In all the general Encyclopedias, the biography and bibliography and criticism of English and American authors is usually copiously given.

In what is called the higher criticism of literature, as has been already intimated, our own language is in some respects deficient. In others it is abundantly supplied. Sir Philip Sydney's *Defence of Poesie* is worthy of a writer who had a poet's phantasy and a critic's delicacy of discrimination. With the exception of Sydney, Dryden is the earliest critic who rose above the mere technics of form and aimed to be at once just and genial, but Dryden's criticisms are too brief and limited to render any satisfactory service. Addison's Papers in *The Spectator* upon Milton's Paradise Lost are examples of a well intended attempt to attain to something higher in criticism than could easily be achieved in those times. Samuel Johnson was an omnivorous as well as an appreciative reader and a discriminating critic. His Lives of the Poets, his remarks upon writers in the Rambler, and his familiar talks concerning them which are recorded by Boswell are fraught with good sense and not wanting in discrimination, but his comprehension of the aims of criticism was limited, and his standard was in many . respects conventional. The so-called British Essayists contain more or less of criticism upon standard and current orators, which certainly did not rise above that of Johnson and Addison. *The Gentleman's Magazine* and the other monthlies, with Dodsley's *Annual Register* neither aimed at, nor attained to anything better.

The establishment of the Quarterly Reviews within the present century gave a powerful impulse to the critical ex-amination of books and the critical study of literature, opening as they did an opportunity for some of the ablest critics of their time, to express their opinions upon the leading authors of the day. The time of the establishment of the first was nearly coincident with the awakening in Great Britain of the new and better criticism, and these reviews were at once the cause and the effect of this awakened spirit. Sir Francis Jeffrey, Sidney Smith, Sir James Mackintosh, Lord Brougham, Lord Macaulay, Robert Southey, and Sir Walter Scott, Sir James Stephen and many others have contributed critical papers of surpassing ability to some one of the leading British Reviews. But most of these reviews were conducted in a political as well as a literary spirit, and many of their best critical papers are written in a tone that is ambitious of smartness and effect in the forms of expression, rather than of justice and candor in their estimates of authors and their works.

In later years this partisan feeling has been greatly softened, and many of the critical papers in these reviews have been composed in the spirit of eminent fairness and honor. A general feeling of homage to public justice has gained a strong hold of many of the leading minds in Eng-land and America, and the trenchant and slashing charac-ter of a review does not always save its injustice and par-tiality from general reprobation"; much less does it com-mand as formerly almost universal praise. While it is true that at present the leading English Quarterlies do not maintain that exclusive prominence in the field of criticism which they formerly held, they are still very ably conducted and contain many papers of masterly superiority from the foremost men of the present time.

The better criticism of England and America, as we have already explained, was either inspired from Germany, or it grew up with that interest in German literature which forced the English critics to confess that in some things England might learn from the continent. The writings of the Schlegels were early translated and read in the English language. Previous to this time, however, Wordsworth had written the profound, and in many respects, just criticisms upon Poetry which are found in his prefaces, appendix and postscript to the earlier editions of his Lyrical Ballads. Coleridge also, soon began to astonish the literary world by his public lectures upon Shakspeare, and by the bold and comprehensive criticisms which are to be found in his *Biographia Literaria*, and his occasional contributions to periodical literature. His conversations with many of the leading writers and critics of his time, were stimulating and attractive, and did much to create a new school of sympathetic and enlightened admirers for the best, and till then, much neglected older English writers. The Retrospective Review, a quarterly devoted exclusively to the criticism and history of the earlier English writers exercised a powerful influence for good. The series is an invaluable acquisition to English critical literature. Walter Savage Landor, in his *Imaginary Conversations*, taught a few select but admiring readers what it is to seek to put one's self in the place of a great writer and a great mind of another nation, and of other times. Prof. John Wilson, better known as Christopher North, invested criticism itself, with the dignity and interest of original creation, by filling his Nodes Ambrosianæ, *and other papers in Blackwood's Magazine with the most enthusiastic and genial criticisms that ever proceeded from an English pen. W. Hazlitt, in spite of his prejudices, gave many examples of a discriminating appreciation of the older and of contemporaneous writers. Leigh Hunt did the same with a far more loving spirit. Mrs. Jameson wrote a whole theory of the varieties of female character in her criticisms of the female personages of Shakspeare, entitled* Characteristics of Women. *Thomas Carlyle almost began his literary life by a delightful article on Burns, in the Edinburgh Review, in which, for once, he wrote English as other people do. Thomas De Quincey through his multitudinous papers of a critical and gossiping character, has done much to stimulate and to gratify interest and curiosity in the literary men of his times. Hartley Coleridge has, if possible, surpassed his father in his sagacious and well-balanced, yet warm and hearty judgments of his favorite authors. Thackeray's* Lectures on English Humorists *has the double merit of opening a new vein and working it successfully. The elder D'Israeli has done not a little to interest the public in literature and in authors by the miscellaneous contributions contained in his* Curiosities of Literature, *his* Amenities of Literature, *and his more methodical essay on the* Literary Character. *N. Drake's* Essays, Memorials of Shakspeare, and Shakspeare and his Times, *are worth consulting, at least, as showing one step in the transition to a better style of criticism. Meanwhile, the excellent work upon Shakspeare of the estimable and industrious Hermann Ulrici has been made known to the English people. Goethe has been extensively read by English* litterateurs who have imbibed his spirit, and been taught by his example. The extensive school of German historians and critics of their patron literature, has also become familiar to not a few Euglish and Americans, and inspired them with a laudable desire to imitate their example in dealing with their own writers.

The French have also taught something in respect to criticism. The comprehensive work of H. Taine upon English Literature, and his other works of art-criticism are genial, and almost recreative. The appreciative and subtle, the acute yet always civilized **St. Beuve** has enforced by abundant and attractive examples, the impression of what criticism may and ought to become. Matthew Arnold has inculcated these same lessons in his **Essays out Criticism; Culture and Anarchy; On the Study of Celtic Literature** better sometimes by his precepts than by his own practice. Interesting examples of what criticism may and ought to be are to be found in the **Hours with the Mystics** by the lamented R. A. Vaughan, in the Prefaces and notes of Henry Taylor, as well as in his **Notes on Books**, and in the **Dublin**

Afternoon Lectures upon Literature and Art which have now reached their fifth annual volume. Indeed there are few volumes in the English language which are better fitted to inspire and instruct the student of literature and of criticism, than the volumes of this series, or which deserve to be more generally known. Prof. David Masson is deserving of especial notice for his excellent volume *The British Novelists*, etc., to which we have previously referred. His *Life of Milton*, of which one volume only has been published, is a mine of critical and historical research on its illustrious subject and his times. His *Recent British Philosophy* is a contribution to literary as well as philosophical criticism. Prof. J. C. Shairp's *Studies in Poetry and Philosophy* are genial and discriminating. E. S. Dallas, under the enigmatical title of *The Gay Science*, has published a work, which though it contains many caprices and oddities, is yet of rare interest so far as it treats of the principles which are fundamental to the critical enjoyment of literature. F. W. Newman *On Homeric Translation* and Matthew Arnold's papers on the same topic, are instructive and stimulating. F. W. Newman's *Miscellanies* contains a series of *Lectures on Poetry* to which we have referred. *Guesses at Truth, The Oxford, Cambridge and Edinburgh Essays, Peter's Letters to his Kins-folk*, Dr. J. Brown's Horce Subsecivæ—better known among us as *Spare Hours*—contain much that is suggestive and inspiring to the critic. To a very large extent the Biographies of literary men include criticisms on their "Works and those of their contemporaries, and some of the most interesting criticisms in the language are found in the familiar letters of distinguished persons concerning the works and authors of the season and the week while each was the novelty of the hour.

In the United States, literary activity has to a large extent taken the form of literary criticism. We have had critics of the old school and of the new. Among those of the old are the prominent contributors to the North American Review, as Alexander and Edward Everett, the brothers W. B. O. and 0. W. B. Peabody, also Rev. Professor A. P. Peabody, Prescott the historian, George Ellis, Francis Bowen, and scores of others. Of the new or modern school the following are prominent: Henry Reed, Horace Binney Wallace, Orestes A. Brownson, Margaret Fuller Ossoli, George Ripley, H. T. Tuckerman, E. P. Whipple, Richard Grant White, Henry N. Hudson and James Russell Lowell. Mr. Reed is conspicuous for his labors on Wordsworth and Shakspeare—Mr. Wallace for his spirited criticisms upon art and philosophy—Mr. Ripley for the very elaborate and genial literary notices which have formed so conspicuous a feature in the New York Tribune for so many years—Mr. Brown-son for the trenchant and aggressive review which was for so many years sustained by his name—Margaret Fuller Ossoli for an enthusiasm which was almost genius—Mr. Tuckerman for the faithful and patient labor which has been bestowed on so many literary and art topics—Mr. Whipple for the careful research and elaboration of his analyses and delineations, especially those in his ***Lectures on the Literature of the Age of Elizabeth***—Mr. Hudson for his knowledge of, and his enthusiasm for Shakspeare and his vigorous way of putting his thoughts—Mr. White for his many explorations into curious literary facts, and his nice discriminations—Mr. Lowell for his masterly though personal ***Fable for Critics***, as also for his discriminating and kindling literary papers. We have by no means named all who deserve notice, but these may suffice. The reader who has followed us thus far, will have learned still farther to seek and find for himself, and to judge what he requires better than we can judge for him.

We ought not in this connection to omit all notice of the history and criticism of the Fine Arts, inasmuch as a critical interest in Art is nearly allied to a taste for literature. The standard English authors in English literature before the days of Ruskin and the Germans, were ***Alison on Taste***, Burke ***On the Sublime and Beautiful***, Price On ***the Picturesque***, Sir Joshua Reynolds' ***Discourses***, Horace Walpole's ***Anecdotes of Painting***, Lanzi's ***History of Painting***, Vasari's ***Lives of the Painters***, Fuseli's ***Sculptors and Architects***, and Hogarth's ***Analysis of Beauty***. But since the German criticism began to make itself felt in Art as well as Literature, we have J. Wincklemann's ***His-tory of Ancient Art***, C. O. Müller's ***Ancient Art and its Remains***, F. T. Kugler's Hand-booh of Painting, {German, Flemish, and Dutch Schools),also ***Hand-booh of Painting in Italy***. More recently W. Lübke's ***History of The Arts***, J. Ferguson's ***Illustrated History of Architecture***, J. H. Parker's ***Glossary of Terms of Architecture***, all of the last four being abundantly illustrated Following in the footsteps of the Germans we have A. W. Lindsay's ***Sketches of***

Christian Art, Mrs. Jameson's **Memoirs of Early Italian Painters, Sacred and Legendary Art, History of our Lord in Works of Art**, C. L. Eastlake's **Contributions to the Literature of the Pine Arts** and other kindred works. We ought not to omit to name Dunlap's **History of the Arts of Design in the United States** and H. T. Tuckerman's **Booh of The Artists**; nor G. W. Samson's **Art Criticism** and S. Spooner's **Art Dictionary**.

Since John Ruskin first took the modern world by storm in his Modern Painters, and began to follow the first impression by a succession of stimulating volumes, the subject of art and criticism generally has been invested with new interest to a multitude of readers who never thought before earnestly concerning either. There is little danger that a very considerable number of Ruskin's readers will adopt his theories in full, or would be injured by them if they should. The exciting, and at the same time elevating character of all his writings, has been acknowledged with enthusiastic appreciation by the great number of readers who feel that they have been wisely taught by him many valuable lessons in the observation of nature as well as in their judgments of art and literature. His works or selections from them, cannot be too warmly recommended for their moral as well as their aesthetic excellence. Now and then a young person may be overborne and swallowed up by Ruskin, but there are very few who have read him with ardor who have not been greatly benefited.

Books on the English Language, and on language in general deserve a passing notice in this place inasmuch as reading on these subjects comes legitimately within the scope of the general title of this chapter. The number of school grammars is well nigh boundless, and among them there is a great variety in respect of excellence. Of Philosophical Grammars of the English language there is a lamentable deficiency. It is in the German language only that we find those which are at all satisfactory and truly scientific. The works of R. G. Latham, and the grammar of "W". C. Fowler are perhaps the best. George P. Marsh's **Lectures on the English Language** and **Origin and History of the English Language**, stand prominent as treatises adopted for general reading. R. C. Trench **On the Study of Words, English Past and Present**, and **Select Glossary of English Words** are instructive and popular books. W. Swinton's ***Rambles among Words***, and Scheie De Vere's ***Studies in English*** are books which excite and gratify curiosity. The attention which has everywhere been given to the study of Anglo-Saxon and of the early English, promises to yield large contributions to this class of works.

In General Philology, which is a subject that interests very many general readers, the following books may be named : Max Müller's ***Lectures on Language, Chips from a German Workshop***, W. D. Whitney's ***Language and the Study of Language***, F. W. Farrar ***On the Origin of Language***, B. W. Dwight's ***Modern Philology***, and J. Stod-dart's ***Glossology***. The study of words in their general aspects and of language is very nearly akin to literary criticism, and careful and critical attention to the style of the authors we read, is itself a most important means of culture, as well as a source of high enjoyment. For this reason such works as Dean Alford's ***The Queen's English***, C. W. Moon's ***Bad English and the Dean's English***, and E. S. Gould's ***Good English*** are well worth reading. The habit of consulting an English Dictionary in reading is not maintained as commonly as it should be by intelligent persons. No single habit is at once so eminently the cause and the indication of careful attention to the language which we use, and an efficient training to the best kind of culture. It involves daily and hourly criticism of the use of an instrument which cannot be correctly and felicitously applied without accurate and careful thinking and active and refined sensibility.

CHAPTER XIX.

BOOKS OF SCIENCE AND DUTY.

PHILOSOPHICAL and ethical reading next claim our at-tention, and those books which aim to enlarge or confirm our convictions of Truth or to convince and incite us with respect to Duty. We use the words philosophical and ethical in a very liberal sense—to define all those works whether longer or shorter, whether graver or less serious, which have for their direct object conviction or action in the light of permanent principles, in contradistinction from those books which narrate facts or address the imagination. We do not include Theological and Religious reading, but reserve these for a separate chapter. We exclude all books and reading in technical or special science, because our design contemplates only a general course of reading, and because, for obvious reasons, the teachers and manuals of the several sciences may be relied on to direct to courses of special and technical study.

We begin with the sciences of Nature, i. e., physical na-ture—for we hold that the universe of Nature includes the spiritual as truly as the material, and that it is inaccurate to restrict the word nature to matter, whether it be hard matter or soft matter, whether it be solid and fixed as adamant or as impalpable and evanescent as the most diffused and diffusible of the gases. Most of the books upon these sciences which are of the highest authority are necessarily technical. They require careful study and exact knowledge. Of these standard treatises there is a very large number, and they are constantly displacing one another, with the very progress of science itself. A few books only come within the range and scope of our discussion, but these few should not be omitted. For the general reader Alexander von Humboldt's ***Cosmos*** is the best single book which gives what was known concerning the physical universe or was regarded as established by scientific methods and scientific evidence, at the time when the illustrious author finished the work which was so splendid *a finale* to his laborious life. This work is very concisely written and is often abstract and technical, but it will well repay slow and careful reading. The History of the progress of the sciences of nature, to the man of philosophical tastes is in the highest degree exciting and instructive, especially when followed in the more recent stages of their rapid and brilliant development. William Whe-well's ***History of the Inductive Sciences from the earliest to the present time***, is the best if not the only compendious work upon this general topic which is accessible. It meets all the wants of the general reader up to the time when it was written; J. F. W. Herschell's ***Preliminary Discourse on the Study of Natural Philosophy***, is a clear and popular position of the methods of studying nature and of the grounds of our confidence in the processes of induction. W. Whewell's ***Philosophy of the Inductive Sciences***, afterwards re-wrought and published under the title of ***History of Scientific Ideas, etc.***, is much more ambitiously metaphy-sical and entirely beyond the reach of the general reader. John Stuart Mill's ***System of Logic Ratiocinative and Inductive***, treats in Book Third of the processes and laws of induction, more carefully and exhaustively than any other work. The defective philosophical system taught in it diminishes very little from its practical value. The sub-stance of Mill's work may be found in abridgements, as W. Stebbing's ***Analysis of Mill's Logic***, and T. Fowler's ***Elements of Inductive Logic***. L. Agassi z's ***Essay on Classification*** is a treatise often referred to in respect to the philosophy of the inductive processes. His ***Methods of Study in Natural History, and Geological Sketches*** are at once popular and scientific. Arnold Guyot's ***Earth and Man conies*** within our rule, for though it treats in special of physical geography it discusses it very largely in its general relations to the history and development of the race. Many of the writings of the lamented Hugh Miller are very attractive to the unscientific reader, even when they are strictly technical, for the interest with which they invest physical research and the light they throw upon its processes. The same is true of many of the writings of Sir Humphrey Davy, Sir Charles Bell, of Richard Owen, Michael Faraday, and J. F. Tyndall. It is to be borne in mind that the press is literally oppressed by the number of superficial books in which the attempt is made to popularize science and to set forth its relations to the imagination and to faith. To uninstructed minds and to those who have only a smattering of knowledge many of these writings are attractive just in proportion to their superfi-cialness and pretension. The style in which they are written is often vicious and inflated, and overloaded with tawdry ornaments. It is not wise either to trust the science taught in such books or to follow the imaginative flights to which they would exalt and inspire, unless their authors are known among scientific men to be men of requisite knowledge and of sound judgment. Although the physical sciences are in their nature severe and in their requisitions exacting, they afford the amplest room for all grades of sciolists and pretenders as well as the widest range for every species of imaginative romancing. Science run mad is the maddest and the most uncontrollable of all forms of madness, as the steadiest and most trustworthy of horses is the most stiff-headed and unmanageable when he goes off in a fright or indulges in an escapade. It is a safe rule not to waste one's time or money on any of these pretentious travesties of scientifi truth, or works of science poetically treated. Among standard books of science in. general and on some of the special sciences, may be named, Mary Somerville's ***The***

Connection of the Physical Sciences, The Mechanism of the Heavens, and *Physical Geography*, L. Euler's *Letters on Natural Philosophy*, D. Olmsted's *Letters on Astronomy*, E. Loomis's *Progress of Astronomy*, J. Liebig's *Familiar Letters on Chemistry*, J. P. Cooke's *Religion and Chemistry*, G. P. Marsh's *Man and Nature*, J. F. Tyndall's *Heat as a mode of Motion, Sound*, H. P. Roscoe's *Spectrum Analysis*, E. L. You-mans', (edr.) *Correlation and Conservation of Forces*, E. F. Burr's Ecce Cælum.

Natural History differs from *Natural Science*, in that it is limited to descriptive classifications of living things and beings, and excludes reasoned theories of the laws and prin-ciples of the inorganic agencies and elements of the physical universe. The reading of works of this description is usually fascinating to children and youth, and should be cultivated assiduously in order to stimulate to the careful study of Botany and Zoology as the powers of observation are matured. In all these branches of study, as in Geology, we have manuals and authors of the highest rank and trust-worthiness, as L. Agassiz, J. D. Dana, A. Gray and A. A. Gould, and many others. That observation of Nature which is within the reach of every person of active mind and curious tastes may be greatly stimulated by reading such books as Gilbert White's *Natural History of Sel-borne*, W. Howitt's *Book of the Seasons*, G. B. Emerson's *Forests and Shrubs of Massachusetts*, Samuel's *Birds of New England*, T. L. Harris' *Insects of Massachusetts*, L. H. Morgan's *The American Beaver*, J. G. Wood's *Illustrated Natural History*, etc., all which are attractive and trustworthy. Such works as those of J. L. Michelet, *The Bird*, and the many prepared by L. Figuier—those published in *The Library of Wonders* from the French, *The Universe* by L. A. Pouchet, never cease to attract and reward the reader, whether young or old, and they render a most important service when they stimulate a family of children, especially if they have a home in the country, to use their eyes and ears in the observation of nature. If rightly used they furnish the happiest illustration of the remarks which we have made, that reading becomes most interesting and instructive when it is interpreted by, as well as when it directs the employments and amusements of the daily life.

We are reminded by this of the important use which may be made of books and reading by those who cultivate the soil. The old and stupid prejudice against "book-farming" has almost entirely passed away. No person who reads this volume will be likely to retain the least remnant of it. A sense of the value of agricultural books and periodicals is now generally diffused throughout the community. It were difficult to decide what are the best books upon the many topics comprehended under this extensive department. Every part of the country has those which are thought to be the best. Every leading journal and newspaper is usually interested in certain favorite writers. Should we attempt to furnish a select list which might be approved for the present year, it would probably be soon displaced in part in the year following. The list which we subjoin has been carefully studied by a compe-tent and discriminating authority who is endorsed by an author who stands high in favor with the farming as well as with the literary world. S. W. Johnson, **How Crops Grow. How Crops Feed**. G. E. Waring, **Draining for Profit**. J. J. Thomas, **Farm Implements**. A. **Gray, Field, Garden and Forest Botany**. W. Darlington, **American Weeds and Useful Plants**. C. L. Flint, **Grasses and For age Plants**. F. Burr, **Field and Garden Vegetables of America**. P. Henderson, **Gardening for Profit**. J. J. Thomas, **Fruit Culturist**. G. Husman, **Grapes and Wine Making**. A. S. Fuller, **Small Fruit Culturist**. J. A. Hoopes, **Forest Tree Culturist. Book of Evergreens**. F. Parkman, **Book of Moses**. E. S. Rand, Jr. **Bulbs. Seventy-five Flowers**. S. Tenney, **Natural History**. R. L. Allen, **Domestic Animals**. C. L. Flint, **Milch Cows and Dairy Farming**. H. W. Herbert, **Hints to Horse-keepers**. W. Youatt, **The Horse**. Harris, **On the Pig**. H. S. Randall, **The Practical Shepherd**. T. W. Harris, **Insects of Massa-chusetts**. A. J. Downing, **Landscape Gardening**. L. L. Langstroth, **The Hive and Honey Bee**. D. G. Mitchell, **My Farm at Edgewood. Wet Days at Edgewood**.

From Agriculture to Psychology and Speculative Phil-osophy seems a long stride. It is a wide leap which carries us from the most concrete to the most abstract of topics. And yet the stride is by no means so long, nor the leap so wide as would appear at first view. The culture of the earth forces us to consider life in the plant and the animal, and we find ourselves before we know it ascending from the soil and the clod into the fascination and mystery of that life which nature sustains by the earth and from the air. The study of life carries us up to finer and more subtle processes and powers so that before we .are aware, we are confronted by the presence of spirit with its wondrous capacities and gifts and its still more wonderful intuitions and beliefs. The analysis of these implicates us in psychological inquiries and metaphysical researches. Ethical principles spring out of the soul's inner being, and conscience and duty are seen to be clothed with authority by the soul and to be enforced by all the indications and utterances of the universe. God himself looks out upon us from all the windows of heaven and is felt by us to be the strength and stability of the fabric of Nature and the institutions of human society.

The mental and moral sciences are often abstruse, but they are not technical and special as are the so-called sciences of Nature, for the reason that the principles and facts with which they have to do are more within the reach of common minds and have a nearer relation to many of the higher interests and feelings of the race. They require less technical preparation in special studies, and hence are more accessible to the judgment and interest of any thoughtful and studious person. An intelligent reader, it is true, is not likely to be destitute of curiosity respecting mechanics or astronomy.. But he is still less likely to be devoid of interest in those speculations which concern the nature of the soul, the sanctions of conscience, the rights and duties of men, the limitations of government and the destiny of the race. All men as soon as they begin to reflect, begin a course of metaphysical activity whether they know or not, and many a plain man whose reading is very limited is ready to be aroused to excited interest in speculative studies and in the history of such inquiries as conducted by others. Wherever men have been made earnest thinkers by theological discussions, political excitements or moral revolutions, there has it been uniformly true that the subject matter of speculative and moral philosophy has awakened a profound and excited interest in the minds of the common men of the community. A great social convulsion, like the so-called Great Rebellion of 1640, the English Revolution of 1688, the American Revolution of 1776, the French Revolutions of 1789 and 1848, or our own Civil War of 1861, forces even the ignorant and unthinking to fall back upon the ultimate principles of political and social obligation and to discuss them with excited interest. It turns a nation of farmers and artisans into a school of acute and disputatious philosophers. The din of preparation for physical conflict in the field is usually interspersed with the hum of excited if not angry discussion and debate. The questions of the suffrage of women, of blacks and whites, of natives and foreigners, cannot be settled without an intelligent reference to the principles of ethical and political philosophy. The occurrence of strikes, the organization of trades unions, the demands of the laborer, and the retorts of the employer force all parties to examine the doctrines and definitions of political and social science. Earnest religious excitements and controversies, whether they end in faith or in unbelief, compel every man who is interested, to a profound philosophical inquiry. All men who think earnestly upon fundamental questions must so far be philosophers. In this way is the fact to be explained, that plain and even unlettered men are so often acute philosophical reasoners and are interested so profoundly in books and reading of a speculative character. This is especially true in a country like ours, so receptive of ideas and so quick to transmit them, all over which so many persons of active minds are profoundly interested in great practical questions and are finding themselves as constantly forced to decide these by a reference to fundamental principles. Hence we explain the fact that there are multitudes of men making no pretence to extensive literary culture who not only take a strong interest in books on these subjects but are qualified to read and judge them with intelligence and discrimination. We do not consult the wants of the learned class, but provide for the occasions of the general reader when we suggest a course of reading in Philosophy.

We begin with the History of Philosophy. While there is no general history in the English language which meets all the wants of the general reader there are several which deserve to be named as worthy of perusal. F. D. Maurice's ***History of Moral and Metaphysical Philosophy*** is perhaps the most readable of any. A. Schwegler's ***History of Philosophy*** translated from the German by Prof. J. H.. Seelye, and a later edition with large additions by J. H. Stirling, is a very good brief manual. ***An Epitome of the History of Philosophy*** from a French manual translated by Prof. C. S. Hurny, which is published in Harper's Family Library, is a convenient but rather dry book of reference. Mr. G. H. Lewes' ***History of Philosophy*** is in some respects more erudite and acute than the work of Mr. Maurice, but it is written too decidedly in the ***negative*** spirit of the ***positive*** school to inspire entire confidence, especially as it is a cardinal doctrine of this school that philosophical speculation is vain and profitless. A translation from the very learned and comprehensive manual of F. Ueberweg is now in course of publication, from which much may be expected of accurate statement and intelligible information. For modern philosophy J. D. Morell's ***Historical and Critical View of the Speculative Philosophy of Europe in the 19th Century*** is a very comprehensive and convenient though not always satisfactory treatise. For the history of the modern German Philosophy H. M. Chalybäus's ***Historical Survey of Speculative Philosophy from Kant to Hegel*** is perhaps as good, *i. e.* as intelligible an account as could be expected from a German historian, of the progress of a series of speculations which are confusedly dark and abstruse. In ancient philosophy in particular "W. A. Butler's ***Lectures on the History of Ancient Philosophy*** are the most satisfactory as they are the most eloquent history which the language can show. Mr. George Grote in his ***History of Greece*** gives a very attractive sketch of Socrates and the Socratic school, while in his very elaborate work on ***Plato, and the other companions of Socrates***, he has drawn out a careful outline of each of his works. Mr. Grote is in many cases unjust to Plato, so far at least as he interprets and judges him by the tenets of the narrow and superficial school of philosophy to which he himself belongs. Mr. G. H. Lewes has devoted a special volume to the contributions of Aristotle to physical science. B. F. Cocker's ***Christianity and Greek Philosophy*** is a valuable discussion of the themes and the achievements of ancient speculation and a comparison of both with those of modern thought and the positive teachings of Christianity. For the history of speculative philosophy in Great Britain nothing better can be named than Dugald Stewart's ***General View of' the Progress of'Metaphysical, Ethical and Political Philosophy***, which as was natural is specially devoted to British metaphysicians, and Sir James Mackintosh's ***General View of the Progress of Ethical Philosophy***, Both of these works are very incomplete and imperfect, though containing much valuable history and criticism. All mere histories of philosophy, are necessarily unsatisfactory by reason of the narrow limits within which the writer is confined. It not unfrequehtly happens that these defects are supplemented by articles in Encyclopedias or by special treatises of a biographical or critical character.

Leaving the History of Philosophy and proceeding to Philosophy itself, the general reader will find translations of the following works ample for the direct knowledge which they give of the teachings and modes of thinking of the most distinguished of the ancient philosophers. W. Whewell's **Select Platonic Dialogues**. R. W. Browne, **Aristotle's Nicomachean Ethics**. T. Hobbes and T. Buckley's **Rhetoric and Poetics. Cicero's Offices, Letters, Tusculan Disputations and De Finibus**, translated by different writers; also the writings of Seneca, Epictetus, Antoninus and the poet Lucretius. Coming to modern times we name the following works as pre-eminently worthy to be read. R. Descartes, **Meditations and Essay on Method. J. Locke's Essay on the Human Understanding**, with V. Cousin's **Lectures on Locke**, known in one translation as Cousin's **Psychology**. T. E. "Webb, **The Intellectualism of Locke**. D. Hume, **Philosophical Treatises**. G. Berkeley, **The Minute Philosopher; The Principles of Human Knowledge**. T. Reid, **Inquiry and Essays**. T. Brown, **Lectures on the Philosophy of the Human Mind**. Dugald Stewart, **Philosophical Works**., I. Kant, **Critic of Pure Reason**} translated by Meiklejohn. J. G. Fichte, **The Science of Know-ledge; The Destination of Man**. Sir William Hamilton, **Lectures on Metaphysics and Logic, also Philosophical and Literary Essays**. H. Calderwood, **Philosophy of the Infinite.** H. L. Mansel, **Limits of Religious Thought; The Philosophy of the Conditioned; Prolegomena Logica**. Godwin Smith, **Letter to H. L. Mansel**. J. H. Stirling, **The Secret of Hegel**. J. S. Hartley's **Observations on Man**. J. Mill, **Analysis of the Human Mind**. J. Mill, **A System of Logic Ratiocinative and Inductive; Examination of Sir William Hamilton's Philosophy**. J. M'Cosh, Ex-amination of Mr. J. L. Mill's Philosophy, being a Defence of Fundamental Truth; The Intuitions of the Human Mind, etc. **J. F. Ferrier,** Institutes of Metaphysics. **Herbert Spencer, First Principles, and** Principles of Psychology. **A. Bain,** The Senses and the Intellect; The Emotions and the Will; Mental and Moral Science; A Compendium of Psychology and Ethics ; Logic, Inductive and Deductive. D. Masson, Recent British Philosophy. **F. Bowen,** Essays. **J. Martineau,** Essays, Philosophical and Theological. These works with the Histories of Philosophy and the numerous critical papers which many of them have occasioned would give the reader a reasonable knowledge of the various schools of opinion which have prevailed in modern Philosophy.

Of Manuals of Psychology we name as in more or less extensive use, those of T. C. Upham, F. "Wayland, L. P. Hickock, Dugald Stewart, Thomas Brown, Sir "William Hamilton, J. Haven, A. Mahan, J. T. Champlin, N. Porter, J. Bascom and A. Bain To Psychology, Physiology has close relations because of the intimate connection between the human body and the human soul. The interest in this science has also of late been greatly increased as the result of materialistic views in respect to life and spirit. The study of life in any of its forms is indeed the best introduction to the study of spirit in any of its manifestations. W. B. Carpenter's *General Physiology and Human Physiology* are very gen-erally accepted as of the highest authority. They are characterized by their encyclopediac character more than by acuteness of discrimination, force of reasoning or comprehensiveness of thought. J. Muller's *Human Phy-siology* is in all these respects incomparably the superior. Very able Manuals have been produced by E. C. Dalton, W. Draper and T. H. Huxley. A more comprehensive treatise is in process of publication by A. Flint. A brief and plausible argument for materialistic views may be found in a tract by T. H. Huxley, *The Physical Basis of Life* and a reply of great ability *As regards Protoplasm* by J. H. Stirling.

Vegetable Physiology is usually treated in works upon Botany. A. Gray's *How Plants grow*, L. H. Grindon's *Phenomena of Plant Life*, H. von Mohl, *The Vegetable Cell*, J. Marcet's *Vegetable Physiology*, J. M. Schleiden's, *The Plant a Biography*, C. Darwin's *Origin of Species*, P. W. Roget's *Animal and Vegetable Physiology* are all works of authority.

In Ethics the contributions to English literature are very numerous, but are almost universally deficient in precision, method and philosophical completeness. We name the most significant writers, and they may be advantageously read in connection with the following critical histories, J. Mackintosh's *Progress of Mbical Philosophy*, W. Whe-well's *History of Moral Philosophy in England*, R. Blakey's *History of Moral Science*, Th:. Jouffroy's *Introduction to Ethics*, The leading writers are: T. Hobbes' *The Leviathan*, R. Cudworth's *Treatise concerning Eternal and Immutable Morality* R. Cumberland's Be Legibus Naturæ, *F. Hute-heson's* Inquiry into the Origin of our Ideas of Beauty and Virtue; Moral Philosophy, *D. Hume,* Inquiry into the Principles of Morality, *Jonathan Edwards',* A Treatise on the Nature of True Virtue, *R. Price's* Review of the Principal Questions in Morals, *A. Smith's* Theory of Moral Sentiments, *W. Paley's* Manual of Moral and Political Philosophy, *J. Bentham's* Principles of Morals and Legislation; Deontology, *J. S. Mill's* Essay on Utilitarianism, *Alex. Smith's* On the Philosophy of Morals, *I. Kant's* Metaphysics of Ethics, (tr. from the German), F. W. Cobbe's *Essay on Intuitive Morals*, an eloquent exposition of the Kantian system, W. Adams' *Elements of Christian Science*, S. S. Laurie's *On the Phil-osophy of Ethics*, M. Hopkins' *Lowell Lectures, also Law of Love and Love as Law*, D. Metcalf's *Nature Foundation and Extent of Moral Obligation*, A. Bain's *Compendium of Ethics*.

Of manuals of the theory and practice of ethics, we name "W. Whewell's *Elements of Morality including Polity*, W. Fleming's *Manual of Moral Philosophy*, F. Wayland's *Moral Philosophy*, L. P. Hickock's *System of Moral Science*, J. Haven's *Moral Philosophy*, J. H. Fairchild's Moral Philosophy, or the Science of Obligation, A. Alex-ander's *Moral Philosophy*,

Politics and Jurisprudence are akin to ethics, and the principles of both these sciences are generally discussed in manuals of duty. The principles of the science of government should be thoroughly considered by every reading man in a republican government. The attempt has been made to introduce the study of the elements of this science into our public schools but with no flattering success, for the reason that the study in its own nature is too abstract and requires too much reflection to be suited for very young persons. The *Political Class Book* by W. Sullivan, a very clear-headed writer, was prepared for use in schools. *Blachstones 'Commentaries* is the text book which introduces every student to the common law of England. It is eminently instructive to every general reader who is not repelled by its length and terminology. J. Kent's *Commentaries on American Law* in its extended or its abridged form is a work of the highest authority. H. S. Maine's *History of Ancient*

Law is a work of a decidedly philosophical character, and traces many of the principles and rules of positive legislation back to their first beginnings; so to speak to their rudimental germs. J. Austin's *Lectures on Jurisprudence* is a work of eminent interest and value. J. N. Pomeroy's *Introduction to Municipal Law* is a popular and thorough treatise.

Of works in political science, the following are worth attention. F. Lieber's *Civil Liberty and Self-government* is a comprehensive and trustworthy manual which ought to be mastered by every intelligent reader. J. Mackintosh, *On the Law of Nature and of Nations*, J. S. Mill, *On Liberty* and *On Representative Government*, J. C. Calhoun, *On Government*, J. Locke, *On Government*, S. Nash, *Morality and the State*, E. Mulford,. *The Nation* are works of greater or less interest and authority. A. De Tocqueville's *Democracy in America* is universally ac-knowledged to be the most sagacious and profound work on American Institutions and American society that has ever been produced. *The Federalist* is a classical work upon the nature and origin of our general government, as are the so-called Madison Papers, which contain a sketch of the debates in the convention which formed the constitution. With this should be connected J. Elliot's *Debates on the adoption of the Federal Constitution in the several State Conventions*, also Geo. T. Curtiss' *Origin of the Constitution of the United States*, also Marshall's *Decisions of Cases* which concerned the interpretation of the same. T. Jefferson's *Memoirs, Correspondence and Miscellanies*, with his *Life* by S. Randall are invaluable to a right understanding and a just estimate of parties in this country. The life and works of Alexander Hamilton give the views of a leader on the opposite side. *W. Sullivan's Letters on Public Characters*, T. Dwight's *The Character of Jefferson as shown by Sis Writings and History of the Hartford Convention* may be consulted with great profit. The writings and speeches of John C. Calhoun and Daniel Webster which relate to the doctrines of nullification and secession are also of the first importance. M. Van Buren's *History of Parties in the United States*, J. A. Hamilton's *Reminiscences*, T. H. Benton's *Thirty Years' View of the United States Government*, J. Buchanan's *President Buchanan's Administration* are all instructive concerning our more recent political history. The treatises and speeches elicited by the recent civil war on both sides, are too recent and too well-known to require to be named, if indeed a selection from such a multitude could easily be made. The publications of the National Loyal League association present the national view with great force and varied ability.

Of treatises upon the English government and constitution W. Bagehot's *The English Constitution* is foremost in thoroughness and authority. E. S. Creasy's *Rise and Pro-gress of the English Constitution*, Lord John Russell's *Eng-lish Government and Constitution*, I. L. De Lolme's Consti-tution of England, are all good books.

The histories of H. Hallam and E. May have been already noticed. E. Burke's *Reflections on the French Revolution* and other writings, J. Mackintosh's Vindieiæ Gallicm, *Guizot's* History of the English-Revolution *and* Causes of Success of the English Revolution of 1640 and 1688 are publications of the first rank. The reader moreover who aspires to pursue an extended course of reading in political science or political history will find no difficulty in selecting the best works upon every topic in either of these de-partments.

In International Law, H. Wheaton's *History of In-ternational Law, and Elements of International Law* are of the highest authority. T. D. Woolsey's *Manual and Text Book* on this topic is universally commended and is brought down to the latest decisions. G. Bemis' *Precedents* of *American Neutrality* and *Hasty Recognition of Rebel Belligerency ; Letters On International Law* by " Histori-cus " and M. Bernard's *British Neutrality* should be consulted on this much vexed topic.

Political Economy is a science much attended to in our country and indeed in all civilized countries. The science of wealth and questions of Exchange and Finance must necessarily be thought of by every intelligent man. The newspapers abound in discussions upon these topics, and the destinies of great political parties hinge upon them. Adam Smith's *Wealth of Nations* is the first in time and almost first in importance. J. S. Mill's *Principles of Political Economy* is a more modern authority.

J. Ricardo, N.W. Senior, R. Whately, H. Fawcett, J. E. McCul-loch, among others, are all very able writers. H. C. Carey, in Essays and his other writings is the able and indomitable advocate of a decided Protective system, while F. Bastiat, in *Popular Fallacies, etc., Sophisms, etc.*, is its scientific foe. F. Bowen, *Political Economy*, and *American Political Economy* is the moderate defender of Protection and A. Perry, *Elements of Political Economy*, is its ingenious and apt opponent. Sociology is a new name for a so-called science which proposes to investigate those social conditions and arrangements whether natural or artificial, which affect the well-being of the community as a whole and that of the individual through the community. It treats of questions of the public health, the public morality and popular education. Active and efficient societies are formed for the furtherance of these objects, and the reports and treatises which they will produce must soon become an important part of our literature. Treatises upon education both special and popular are very abundant in our country, and are brought before the notice of all readers of newspapers. There remains to be considered a very large class of works of a more or less decidedly practical character, which in the language of Bacon come home " to men's business and bosoms." Many of these works are more or less Ethical in their influence and character, and may be classed under treatises or suggestions relating to the minor morals. They must almost of necessity be Ethical, for all those writings which propose to teach men how they ought to think and act in respect to any matter whatever must recognize more or less distinctly some standard of duty or some obligation enforced by duty. But these works treat of the minor rather than of the greater morals, of the lesser interests and ends of life, rather than of those commanding objects and aims which are universally and seriously enforced by morality and religion. Lord Bacon's *Essays, Civil and Moral*, stands confessedly at the head of all works of this class in English literature. It is in a sense properly taken as a model for all, and is one of the wisest and most thoughtful books for men of every condition and every age. It has been edited by Archbishop Whately with abundant comments, all of a solid and interesting character. Whately's edition may be fitly called Bacon adapted to modern times, by a writer of marked good sense. Whately's comments are never unworthy of Bacon. Of books of the class we have in mind, there are hundreds if not thousands in the English language. They are in a sense the legitimate and most characteristic product of the practical tendencies of the English people. They reflect that freedom in criticism and discussion which for so many-ages has been asserted by English writers, enforced by public opinion and secured by the laws. We can only set down a few of the best, somewhat after the order of time, and shall doubtless omit scores if not hundreds of great value. Roger Ascham, *The Schoolmaster; Toxophilus*. T. Fuller, *Holy and Profane State; Good Thoughts in Bad Times*. T. Brown, *Religio Medici*. O. Feltham, *Resolves, Moral and Political*, etc. A. A. Shaftesbury, *Characteristics*. Daniel De Foe, *The Family Instructor, Political* and other *Tracts*. D. Hume, *Essays. The British Essayists* from Addison to V. Knox. M. Montaigne, *Essays*. I. Watts, *On the Improvement of the Mind*. B. Franklin, *Essays*. William Cobbett, *Miscellaneous Works*. W. Irving, *The Sketch Book*, etc., etc. J. Den-nie, *The Lay Preacher*. E. Sampson, *The Brief Remarker*. S. T. Coleridge, *The Friend* and other works. J. Wilson, Nodes Ambrosianæ *and other works. C. Lamb,* Essays of Elia. *Leigh Hunt,* The Indicator *and other works. T. Hood,* Whims and Oddities, *and other works. W. Hazlitt,* Essays and Criticisms. *T. De Quincey,* Confessions of an Opium Eater *and a score of works besides. T. Carlyle,* Critical and Miscellaneous Papers, Sartor Resar-tus, *etc. J. Foster,* Essays. *Isaac Taylor, Home* Education *and other works. W. Channing,* On Self-Culture *and other writings. Anon.,* Self-Formation or History of the Growth of an Individual Mind. *H. Taylor,* The Statesman *and other writings. Arthur Helps,* Friends in Council *and other works. Mrs. Ellis,* Women of England, *etc. Anon.,* Small Books on great Subjects. *John Ruskin's* Writings. *C. J. and A. Hare,* Guesses at Truth. *C. C. Colton,* Lacon. *H. Davy,* Consolations in Travel, Salmo-nia. *L. Withington,* The Puritan. *H. Coleridge,* Essays and Marginalia. *John Brown,* Horæ Subsecivæ, *or* Spare Hours. *H. B. Wallace,* Papers in Art and Criticism. *F.Saunders,* Salad for the Solitary, etc. G. Mogridge, (Old Humphrey) various works. D. M. Mulock, *A Woman's Thoughts about Woman*. M. Fuller Ossoli, *Papers on Lit-erature and Art, etc*. N. P. "Willis, *Various works*.. W. Legget, *Writings*. P. Bayne, *Essays*. H. Bushnell, *Work and Play*. H. W. Beecher, *Life Thoughts; Star Papers*. R. "W. Emerson, *Conduct of Life* and other works. E. P. Whipple, *Essays and Reviews*. D. G. Mitchell, (Ik. Marvel) *Reveries of a Bachelor* and other writings. A. Froude, *Short Studies on Great Subjects*. A. R.

Hope, **Book about Dominies**. **Book about Boys**. D'Arcy Thompson, Day **Dreams of a Schoolmaster** and other works. A. H. Boyd, {The Country Parson) Miscellaneous Volumes. **"William Smith,** Thorndale, or the Conflict of Opinions, Gravenhurst. *J. G. Holland,* Letters of Timothy Titcomb, etc.

CHAPTER XX.

RELIGIOUS BOOKS AND SUNDAY READING.

WE approach both these topics with some hesitation. We do not expect that what we write will be understood by all our readers, or will be accepted by all who under-stand it. Very many persons who are intelligent upon a variety of other subjects never think or read with earnestness upon religion, although in the words of Daniel Webster, "the noblest theme that can occupy the intellect of man is man's relations to God." Lord Bacon also says in sober earnestness that " Theology is the haven and Sabbath of all man's contemplations." Religion and its truths, its theologies and its ethics, its histories and its biographies, its poetry and its criticism, are despised by many otherwise well and even highly cultured persons as the offspring of a fond imagination, a credulous superstition or a timid traditionalism. Or all these are disliked as imposing unwelcome restraints upon the pursuits and passions by which too many are controlled; perhaps they are scorned with passionate contempt from some inherited or conventional associations. There are not a few skeptics or rejectors of Christianity who if honest would be forced to confess with Hume, that they had never read the New Testament through with intelligent attention. On the other hand, there are not a few earnestly and actively religious people who rarely read earnestly upon the very subject which occupies their best emotions and inspires their best activities, either because they never read upon any subject with intelligence and effect, or because they have been trained to conceive that the exercise of a very active intelligence upon religious topics is inconsistent with warm emotion or a confiding faith. Hence the religious reading which they allow themselves is be-low their intelligence, and **done** rather for the purpose of exciting devotional feelings or spending a half hour over a quantum of religious phraseology than for the ends of intelligent conviction and reasonable emotion.

They read history, biography, novels, poetry and criticism on the most liberal scale and with excited wakefulness, but their religious reading is limited to one or two books of de-votion or a few second-rate biographies of second-rate and goodish people. Others perhaps never care or never dare to read any religious book unless it has the *imprimatur* of their own religious communion. The Romanist is by necessity almost precluded from any other than Catholic literature. If the reader is a Methodist he is likely to read only such books as are issued by the " Book Concern," if a Presbyterian, to believe only in the blue-backed volumes of " the Publication Society," if an Episcopalian he ignores all works except those written or sanctioned by Churchmen, or if he is a Liberal Christian he may have a traditional and very illiberal contempt for every literary production that proceeds from the so-called Orthodox. A very large class of Christians are so intensely practical or evangelical as to be conscientiously jealous of the exercise of earnest thinking upon religious truth or duty, and are offended by every book which would either awaken or stimulate the intelligence, or requires its vigorous exercise in order to be understood. It must be confessed that religious emotion as such, like every other description of emotion, is not of itself friendly to, or promotive of the exercise of intellectual energy. The fact has been noticed by Coleridge that the fond indulgence of religious feeling has often brought a species of dry rot into a noble intellect by the force of simple stagnation. We hold that this is unnatural and abnormal—nay more, that this happens not only by error but by sin, and that as a consequence the religious character itself becomes one-sided and degenerate. We contend that if a man dwarfs or blinds or stupefies his intellect in order to attain to earnest and sustained religious feeling— especially if he uses vigorous thinking and earnest reading upon other topics and dares not to do it or is disinclined to do it upon religious themes—he will sooner or later suffer lamentably in his religious faith and fervor. We assert that it is the duty of every one who reads with zest and curiosity upon other subjects, to read with earnestness and with freedom upon religious themes. We would even go farther and assert that the cause of the decline and fervor in very many persons of active and imaginative minds is that they do not give to religious subjects the same activity which they bestow upon subjects of inferior interest. The injunction " give atten-tion to reading " has a wider reach and is supported by a greater variety of reasons than is usually thought.

If what we have said should have disturbed the feelings of any, we hasten to relieve them by adding that we do not propose to discuss any questions which relate directly to special theological creeds or to ecclesiastical or denomi-national divi-sions. We assume indeed, as we have already explained, that the Christian History is true and that Christ is the proper object of confidence, reverence, and gratitude. This being premised, we proceed to speak respecting the selection and reading of religious, *i. e.* Christian books.

Religious books may be divided into four classes: *good* books, *i. e.* books which are very good—*goodish* books— books which are *good for nothing*—books which are *worse than nothing*.

Good books are such as are positive and conspicuous for one or all of three merits—merits of thought, feeling, and diction. Every good book can show a raison dêtre. There is some occasion for its being produced and read. Good books invari-ably bear marks of having originated in a gifted mind—in a mind set apart by na-ture or called of God to speak to one's fellow-men by reason of the gift of genius or of earnestness. They show the signs of this calling and these gifts, and awaken a response in the ear and the hearts of the truly earnest or the truly cultured of those who hear them, and thus prove there was an occasion for their being written.

Goodish booKs are books of second-hand goodness—books that are conscious-ly or unconsciously imitated from good books —books that repeat old thoughts, by stupid and servile copying, or with such original variations as despoil them of their freshness and life—books which seek to express simple and familiar emotions with-out just or real feeling— books which strain out affected conceits, or extravagant im-agery with some empty ambition of originality—books whose authors are will-ing to gain the admiration of the uncultured and the half cultured by any extrava-gance of thought or diction. Above all, they are books which utter the words of religious feeling, when the writer does not really possess it, or possessing it describes the objects of his excited emotion in borrowed or stereotyped phraseology. Such books are deformed by more or less of *cant* in the strict and proper acceptation of that term, as characterizing an unsuccessful attempt to sing what another sings heartily and sings well. Goodish books 'may have more or less positive merit, with all their strained and factitious untruth—they may be eminently useful to readers who do not observe their defects or are not offended by them, who do not require anything better, or who may have a taste so perverted as to prefer them to good books, even though good books would be far better for them. There is unhappily, in the religious world, a very large class of books of whom the remark of a shrewd observer will hold, u men who are simply and earnestly good, I like exceedingly, but goodish. men or those who put on airs of goodness, not at all."

Religious books which are ***good for nothing*** are such as are stupid in thought, feeble in emotion, false in imagery, vulgar in illustration or uncouth and illiterate in diction, and which are so deficient in all these particulars as to be incapable of doing good to any one which might not be done far more efficiently by books that are better or those less open to objection. Books of this description are very numerous. They are produced by the ton. They thrust themselves in your face in every bookseller's shop. They are obtruded upon your notice by weak but well-meaning people at every corner. That they serve some useful purpose to very many people does not disprove that they are good for nothing, provided we can show that a good or a goodish book would have answered the same purpose better or equally well.

Religious books that are ***worse than nothing*** are such as are positively offensive from defects so gross as to be obvious to people of very moderate cultivation. All books belong to this class which are false in sentiment, fraudulent by overstatement or by suppression, wooden or scholastic in phraseology and conception, dishonest in the caricature or misrepresentation of opponents whether infidel or fellow-Christian, unsound in reasoning, hysterical in emotion, doggerel in verse, or sensational and extravagant in prose. These all dishonor true religion either by conspicuous errors, a bad spirit, bad taste, bad manners or bad English. Whatever partial or occasional good they may seem to effect among people who are not aware of their falsehood, or are not offended by their extravagance, would be done more effectually by other books, while the positive evil they occasion to the bigoted, the undevout and the scoffer is fearful to think of.

Two questions here suggest themselves as worth the asking. "Why is the number of inferior religious books propor-tionately so great ? and why are such books treated with greater consideration than inferior books upon other sub-jects? The first of these questions is easily answered. The reasons which explain the production and use of inferior books of any description explain with especial significance the demand for religious books. The demand accounts for the supply. Incompetent men will write mean books on religious topics, as they do upon all topics, with the best intentions and with intentions which are none of the best, and incompetent judges will read such books without being aware of their inferiority, and may even prefer the inferior to the superior. The goodness of the aim often hides from the well-intentioned author and reader the essential inferiority of the author and critic. The public teachers of religion are also by the necessities of their profession, more or less practised in literary composition. Very many are surrounded by circles of kindly-disposed and even admiring friends, who feel a special interest in everything which comes from them. Many a preacher becomes an author who has no other call to this vocation than the call of an admiring congregation for a volume of discourses, or of sermons turned into lectures or essays. He yields to the call, either because he mistakes it for the call of a wider circle, or because he desires to gratify the kindly preferences of his friends, or because he knows that they will read with a special interest a tract or book written by himself.

The reasons why inferior books upon religious topics are treated with especial forbearance are the following:

First of all, there is the general disposition to consider the goodness of the end which every such book contemplates, and to overlook the question, whether the book in hand is fitted to promote the end. Even though the book is painfully weak or commonplace, or bristles with shocking extravagances of style and conception, it is charitably said of it, "perhaps it may do good with some people;" and therefore is it exempt from the criticism which it deserves. Those who see its weakness allow it to pass—if they sympathize with its aims, from charity—if they despise its ends, from simple disdain. Many fail to see that the book is weak because of their interest in or their contempt for these ends. In view of such considerations criticism is either unconsciously disarmed, or distinctly repressed when it is called for.

It is in place here to notice, that motives which are far from being worthy often present themselves under the guise of an appeal to the religious feelings. A book that is written in the interest of a religious sect or party, a book that is published by our favorite publishing society or which is in any way identified with our church or denomination may lead the critic and the public for whom he writes to be tolerant of defects which in the books of another party or society or church he would be sharp-sighted to observe and foremost to expose.

It is also to be observed that not a few good or goodish people, in their conceptions and judgments of religious literature, seem conscientiously and even religiously to dis-regard the relation of means to ends. They reason that because now and then a weak book or a weak and offensive passage in a book has caught the attention, or wakened a response of feeling in some person who was without religious thought or feeling,—therefore no relation is re-cognizable between argument and conviction, persuasion and assent, eloquence and impression, or genius and edification. Some religionists seem to labor under the impression that too great a measure of logic, eloquence or genius is not to be desired, lest they should usurp the place of mysterious and undiscerned agencies of a higher character. For this reason, though they, in all cases, somewhat inconsistently require that the English should be grammatical, they contend that the diction should not be too fine or too eloquent; though they would think it well that there should be a certain degree of logical coherence and eloquent exposition, they are religiously offended if these excellencies are too conspicuous. That such an attitude is purely sanctimonious and in so far irreligious, we shall waste no words to prove. The conditions of success are as truly observed in the sphere of religious thought and feeling as in any other, although they are at times dispensed with or over-borne by special interpositions. Such interpositions are not furnished to sanction intellectual laziness, or careless English, or inapt logic, much less to justify those enormities of platitudinous commonplace and sensational infla-tion which are so largely represented in some departments of religious literature. For man to crown his indolence or unculture with the aureole of superior spiritual sanctity is to dishonor his Creator in the most sacred of operations, as well to dis-honor his own human powers by one of the most debasing of untruths. If there is no connection between un-cleanliness and godliness there can be none between careless diction, blundering logic, and tumid eloquence, and the special power or presence of the divine Spirit.

So far is it from being true that earnest feeling requires or tends to promote an inferior literature, it may be shown that the quality of religious literature degener-ates, in connection with the decay of religious earnestness. While it must be con-ceded that the ends immediately proposed by religious orators, poets, and essayists, are practical rather than literary, it is also as true, that it is only when faith is earnest and zeal is ardent, that eloquence is overpowering, poetry sublime, and argument irresistible, because it is only at such times that the noblest human energies are strongly aroused by the highest objects. It is only by men thoroughly aroused and inspired that the great works of religious literature have been produced. But when faith and fervor decline, then twaddle and cant take their place, religious books abound in imitated thoughts, in solemn formalisms, in sanctimonious utterances and tiresome platitudes. It is at such times that books are manufactured to order, not produced by inspiration. They are brought into being because godliness tends to reputation or to " gain," not because the writer " believes and therefore speaks." No mistake can be more serious than to suppose that the production of shoals of infe-rior religious books is a sign of religious progress. The exact opposite may be true.

But enough of this fault-finding: It were wiser and more useful to notice some of the signs or tests by which good religious books can be distinguished from those which are inferior or worthless.

Good religious books should have the stamp of individu-ality. They should express the writer's individual thoughts and feelings. They should come from a person who has something to say which is his own, and is neither the affected nor the unconscious repetition of the thoughts of another. This is the true conception of what we call originality and freshness, which are closely allied to genius. An author may be defective in respect to literary culture, and range of knowledge, and yet if he has these, he is usually worth reading. The sources of fresh and individual thoughts on religious themes, are more universally accessible to all men, than in respect to any other, because they are all found in God and nature, in Christ and the Scriptures ; and in the soul of man as moved by each and all of these objects. A devout thought if it is a writer's own, is often a stroke of genius. Hence the power of such writers as Bunyan and Defoe. But real originals should be distinguished from the factitious and imitated. As real originality in religion is always fresh and dewy, and is always greatly to be desired—so the factitious is to be avoided and rejected. The sensational, the strained, and the bizarre are often present in religious writing for the reason that many authors seek to shun the commonplace, by running . into a variety of unnatural extravagances and excesses. Hence the intellectual antics and vulgarities of every description which infest the pulpit and degrade religious books and newspapers. A fresh writer like Coleridge, Carlyle, Emerson, Robertson or Ruskin, cannot appear without exciting a host of imitators in style and illustration. Many in almost every religious congregation are agape for what they call or conceive to be originality in a preacher. It should ever be remembered that while in all departments of writing, sincerity, (and, therefore, simplicity,) is a sign of genius, this is emphatically true in religious writing.

Another sign of a good religious book is its freedom from phraseology that is needlessly technical and stereotyped. Theology and religion must certainly have their appropriate terms; truths and emotions that are so marked and uniform must necessarily shape for themselves certain words with a fixed and definite import. To those persons to whom this import is unfamiliar or distasteful these terms must seem strange. As the terms that are necessary in music or art or any of the sciences are strange and even uncouth to those who concern themselves with neither—as the language of the lover is an unknown speech to those who have never felt his emotions, so must the language of the humble and devout be offensive to the proud and the godless. The incubus upon religious literature is not the use of such terms when they do express thought and feeling, but when they fail to express either. The same evil ensues when terms of thought are used simply to manifest feeling with little or no intelligence, and when customary phrases are repeated with little or no significance. The repetition of " stock phrases " such as are taken from the Scriptures out of all proper connection, or are borrowed from the current private dialect of any religious communion, is what we have already noticed, as the offense of multitudes of religious books to men of culture and good sense. The sensitive and sensible John Foster was so painfully affected by this feature of much of the religious literature of his time that he made it the theme of one of the ablest of his Essays. An important point will be gained when this conventional and factitious religious dialect is discarded by all good writers. This result will be hastened if buyers and readers make it a test of a good religious book that it is free from technical or canting phraseology.

A good religious book is always stimulating to thought and elevating to the imagination. A book that does not make us think and feel and aspire—that does not exalt us by the grandeur of its objects and ennoble us by the aspirations of duty, that does not aid us to soar upwards towards God is not a good religious book however pious its tone or pretentious its phraseology. It is the appropriate function of a good religious book to accomplish all these objects, and whatever book fails of these ends cannot be good of its kind. When we say that a good book should stimulate thought we do not mean that it should be scholastic or theological or obtrusively intellectual; least of all that it should swell with the meretricious airs of what is called originality; but we do intend that it should offer thoughts which are fitted to stir and quicken while they overawe and sober the intellect. We do not mean that these thoughts should be other than practical, for truths of practice and duty especially when they search the heart and purify the motives are of all truths the most quickening, but we do intend that they should take hold of the mind with a strong and definite grasp. When we say a good book should elevate the imagination we do not intend that it should make man proud, but that it should make him humble. This it will do most effectually if it confronts him with ideas that take away the thoughts of self, that subdue him to repentance while they encourage him to faith. It is also eminently fitting that a good religious book should have all the accessories which are found in a pure and elevated diction; that it should suggest no offen-sive or degrading associations; that it should be free from all suggestions of coarseness, egoism or vulgarity. It is natural to add that a book may be a good book for one man which is not good for another, and that no man is bound by religious duty to make a book seem good to himself which reasonably offends his judgment, his taste or his imagination.

Of the few classes of religious books of which we may venture to speak, we name first those which relate to Theism and the Christian History. With subjects of this class every reader should be more or less conversant, and inasmuch as the methods of discussing them have materially changed within the present century, there is occasion for careful selection if we would read the books which are best fitted for the present generation. While in one sense it cannot be conceded that scientific Atheism, Pantheism or Infidelity are more formidable at present than formerly, inasmuch as true science and a thoroughly scientific spirit are favorable to neither, it cannot be denied that not a few are shaken in their faith in both Theism and Christianity, by what they regard as the teachings and deductions of Science. Upon the existence and moral Government of a Personal God may be consulted, the so-called Burnett Prize Essays of 1854, *i. e.* R. A. Thomp-son's ***Christian Theism and*** J. Tulloch's ***Theism***. To these may be added J. Buchanan's ***Modern Atheism***. The so-called ***Bridgewater Treatises*** are all very able works of their kind, although their science is a little antiquated.

C. Babbage, ***Ninth Bridgewater Treatise***, F. Wharton, ***Theism and Skepticism***, W. Whewell, ***Indications of a Creator***, J. McCosh and G. Dickie, ***Special Types and Ends in Creation***, W. Paley, ***Natural Theology***, Lord Brougham, ***Discourses on Natural Theology***, G. Berkeley, ***The Minute Philosopher***, F. Bowen, ***Lowell Lectures***, I. Kant, ***Critique of Pare Reason***, T. Chalmers, ***Natural Theology***, B. Pascal, ***Thoughts on Religion***, F. Burr, ***Ecce Caelum***, J. Butler, ***Analogy of Natural and Revealed Reli-gion***, N. W. Taylor, ***On the Moral Government of God***, J. McCosh, ***On the Method of the Divine Government***, H. L. Mansel, ***The Limits of Religious Thought***, F. D. Maurice, ***What is Revelation***, Goldwin Smith, ***Rational Religion***, H. Calderwood, ***Philosophy of the Infinite***, A. T. Bledsoe, ***Theodicy***, J. Young, ***Evil not from God***, A. S. Farrar, ***Science and Theology***,

The Duke of Argyll, ***The Reign of Law***, J. D. Morell, ***The Philosophy of Religion***, S. T. Coleridge, ***Aids to Reflection*** are all worth reading.

Upon the evidences of Christianity may be named W. Paley, ***The Evidences of Christianity***, T. Chalmers, ***Chris-tianity***, from the Ed. Encyclopedia, W. L. Alexander, ***Christ and Christianity, "Ecce Homo"*** J.R.Beard, ***Voices of the Church in reply to D. F. Strauss***, G. Uhlhorn, ***Modern Representations of the Life of Jesus***, E. Erskine, ***Remarks on the Internal Evidence of Revealed Religion***, (very good), G. P. Fisher, ***Essays upon Supernatural Christianity***, (good on Modern Critical Objections,) J. Young, ***The Christ of History***, (very good), C. Tischendorf, ***When were our Gospels written***. R. Whateley, ***Historic Doubts***, J. B. Walker, ***Philosophy of the Plan of Salvation ; Philosophy of Skepticism***, A. Norton, ***The Genuineness of the Gospels***, (clear and solid),W. E. Channing, ***The Evidences of Christianity***, A. P. Peabody, ***Christianity the Religion of Nature***, J. Freeman Clark, ***Steps of Belief***, J. B. ***Moz-ley, Lectures on Miracles***, R. C. Trench, ***Notes on Miracles, Aids to Faith, Tracts for Priests and People***, H. Bush-nell, Nature and the Supernatural, (eloquent and elevating), B. F. Westcott, ***The Gospel of the Resurrection***, O. Gregory, ***Evidences of Revealed Religion***, D. Wilson, ***Evidences of the Christian Religion***, M. Hopkins, ***Evi-dences of Christianity***, W. Paley, Horæ Paulinæ***, J. J. Blunt,*** Undesigned Coincidences***, C. Rogers,*** Eclipse of Faith; Defence of do. (against F. W. Newman), Albert Barnes, Evidences of Christianity in the l$th Century***, E. Dodge,*** Evidences of Christianity***, Isaac Taylor,*** The Restoration of Belief***, R,. Yanghan,*** The Way of Rest***, C. Walworth,*** The Grentle Skeptic***, N. Wiseman,*** Lectures on Science and Revealed Religion***, J. Leland,*** Deistical Writers***, A. S. Farrar,*** Critical History of Free Thought, The Boston Lectures on Christianity and Skepticism.

Christian believers of all sects and all shades of opinion agree in recommending the critical and historical study of the Scriptures as of the highest interest and importance. Indeed many, not to say most of those even who reject the claims of the Scriptures to a supernatural origin and authority, do not hesitate to accord the highest significance to these books as literature and as movers of opinion and feeling in all ages. Whatever in books or reading promises to cast any light upon the history and antiquities, the sentiments and opinions, the facts and characters which we find in these books, is generally acknowledged to be of the highest significance and interest. This estimate is neither vague nor superficial, nor is it held as a tradition or a truism. It is not the result of a blind or fond preference, but of enlightened and rational judgment. The attacks of unbelief upon the Christian history, the movements of a negative anti-supernaturalism against the positive acceptance of the supernatural and the miraculous, have involved the sharpest historical criticism of every point pertaining to the Scripture narratives and have invested with deep interest every discussion and every treatise that relate to subjects of this sort. Who was Moses? Whence came the Jewish economy? Who was David? How did it happen that he wrote such wonderful poetry and anticipated so great a successor in his own lineage ? Who were the Prophets ? Whence came their insight into the moral and religious import of passing events and their capacity to exhort and rebuke with such penetrating truth and startling energy ? Whence their foresight into the future and their rapt anticipations of the emergence and the triumphs of a spiritual kingdom of God ? Again, who was Jesus ? What were His estimates and His assertions concerning Himself? How did He justify and enforce these claims ? At what points did He touch, and how did He adapt Himself to the great movements that preceded His own times ? By what means did He lay hold of the thought and feeling of all succeeding generations ? These questions are not to be set aside by the intelligent reader as the hackneyed themes of pulpit harangues nor as truisms that are become familiar to every Sunday-school child, nor as convenient topics for shallow platitudes, or the croaking jeremiads of morbid or one-sided devotees, but they are inquiries which are fitted to arouse the curiosity and to hold the attention of every manly thinker and reader. " 'Tis true, 'tis pity, and pity 'tis, 'tis true" that multitudes who read intelligently and thoughtfully upon other subjects, thrust aside these questions with contemptuous disdain, or accept with a grateful and silly confidence the oracular dicta of extemporizing dogmatists. It is also true that many who believe in a supernatural Christ do not appreciate the intellectual reach and import of their faith. The Scriptures are perused by multitudes in a negligent, mechanical and traditional spirit which involves little intelligence and less curiosity. Even the great mass of those who aspire to interpret them to others have limited conceptions of the historical and intellectual wealth of the wonderful writings which they at-tempt to expound. Of books relating to the Scriptures it is emphatically true that there are a few which *are* books, and multitudes which are *no books*, but mere copies and dilutions of those which are books indeed. Of the best of them it may be said that they require a more awakened intelligence and a more vivid imagination than often accompany their use, however diligent and well intended this may be.

The following may be named as useful aids for the English reader in the general study of the Scriptures. We omit the notice of commentaries of every kind for the reasons already given. W. Smith's *Bible Dictionary*, 3 Vols., is a work which stands foremost as an encyclopedia of biblical history and criticism. The edition by H. B. Hackett and E. A. Abbot is the best. S. W. Barnum's *Comprehensive Dictionary of the Bible* is an extensive and excellent dictionary founded on Smith with many valuable additions. Either of these works may take the place of many separate treatises on the separate books of the Scriptures, as well as upon Scriptural Geography, History and Antiquities. J. McClintock and J. Strong's *Encyclo-pedia of Biblical Literature*, when complete will be an excellent book of reference, P. Fairbairn's *Imperial Bible Dictionary*, and J. Kitto's Cyclopedia of *Biblical Literature* (edited by W. L. Alexander) are of the highest authority. We have named already the histories by Ewald and Stanley, also Helon's *Pilgrimage*, and Herder's *Spirit of Hebrew Poetry*, all of which are as relevant to the student of the Scriptures as to the reader of history. Eobinson's *Biblical Geography*, Stanley's *Egypt and Palestine*, and Thomson's *The Land and the Book* should be named also in this connection. H. C. Conant's *History of the English Bible*, and B. F. Westcott's *History of the English Bible*, are books of authority. G. F. Townsend's *The Bible in Chronological order*, H. Alford's *How to Study the New Testament*, B. F. Westcott's *Study of the Gospels*, S. J. Andrews' *Life of our Lord*, A. Neander's *Life of Christ* and *Planting and Training of the Church*, W. J. Conybeare's and J. T. Howson's *Life and Epistles of St. Paul*, E. H. Plumptre's *Christ and Christendom*, E. De Pressensé's *Jesus Christ* and *The Religions before Christ*, C. Hardwick's *Christ and other Masters*, T. Lewis, *The Divine Human in the Scriptures* are all works of interest and authority. ***The Psalms chronologically arranged by Four Friends***. J. Mur-dock's ***The New Testament from the Syriac***, The Translations of the Psalms and other books of the Old Testament and of the whole of the New, by G, R. Noyes, are valuable auxiliaries in the study of the Bible.

In respect to Books of edification and devotion a few hints may be allowed without overstepping the rules which we have prescribed to ourselves, or offending the prepossessions of any religious communion. No man need, we would almost say no man should, read books which contain few clear and definite thoughts or whose thoughts are not elevating and quickening. There is nothing more deadening to the religious sensibilities or more depressing to the whole character than the attempt to arouse spiritual feeling by a devotional book which is stupid, weak or belittling. It is difficult enough for the soul when it is aided by every accessory to rise in spiritual flights or to keep those heights which it is competent to gain. It is doubly foolish for it to encumber or degrade itself by any superfluous hindrances. A devotional and practical manual should have an intellectual as well as a spiritual tone, for in order to gain edification and elevation for the feelings the intellect must be quickened and refreshed. Next Devotional works should not only be stimulating to thought, but they should be elevating in style and imagery. This is eminently true of Hymns and sacred Poetry. Roundell Palmer's ***Book of Praise***, and many choice collections from Latin and German Hymns have brought within the reach of every earnest Christian the means of satisfying his taste while they cultivate the spiritual feelings or express them in acts of worship. Watts, Doddridge, Ken, Cowper, and Heber, C. Wesley, Bonar, C. Elliott, R. Palmer and many others have given us too many pure and high-toned hymns to make it necessary now to resort to religious doggerel. The most elevated moods and attitudes of the soul should be honored as well as sustained by the choicest accessories of language and rhythm. Good religious poetry and biography usually serve most effectually the purposes of edification and devotion. ***The Confessions of St. Augustine, The Imitation of Christ***, Taylor's ***Holy Living and Dying***, Bp. Wilson's ***Sacra Privata*** and ***Maxims of Piety and Christianity, The Whole Duty of Man***, Baxter's ***Saints' Rest, Howe's Blessedness of the Righteous***, and W. Law's ***Serious Call*** have stood the test of time. Arnold's ***Sermons on the Christian Life***, Bushnell's ***Sermons for the New***

Life, C. J. Yaughan's well known Volumes *Christ the Light*, etc, Hopkins' *Lessons from the Cross*, Taylor's *Christian Aspects of Faith and Duty* are specimens of varied types of modern practical works.

A word or two may be added touching reading for Sundays. We trust we shall offend none of the advocates for the strictest religious use of the Lord's day, when we suggest that every reader should make a business and a conscience of having his Sunday reading intellectually profitable and stimulating as well as spiritually devout. Laziness and dawdling have no affinity with true worship or the girding up of the inner man for the moral and religious conflicts of the succeeding week-days. Mysticism, pietism and asceticism all weaken the manhood and so bring insidious poison into the ethicaj and religious life. The exercise of the intellect on some question in Theology, some scriptural exposition, or Christian history, some quickening biography or Christian poem, and doing this earnestly and systematically is greatly to be recommended in place of the desultory meditation, the reading of goodish books, and the sometimes not even goodish religious newspapers, or the meaningless religious gossip which use up and degrade so many bright hours of so many Sundays. The mechanic and laborer, the clerk and the apprentice, the merchant and the professional man, every one who is so far subjected to task work as to find little time for continuous reading on week-days ought to make his Sundays as available as possible for intellectual excitement and en-larged information upon religious themes as well as for simple edification. Let such seek in their religious reading on Sundays for invigorating thoughts, for valuable information, for elevating impressions of character, for lofty sentiments of resolve and aspiration, with which to store the mind for the week of conflict and worldliness, of temptation and meanness to which they will certainly be exposed. No classes of subjects are so suitable for Sunday reading in combining rest and refreshment with elevating and stimulating influences as good religious biography, enlightened and liberal Church History and superior religious poetry. No subject needs attention so much from the more gifted and best cultured minds, as the preparation of religious books for Sunday use, that the day may be set apart from other days not only by its appropriately religious duties, but may become more effactually a day for spiritual culture in its more enlarged and highest signification. An attempt has been made to provide a

Sunday Library, on this theory, by the publishers Macmillan, which may enable the reader to understand our ideal. This ideal other publishers and writers may more perfectly realize. These 'hints are all that we dare allow ourselves upon a subject in regard to which opinions differ so widely and suspicions and offense may be so easily aroused,

CHAPTER XXI.

NEWSPAPERS AND PERIODICALS.

THE rapid growth and the enormous increase of News-papers and Periodical journals make it necessary to discuss them separately, freely and at some length. With very many persons they have very largely taken the place of books and have induced peculiar habits of reading and of thinking, which modify the estimate and the use that are accorded to the books which continue to be read. There are many persons now living, who were bred in the wealthiest and most accessible country towns even of New-England, who can remember when the most intelligent families were content with a single weekly newspaper, issued from the nearest city or shire town. Perhaps a religious weekly was added, after religious newspapers began to be published. One or two households besides that of the clergyman or lawyer might take a Monthly as the ***Analectic Magazine***, or possibly a Quarterly as the newly initiated ***North American*** Review; or perhaps one family read the ***London Quarterly*** and another the ***Edinburgh***, which were then reproduced, the one in drab, and the other in blue and yellow. A daily newspaper except in the large commercial cities was unknown and unthought of, and a copy rarely found its way into the most accessible towns of the ' largest size. A Semi-weekly New York or ***Boston Advertiser***, or a ***Philadelphia Gazette***, was the height of luxury in the country towns.

But all this is now bravely changed in England and America—so far as newspapers are concerned, more em phatically in America than in England. The United

States is the paradise of newspapers, if a rank and rapid growth indicates a paradise. A daily newspaper has become a necessity of life to every city and every extemporized village on the extreme frontiers of civilization. As a medium for learning and telling news and for the manufacture and the retail of gossip, the newspaper has taken the place of the fountain and the market-place of olden times; and in times more recent, of the town-pump, the grocery and the exchange; as well as of the court-house and the cross roads of a more scattered population. We cannot finish our breakfast without the local daily, whether it be metropolitan or provincial. If we do business in the city and sleep in the country, we must despatch two or three dailies on our way to the office or the countingr-room, and we reconsider and review the day by a glance at the evening journals. Instead of reading books, many read reviews of books; instead of patiently perusing history, many cram from summaries or digests in the form of partisan or critical articles. Every leading monthly has its serial novel with which to tantalize the reader and to prolong the tale; which frequently breaks off at an exciting crisis, in order to hold the tale and the periodical prominently before the minds of the greatest number of readers. Brilliant poems are secured to sell a single number. Telling articles on politics, finance and theology are no longer published in pamphlets as formerly, but they are sought for to give character to a Quarterly. Editors' " book tables," "easy chairs," "quarterly or monthly summaries" are relied upon to indicate, or regulate the current of public opinion as well as for the circulation of a variety of gossip and the discharge of. any redundant editorial humor, which is various in the quality of its effervescence and pungency. The shy girl of the country, and the bold girl of the town, the fast girl of the period and the brassy girl of the promenade all study the fashions in some newspaper or magazine, to which are appended a flashy poem, a sensational tale and a flaunting essay. To meet the wants of those whose intellectual digestion is weak, but whose moral sense is scrupulous, newspapers of a very light pabulum are furnished, strongly flavored with a tremendously exciting story and several highly exalted essays and extracts of wonderful adventures; and these papers penetrate all parts of the country, by the force of enterprise and effrontery. The fast life which we are rightly accused of living is rendered trebly fast by the number of newspapers and journals, which allow us no repose when we seem to be at leisure either for a cheerful conversation with our fellows, or for a quiet chat with ourselves or with quiet and elevating books. The Home Library has become a place in which to read newspapers and periodicals, and sometimes its shelves contain little more than the bound volumes of the quarterlies or monthlies which a few years have accumulated.

Inasmuch as people will read newspapers and journals as well as books, and often in the place of books, it seems worth the while and almost necessary to offer some hints in respect to their value and the best or least harmful way in which they can be used. We begin with the Quarterly and Monthly journals.

The modern Quarterlies when they came into being were an inevitable necessity. The Edinburgh Review appeared as the organ of a liberal and progressive literary and political party, and it fitly ushered in the present century. The zeal and boldness of the Edinburgh as the organ of the Whigs, called forth from the Conservatives the London Quarterly and Blackwood's Magazine. Then followed the quarterlies and monthlies which were made the organs of religious parties and denominations and also of special philosophical and theological opinions. The primary object of the most of these magazines was to furnish thorough criticisms of books of current literature, and well-considered articles upon the various topics of politics and reform in which the public were interested. In process of time, the scope of these reviews was somewhat enlarged, and they received papers of a general character upon any subjects to which certain writers had devoted special attention. In this way they became in part nothing more than a periodical vehicle for the issue of pamphlets or brief treatises. In consequence, many a writer who in earlier times would have published his book, which might be longer or shorter, now publishes a labored article. The convenience and the regularity of the review stimulates to the production of many treatises which would not otherwise have been written. Its limits and its popular character requires that the article should be condensed and spirited. This has created a peculiar style of writing—bold, trenchant, and antithetic, often eloquent and able, but always positive and unqualified. Condensed summaries take the place of long disquisitions, brief and pithy statements of expanded arguments, and bold and square assertions of guarded and qualified inductions. In the Edinburgh Review, Sidney Smith, Jeffrey and Macaulay were representative writers; in the London Quarterly, Gilford, Southey and Croker; in Blackwood, Lockhart and Wilson were master spirits. The North American Review aspired at a purely literary character and influence with no pronounced political sympathies. Buck-minster, Ticknor, Sparks, and the Everetts were its characteristic writers.

The influence of these reviews upon the intellectual habits of their readers, especially of those who have read them from their youth, has been not inconsiderable. With many, they have displaced not a few of the books which had previously been considered essential in the reading of every well-informed man. Instead of reading a history with care and in detail, many have been content to learn from a review its chief positions, its general aims and some of its more striking passages. In place of reading the original papers or documents on both sides of a controversy on politics or finance, it has been found more expeditious and convenient to read the summing up of a reviewer even though it was notorious that he wrote in the spirit of an advocate. The mastery of a distinguished author, which by the old-fashioned method could only be achieved by long and laborious processes is now seemingly achieved at a few hours' sitting, by the aid of the able and exhaustive critic who has condensed the chief results and principles into a brief essay. Instead of going to original sources of evidence, or hearing both sides of a contested question, it is more convenient to take the impressions of a writer who has volunteered to perform the labor for the reader. If the reader is not satisfied with reading a single article, he can find two or more on opposite sides, of nearly equal ability and research, and in this way form his own conclusions with comparative facility.

It must be acknowledged that periodicals are in many respects a great intellectual convenience. They abbreviate labor and place the results of the research of a few at the service and disposal of the many. They sometimes facilitate the research of the student by directing him to the original sources of which he may desire to avail himself. Oftentimes an article is better than a book. Especially is this the case when the subject is out of our line and we have time neither to look up authorities nor to study them. Many of the most intelligent of readers are remote from libraries and are unable to borrow or to purchase the books which furnish the information or the estimates which they desire. In a multitude of instances similar to these the modern review or journal serves the most important purposes. It has greatly diffused information, abbreviated labor, and quickened thought. No man of sense would think of dispensing with its aid or of depriving himself of the gratification and stimulus which it furnishes. On the other hand:

The excessive or even the constant reading of the best reviews exposes to certain special dangers. First of all, it tends to make the reader superficial so far, at least, as it accustoms him to take up with second-hand information and authorities. In respect to history and argument— whether testimony concerning facts or reasoning to conclusions are required—the man who does not go to original sources, is liable in spite of himself to receive inadequate or one-sided impressions. The habit of taking one's knowledge or opinions at second-hand induces the feeling of submission and dependence, which can neither be hindered nor disguised by the excessive confidence not to say effrontery with which the habit is usually accompanied.

It tends to make a man a partisan in his opinions and feelings. The attitude of the writers whom he reads is more frequently a partisan attitude, and it is natural that it should be. The habitual reader of one-sided arguments— especially if he be himself devoted to the general views of the journal in which he most confides— will be likely to be formed and fixed insensibly to partisan ways of looking at every subject. It can hardly fail to be true that one should be moulded to partisan habits who is familiar with one-sided and partisan literature.

Again : the exclusive reading of this specks of literature may expose to skepticism or indifference concerning Truth of every kind. To avoid narrowness and bigotry the reader seeks to study a subject on every side. By doing this he incurs the opposite danger of losing his confidence in positive truth and earnestness in his own convictions. No evil should be more earnestly deprecated than the evils of intellectual libertinism or skepticism in respect to the great principles of moral, political and religious truth. But to none is the quick-minded and susceptible reader more exposed, who runs rapidly over the arguments on both sides of great questions, all of which are second-hand so far as authorities are concerned, all of which are partisan, all of which are contemptuous of their opponents, while all are equally confident and pronounced. The reader who begins the study of all sides through the medium of opposing periodicals, may at first be ingenuous, simple and earnest. Reading rapidly as he may because the articles are brief, passing quickly to the counter-article without having given to the first sufficient reflection, and so to the next, he finds himself dazed, confused and uncertain. If he goes no farther, he will at least be in danger of concluding that no truth can be an established truth, on both sides of which so much can be said, and may finally rest in the desperate and despicable attitude of having no opinions whatever in respect to the most important questions. Meanwhile he baptizes his weakness with a name of strength. He calls that liberality which is truly libertinism. No single agency has been more efficient in the present century in diffusing this spirit among reading circles than the habits induced by the extensive and many-sided reading of second-hand literature. Men who are quick-witted and curious withal, and who desire to know all sides, rush through reviews and books which are nothing better than extended journalistic articles—books which are written in the bold, unfair .and declamatory style which review writing has bred, and the habit of review reading demands —and return with the report: " We have gone everywhere with the inquiry, What is truth? and have not yet found an answer; there is no truth except, perhaps, in some blind instincts or scanty intuitions which are as blind; the structures which law-givers and priests and teachers bid us receive and which the experience of other generations had confirmed are all built upon the sand." The flippant dogmatism of most of the sophists of our time who so freely, so confidently and apparently so learnedly, dispose of the old philosophies, the old religions, the old laws, the old educations, the old manners, and even the old decencies of life, finds its readiest converts in the *litterateurs* who have been inflated with conceit or paled with skepticism from feeding exclusively on the second-hand literature which the modern review has engendered.

The influence of the style and diction which the modern review has required and cultivated, should not be passed over. This diction is shaped too exclusively for immediate effectiveness to be altogether salutary in its influence. The pungent and pithy antitheses, the slashing and unqualified assertions, the biting satire, and the caustic humor, no less than the laudatory panegyrics, the ambitious rhetoric and the studied periods, which many very successful reviewers have employed, are all bad examples of style, even if they are not positively offensive to any one who seeks to retain his intellectual integrity or a candid and truth-loving spirit. Any community or generation of readers must be in a bad way which gives itself up too exclusively to a school of writers who value effectiveness more highly than truth. It would not be difficult to show that no little demoralization of thought has come in as the in-direct result of the demoralization of style which the review has effected,—that it has infected books of history, philosophy and physics with a vicious rhetoric, that is essentially superficial and sophistical, glazing not merely the forms of expression with a false brilliancy, but making the matter rotten to the core.

If it is not wise to allow our grave reading to be given exclusively or in large proportion to the reviews, it follows that too much of our lighter reading should not be devoted to the less solid magazines. With all the ability by which they are distin-guished and the variety of excellence which they have achieved, they cannot be the staple of one's reading without serious evil. Brilliant and various as they are, often profound and sagacious, abounding as they do with the choicest productions of the most gifted writers, they are too desultory, their subjects are treated too briefly and superficially, their tone is often too flippant and sensational, their judgments are too uncertain and unsound, to furnish the principal reading of any person; least of all, of any young person. The young man or the young lady whose solid reading is limited to the very best of these magazines will doubtless find in them much intellectual excitement and no little good, but not without attendant evil. The knowledge and education may be varied and useful, but the school remains superficial and narrow. If on the other hand they find their best reading in the magazine of a lower grade their reading must be poor indeed; little better than a showy flippancy can come of it, if nothing worse.

But what shall be said of the newspapers ? First, that they vary widely, from the very good down to those which are contemptibly, not to say offensively poor. Among these various grades there is ample room for selection, from the leading metropolitan or provincial newspaper which is characterized by more or less of ability and principle, down to the sheet—whether in city or country—which reflects the vulgar illiteracy of a low or uncultured community, as well as flatters its self-conceit and panders to its interests ; from the high-toned religious or literary journal down to one that is desperately partisan in either of these spheres.

Second, newspapers are not only a great convenience but an absolute necessity of modern life and civilization. The overwrought and jaded brain may compel its possessor to escape from the news and their excitements by a voyage that parts him from the mail and the carrier, or ' he may plunge into the wild retreat into which neither penetrate, but the call for the last newspaper is the first symptom that the brain is slightly refreshed by its rest. The comprehensive survey which the morning news gives us of what happened yesterday in every part of the world enlarges immensely our intellectual vision; training us to the habit of thinking habitually of the concerns of all the world besides—and not only to the habit of thinking of them but of comparing and adjusting one with another. It sends the imagination round the world " in less than forty minutes," bringing before it Englishman and Arab, French and Tartar, Prussian and Chinese with their varieties of interests and civilization. This frequent and comprehensive review of the whole world stimulates the intelligence to discriminate and compare, as well as to search for principles and laws. It induces tolerance for the principles and ways that differ from our own, charity towards the whole family of man, despite of intellectual differences, conflicting interests and hostile passions.

Third, the newspaper wherever it is free, is at present very largely the educator and controller of public sentiment, and hence has become a most potent instrument and depositary of power. The editor is at this moment apparently more influential than preachers, judges or legislators. He is mightier than all these united. The confiding reader of a favorite newspaper often tests the 6ermons of Sunday by the chapter and verse of the leading articles of the week. He tries his elected rulers and judges before the bar of the newspapers. He accepts and rejects his lawmakers and the laws which they make according to the revision of the editorial court of appeals. The newspaper press makes war and peace, writes up and down the value of property and destroys or defends reputation.

It may be said indeed that this power is not unlimited, because the press can regulate public opinion only so far as it reflects it and adapts itself to it. It may be urged that the editor controls and directs the great agencies of modern life only as he skillfully anticipates and interprets them, that he can command these only as man commands the laws of nature, by first understanding and then obeying them. This to a certain extent is true, but it is also true that the press can inflame and excite agencies which but for its influence would have slumbered forever, that it can unite and concentrate forces which would have been feeble so long as they were scattered, that it can give courage and boldness to men and to causes which but for its inspiriting influence, would have been perpetually cowed and repressed. It may also be said that whenever the press is free it cannot mislead, for falsehood can be met by truth, sophistry can be refuted by sound reasoning, party tricks can be exposed, dishonesty can be made public, and in the long run the truth and the right will prevail. This may be true in the long run, but the time required may be too long for the public good. Meanwhile, so far as the individual and a single generation are concerned the press has ample room to delude, to degrade and to destroy. It can deliberately and persistently flatter the vile, and hoodwink honest men. It can act the part of the demagogue and the seducer and the venal advocate. It can suppress the truth by conscious villainy and it can set off error in false colors and with factitious rhetoric. It can lower education and debauch public and private morals. It can dishonor the noblest characters among the dead and the living. It can induce skepticism in whatever is sacred or venerable, by sneering and sophistry, and can adroitly conceal both. In the name of science and taste and progress it can vulgarize and degrade and put back all these for a century.

Fourth, many newspapers whose influence is not incon-siderable are low in their intellectual tone. "While there is room in the editorial profession for the exercise of the most consummate power and the most varied qualifications, it is possible to be what is called a successful editor with scanty knowledge and limited abilities. Application is necessary and a certain energy of endurance in small work. If to this be added the tact at knowing what will please, and what is called the knack of writing an editorial, success is certain under circumstances ordinarily favorable. That a multitude of newspapers do not exhibit any considerable intellectual power or knowledge is too obvious to require proof. Their readers recognize the indications of dullness and incompetency. Feebleness of judgment and the want of discrimination and intellectual force betray themselves in every column. Silliness and bad taste sometimes break out in oppressive manifestations, and general impotency are everywhere exhibited. And yet for all these weaknesses, industry, business talent, and tact in understanding the demands of the public and skill in supplying these demands may so far compensate for these glaring defects as to gain for the paper an extensive circulation and no little influence. Fifth, many newspapers are animated by a spirit that is more or less insincere. Their editors and leading writers have few convictions, *i. e.*, few opinions which they hold with earnestness and regard as of pre-eminent importance. They profess to hold the principles of their party whether political or religious. But all they mean by this is that their paper is pledged as the organ of the party or its platform, and is thereby committed to the duty of publishing those facts and arguments which favor these opinions, and of suppressing or skillfully managing those which make against them. Public opinion is to a large extent regarded as an effect which can be moulded and manipulated. The influence of a paper is cast in favor of a particular movement or is thrown against it, by arts which are perfectly well understood in the editor's closet. The habit of thus manipulating public opinion, if it never leads to trading in it,— the consciousness of laying plans and of executing them to arouse public sentiment in a given direction or to give it a dexterous turn in favor of a measure or a man—is not over friendly to that solidity and ardor cf sentiment which usually characterizes strong convictions or earnest principles. The necessity of writing upon many subjects in which the writer cannot feel a special interest induces the habits and temper of the advocate with his factitious simulations and artificial excitements. The discerning reader finds only now and then a leader which bespeaks the solid convictions of a high-toned and earnest man, which is written because these cannot be repressed, and which seizes hold of the mind with that power which earnestness always excites. In other articles there may be ability, research and strength; the subjects may be fairly treated and exhaustively presented, but the impression is not of a strong nature thoroughly aroused.

This insincerity is manifested in its extremest form when it produces the modern ***Bohemian***, or the soldier of fortune in the service of the newspaper press, who is ready for an engagement whenever it offers, provided the pay is sure and good, and sometimes when it is neither, provided the "provant"—as the famous Dugald Dalgetty, an illustrious member of the fraternity termed it—is ample and well-moistened. He is a person of no mean qualifications, but smart rather than solid and apt rather than trustworthy. He has received an education more or less accomplished from the finished classical culture of the English university down to the scanty but stimulating curriculum of the printing and editorial room. He has a facile command of the pen, a good memory, a ready wit and infinite volubility. His assurance is unbounded and his principles and his sense of consistency never stand in the way of any engagement. He does not hesitate to write leaders at the same time in the organs of two opposing parties—for and against protection or national banking, or whatever doctrine divides the parties of the day. He is ready to applaud and to defame any man for hire and to extol and depress the same man in two successive weeks according to his engagement. He is a regular **Swashbuckler**; the instrument of his power is what is called a trenchant style, with ready command of images, allusions and historic parallels, and a capacity for **blatherskite** which is inexhaustible. He is, of course, thoroughly insincere. He has no convictions except upon a single point, and that is that those who pretend to have any, are either weakly self-deceived or self-conscious knaves. And yet no class of writers use the vocabulary of earnestness and honesty more fervently and impressively than he. The Bohemian whom we have described is one of the ex-tremest type. There may be few examples of one who is so thoroughly consistent, but so far as the modern newspaper is insincere, so far is it animated by his spirit. We do not assert that all newspapers are insincere. On the contrary, there are not a few in which earnest convictions and positive opinions are everywhere conspicuous. The tone of such journals is unmistakable. One feels the presence of real, not pretended sincerity the moment he takes up such a sheet. Sincerity not only rings through the editorials but it controls the selection and is apparent in the very arrangement of its articles.

Sixth, the modern newspaper so far as it is insincere is immoral and demoralizing. There are other reasons why it is exposed to this charge. It is confessed that newspapers are often unscrupulous in their statements of fact, that they suppress the truth when it makes against them and overstate that which would be in their favor. It is notorious that the partisan temper and partisan tactics very largely regulate the conduct of many so-called organs not only of political but of religious parties. The newspaper descends to inexcusable personalities,—both the pure and indecent and the trivial and belittling. It often delights in vituperation. It even makes this to be its duty. No sooner is a man conspicuous by holding a public position or is named as a candidate for it, than his private character and affairs are made matters of public comment, either to flatter his vanity or to gratify the insane passion for gossip which rules the public taste, or to excite the prejudice and contempt of his opponents. Vituperation of one's antagonist in politics or religion is esteemed one of the cardinal virtues, if we may judge from the practice of many journals. The more freely it is indulged the more satisfactorily is the writer thought to discharge his duty and the more completely is homage paid to public justice.

If a newspaper is devoted to some public reform in the service of morality or freedom, or in vindication of the rights of some class which is thought to be oppressed, it takes the largest liberty of vituperation and discharges its energetic denunciations in the manner of a brawling prophet. The end sanctifies the means. " Are not the enemies of the proposed reform, enemies of all truth and does not fidility to our cause require us to denounce them as such ? " Of not a few of these self-asserted and conspicuous champions of reform it is eminently true that their habit of deliberately and persistently denouncing their opponents in terms of unlicensed vituperation has become so much a second nature as to vitiate all their other excellences, and to make the very organs of moral and political reform to be the instruments of private and public demoralization. Of many of these advocates and organs it is not easy to decide whether the devil has in fact taken orders among the reformers or whether the reformers have taken " to serving the Lord as if the devil were in them."

It is not an unheard of thing that a paper edited with consummate ability and that promised to be of high tone in respect of manners and morals, has with apparently cool and deliberate resolve given itself to the project of forcing itself into notoriety by a variety of sensational devices, and pre-eminently by dragging before the public scandalous rumors and more scandalous transactions, as well as by grossly assailing the characters of public men, and following them and their friends with persistent slander.

The influence of a newspaper cannot but be demoralizing, however able its correspondence, or prompt and trustworthy its news, if the presiding genius of its editorial sanctum be a grinning, sneering ***Mephistopheles***, and the tone of the articles composed under this inspiration be that of persistent banter of everything which honest men reverence and brave men are ready to die for; the audacious drollery of which moves the whole community to laughter, even when it moves honest men to virtuous wrath. A Harlequin may be allowed in his place, but we cannot welcome him in our churches or our oratories, to sneer when we desire to worship; or find him congenial to those sober moments when life at least is real and earnest, even if conscience and God are not.

Seventh, that some newspapers conspicuously rejoice in bad examples of English style need hardly be added. This might be inferred if it were not so notorious. Where there is insincerity, untruth and defect of principle there must be more or less of bad English. While a few are models of clear, unpretending, direct and nervous English, not a few are representatives of every description of excess and overdoing, of carelessness and pretension, of extravagance and " blatherskite," which are an offence to the lovers of a pure and simple diction.

From these facts, the following may be derived as rules in respect to the use of newspapers.

First. It is worse than unwise to allow newspapers to be one's sole reading. The temptation to do this is very strong, and many yield to it. Men immersed in business seem often shut up to this by necessity. Even professional men who read or consult not a few books in the way of duty allow the newspapers to take the place of other reading. The merchant reads the money articles of the newspaper, but rarely if ever a book upon banking or political economy. The farmer reads his agricultural journal, but never a treatise. As to the politicians, both small and great, it is enough for them to consult the current histories of domestic campaigns and foreign entanglements which the papers furnish, without looking into books for the history of the remoter past which has prepared the way for the present and alone can explain it. Even if the leader is more instructive and more to the point than any book could be, the book may be better because it opens a wider range of considerations and so tends to enlarge the mind. The newspaper is written more in the spirit of an advocate than even a very one-sided book. The writer for the newspaper usually dogmatizes more and is more positive than the author. The standard of manners and of temper is usually far lower in the one than in the other. The style of the book is ordinarily better. The best newspaper style suffers under the necessity of compression or it abuses the liberty of indefinite expansion and verbiage. The newspaper deals with the present, and is hurried, narrow, confident and bustling. The book has to do with all times— the past, the present and the future,—and is in so far more calm, elevated and saga- cious. For these and other reasons it is observed that the reader of newspapers only is more usually positive, conceited and flippant than the man who is also a reader of books. Second. One should read good newspapers in preference. "We mean not only those which are able in thought and pure in style, but those whose principles are pronounced and whose manners are elevating. Many say and think: " It is only a newspaper; of what consequence is it? We only glance at it for a moment or run through it for an hour and then lay it aside. If its bad logic its unsound doctrines its vile insinuations and its profane banter were in a book we would not tolerate the book for a moment, but I and my children know, it is only the so or so, and we let its unwisdom and its foulness pass for what they are worth." Mr. A. would not tolerate slander or mean personalities for a moment in conversation at his table, and yet Mr. A. takes a paper for himself and his children which distribute both as freely and as maliciously as an audacious villain ejects vitriol into the eyes or upon the apparel of passers by. He would not allow his family to read a book that should gravely attack or sneeringly scoff at his faith lest it should leave some unfavorable impressions, but he allows the daily slime of an insinuating newspaper to hold their thoughts and to possess their imagination by a daily lesson and for a much longer time than the lessons of Scriptures which are allotted to the morning and evening devotions of his household.

Third. One should use the newspaper as a servant and not as a master. Many confiding souls believe all that the newspaper tells them and think it their duty to justify and defend all its statements, because forsooth it is the paper which they subscribe for or which is the organ of their party. In like manner some go so far as to feel bound to read every paper through. Neither is wise nor even safe. No obligation rests upon any man to read or to believe the whole of what any, even the best of newspapers may contain. The haste with which its news is gathered and its opinions are expressed, the very great extent to which the most honest and best qualified managers are dependent upon the fidelity of others, to say nothing of the force of the passions and prejudices of the hour and the demands of the party or the public whose good will the paper is desirous to secure, all these constitute it an unsafe guide to be implicitly believed or followed. If it is often wise to regard our books with a kind of suspicion and to guard against their excessive influence, much more should we do the same with respect to our newspapers, even if they are the best.

We have questioned whether the saying were altogether true that, " No man is the wiser for his *books* until he is above them." We cannot question that it is true of news-papers.

Fourth. Every one should remember that he is to some degree responsible for the character of the issues from the newspaper press. The newspapers of a country it should never be forgotten are no worse or better than the people would have them to be. They are a reflex of the knowledge and tastes of the majority of their readers. We cannot resist this inference however humiliating at times it may be. More than one intelligent defender of our country in Europe has been arrested and disturbed in his argument by the question, " How do you explain the fact that such and such a newspaper has so extensive a circulation among your people?" It would be well if every man who buys or reads a newspaper would think of this question and of the lessons of duty and honor which it suggests.

CHAPTER XXII.

THE LIBRARY.

EEADERS of books desire to become the owners of books. The pleasure and advantage which are derived from the use of a volume, prompt to the wish that it may be constantly within reach. Hence, books like everything else which is desirable come to be sought for and valued as property. The child is not satisfied with using a picture-book, he must call the book his own. The persistent *litterateur* and the veteran scholar value no purchase or gift so highly as a rare or elegant volume. The enthusiastic and devoted reader, if he has the means and the spirit of independence, usually becomes the buyer and owner of books. Every reader gathers about himself something of a library. Every community so soon as it rises above the most pressing and immediate wants, feels the need of a collection of books which may supply its higher necessities. We cannot therefore properly dismiss our theme of *Books and Reading* without also considering *The Library*.

We begin with *the personal or private Library*. The thought which first suggests itself is the very obvious one, that the size of a library when collected by a single person for his private use depends on his means, his liberality, his feeling of independence, his duties and relations to others, and the comparative estimate which he places upon books; not upon any one of these, but upon all united. A man comparatively poor, may contrive to acquire a larger collection of books than a man who is rich, simply because he cares more for them, and in order that he may possess them is willing to forego many other possessions and enjoyments, On the other hand a man of ample means and of decided literary tastes may deny himself the convenience and luxury of a library for such reasons of duty as would lead him to forego other conveniences or luxuries.

It is the quality not the size of the private library in which we are most nearly interested. Some persons buy books chiefly *for use*, and the library which they collect is conspicuously professional. The physician must at least have his treatises on physiology, surgery and the materia medica; the lawyer cannot dispense with a copy of the Statutes or with a book of legal forms; the clergyman, provided he can read, must own a Bible, a commentary and a concordance. These indispensables naturally expand into those formidable libraries which are strictly professional; libraries which are "*caviare* to the general;" but which to the individual worker with the brain, are literally his "tools of trade." However unintelligible and uninteresting such a library is to a layman, it is full of interest and importance to the artist, the mechanic, or any other professional worker.

Often persons collect books for *enjoyment*. It is to them a luxury and delight to read history and biography, fiction and poetry, eloquence and criticism. To have a large col-lection of books of all these descriptions constantly within their reach, is to have at hand treasures and luxuries with which nothing else deserves to be compared. They say with another, " I no sooner come into the library but I bolt the door to me, excluding lust, ambition, avarice, and melancholy herself, and in the very lap of eternity, amongst so many divine souls, I take my seat with so lofty a spirit and sweet content that I pity all our great ones, and rich men that know not this happiness."

Still other persons buy books for show. They like the sight of elegant books in substantial and costly bindings. The show itself is pretty to the eye and the associations are grateful to the mind, that knows enough of the use and value of books to be flattered by the company with which the possession of books connects the owner. It is gratifying to gaze upon the stately folios as they support the elegant yet substantial octavos, and these the compact and genteel duodecimos, and these the daintier sizes—to behold some in polished calf, skilfully tooled in figures of arabesque; others in levantine turkey, rich with its deeply grained colors ; others in the gayer hues of the French *chagrin*, bright with red and green and blue; and others still in the many varieties of German finish; and others distinguished by the Roman vellum, delicately set off with its tracery of gilt. It is a proud act for the owner of such an expensive collection to introduce a friend or a guest to his treasures with their appropriate accessories of illustrated works, choice engravings, illuminated missals, etc., and to count up the cost of his expenditures in honor of letters and art.

Others still, buy *for curiosity* and *for rareness*. Learned and sharp-cut Elzevirs, elegant Aldines, much sought *Incunabula, Editiones principes*, books with autographs or annotations of former owners famous in literature, books made up by mosaic handicraft of illustrations collected far and near, tall paper copies, survivors of scanty or exhausted editions, all these are bought with princely liberality and are exhibited with natural pride to the select few who can judge and estimate them as only diamond fanciers estimate diamonds.

Others buy a Library for the convenience of their families or friends; being themselves too busy to have much to do with books or having no decided taste for books, but desiring to cultivate their tastes or enlarge their knowledge and usefulness.

The personal Library is often in a sense the embodiment of the spirit of its collector and owner. It certainly is a striking manifestation of his tastes, habits, character and pursuits. This is always true if the Library is collected with any special zeal, and the owner is free to indulge his special proclivities. We can usually interpret the tastes and principles of a man,—often we can discover his crotchets and prejudices by simply inspecting his library. The mass of his collection may be such books as "no gentleman's library should be without;" but the discerning eye will spy out here and there a volume or a series— perhaps in some private corner—which reveal his peculiar tastes and his inmost feelings. Very often the indications are so obvious as to need no special sagacity for their interpretation. Even if the library is not prevailingly pro-fessional, it will reveal to the hasty observer of its shelves, whether its owner is mathematician, physicist or linguist, and in what speciality of each; and this whether he is a proficient or amateur. If he is devoted to history, his library will show it, and will also make known the kind of history in which he delights. The lover of poetry, or fiction or literary criticism, and the man of many-sided and universal tastes will be as distinctly revealed. The dominant tastes, the ruling aims, the controlling principles can often be gathered from the presence or absence of certain classes of books. With equal distinctness the fact is proclaimed whether he is a believer in God or in Nature, in Christ or in Humanity. If he is a Christian believer, his theological creed and his religious earnestness may be conjectured with similar confidence.

By the same rule the growth of a library when it is un-constrained by hindrances or influences from without, is a record and memorial of the growth and changes of the owner's intellect and tastes, and perhaps of sudden or gradual transformations in his aims and principles. If he has retained his early school books and with them the tales and lives which delighted his childhood, these well thumbed and tattered volumes will tell to him at least, a story of the delight with which he read and re-read Robinson Crusoe, the Arabian Nights, the adventures of Philip Quarles or the memoirs of Baron Trenck; or perhaps of the ardent zeal for knowledge which led him to labor with his own hands that he might buy his first Greek Grammar or a better Greek Lexicon. It is often a wonder to the fastidious observer or the careful housekeeper, who look at books with the bodily eye, why in an expensive and luxurious library there is often carefully preserved some shelf of these worthless and battered volumes which they would consign to the paper maker or the flames. They little know what precious memories are stored upon that shelf and gather about each of those soiled and damaged books. But the books which most vividly bring back to the owner his youthful self will be those few favorite authors, which he longed so earnestly to possess when he first conceived the idea of forming a library of his own. How often did he ponder the questions, What book or books did he care most to possess? or Which could he afford to buy? How often did he go into the book-shop and gaze upon and handle the much coveted volume! It may have been some work of a poet like Byron or Scott, who had first waked in his soul the feeling for poetry, or an old philosopher like Butler or Berkeley, or a new philosopher like Coleridge, or a newer sage like Carlyle or Emerson. What fresh and fervid associations are wakened within him as the identical volumes are taken in hand which twenty or forty years before he carried home without weariness and installed upon his empty shelves with such positive delight. Upon these shelves they still remain. Though they have been almost crowded out by other favorites they never can be thrust wholly aside, for they hold their place as witnesses and memorials of tastes and moods which can never be forgotten, though they may have been long outgrown. Other shelves testify to later passages in his life's progress; one to an awakened passion for history, another to a newly kindled zeal for literary criticism. In one division stand the sophists who weakened the faith of the owner in the fixed principles and the severe moralities of his childhood's faith. In another the wise teachers who recovered him from these sophistries and bewilderments. The field of the intellectual activities and the objects of the prevailing tastes of one decade of his life are here. Those of another are there. One group of books was purchased in the excitement of a zeal and of ardent purposes which were soon dissipated into irresolution and sloth. As the eye of the industrious reader runs along the shelves of his library in an hour of musing, it can read upon them the successive passages that make up the history of his life. In view of facts like these it is not in the least surprising that so many have cleaved to their libraries with so fond an affection, and have learned to conceive of them as parts of themselves, as in a sense visible and tangible embodiments of their own being; or that they part from their beloved books with especial tenderness when they part from their lives. Many a student will understand and appreciate the desire of Prescott the historian that when arrayed for the grave he might be left alone .in the library which had been so long the scene of his labors and the object of his zealous care.

The preservation of a library to another generation, espe-cially if it was carefully selected or was the object of its owner's special affection, is to many a matter of no little im-portance—with no less reason surely than the preservation of silver or other heirlooms which belonged to a parent or near relative. The latter witness to the taste of the owner as to material form or workmanship, or perhaps are interesting memorials of the arts of another generation. The other is a memorial of the intellectual and moral tastes of the spirit as-well as an image of the culture and the products of the generation in which he lived. The haste and apparent heartlessness with which the libraries of students and literary men are often broken up after their death is something surprising and offensive. To know that the library of Scott still stands in Abbotsford, that the library of Daniel Webster remains unsold in Marshfield, that the library of. Theodore Parker is kept intact and unbroken in the Boston city collection, that the library of Charles Julius Hare stands by itself in the library of Trinity College at Cambridge, is far more satisfactory to our feelings than it is to hear that the libraries of Thackeray and Dickens were sold and distributed within a few months after the death of each. The extravagant prices at which many of their books were sold must have been more satisfactory to their heirs than the fact that they were willing to sell the books at all, is pleasing to the admirers of their former owners. It would seem, at least, that the disintegration of a beloved library which has been the outgrowth of a read-ing life and is itself a transcript of its history might sometimes be delayed a few months longer, out of decent respect to the associations with which it is hallowed. It not uiifre-quently happens that it passes unbroken into the library of some public institution, and remains as an honored memorial of the individual and his times; of his own liberality or that of his family. The library of a reading clergyman, which has been consecrated alike by his love of books and his love of his people, if he dies among them, should never be disposed of except to become the permanent possession of the parish.

Thoughts of the personal library suggest those of its natural enemies, the ***book-borrower***, who delays or forgets to return the books which he borrows—and the ***book-stealer***, who never intends to restore the books which have come into his possession by accident or design. Wide laeunæ *gaping for months or years testify to the carelessness of the book-borrower, and the impatient and sometimes indignant reflections of the owner as these unfilled places and broken sets meet his eye, testify to his sense of abused kindness and confidence. May the shadow of the book-borrower very soon be less or may his habits speedily be reformed! May the succession speedily be broken and his lineage be altogether cut off! As to the book-stealer; the enormity of his offense cannot be expressed in language. Words would fail altogether to set forth his ill-desert and infamy. The* Book-collector *and the* Biblio-maniac have been too often commemorated to receive more than a passing tribute of respect. We honor their zeal and admire their eccentricities, for we see in their excesses only the luxuriance of noble impulses and worthy aspirations. They are the auchorets of literature, the devotees whose very excesses reprove and put to shame the coldness and negligence of ordinary worshipers.

From the library of the individual we pass to the library of the household, from the private to the ***home library***. Every home should have its library even if it does not comprise a score of volumes. " A house without books," says H. W. Beecher, "is like a room without windows. No man has a right to bring up his children without surrounding them with books if he has the means to buy them. A library is not a luxury but one of the necessaries of life. A book is better for weariness than sleep;— better for cheerfulness than wine;— it is often a better physician than the doctor, a better preacher than the minister, a better sanctuary than the drowsy, church." The presence of good books in any house is a sign of elevation and a perpetual reminder of the wants and aspirations of the higher nature. Books lay hold of the intellect and character in ways that can neither be anticipated nor traced. The child that grows up in the presence of books will feel their power almost before he is allowed to open them. If books are provided in a house, some one, at least, of the family will develop a taste for reading them. The entire household will by degrees form the habit of consulting books, and of answering from books the many questions suggested by conversation or the newspapers. The irrepressible zeal for reading manifested by a single member of the family will excite the envy or the emulation of the remainder. Leisure hours which might have been wasted in indolence or worse than wasted in sin will be beguiled by the tale or instructed by the history. The conversation of the household will concern more profitable themes than the gossip of the hour. Higher aims and ideals will be proposed. Contentment, industry and frugality may be learned from books. The lessons of duty are taught and the aspirations of piety evoked by a good home library. Such a library will stimulate and direct the desire to embellish the house and decorate the grounds. It will encourage intelligent skill in the management of one's trade or profession and even in regulating the economies of the household. By its presence and influence the family will rise to a higher plane of true culture and the realization of a more intelligent moral and Christian life. There is no good economy in dispensing with a library. It is almost better to dispense with a carpet. It is certainly cheaper to do without a new set of fashionable furniture. " I should like of all things to spend from three to five hundred dollars in a library" said a gentleman in active business, with some thousands of capital at his command, " but I cannot afford the interest of the investment." He did not reflect that the house, the furniture and the equipage which he could not forego, were all an investment of capital, returning no rents in money, but manifold in comfort and civilization. It may not be wise to spend a large amount of money at once upon a library, but it is wise to regard books among the necessaries of life and to allow the library to come in for its share of the outfit of the household, as well as for its portion of the yearly expenses. A few books, at least, should be found in every home, and kept constantly within reach, however ample are the facilities furnished by the public library. These books no family should be content to be without for a day. They are so to speak the foundation stones of the library. An English dictionary, a good atlas, an encyclopedia of some sort are among these books. We assume that the house will have a Bible and some kind of a commentary or Bible dictionary. Beyond these no directions can be given in respect to the home library, which cannot be gathered from the discussions of the several topics, of which we have treated. ***Brief Suggestions for Household Libraries*** is the title of a useful tract issued in 1867 by G. P. Putnam & Son, to which are appended specimen catalogues of libraries of different sizes, the first of 350 volumes, the second of 500 additional volumes, and the third of 450 more; to which are appended.the titles of "a collection of 50 volumes of useful and desirable books in economical and compact editions for a young man's book shelves." This tract was a useful guide for the time when it was issued, and with additions from books since published, may do good service.

The Home Library should have a place for its contents, even if it is no larger than a candle-box or occupies only a single shelf. The light of the house should stand upon a candlestick. The household Penates should be honored with a shrine, whether the home be hired apartments, a rude cabin or a contracted cottage. The fountain of intelligence and refinement should be found in a place that is convenient, neat and tasteful, whether this place is a tidy corner of the kitchen, a tasteful recess in the sitting room or a separate apartment. If the library has a room by itself, this should be suitably furnished and decorated, not too daintily for common and comfortable use, but cheerfully and attractively to the eye and the mind. It should at times be the resort of the children and the gathering-place of chosen friends, that books and the use of books may be associated with innocent pleasures and common duties.

The books of the Home Library should be choice books and in general select and standard volumes. The books of one house, whether there is a score or a thousand, will reveal the fact that they have been picked up by chance, either at the solicitations of the persistent book agent or the suggestions of a vagrant fancy. Those of another indicate at a glance that they were chosen with definite purposes and by a discriminating judgment. If the home remains to the second or third generation, let not the library be scattered, but let the books of the preceding generation testify to the intelligence and the refinement of those whose spirits are gathered with the dead. With the portraits of the persons of parents and relatives, there should always be connected the books which represent their inner life. Manifold are the thoughts and instructive the musings which are suggested by the family library in the few homes in which it is retained in the ownership of the successive generations.

The Home Library suggests the ***library of the community***, whether this community be a neighborhood, a school, a parish, a village, a city, a college or a State.

The establishment of a neighborhood or a village library is as natural and almost as necessary as the setting up of a grist mill or a town pump. When individuals and families sensibly feel the want of books and cannot supply them from their separate resources, they proceed to provide a common supply. The social library indicates an advance in civilization in respect to the development of wants and the capacity to supply them. It was an epoch in the history of certain of the older states when such libraries began to be common. This was not far from that awakening into life which terminated in the war of independence. The ew communities that went out from those of the older states which had school-houses and social libraries, established both, long before their log houses disappeared. Daniel Webster's intellectual growth was nourished from the little library which his father started in the beginnings of a pioneer settlement, when books were few and costly. Dr. Franklin contributed largely to the establishment of these social libraries. In 1731 he and some few of his friends in Philadelphia procured fifty subscribers of forty shillings each as capital, and ten shillings a year for forty years. In 1742 a charter was obtained, and the number of subscribers was increased to one hundred. "This was the mother of all the North American subscription libraries now so numerous." "These libraries," Franklin adds, "have improved the general conversation of the Americans, made the common tradesmen and farmers as intelligent as most gentlemen in other countries, and perhaps have contributed in some degree to the stand so generally made throughout the colonies in defence of their privileges." In 1786 Dr. Franklin made a present of 116 volumes to the town of Franklin in Massachusetts which took his name; on occasion of which gift, the Pastor preached a sermon upon the text " Show thyself a man." Eighty years ago it was observed by a traveler, of the people of this country, "It is scarcely possible to conceive the number of readers with which every little town abounds. The common people are on a footing in point of literature with the middle ranks of Europe." Subscription or share-holders' libraries existed in almost all the towns of New England at the beginning of the present century. The consequences were that there was no little activity of thought, especially in regard to history, politics and theology. The curiosity of the youth of both sexes was stimulated as well as their taste for imaginative literature. Those who were especially fond of reading had ample leisure. The books in these libraries were solid and substantial. Though their number was not great and their contents not over exciting, yet they awakened such a measure of solid and thoughtful intelligence as has been known in but few other communities in the world's history. One of these village libraries the writer has abundant occasion to remember. It was founded in 1795, and still survives, numbering with all its losses by use and sale and distribution nearly two thousand, among which are several of the original well-worn volumes. At the time referred to it consisted of some seven hundred books all bound in leather and carefully protected by an additional cover of brown sheep skin. The books were kept in substantial and locked cases, in the front and rear halls of an old-fashioned square dwelling-house. The meetings for drawing and returning books were held on the first Sunday evening of every month. The share-holders or their representatives assembled in the ample kitchen which was always made tidy and cheerful for this grave assembly of the chief personages of the village. As one and another dropped in, each with his monthly load of books (three was the quota) and saw them credited, he took his place in the circle which speedily numbered some twenty or thirty. Conversation had already started in knots or in common, upon the topics of fresh interest at home or abroad, in which the freest interchange of opinion was indulged. This exchange was immeasurably superior to that of the modern newspaper for the vividness and interest of the impression. To boyish ears and minds, the revelations of character and the utterances of novel thoughts were most instructive and exciting. When the hour for receiving books arrived, the names were drawn by lot, and the person whose name was first had the choice of all the library. The newest books were naturally preferred. Every book as it was drawn was set up for a bid, which rarely in those frugal times exceeded more than eight or ten cents, after the sharpest competition even for the last of the Waverly series. But all this has gone by. The library now stands in the office of the Town Clerk, is open at all hours, and the excitements of the "library meeting" have vanished forever.

In many of the cities, these subscription libraries have grown to very expensive and valuable collections. The Boston Athenaeum, and the Society Library of New York, are of this character. Some of these have been opened the public on payment of annual subscriptions. More recently, public libraries in cities and large villages have been founded by public-spirited individuals who have subscribed liberally for a building and the purchase of books, which have been made available to any one by the payment of an annual fee. Young Men's Institutes and similar Associations, have formed libraries substantially upon this plan, with the addition of courses of lectures, at first for instruction and improvement, more recently for amusement and pecuniary gain. Circulating or lending libraries have usually been individual enterprises. In England-two or three large establishments purchase several hundred copies of every popular book and send them to subscribers in every part of the kingdom.

Book clubs are often a good substitute for a social library where none exists, or a supplement to it when a few neighbors wish to read a special class of books which the library cannot furnish or cannot furnish readily. It is easy to organize a book club with no more than five persons if they will agree to pay in an annual subscription and buy a few books. On the fly leaf paste the following directions over a printed or written list of the names of partners, in the order of their residence, with blank columns for entering the date when the book was received and when it was sent to the next neighbor. " ***Books to be forwarded on Saturday. Books may be retained 14' days for the first reading, 28 days for the second reading. Five cents fine for each day's detention over*** 14." "When the book has gone the round it should be sent to the librarian, and when the company please to order it, the books can be disposed of by lot or by sale. The volume from which these regulations were copied is numbered 1481, and the club has existed for some thirty years.

An important impulse has been given to the establishment of libraries in con- nection with the increased interest awakened in our Public Schools. In some of the states the effort has been made to provide every school district with a library which should not only be adapted to the wants of those attending upon the schools but to the necessities of the whole community. In the State of New York particularly, considerable appropriations have been made by the legislature with the design of establishing libraries " not so much for the benefit of children attending school, as for those who have completed their common school education. The main design was to throw into school districts, and to place within reach of all the inhabitants, a collection of good works on subjects calculated to enlarge their understandings and store their minds with useful knowledge." The suggestion was very natural that the school system which furnished elementary instruction for the young might proper- ly continue to minister light and knowledge with the advancing years of successive school generations. It was also believed that the money and organization required- for the sustentation of a school might be advantageously used for the support of a public library. The plan has been tried with varying success. The objections are obvious. School teachers and school committees are not necessarily the most suit- able trustees for the management of a library for all classes of readers. They would naturally be tempted to allow too large a share of the library to books required by teachers and adapted to young persons. In ordinary school districts says a compe- tent witness, "Experience proves that it is impracticable to maintain libraries for general reading: They are usually too feeble to awaken popular interest, or claim proper care or protection. By uniting the interests and resources of a whole town, suitable cases, room or building, and a responsible librarian are secured. Among a dozen districts, each library grows diminutive, and at length the books are scattered beyond recall." (Rev. B. G. Northrop, ***School Report for Conn***. 1868.) An experi- ment made to establish public libraries in the State of Rhode Island as an auxiliary to, but not as a part of the public school system, was successful in every town except four. It was backed by the liberal contributions of individuals, but its success was owing to the untiring zeal for four years, 1846-1849, of the then school commissioner, Hon. Henry Barnard.

Out of this movement for school Libraries another has grown into form, the establishment of free Town Libraries by the action of the towns themselves. Its history is not uninteresting. In 1847, Rev. Francis Wayland, doubtless excited by the movement then in progress in Rhode Island, tendered five hundred dollars to the town in Massachusetts which bore his name, " on condition that its citizens should secure an equal amount for a town library." More than the sum required was raised by subscription. But as doubts were raised about the right of a town to tax its inhabitants for a library building, Rev. John B. Wight, a representative from the town in 1851, procured the enactment of a law authorizing cities and towns to establish and maintain public libraries. This has led to the formation and enlargement of many libraries, some of which have been generously endowed by private munificence as well as by public taxation. In not a few cities and villages of several states the library is established in the affections of the community. . Not only is it generously supported, but the books which it contains are extensively used by a large number of the inhabitants. In Boston the Public Library is pointed out to the visitor as the pride of the city. In Springfield a handsome building has been erected containing a valuable library, which is maintained by the city and is free to all. In Stockbridge and Lenox, buildings appropriate and substantial contain the village libraries which private generosity and public taxation have provided and sustained. In not a few of the cities and large towns the name of some public-spirited citizen or former resident is remembered by the Library which is called after his name. The name of Logan is thus honored in Philadelphia, the name of *Astor* in New York, the name of Watkinson in Hartford, of *Bronson* in Waterbury, of *Otis* in Norwich and of *Cheney* in South Manchester, the names of *Jackson* and *Goodrich* in Stockbridge, and the name of *Peabody* in Danvers and Baltimore. There is scarcely a village in the older settlements from which some citizen has not gone forth who has acquired a fortune more or less ample. If he would be honorably remembered among the scenes of his childhood and youth he can accomplish his desire in no way so usefully as by erecting a simple fire-proof building, and founding a village library. We have already observed how hard it is for the student to part from his books—and how painful the thought that his library must be scattered. This can be avoided by giving one's library to the collection of the parish or the town, or by depositing it in the care of some public institution. The learned library of the Mathers still remains in the Antiquarian Hall at Worcester to testify to the learning of its collectors and the lore of their times. The library which Rev. Thomas Prince gathered with such pains and expense for fifty years was kept by the church of which he was pastor for more than three quarters of a century, and is now committed to the public library of Boston. A choice library carefully collected by a country clergyman in New England was given by his widow to an infant university in Oregon.

It will be thought, perhaps, that we ought not to overlook the Sunday-school Library. "We had designed to speak of this and of juvenile literature in general, but the subjects are too important to be disposed of in a chapter. That children are over-stimulated with reading we do not doubt. That the quality is often as objectionable as the quantity of their books is no less clear to our minds. We are equally well satisfied that the Sunday-school and juvenile library too often take the place of the home and the public library; and indeed, that children are pampered to so great an excess that their appetite for good reading is not infrequently ruined. It becomes of less consequence that the supply of wholesome books for such adults is often cut short by the expenditure required to still the imperious cries of the young Olivers for " more."

The college and university library must not be left without notice. We offer no argument for their utility. It is self-evident that without a complete library no institution of learning can attain the highest rank, or continue to attract or educate scholars of finished culture.

We began these papers by introducing a savage to a public library. We cannot more appropriately conclude them than by imagining a thoughtful scholar to take his place. The same objects meet the bodily eye, but very different are the thoughts which the books awaken in the soul that has been refined and enriched by the culture which books impart. They recall the history and achievements of the forgotten past. Every volume suggests a living author who thought and toiled in history, or speculation, or experiment; in eloquence, or poetry, or fiction. At the reading cf the titles the scholar thinks of these men as still living, then of the generation of men among whom they labored, then of their honorable fame or their deserved infamy, of their pure aspirations or their de-basing passions, of their greatness or their meanness, of their precious legacy of solid truth and quickening emo-tions or of pernicious sophistry and vile suggestions. The topic has been often treated of, but by no writer more briefly and effectively than by Southey in the lines which a house filled with *books* and a life devoted to *reading* were fitted to inspire.

My days among the dead are past ;
Around me I behold, Where'er these casual eyes are cast,
The mighty minds of old. My never-failing friends are they, With whom I converse day by day.

With them I take delight in weal,
And seek relief in woe ; And while I understand and feel
How much to them I owe, My cheeks have often been bedew'd With tears of thoughtful gratitude.

My thoughts are with the dead ; with them
I live in long-past years; Their virtues love, their faults condemn,
Partake their hopes and fears; And from their lessons seek and find Instruction with an humble mind.

My hopes are with the dead: anon
My place with them will be, And I with them shall travel on
Through all Futurity: Yet leaving here a name, I trust, That will not perish in the dust.

The Codes Of Hammurabi And Moses
W. W. Davies

QTY

The discovery of the Hammurabi Code is one of the greatest achievements of archaeology, and is of paramount interest, not only to the student of the Bible, but also to all those interested in ancient history...

Religion   **ISBN:** *1-59462-338-4*   **Pages:132**

MSRP $12.95

The Theory of Moral Sentiments
Adam Smith

QTY

This work from 1749. contains original theories of conscience amd moral judgment and it is the foundation for systemof morals.

Philosophy **ISBN:** *1-59462-777-0*   **Pages:536**

MSRP $19.95

Jessica's First Prayer
Hesba Stretton

QTY

In a screened and secluded corner of one of the many railway-bridges which span the streets of London there could be seen a few years ago, from five o'clock every morning until half past eight, a tidily set-out coffee-stall, consisting of a trestle and board, upon which stood two large tin cans, with a small fire of charcoal burning under each so as to keep the coffee boiling during the early hours of the morning when the work-people were thronging into the city on their way to their daily toil...

Pages:84

Childrens   **ISBN:** *1-59462-373-2*   *MSRP $9.95*

My Life and Work
Henry Ford

QTY

Henry Ford revolutionized the world with his implementation of mass production for the Model T automobile. Gain valuable business insight into his life and work with his own auto-biography... "We have only started on our development of our country we have not as yet, with all our talk of wonderful progress, done more than scratch the surface. The progress has been wonderful enough but..."

Pages:300

Biographies/   **ISBN:** *1-59462-198-5*   *MSRP $21.95* www.bookjungle.com *email: sales@bookjungle.com fax: 630-214-0564 mail: Book Jungle PO Box 2226 Champaign, IL 61825*

The Art of Cross-Examination
Francis Wellman

QTY

I presume it is the experience of every author, after his first book is published upon an important subject, to be almost overwhelmed with a wealth of ideas and illustrations which could readily have been included in his book, and which to his own mind, at least, seem to make a second edition inevitable. Such certainly was the case with me; and when the first edition had reached its sixth impression in five months, I rejoiced to learn that it seemed to my publishers that the book had met with a sufficiently favorable reception to justify a second and considerably enlarged edition. ...

Pages:412

Reference   ISBN: *1-59462-647-2*   *MSRP $19.95*

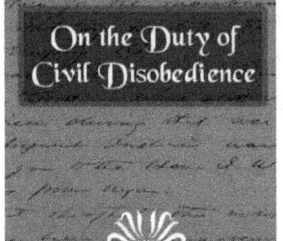

On the Duty of Civil Disobedience
Henry David Thoreau

QTY

Thoreau wrote his famous essay, On the Duty of Civil Disobedience, as a protest against an unjust but popular war and the immoral but popular institution of slave-owning. He did more than write—he declined to pay his taxes, and was hauled off to gaol in consequence. Who can say how much this refusal of his hastened the end of the war and of slavery ?

Law   ISBN: *1-59462-747-9*   **Pages:48**

MSRP $7.45

Dream Psychology Psychoanalysis for Beginners
Sigmund Freud

QTY

Sigmund Freud, born Sigismund Schlomo Freud (May 6, 1856 - September 23, 1939), was a Jewish-Austrian neurologist and psychiatrist who co-founded the psychoanalytic school of psychology. Freud is best known for his theories of the unconscious mind, especially involving the mechanism of repression; his redefinition of sexual desire as mobile and directed towards a wide variety of objects; and his therapeutic techniques, especially his understanding of transference in the therapeutic relationship and the presumed value of dreams as sources of insight into unconscious desires.

Pages:196

Psychology   ISBN: *1-59462-905-6*   *MSRP $15.45*

The Miracle of Right Thought
Orison Swett Marden

QTY

Believe with all of your heart that you will do what you were made to do. When the mind has once formed the habit of holding cheerful, happy, prosperous pictures, it will not be easy to form the opposite habit. It does not matter how improbable or how far away this realization may see, or how dark the prospects may be, if we visualize them as best we can, as vividly as possible, hold tenaciously to them and vigorously struggle to attain them, they will gradually become actualized, realized in the life. But a desire, a longing without endeavor, a yearning abandoned or held indifferently will vanish without realization.

Pages:360

Self Help   ISBN: *1-59462-644-8*   *MSRP $25.45*

QTY

The Rosicrucian Cosmo-Conception Mystic Christianity *by Max Heindel*   ISBN: *1-59462-188-8*   **$38.95**
The Rosicrucian Cosmo-conception is not dogmatic, neither does it appeal to any other authority than the reason of the student. It is: not controversial, but is: sent forth in the, hope that it may help to clear...   New Age/Religion Pages 646

Abandonment To Divine Providence *by Jean-Pierre de Caussade*   ISBN: *1-59462-228-0*   **$25.95**
"The Rev. Jean Pierre de Caussade was one of the most remarkable spiritual writers of the Society of Jesus in France in the 18th Century. His death took place at Toulouse in 1751. His works have gone through many editions and have been republished...   Inspirational/Religion Pages 400

Mental Chemistry *by Charles Haanel*   ISBN: *1-59462-192-6*   **$23.95**
Mental Chemistry allows the change of material conditions by combining and appropriately utilizing the power of the mind. Much like applied chemistry creates something new and unique out of careful combinations of chemicals the mastery of mental chemistry...   New Age Pages 354

The Letters of Robert Browning and Elizabeth Barret Barrett 1845-1846 vol II   ISBN: *1-59462-193-4*   **$35.95**
by Robert Browning and Elizabeth Barrett   Biographies Pages 596

Gleanings In Genesis (volume I) *by Arthur W. Pink*   ISBN: *1-59462-130-6*   **$27.45**
Appropriately has Genesis been termed "the seed plot of the Bible" for in it we have, in germ form, almost all of the great doctrines which are afterwards fully developed in the books of Scripture which follow...   Religion/Inspirational Pages 420

The Master Key *by L. W. de Laurence*   ISBN: *1-59462-001-6*   **$30.95**
In no branch of human knowledge has there been a more lively increase of the spirit of research during the past few years than in the study of Psychology, Concentration and Mental Discipline. The requests for authentic lessons in Thought Control, Mental Discipline and...   New Age/Business Pages 422

The Lesser Key Of Solomon Goetia *by L. W. de Laurence*   ISBN: *1-59462-092-X*   **$9.95**
This translation of the first book of the "Lemegton" which is now for the first time made accessible to students of Talismanic Magic was done, after careful collation and edition, from numerous Ancient Manuscripts in Hebrew, Latin, and French...   New Age/Occult Pages 92

Rubaiyat Of Omar Khayyam *by Edward Fitzgerald*   ISBN:*1-59462-332-5*   **$13.95**
Edward Fitzgerald, whom the world has already learned, in spite of his own efforts to remain within the shadow of anonymity, to look upon as one of the rarest poets of the century, was born at Bredfield, in Suffolk, on the 31st of March, 1809. He was the third son of John Purcell...   Music Pages 172

Ancient Law *by Henry Maine*   ISBN: *1-59462-128-4*   **$29.95**
The chief object of the following pages is to indicate some of the earliest ideas of mankind, as they are reflected in Ancient Law, and to point out the relation of those ideas to modern thought.   Religion/History Pages 452

Far-Away Stories *by William J. Locke*   ISBN: *1-59462-129-2*   **$19.45**
"Good wine needs no bush, but a collection of mixed vintages does. And this book is just such a collection. Some of the stories I do not want to remain buried for ever in the museum files of dead magazine-numbers an author's not unpardonable vanity..."   Fiction Pages 272

Life of David Crockett *by David Crockett*   ISBN: *1-59462-250-7*   **$27.45**
"Colonel David Crockett was one of the most remarkable men of the times in which he lived. Born in humble life, but gifted with a strong will, an indomitable courage, and unremitting perseverance...   Biographies/New Age Pages 424

Lip-Reading *by Edward Nitchie*   ISBN: *1-59462-206-X*   **$25.95**
Edward B. Nitchie, founder of the New York School for the Hard of Hearing, now the Nitchie School of Lip-Reading, Inc, wrote "LIP-READING Principles and Practice". The development and perfecting of this meritorious work on lip-reading was an undertaking...   How-to Pages 400

A Handbook of Suggestive Therapeutics, Applied Hypnotism, Psychic Science   ISBN: *1-59462-214-0*   **$24.95**
by Henry Munro   Health/New Age/Health/Self-help Pages 376

A Doll's House: and Two Other Plays *by Henrik Ibsen*   ISBN: *1-59462-112-8*   **$19.95**
Henrik Ibsen created this classic when in revolutionary 1848 Rome. Introducing some striking concepts in playwriting for the realist genre, this play has been studied the world over.   Fiction/Classics/Plays 308

The Light of Asia *by sir Edwin Arnold*   ISBN: *1-59462-204-3*   **$13.95**
In this poetic masterpiece, Edwin Arnold describes the life and teachings of Buddha. The man who was to become known as Buddha to the world was born as Prince Gautama of India but he rejected the worldly riches and abandoned the reigns of power when...   Religion/History/Biographies Pages 170

The Complete Works of Guy de Maupassant *by Guy de Maupassant*   ISBN: *1-59462-157-8*   **$16.95**
"For days and days, nights and nights, I had dreamed of that first kiss which was to consecrate our engagement, and I knew not on what spot I should put my lips..."   Fiction/Classics Pages 240

The Art of Cross-Examination *by Francis L. Wellman*   ISBN: *1-59462-309-0*   **$26.95**
Written by a renowned trial lawyer, Wellman imparts his experience and uses case studies to explain how to use psychology to extract desired information through questioning.   How-to/Science/Reference Pages 408

Answered or Unanswered? *by Louisa Vaughan*   ISBN: *1-59462-248-5*   **$10.95**
Miracles of Faith in China   Religion Pages 112

The Edinburgh Lectures on Mental Science (1909) *by Thomas*   ISBN: *1-59462-008-3*   **$11.95**
This book contains the substance of a course of lectures recently given by the writer in the Queen Street Hall, Edinburgh. Its purpose is to indicate the Natural Principles governing the relation between Mental Action and Material Conditions...   New Age/Psychology Pages 148

Ayesha *by H. Rider Haggard*   ISBN: *1-59462-301-5*   **$24.95**
Verily and indeed it is the unexpected that happens! Probably if there was one person upon the earth from whom the Editor of this, and of a certain previous history, did not expect to hear again...   Classics Pages 380

Ayala's Angel *by Anthony Trollope*   ISBN: *1-59462-352-X*   **$29.95**
The two girls were both pretty, but Lucy who was twenty-one who supposed to be simple and comparatively unattractive, whereas Ayala was credited, as her Bombwhat romantic name might show, with poetic charm and a taste for romance. Ayala when her father died was nineteen...   Fiction Pages 484

The American Commonwealth *by James Bryce*   ISBN: *1-59462-286-8*   **$34.45**
An interpretation of American democratic political theory. It examines political mechanics and society from the perspective of Scotsman James Bryce   Politics Pages 572

Stories of the Pilgrims *by Margaret P. Pumphrey*   ISBN: *1-59462-116-0*   **$17.95**
This book explores pilgrims religious oppression in England as well as their escape to Holland and eventual crossing to America on the Mayflower, and their early days in New England...   History Pages 268

QTY

The Fasting Cure *by Sinclair Upton*   ISBN: *1-59462-222-1* **$13.95**
*In the Cosmopolitan Magazine for May, 1910, and in the Contemporary Review (London) for April, 1910, I published an article dealing with my experi-
ences in fasting. I have written a great many magazine articles, but never one which attracted so much attention... New Age/Self Help/Health Pages 164*

Hebrew Astrology *by Sepharial*   ISBN: *1-59462-308-2* **$13.45**
*In these days of advanced thinking it is a matter of common observation that we have left many of the old landmarks behind and that we are now pressing
forward to greater heights and to a wider horizon than that which represented the mind-content of our progenitors...   Astrology Pages 144*

Thought Vibration or The Law of Attraction in the Thought World   ISBN: *1-59462-127-6* **$12.95**

by William Walker Atkinson   *Psychology/Religion Pages 144*

Optimism *by Helen Keller*   ISBN: *1-59462-108-X* **$15.95**
*Helen Keller was blind, deaf, and mute since 19 months old, yet famously learned how to overcome these handicaps, communicate with the world, and
spread her lectures promoting optimism. An inspiring read for everyone...   Biographies/Inspirational Pages 84*

Sara Crewe *by Frances Burnett*   ISBN: *1-59462-360-0* **$9.45**
*In the first place, Miss Minchin lived in London. Her home was a large, dull, tall one, in a large, dull square, where all the houses were alike, and all the
sparrows were alike, and where all the door-knockers made the same heavy sound...   Childrens/Classic Pages 88*

The Autobiography of Benjamin Franklin *by Benjamin Franklin*   ISBN: *1-59462-135-7* **$24.95**
*The Autobiography of Benjamin Franklin has probably been more extensively read than any other American historical work, and no other book of its kind
has had such ups and downs of fortune. Franklin lived for many years in England, where he was agent...   Biographies/History Pages 332*

Name	
Email	
Telephone	
Address	
City, State ZIP	

☐ **Credit Card**   ☐ **Check / Money Order**

Credit Card Number	
Expiration Date	
Signature	

Please Mail to: Book Jungle
PO Box 2226
Champaign, IL 61825
or Fax to: 630-214-0564

ORDERING INFORMATION

web*: www.bookjungle.com*
email*: sales@bookjungle.com*
fax*: 630-214-0564*
mail*: Book Jungle PO Box 2226 Champaign, IL 61825*
or PayPal *to sales@bookjungle.com*

Please contact us for bulk discounts

DIRECT-ORDER TERMS

**20% Discount if You Order
Two or More Books**
Free Domestic Shipping!
Accepted: Master Card, Visa,
Discover, American Express

www.ingramcontent.com/pod-product-compliance
Lightning Source LLC
Chambersburg PA
CBHW081145020726
47504CB00009B/2006